Winner of THE SCOTIABANK GILLER PRIZE

Winner of THE GOVERNOR GENERAL'S AWARD

Shortlisted for THE MAN BOOKER PRIZE

Shortlisted for THE BAILEYS WOMEN'S PRIZE for Fiction

Shortlisted for THE RATHBONES FOLIO PRIZE

A *NEW YORK TIMES* NOTABLE BOOK

A *GLOBE AND MAIL* BEST BOOK

NATIONAL BESTSELLER

"*Do Not Say We Have Nothing* reminds us what fiction can do for the truth. It speaks to the humanity that continues even in the harshest, most self-destructively paranoid conditions, and it shows how the savagery of destroying culture comes hand in hand with the destruction of human bodies."
NEW STATESMAN

"A magnificent epic of Chinese history, richly detailed and beautifully written."
THE TIMES

Praise for

DO NOT SAY WE HAVE NOTHING

"[A] gorgeous intergenerational saga. . . . Should any doubt remain, *Do Not Say We Have Nothing* will cement Madeleine Thien as one of Canada's most talented novelists. . . . Thoroughly researched . . . riveting and lyrical." *The Globe and Mail*

"Resonant, heartbreakingly beautiful. . . . We will be reading this book for the next century." Kevin Patterson, *The Walrus*

"A literary epic. . . . That such a diffuse tale should prove shattering serves as testament to Thien's formidable storytelling skills. . . . *Do Not Say We Have Nothing* . . . will enthrall just about any reader." *Toronto Star*

"Skillfully and elliptically told. . . . *Do Not Say We Have Nothing* . . . show[s] Thien at the height of her abilities." *National Post*

"By the time you've passed through each portal of *Do Not Say We Have Nothing* . . . neither your sense of self nor your consciousness will remain the same. . . . It is difficult to say which is the more potent in this rich, complex and lyrical novel, Thien's characterization or storytelling powers, the sheer lyrical beauty of her writing or her perception. . . . Read it once and weep. Read it twice and marvel." *South China Morning Post*

"Mythic yet realistic, panoramic yet intimate, intellectual yet romantic– Thien has written a concerto dauntingly complex and deeply haunting." *Kirkus Reviews* (starred review)

"This is a resplendent, epic masterpiece of a novel that brings to light a dark period of Chinese history through wit, humour and nuanced storytelling. The characters linger long after the last page." Alice Pung, author of *Unpolished Gem*

Madeleine Thien

DO NOT SAY
WE HAVE
NOTHING

A Novel

VINTAGE CANADA

VINTAGE CANADA EDITION, 2017

Published by Vintage Canada, a division of Penguin Random House
Canada Limited, in 2017. Originally published in hardcover by Knopf Canada,
a division of Penguin Random House Canada Limited, in 2016, and simultaneously
in the United Kingdom by Granta. Distributed in Canada by
Penguin Random House Canada Limited, Toronto.

Vintage Canada with colophon is a registered trademark.

www.penguinrandomhouse.ca

LIBRARY AND ARCHIVES CANADA CATALOGUING IN PUBLICATION

Thien, Madeleine, 1974– , author
Do not say we have nothing / Madeleine Thien.

ISBN 978-0-345-81043-4
eBook ISBN 978-0-345-81044-1

I. Title.

PS8589.H449D65 2017   C813'.6   C2015-908538-1

Book design by CS Richardson

Image credit: © Cate McRae/Arcangel Images

Printed and bound in the United States of America

2 4 6 8 9 7 5 3 1

VINTAGE CANADA | Penguin Random House

For my mother and father and Katherine and Rawi

PART ONE

There are a thousand ways to live. Just how many do the two of us know?

—ZHANG WEI, *The Ancient Ship*

Of all the scenes that crowded the cave walls, the richest and most intricate were those of paradise.

—COLIN THUBRON, *Shadow of the Silk Road*

IN A SINGLE YEAR, my father left us twice. The first time, to end his marriage, and the second, when he took his own life. That year, 1989, my mother flew to Hong Kong and laid my father to rest in a cemetery near the Chinese border. Afterwards, distraught, she rushed home to Vancouver where I had been alone. I was ten years old.

Here is what I remember:

My father has a handsome, ageless face; he is a kind but melancholy man. He wears glasses that have no frames and the lenses give the impression of hovering just before him, the thinnest of curtains. His eyes, dark brown, are guarded and unsure; he is only 39 years old. My father's name was Jiang Kai and he was born in a small village outside of Changsha. Later on, when I learned my father had been a renowned concert pianist in China, I thought of the way his fingers tapped the kitchen table, how they pattered across countertops and along my mother's soft arms all the way to her fingertips, driving her crazy and me into fits of glee. He gave me my Chinese name, Jiang Li-ling, and my English one, Marie Jiang. When he died, I was only a child, and the few memories I possessed, however fractional, however inaccurate, were all I had of him. I've never let them go.

In my twenties, in the difficult years after both my parents had passed away, I gave my life wholeheartedly to numbers–observation, conjecture, logic and proof, the tools we mathematicians have not only to interpret, but simply to describe the world. For the last decade I have been a professor at Simon Fraser University in Canada. Numbers have allowed me to move between the unimaginably large and the magnificently small; to live an existence away from my parents, their affairs and unrequited dreams and, I used to think, my own.

Some years ago, in 2010, while walking in Vancouver's Chinatown, I passed a store selling DVDs. I remember that it was pouring rain and the sidewalks were empty. Concert music rang from two enormous speakers outside the shop. I knew the music, Bach's Sonata for Piano and Violin No. 4, and I was drawn towards it as keenly as if someone were pulling me by the hand. The counterpoint, holding together composer, musicians and even silence, the music, with its spiralling waves of grief and rapture, was everything I remembered.

Dizzy, I leaned against the glass.

And suddenly I was in the car with my father. I heard rain splashing up over the tires and my father, humming. He was so alive, so beloved, that the incomprehensibility of his suicide grieved me all over again. By then, my father had been dead for two decades, and such a pure memory of him had never come back to me. I was thirty-one years old.

I went inside the store. The pianist, Glenn Gould, appeared on a flatscreen: he and Yehudi Menuhin were performing the Bach sonata I had recognized. There was Glenn Gould hunched over the piano, wearing a dark suit, hearing patterns far beyond the range of what most of us are given to perceive, and he was . . . so familiar to me, like an entire language, a world, I had forgotten.

In 1989, life had become a set of necessary routines for my mother and me: work and school, television, food, sleep. My father's first departure happened at the same time as momentous events occurring in China, events which my mother watched obsessively on CNN. I asked her who these protesters were, and she said they were students and everyday people. I asked if my father was there, and she said, "No, it's Tiananmen Square in Beijing." The demonstrations, bringing over a million Chinese citizens into the streets, had begun in April, when my father still lived with us, and continued after he disappeared to Hong Kong. Then, on June 4th, and in the days and weeks following the massacre, my mother wept. I watched her night after night. Ba had defected from China in 1978 and was forbidden from re-entering the country. But my incomprehension attached itself to the things I could see: those chaotic, frightening images of people and tanks, and my mother in front of the screen.

That summer, as if in a dream, I continued my calligraphy lessons at the nearby cultural centre, using brush and ink to copy line after line of Chinese poetry. But the words I could recognize— big, small, girl, moon, sky (大, 小, 女, 月, 天)—were few. My father spoke Mandarin and my mother Cantonese, but I was fluent only in English. At first, the puzzle of the Chinese language had seemed a game, a pleasure, but my inability to understand began to trouble me. Over and over, I wrote characters I couldn't read, making them bigger and bigger until excess ink soaked the flimsy paper and tore it. I didn't care. I stopped going.

In October, two police officers came to our door. They informed my mother that Ba was gone, and that the coroner's office in Hong Kong would handle the file. They said Ba's death was a suicide. Then, quiet (qù) became another person living inside our house. It slept in the closet with my father's shirts, trousers and shoes, it guarded his Beethoven, Prokofiev and Shostakovich scores, his hats, armchair and special cup. Quiet (闃) moved into our minds and stormed like an ocean inside my mother and me. That winter, Vancouver was even more grey and wet than usual, as if the rain was a thick sweater we couldn't remove. I fell asleep certain that, in the morning, Ba would wake me as he always had, his voice tugging me from sleep, until this delusion compounded the loss, and hurt more than what had come before.

Weeks crept by, and 1989 disappeared inside 1990. Ma and I ate dinner on the sofa every night because there was no space on our dining table. My father's official documents–certificates of various kinds, tax declarations–had already been organized, but the odds and ends persisted. As Ma investigated the apartment more thoroughly, other bits of paper came to light, music scores, a handful of letters my father had written but never sent ("Sparrow, I do not know if this letter will reach you, but . . .") and ever more notebooks. As I watched these items increase, I imagined my mother believed that Ba would reincarnate as a piece of paper. Or maybe she believed, as the ancients did, that words written on paper were talismans, and could somehow protect us from harm.

Most nights, Ma would sit among them, still in her office clothes.

I tried not to bother her. I stayed in the adjoining living room and heard, now and then, the nearly soundless turning of pages.

The qù of her breathing.

Rain exploding and slicing down the window panes.

We were suspended in time.

Over and over, the No. 29 electric bus clattered past.

I fantasized conversations. I tried to imagine Ba reborn in the underworld, buying another new diary, using a different currency, and slipping his change into a new coat pocket, a lightweight coat made of feathers or maybe a cloak of camel wool, a coat sturdy enough for both heaven and the underworld.

Meanwhile, my mother distracted herself by trying to find my father's family, wherever they might be, to tell them that their long-lost son or brother or uncle no longer survived in this world. She began searching for Ba's adoptive father, a man who had once lived in Shanghai and had been known as "the Professor." He was the only family Ba had ever mentioned. The search for information was slow and painstaking; there was no e-mail or internet back then and so it was easy for Ma to send a letter but difficult to obtain a true answer. My father had left China a long time ago and if the Professor were still alive, he would be a supremely old man.

The Beijing we saw on television, with mortuaries and grieving families, with tanks stationed at the intersections, bristling with rifles, was a world away from the Beijing my father had known. And yet, I sometimes think, not so different after all.

It was a few months later, in March 1990, that my mother showed me the Book of Records. That night, Ma was seated at her usual place at the dining table, reading. The notebook in her hand was tall and narrow, the dimensions of a miniature door. It had a loose binding of walnut-coloured cotton string.

Long past my bedtime, Ma suddenly noticed me.

"What's wrong with you!" she said. And then, confused by her own question: "Have you finished your homework? What time is it?"

I had finished ages ago and had been watching a horror movie on mute. I still remember: a man had just been killed with an ice pick. "It's midnight," I said, disturbed, because the man had been soft as dough.

My mother extended a hand and I went to her. She closed one arm around my waist and squeezed. "Do you want to see what I'm reading?"

I leaned over the notebook and stared at the gathering of words. Chinese characters tracked down the page like animal prints in the snow.

"It's a story," Ma said.

"Oh. What kind of story?"

"I think it's a novel. There's an adventurer named Da-wei who sets sail to America and a heroine named May Fourth who walks across the Gobi Desert . . ."

I stared harder but the words remained unreadable.

"There was a time when people copied out entire books by hand," Ma said. "The Russians called it samizdat, the Chinese called it . . . well, I don't think we have a name. Look how dirty this notebook is, there's even bits of grass on it. Goodness knows how many people carried it all over the place. . . . it's decades older than you, Li-ling."

I wondered: What wasn't? I asked if this notebook had been copied by Ba.

My mother shook her head. She said the handwriting was beautiful, the work of a refined calligrapher, while my father's writing was only so-so. "This notebook is one chapter from something longer. Here it says: Number 17. It doesn't say who the author is, but look, here's a title, the Book of Records."

She set the notebook down. On the dining table, my father's papers had the appearance of whitecaps, surging forward, about to crest off the surface and explode onto the carpet. All our mail was here, too. Since the New Year, Ma had begun receiving letters from Beijing, condolences from musicians in the Central Philharmonic who had only lately learned of my father's death. Ma read these letters with a dictionary at hand because the letters were written in simplified Chinese, which she had never learned. Educated in Hong Kong, my mother had studied the traditional Chinese script. But on the mainland, in the 1950s, a new, simpler script had become law in Communist China. Thousands of words had changed; for instance, "to write" (xiě) went from 寫 to 写, and "to know" (shí) went from 識 to 识. Even "Communist Party" (gòng chǎn dǎng) went from 共 產 黨 to 共 产 党 . Sometimes Ma could see the word's former self, other times she guessed at meanings. She said it was like reading a letter from the future, or talking to someone who had turned their back on her. All this was complicated by the fact that she rarely read in Chinese anymore, and expressed most of her thoughts in English. She didn't like my speaking Cantonese because, as she said, "Your accent is completely crooked."

"It's cold in here," I whispered. "Let's put on our pyjamas and go to bed."

Ma stared at the notebook, not even half-listening.

"Mother will be tired in the morning," I persisted. "Mother will hit snooze twenty times."

She smiled but her eyes beneath her glasses tightened against something. "Go to bed," she said. "Don't wait up for Mother."

I kissed her soft cheek. She said, "What did the Buddhist say to the pizza maker?"

"What?"

"Make me one with everything."

I laughed and groaned and laughed again, then shivered, thinking of the victim on the television, his doughy skin. Smiling, she nudged me firmly away.

Lying in bed, I considered several facts.

First, that in my grade five class, I was an entirely different person. I was so good-natured and well-adjusted there, so high-achieving, I wondered if my brain and soul were separating.

Second, that in poorer countries, people like Ma and me would not be so lonely. On television, poor countries were crowded places, overloaded elevators trying to rise to the sky. People slept six to a bed, a dozen to a room. There you could always speak your thoughts out loud, assured that someone would hear you even if they didn't want to. In fact, the way to punish someone might be to remove them from their circle of family and friends, isolate them in a cold country, and shatter them with loneliness.

Third, and this was not a fact but a question: Why had our love meant so little to Ba?

I must have slept because I woke abruptly to see Ma leaning over me. Her fingertips wiped my face. I never cried in the day-time, only at night.

"Don't be like this, Li-ling," she said. She was mumbling a lot of things. She said, "If you're trapped in a room and nobody is coming to save you, what can you do? You have to bang on the walls and break the windows. You have to climb out and save yourself. It's obvious, Li-ling, that crying doesn't help a person live."

"My name is Marie," I shouted. "Marie!"

She smiled. "Who are you?"

"I'm Li-ling!"

"You're Girl." She used my father's pet name for me, because the word 女 meant both girl and daughter. He liked to joke that, where he came from, the poor didn't bother to name their daughters. Ma would smack his shoulder and say, in Cantonese, "Don't fill her head like a garbage can."

Protected in her arms, I curled once more towards sleep.

Later I woke to the sound of Ma mumbling run-on thoughts and she was cackling. These winter mornings were so lightless, but Ma's unexpected laugh cut through the room like buzzing from the electric heater. Her skin had the fragrance of clean pillows, of the sweet osmanthus cream that she used.

When I whispered her name, she mumbled, "Heh." And then, "Heh heh."

I asked her, "Are you walking on land or in the sea?"

Very distinctly, she said, *"He's here."*

"Who?" I tried to see into the darkness of the room. I truly believed that he was here.

"Adoptive man. That hmmm. That . . . *Professor.*"

I held tight to her fingers. On the other side of the curtains, the sky was changing colour. I wanted to follow her into my father's past, and yet I didn't trust it. People could walk away towards illusions, they might see something so entrancing they would neglect to turn around. I feared that, like my father, she would no longer remember the reasons for coming home.

Life outside—the start of a new school year, the regularity of tests, the pleasures of math camp—continued as if it would never cease, driven forward by the circular world of seasons. My father's summer and winter coats still waited beside the door, beneath his hats and above his shoes.

In early December, a thick envelope arrived from Shanghai and Ma once again sat down with her dictionary. The dictionary is a small-format, extremely fat hardback with a green-and-white cover. The pages, as I turn them, are diaphanous, and seem to weigh nothing. Here and there, I find a spot of grease or a ring of coffee, from my mother's cup or perhaps my own. Each word is filed under its root, also known as a radical. For instance, 門 means gate, but it is also a radical, that is, the building block for other words and concepts. If light, or the sun 日, shines through the gate, we have space 間. If there is a horse 馬 inside the gate, this is an ambush 闖, and if there is a mouth 口 inside the gate, we have a question 問. If there is an eye 目 and a dog 犬 inside, we have quiet 闃.

The letter from Shanghai was thirty pages long and written in a spidery hand; after some minutes I tired of watching my mother struggle through it. I went to the front room and gazed at the neighbours. Across the courtyard, I saw a miserable Christmas tree. It looked like someone had tried to strangle it with tinsel.

Rain gusted and the wind whistled. I brought my mother a glass of eggnog.

"Is it a good letter?"

Ma set the pages down. Her eyelids looked swollen. "It's not what I expected."

I ran my finger across the envelope and began to decipher the name on the return address. It surprised me. "A woman?" I asked, suddenly afraid.

My mother nodded.

"She has a request," Ma said, taking the envelope from me and shoving it beneath some papers. I moved closer as if she was a vase about to slide off the table, but Ma's puffy eyes conveyed an unexpected emotion. Comfort? Or maybe, and to my astonishment, joy. Ma continued: "She's asking for a favour."

"Will you read the letter to me?"

Ma pinched the bridge of her own nose. "The whole thing is really long. She says she hasn't seen your father in many years. But, once, they were like family." She hesitated on the word *family*. "She says her husband was your father's composition teacher at the Shanghai Conservatory of Music. But they lost touch with one another. During the difficult years."

"What difficult years?" I began to suspect that any favour would involve American dollars or a new refrigerator, and feared that Ma would be taken advantage of.

"Before you were born. The 1960s. Back when your father was a music student." Ma looked down with an unreadable expression. "She says that your father made contact with them last year. Ba wrote to her from Hong Kong a few days before he died."

A string of questions rose in me. I knew I shouldn't pester her but at last, because I wished only to understand, I said, "Who is she? What's her name?"

"Her surname is Deng."

"But her given name."

Ma opened her mouth but no words came out. Finally, she looked me straight in the eye and said, "Her given name is Li-ling."

She had the same name as me, only it had been written in simplified Chinese. I reached for the letter. Ma put her hand firmly over mine. Forestalling my next question, she lunged ahead. "These thirty pages are about the present not the past. Deng Li-ling's daughter arrived in Toronto but her passport can't be used. Her daughter has nowhere to go, she needs our help. Her daughter . . ." Nimbly, Ma slid the letter into its envelope. "Her daughter will come and live with us for a little while. Do you understand? This letter is about the present."

I felt sideways and upside down. Why would a stranger live with us?

"Her daughter's name is Ai-ming," Ma said, trying to lead me back. "I'm going to telephone now and arrange for her to come."

"Are we the same age?"

Ma looked confused. "No, she must be at least nineteen years old, she's a student. Deng Li-ling says that her daughter . . . she says that Ai-ming got into trouble in Beijing during the Tiananmen demonstrations. She ran away."

"What kind of trouble?"

"Enough," my mother said. "That's all you need to know."

"No! I need to know more."

Exasperated, Ma slammed the dictionary shut. "Who brought you up? You're too young to be this nosy!"

"But–"

"Enough."

Ma waited until I was in bed before she made the telephone call. She spoke in her mother tongue, Cantonese, with brief interjections of Mandarin, and I could hear, even through the closed door, how she hesitated over the tones which had never come naturally to her.

"Is it very cold where you are?" I heard Ma say.

And then: "The Greyhound ticket will be waiting for you at . . ."

I took off my glasses and stared out the blurred window. Rain appeared like snow. Ma's voice sounded foreign to me.

After a long period of silence I re-hooked my glasses over my ears, climbed out of bed and went out. Ma had a pen in her hand and a stack of bills before her, as if waiting for dictation. She saw me and said, "Where are your slippers?"

I said didn't know.

Ma exploded. "Go to bed, Girl! Why can't you understand? I just want some peace! You never leave me alone, you watch me and watch me as if you think I'll . . ." She slapped the pen down. Some piece of it snapped off and ran along the floor. "You think I'm going to leave? You think I'm as selfish as he is? That I would ever abandon you and hurt you like he did?" There was a long, violent outburst in Cantonese, then: "Just go to bed!"

She looked so aged and fragile sitting there, with her old, heavy dictionary.

I fled to the bathroom, slammed the door, opened it, slammed it harder, and burst into tears. I ran water in the tub, realizing that what I really wanted was, in fact, to go to bed. My sobs turned to hiccups, and when the hiccups finally stopped, all I heard was water gushing down. Perched on the edge of the tub, I watched my feet distort beneath the surface. My pale legs folded away as I submerged.

Ba, in my memory, came back to me. He pushed a cassette into the tape player, told me to roll down the windows, and we sailed down Main Street and along Great Northern Way, blaring Beethoven's "Emperor" Concerto, performed by Glenn Gould with Leopold Stokowski conducting. Tumbling notes cascaded down and infinitely up, and my father conducted with his right hand while steering with his left. I heard his humming, melodic and percussive, DA! DA-de-de-de DA!

Da, da, da! I had the sensation that, as we paraded triumphantly across Vancouver, the first movement was being created not by Beethoven, but by my father. His hand moved in the shape of 4/4 time, the cliff-hanging thrill between the fourth beat and the first,

and I wondered what it could mean that a man who had once been famous, who had performed in Beijing before Mao Zedong himself, did not even keep a piano in his own home? That he made his living by working in a shop? In fact, though I begged for violin lessons, my father always said no. And yet here we were, crossing the city embraced by this victorious music, so that the past, Beethoven's and my father's, was never dead but only reverberated beneath the windshield, then rose and covered us like the sun.

The Buick was gone; Ma had sold it. She had always been the tougher one, like the cactus in the living room, the only house-plant to survive Ba's departure. To live, my father had needed more. The bath water lapped over me. Embarrassed by the waste, I wrenched the tap closed. My father had once said that music was full of silences. He had left nothing for me, no letter, no message. Not a word.

Ma knocked at the door.

"Marie," she said. She turned the handle but it was locked. "Li-ling, are you okay?"

A long moment passed.

The truth was that I had loved my father more. The realiza-tion came to me in the same breath I knew, unquestionably, that my father must have been in great pain, and that my mother would never, ever abandon me. She, too, had loved him. Weeping, I rested my hands on the surface of the water. "I just needed to take a bath."

"Oh," she said. Her voice seemed to echo inside the tub itself. "Don't get cold in there."

She tried the door again but it was still locked.

"We'll be okay," she said finally.

I wanted, more than anything, to wake us both from this dream. Instead, helplessly, I splashed water over my tears and nodded. "I know."

I listened to the sound of her slippers diminish as they padded away.

On the 16th of December, 1990, Ma came home in a taxi with a new daughter who wore no coat, only a thick scarf, a woollen sweater, blue jeans and canvas shoes. I had never met a Chinese girl before – that is, one who, like my father, came from real main-land China. A pair of grey mittens dangled from a string around her neck and swayed in nervous rhythm against her legs. The fringed ends of her blue scarf fell one in front and one behind, like a scholar's. The rain was falling hard, and she walked with her head down, holding a medium-sized suitcase that appeared to be empty. She was pale and her hair had the gleam of the sea.

Casually I opened the door and widened my eyes as if I was not expecting visitors.

"Girl," Ma said. "Take the suitcase. Hurry up."

Ai-ming stepped inside and paused on the edge of the door-mat. When I reached for the suitcase, my hand accidentally touched hers, but she didn't draw back. Instead, her other hand reached out and lightly covered mine. She gazed right at me, with such openness and curiosity that, out of shyness, I closed my eyes.

"Ai-ming," Ma was saying. "Let me introduce you. This is my Girl."

I pulled away and opened my eyes again.

Ma, taking off her coat, glanced first at me and then at the room. The brown sofa with its three camel-coloured stripes had seen better days, but I had spruced it up with all the flowery pil-lows and stuffed animals from my bed. I had also turned on the television in order to give this room the appearance of liveliness. Ma nodded vigorously at me. "Girl, greet your aunt."

"Really, it's okay if you call me Ai-ming. Please. I really, mmm, prefer it."

To placate them both, I said, "Hello."

Just as I suspected, the suitcase was very light. With my free hand, I moved to take Ai-ming's coat, remembering too late she didn't have one. My arm wavered in the air like a question mark. She reached out, grasped my hand and firmly shook it.

She had a question in her eyes. Her hair, pinned back on one side, fell loosely on the other, so that she seemed forever in profile, about to turn towards me. Without letting go of my hand, she manoeuvred her shoes noiselessly off her feet, first one then the other. Pinpoints of rain glimmered on her scarf. Our lives had contracted to such a degree that I could not remember the last time a stranger had entered our home; Ai-ming's presence made everything unfamiliar, as if the walls were crowding a few inches nearer to see her. The previous night, we had, at last, tidied Ba's papers and notebooks, putting them into boxes and stacking the boxes under the kitchen table. Now I found the table's surface deceitfully bare. I freed my hand, saying I would put the suitcase in her bedroom.

Ma showed her around the apartment. I retreated to the sofa and pretended to watch the Weather Channel, which predicted rain for the rest of the week, the rest of 1990, the rest of the century, and even the remainder of all time. Their two voices ran one after the other like cable cars, interrupted now and then by silence. The intensity in the apartment crept inside me, and I had the sensation that the floor was made of paper, that there were words written everywhere I couldn't read, and one unthinking gesture could crumple this whole place down.

We ate together, seated around the dining table. Ma had removed a leaf, transforming the table from an egg to a circle. She interrupted her own rambling to give me a look that said, *Stop staring.*

Every now and then, my foot accidentally kicked one of the boxes under the table, causing Ai-ming to startle.

"Ai-ming, do you mind the cold?" Ma said cheerily, ignoring me. "I myself never experienced winter until I came to Canada."

"Beijing has winter but I didn't mind it. Actually, I grew up far away from there, in the South where it was humid and warm, and so when we moved to Beijing, the cold was new to me."

"I've never been to the capital, but I heard the dust flies in from the western deserts."

"It's true." Ai-ming nodded, smiling. "The dust would get into our clothes and hair, and even into our food."

Sitting directly across from her, I could see that she really was nineteen. Her eyes looked puffy and her expression reminded me, unexpectedly, of Ma's grieving face. Sometimes, I think, you can look at a person and know they are full of words. Maybe the words are withheld due to pain or privacy, or maybe subterfuge. Maybe there are knife-edged words waiting to draw blood. I felt like both a child and a grown-up. I wanted Ma and me to be left alone but, for reasons I couldn't explain, I also wanted to be near Ai-ming.

"What is the 'ming' of Ai-ming?" I asked in English, kicking a box for emphasis. "Is it the 'ming' that means to understand, or the 'ming' that means fate?"

They both looked at me.

"Eat your chicken," Ma said.

The daughter studied me, a pleased expression on her face. She drew a shape in the air between us, 明. The sun and the moon combined to make understanding or brightness. It was an everyday word.

"My parents wanted the idea of ài míng," she said. "'To cherish wisdom.' But you're right, there's a misgiving in it. An idea that is . . . mmm, not cherishing fate, not quite, but accepting it." She picked up her bowl again and pushed the tip of her chopsticks into the softness of the rice.

Ma asked her if there was anything she needed, or if there was something she would like to do.

Ai-ming put down her bowl. "To be honest, I feel as if it's been a long time since I had a good night's sleep. In Toronto, I couldn't rest. Every few weeks I had to move."

"Move house?" Ma said.

Ai-ming was trembling. "I thought . . . I was afraid of the police. I was frightened they would send me back. I don't know if my mother was able to tell you everything. I hope so. In Beijing, I didn't do anything wrong, anything criminal, but even so . . . In China, my aunt and uncle helped me leave and I crossed the border into Kyrgyzstan and then . . . you bought my ticket here. Despite everything, you helped me . . . I'm grateful, I'm afraid I'll never be able to thank you as I should. I'm sorry for everything . . ."

Ma looked embarrassed. "Here," she said. "Eat something."

But a change had come over Ai-ming. Her hands were shaking so hard, she couldn't manage her chopsticks. "Every day I go back and think things over but I can't understand how I arrived here. It's as if I'm a fugitive. At home, my mother is struggling. I'm afraid to sleep . . . sometimes I dream that none of this really happened but then waking up becomes a nightmare. If my mother had me with her, if only my father was alive, if only he hadn't . . . but the most important thing is that I make something of myself because, right now, I have nothing. I haven't even got a passport. I'm afraid to use the one I had before, it's not . . . legal. It wasn't mine but I had no choice. I heard that if I could get across the border into the United States, there's an amnesty for Chinese students and I might qualify. Even if I have nothing I'll pay everything back, I swear it. I promise."

"Zhí nǔ," Ma said, leaning towards her. The words confused me. They meant "my brother's daughter," but Ma had no brothers.

"I wanted to take care of them but everything changed so quickly. Everything went wrong."

"There's no need to defend yourself here," Ma said. "We're family and these are not just words, do you understand? These are much more than words."

"And also," Ai-ming said, turning pale, "I'm truly sorry for your loss."

My mother and Ai-ming looked at each other. "Thank you," Ma said. The sudden tears in her eyes stilled everything inside me. Despite all we had been through, my mother rarely wept. "And I'm so sorry for yours. My husband loved your father very much."

On the first Saturday that Ma didn't have to work, she went downtown and came home with socks, sweaters, a pair of winter shoes and a coat. In the beginning, Ai-ming slept a great deal. She would emerge from Ma's bedroom with jumbled hair, wearing a pair of my leggings and an old T-shirt of Ma's. Ai-ming was afraid to go outside, so weeks passed before she wore the new shoes. The coat, however, she wore every day. In the afternoons, she read a lot, sitting at the kitchen table with a stack of my father's books. She read with her hands in her coat pockets, and used a cleaver to keep the book flat. Her hair sometimes slid forward and blocked the light, and she would wind it up and tuck the bundle inside the neck of her sweater.

One night, after she had been with us about a week, she asked Ma to cut her hair. It was just after Christmas, I remember. Since school was out, I spent most of my time eating chocolate Turtles in front of the television. Ma ordered me to come and spray Ai-ming's hair with water from the plastic bottle, but I refused, saying that our guest's hair should be left alone.

The women laughed. Ai-ming said she wanted to look modern. They went into the kitchen and laid down sheets of newspaper, and Ai-ming removed her coat and climbed up onto a footstool so that her long hair could fall freely into Ma's scissors. I was watching an episode of The A-Team and the cold swish of the scissors, as well as their giggling, made it impossible to concentrate. At the first commercial break, I went into the kitchen to check their progress.

Ai-ming, hands folded as if she were praying, rolled her eyes towards me. Ma had cut about a third of her hair, and the long, wet ends lay on the floor like massacred sea creatures. "Oh," I said, "how could you?"

Ma lifted her weapon. "You're next, Girl."

"Ma-li, it's almost the New Year. Time for a haircut." Ai-ming had difficulty saying Marie, and so had chosen the Chinese variant which, according to the dictionary, meant "charming mineral."

Just then, Ma detached another sizeable chunk of hair. It fluttered, as if still breathing, to the floor.

"It's Canadian New Year. People in Canada don't get haircuts at New Year's. They drink champagne."

Each time Ma pulled the trigger of the plastic bottle, a fine mist shrouded Ai-ming, who squeezed her eyes tight against the cold. As I watched, Ai-ming transformed before my eyes. Even the pallor of her skin began to seem less dire. When she had cut to shoulder length, Ma began shaping bangs that slanted across Ai-ming's forehead in a decidedly chic way. She was very, very beautiful. Her eyes were dark and unclouded and the shape of her mouth was, just as the poets say, a rose against her skin. There was a flush to Ai-ming's cheeks that had not been there an hour before, colour that spread each time Ma gazed at her for long moments, assessing her handiwork. They had forgotten all about me.

When I went back to the other room, the credits were rolling on *The A-Team*. I collapsed on the couch and pulled my knees up to my chest. Festive lights shone in almost every window but ours, and I had the sensation that our apartment was under scrutiny by residents of a UFO, unsure whether to land in Vancouver or fly on. The aliens in my spaceship were asking themselves: Do they have soda? What kind of food do they eat? Maybe we should wait and return in spring? *Land*, I told them. *People aren't made to float through the air. Unless we know the weight of our bodies, unless we feel the force of gravity, we'll forget what we are, we'll lose ourselves without even noticing.*

Ai-ming had been reading one of my father's bilingual poetry books. I picked it up now, a book familiar to me because I had used it in my calligraphy lessons. I paged through it until I came to a poem I knew, words my father had underlined,

Watch little by little the night turn around.
Echoes in the house; want to go up, dare not.
A glow behind the screen; wish to go through, cannot.
It would hurt too much, to see the swallow on her hairpin.
Truly shame me, to see the phoenix in her mirror.
To Hengtang I return at dawn
Fading like light on a jewelled saddle.

I read the poem twice through and closed the book. I hoped that my father, in the afterlife to which he had gone, was also celebrating Christmas and the New Year, but I feared that he was alone and that, unlike Ai-ming, he had not yet found a family to protect him. Despite my anger at him, despite the pain that wouldn't leave me, I could not shake my longing for his happiness.

It was inevitable, of course, that Ai-ming would discover the boxes under the table. In January, I came home from school and found my father's papers completely exposed–not because she had moved them, but because she had pushed the dining table backwards. One of the boxes had been completely emptied. Ba's diaries, spread across the table, reminded me of the poverty of the Vancouver flea market. Worse, Ai-ming could read every character while I, his only daughter, couldn't read a single line.

She was making cabbage salad and had grated so much horseradish that I wondered whether the cabbage would actually fit.

I said that I didn't know if my stomach could handle that much horseradish.

She nodded distractedly and flung the cabbage in, tossing it wildly. Everything flew up in the air and rained down into the bowl. Ai-ming was wearing Ma's "Canada: The World Next Door" apron, and her winter coat underneath.

She went to the table. "Once, when I was very small, I met your father."

I remained where I was. Ai-ming and I had never spoken about Ba. That she had known him, that she had never thought to mention this to me before, filled me with a disappointment so intense I could hardly breathe.

"This afternoon," she said, "I started looking inside these boxes. These are your father's things, aren't they? Of course, I knew I should ask your permission, but there were so many notebooks."

I answered without looking at her. "My father moved to Canada in 1979. That's twelve years of papers. A whole life. He hardly left us anything."

"I call this the room of zá jì," she said. "The things that don't fit. Bits and pieces . . ."

Inside my head, to calm the shivering that had started in my chest and was now radiating to my limbs, I repeated, over and over, the words Ai-ming had used but which I had never heard before: zá jì.

"You understand, don't you?" she said. "The things we never say aloud and so they end up here, in diaries and notebooks, in private places. By the time we discover them, it's too late." Ai-ming was holding a notebook tightly. I recognized it at once: it was tall but thin, the shape of a miniature door, with a loose binding of cotton thread. The Book of Records.

"So you've seen this before?" When I still didn't answer, she smiled sadly at me. "This is my father's handwriting. You see? His writing is so effortless, so artful. He always wrote with care, even if the character was an easy one. It was his nature to be attentive."

She opened the notebook. The words seemed to float on the surface and move of their own accord. I backed away. She didn't need to show me, I knew what it looked like.

"I have my own zá jì," she continued. "But it's everywhere now, and I don't know how to contain it. Do you know why we keep records, Ma-li? There must be a reason but what good does it do to keep such insignificant things? My father was a great composer, a great musician, but he gave up his talent so that he could protect me. He was an upright and sincere person and even your father wanted to keep a part of him. Even your father loved him. But they let him die. They killed him as if he were an animal. How can anyone explain this to me? If my father were alive, I wouldn't be here. I wouldn't be alone. And your father, he wouldn't have . . . Oh, Ma-li. I'm sorry. I'm so sorry."

Ai-ming did something I had not seen her do since her arrival more than a month ago. Not only did she weep, but she was too overcome to turn away or cover her face. The sound disturbed me so much, a low keening that dismantled everything. I thought she was saying, "Help me, help me." I was terrified that if I touched her, her pain would swell inside my body and become my own forever. I couldn't bear it. I turned away from her. I went into my bedroom and closed the door.

The room felt very small. *Family*, I whispered to myself, was a precious box that could not open and close at will, just because Ma said so. Ba's picture on my dresser hurt me so much. No, it wasn't the picture of him, but the feeling it caused, this chafing emotion that turned everything, even my love for Ma and Ai-ming, bitter. I wanted to throw the picture on the floor but I was afraid that it was real, that it contained my father himself, and if I damaged it, he would never be able to come home. The rain outside hammered against my thoughts. Down the windowpane, it changed and slipped, and all those rivulets of water, growing large and small, joining and shivering, began to confuse and mesmerize me. Was I as insignificant as that? Would I ever change anything? I suddenly remembered the scent of my father, a sweetness like new leaves or freshly mown grass, the smell of his soap. His voice with its oddly formal syntax, "What does daughter wish to say to Father? Why is daughter crying?" His voice like no voice that had ever lived.

I remembered, against my will, how I'd overheard Ma saying that when Ba was found, he'd had almost no belongings. She'd been speaking on the telephone, long distance, to a friend in Hong Kong. She said that the suitcase, full when he left, was empty. He'd gotten rid of everything, including his wedding ring, his Sony portable CD player and his music. He hadn't even been carrying a photograph of us. The only note he left was not a goodbye. All it said was that there were debts he couldn't pay, failures he couldn't live with, and that he wished to be buried in Hong Kong, at the Chinese border. He said that he loved us.

Once each year, my father used to take us to the symphony. We never had good seats but Ba said it didn't matter, the point was to be there, to exist in the room while music, however old it might be, was being renewed. Life was full of obstacles, my father used to tell me, and no one could be sure that tomorrow or next year, anything would remain the same. He told me that, when he was a young boy, his adoptive father, the Professor, had gone with him to the symphony in Shanghai and that the experience had changed him forever. Inside him, walls that he had never realized existed suddenly revealed themselves. "I knew I was destined to have a different kind of life," he said. Once he became aware of these walls, all he could think about was how to pull them down.

"What walls?" I had asked.

"Mìng," he said. "Fate." It was only later, when I looked up the word again, that I saw that mìng 命 meant fate but it also meant life.

The knock on the door brought me back to the rain, to the room and myself.

"Ma-li," Ai-ming began, sitting at the foot of my bed. She had turned the desk lamp on, and she looked like a pale shadow I had cast. "I shouldn't have read your father's diaries. This is what I wanted to tell you. I'm truly sorry, Ma-li. Please forgive me."

The quiet intensified. I was sitting as far away from her as I could, on top of my pillows.

Ai-ming whispered, "I am truly a very fearful person."

"What are you afraid of?"

"That your mother will ask me to leave. I can't survive by myself again. I know I can't."

Shame welled up in me. Her words reminded me, somehow, of Ba. "You're family, Ma said so."

"It's just, Ma-li, our lives are confused. And there is this . . . heartbreak between your family and mine."

I nodded as if I understood.

Ai-ming continued, "My father loved music, like yours. He used to teach at the Shanghai Conservatory, but that was before I was born."

"What did he do afterwards?"

"He worked in factories for twenty years. First, he built wooden crates and, later on, he built radios."

"I don't understand. Why would he do that if loved music?" The rain was falling so hard it was hitting the window like flecks of silver. Without warning, I pictured Ma waiting at the bus stop, her coat sticking to her, the wind and the wet chilling her bones.

"I met your father," Ai-ming said, evading my question. "When I was a little girl, Jiang Kai came to my village. My father was very happy to see him after so many years. It was 1977 and Chairman Mao had died and it was the beginning of a new era. Many things were changing but, even so, my father was careful about showing his emotions. But I saw how much Jiang Kai's visit meant to him, and that's why I've always remembered it. And then, after my father died, Jiang Kai called us. Your Ba was in Hong Kong. I spoke to him on the telephone."

"Ai-ming, I don't want you to talk about my Ba. I never, never want to hear his name."

"Mmmm," she said. She put her hands inside her coat pocket and immediately took them out again.

"Why are you always so cold!?" I asked, confused.

She clapped her hands together to warm them. "I left Beijing in winter and I think the cold got stuck in my bones because I can't get warm anymore. My mother and my grandmother helped me leave China. They were afraid because . . . I couldn't pretend. I couldn't go on as if nothing had changed." Ai-ming burrowed further inside her coat. She looked terribly young and alone.

"You miss your mother a lot, don't you?"

Ai-ming nodded.

Something clicked in my mind. I clambered off the bed and went out. The notebook with her father's writing, the Book of Records, was easy to find. I picked it up, knowing it would please her. But when I offered the notebook to Ai-ming, she ignored me.

I tried again. "Ma told me it's a great adventure, that someone goes to America and someone else goes to the desert. She said the person who made this copy is a master calligrapher."

Ai-ming emerged from coat. "It's true my father had excellent handwriting, but he wasn't a master calligrapher. And anyway, no matter how beautiful the Book of Records is, it's only a book. It isn't real."

"That's okay. If you read it to me, I can improve my Chinese. That's real."

She smiled. After a few moments of turning pages, she returned the notebook to the bedcover, which had become a kind of neutral ground between us. "It's not a good idea," she said. "This is Chapter 17. It's useless to start halfway, especially if this is the only chapter you have."

"You can summarize the first sixteen chapters. I'm sure you know them."

"Impossible!" But she was laughing. "This is how I used to badger my grandmother into doing things she had no intention of doing."

"Did your grandmother give in?"

"Occasionally."

I pulled the blanket around me as if the question was settled.

"Before you feel too comfortable," Ai-ming said, "I should tell you that my grandmother was known to everyone as Big Mother Knife."

"That's not a real name!"

"In this story, every name is true." She tilted her head mischievously. "Or should I be saying Girl? Or Ma-li? Or Li-ling? Which one is your *real* name?"

"They're all real." But even as I said the words, I doubted and wondered, and feared that each name took up so much space, and might even be its own person, that I myself would eventually disappear.

Perplexed, I curled up into the empty space between us. Ai-ming was still turning the pages of the notebook. I asked what Big Mother Knife looked like. Ai-ming stroked my hair and thought for a moment. She said that everything about Big Mother was both big and small: long eyebrows over slender eyes, a small nose and big cheeks, shoulders like hilltops. From the time Big Mother Knife was a little girl, she had curled her hair; by the time she was old, the curls were so fine and thin they seemed made of air. Big Mother had a jackdaw laugh, a terrible temper, and a shouting voice, and even when she was a small child, nobody dared to treat her lightly.

I closed my eyes and Ai-ming set the notebook aside.

In teahouses and restaurants, Big Mother Knife and her younger sister, Swirl, could sing harmonies so bewitching that problems large and small disappeared beneath the enchantment of their voices. They travelled from town to village, Ai-ming said, performing on makeshift stages, their dark hair bright with flowers or strings of coins. Story cycles like *The Water Margin* or *Wu Song Fights the Tiger* could last a hundred chapters, and the old storytellers could spin them out over months, even years. Listeners couldn't resist; like clockwork they arrived, eager to hear the next instalment. It was a time of chaos, of bombs and floods, when love songs streamed from the radios and wept down the streets. Music sustained weddings, births, rituals, work, marching, boredom, confrontation and death; music and stories, even in times like these, were a refuge, a passport, everywhere.

≡

IN THOSE DAYS, your village might change hands every few weeks, one day to the Communists, the next to the Nationalists, the next to the Japanese. How easy it was to mistake your brother for a traitor or your beloved for an enemy, to fear that you yourself were born in the wrong moment of history. But in the teahouses, anyone could share a few songs, anyone could lift their wine cup and toast the validity and the continuity of love. "People knew family and kinship were real," Big Mother said. "They knew regular life had once existed. But no one could tell them why, just like that, and for no good reason at all, everything they cared for was being ground to dust."

She was eighteen when she named her newborn baby Sparrow, a humble name rarely used for boys. The little sparrow was a bird so common that gods and men, idealists and thieves, Communists and Nationalists, would pass over him in disdain. The peaceful sparrow was weightless because he had no baggage to carry and no messages to deliver.

Throughout his childhood, Sparrow was startled awake in little towns. Teahouse patrons shouted drunkenly beside his mother and aunt, the men thundering like trombones and the women trilling like flutes. By the age of five, he was earning his keep, performing "Song of the Cold Rain" or "In That Remote Place," ballads so stirring that even those with nothing but dust in their pockets tried to feed him something, a nibble of turnip or a crust of bread, or even a puff from their foot-long tobacco pipes. "Here is the little sand sparrow (or golden wing, or red sparrow or stone sparrow)," the grandmothers would say, "come to peck at our hearts again."

Once, in the chaos, they passed a troupe of blind musicians in an abandoned village. The troupe walked–hand to elbow, elbow to hand–guided by a sighted girl who was only eight or nine years old. Sparrow asked his mother how the blind musicians, swaying forward like a rope in the dust, could hide themselves when the warplanes came, strafing houses and refugees, trees and rivers. Big Mother answered brutally, "Their days are numbered. Can a single hand cover the sky?" It was true. Year after year, the roads cratered and collapsed, entire towns vanished, crushed into the mud, leaving behind only garbage, dogs and the putrid, sickly sweet smell of bodies numbering in the hundreds, the thousands, and then the millions. And yet the lyrics of ten thousand songs ("You and I are forever separated by a river / my life and thoughts go in two directions . . .") crowded out everything in Sparrow's memory so that, as an adult, he retained very few memories of the war. Only this troupe of blind musicians could not be erased. Once, at the start of the war and then, astonishingly, near the end, they had reappeared with the sighted girl, now a teenager, coming from nowhere, disappearing to nowhere, a ribbon slipping endlessly between the buildings, their instruments humming as they passed. Were they real? Without realizing it, had he, Big Mother and Swirl, like the musicians, found a way to survive by becoming entirely unseen?

It was 1949 and the civil war was staggering to its conclusion. They were in a town by a large river, and outside, the melting ice made a sound like all the bones in China cracking. At one point, between songs, Big Mother's face appeared, upside down, wide and soft, peering under the table.

She gave him a single pear syrup candy. "This will keep your voice sweet," she whispered. "Remember what I say: music is the great love of the People. If we sing a beautiful song, if we faithfully remember all the words, the People will never abandon us. Without the musician, all life would be loneliness."

Sparrow knew what loneliness was. It was his cousin's small corpse wrapped in a white sheet. It was the man on the sidewalk who was so old he couldn't run away when the Reds came, it was the boy soldier whose decapitated head sat on the city gates, deforming and softening in the sun.

Waiting, Sparrow perfected his library of songs, singing to himself, "My youth has gone like a departing bird . . ."

Months later, when Chairman Mao stood atop the gate of Tiananmen Square, shouts of joy erupted through the airwaves. The radio carried the Chairman's melodic voice into streets and homes, even under the tables where Sparrow felt he had waited forever, and proclaimed a new beginning, a Communist society, and the birth of the People's Republic of China. The words wrapped like a filament around every chair, wrist and plate, every cart and person, pulling all their lives into a new order. The war was over. His mother dragged him into the open, embraced him so hard he couldn't breathe, she wept and gave him so many candies his head spun. The very next morning, they took to the roads once more, walking home to Shanghai.

After vanishing for years, Sparrow's father returned a revolutionary hero. Ba Lute was a tower of a man, round as well as tall, with wide hands, thick feet, and startling triangular-shaped eyebrows. A Flying Horse cigarette was forever crushed between his meaty lips. But the soft waves of jet black hair that Big Mother had once described to Sparrow had disappeared; his father's enormous bald head gleamed like the moon.

On their first meeting, his father plucked Sparrow from the ground and flew him over his head. "I was a book of zero when I joined the Party!" Ba Lute shouted. Sparrow tried not to vomit. He had always been a slight boy, and this slightness now convinced his father that Sparrow was still a little child. "I was a pig's ear!" his father cried, strangely triumphant. "But our Supreme Party crushed me down and made me new again. I was reborn by the blood of my brothers in the People's Liberation Army! Long live the Communist Party! Long live Chairman Mao Zedong, the Red Sun, the Great Saving Star!"

Held aloft in the air, Sparrow gazed at his father in painful, dizzying devotion.

The Party favoured them with a traditional laneway house, not far from the Shanghai Conservatory of Music. It was two storeys, with an inner courtyard and spacious side wings, with room enough for five families, yet despite the dire housing shortage, only two other people shared the courtyard: a husband and wife surnamed Ma, who had lost all three sons in the fighting. Together with Ba Lute, they painted the words, "Trust the Party in Everything" on their common brick wall, their feet tapping an intricate rhythm all the while.

Big Mother was the only one who didn't have the heart for music. Here in her childhood city, she found herself dreaming of her dead parents and her missing brothers, of Swirl's lost husband and child, fantasizing that they, like Ba Lute, would miraculously appear. She was going blind in one eye ("From looking at you," she told her husband) and she saw that her youth, those years of catastrophe and flight, of running along a precipice, had come to an end. Gone were the crushing sorrows and terrors, and gone, too, was her independence. She feared she had no idea how to live in peace.

Worse, she had somehow ended up married to the king of slogans. Everything was ideological with the man. Ba Lute demanded shoes made of humble straw rather than everyday cloth and, in addition to committing the blackboard news to memory, he read the *Jiefang Daily* religiously, his arms open as if to hug the words of Chairman Mao. The Great Helmsman, her husband informed her one morning, had said love was no excuse for withholding criticism.

"When did I ever spit the word *love* at you?" she said. "You Communists are all delusional."

Aghast, her husband twitched his cigarette at her. "If you had seen me at Headquarters, you would know how my comrades respected me!"

"Forgive me . . . I was lugging your son around on my back. I walked five thousand li hoping to trip over your big face again! Meanwhile, where were you? Off at 'Headquarters,' playing the piano and dancing polkas. You melon! Who's the true revolutionary hero?"

He dismissed her. It didn't matter. Their incompatible love made her feel hollow, as if the world had turned out to be flat after all. In honour of her husband's hero status, Big Mother Knife had been assigned an excellent administrative job at the Shanghai No. 2 Electric Wire Company. The twice-daily political meetings were so endless and excruciating she wanted to stick her fingers in the sockets.

By now, Sparrow was eleven years old, and his parents' arguments floated past him as lightly as a whistle of wind. In addition to his regular schoolwork, Ba Lute was tutoring him in music theory and jianpu, a notation using numbers, lines and dots

which Sparrow had first encountered when he was three years old, long before any other writing had entered his life. His father said that jianpu notation was accessible to everyone, and even the humblest daughter of the humblest peasant could read it. Numbers could describe another world. Now, while his father sulked and his mother shouted, he swayed at his desk, singing and singing again this exhilarating music in front of him, his audition piece for the Shanghai Conservatory of Music. Every hair on his head seemed to flutter like wings. The score his father had given him to learn was Bach's *Violin Concerto in A minor*, arranged for the Chinese two-stringed violin, the erhu.

2

BY FEBRUARY, AI-MING HAD been with us only two months, but it felt as if she had been there always. One night, I remember, Shostakovich's *Symphony No. 5* came on the radio. Partway through the third movement, Ai-ming sat down and gazed into the speakers as if into the face of a person she knew. Even I, as young as I was, felt disturbed by the music and the emotions it communicated. Or perhaps this is all hindsight, because later, through the Book of Records, I learned that Shostakovich had written this symphony in 1937, at the height of Stalin's Terror when more than half a million people were executed, including some of Shostakovich's closest friends. Under terrible pressure, he composed the symphony's third movement, a largo that moved its audience to tears by restating and dismantling the theme of the first movement: what initially had seemed simple and familiar, even artless, was turned inside out and refolded into another dimension. The first movement had been deceptive. Inside, concealed and waiting to be heard, were ideas and selves that had never been erased.

I was doing the dishes when the movement began, and at its close they were still unfinished, my hands wrinkled in the cold water, my fingers relaxed against the serrated edge of a knife.

"When I was little," Ai-ming said, standing up, "the radio played only eighteen pieces of approved music. Nothing else. We called them the yàngbǎnxì, revolutionary operas. But often, Ma-li, I would catch my father listening to illegal music."

Her father, the sparrow. "Listening like a bird?" I asked, immersed in the story that was now part of our day-to-day routine.

Unexpectedly, she sang a line of notes, and the music, as natural to her as breathing, contained both grief and dignity. It seemed to expand inside my thoughts even as it disappeared; it was so intimate, so alive, I felt I must have known it all my life. When I asked her if it was Shostakovich, she smiled and said no. She told me this music came from her father's last composition. "That's how Sparrow was, he wanted to exist through music, too. When I was small, he played his hidden records only at night, never in the day. In the village where I grew up, the nighttime sky felt everlasting."

"But, Ai-ming, how can *music* be illegal?" The idea seemed so absurd, I almost laughed.

She frowned at the dishes in the sink which appeared to have multiplied rather than diminished, took the washcloth and shifted me firmly aside. She let the cold water out and started again.

Many nights, Ai-ming said, ignoring my question, her father's music pulled her from sleep. Sparrow, she slowly pieced together, had been one of Shanghai's most renowned composers. But after the Conservatory was shut down in 1966 and all five hundred of its pianos destroyed, Sparrow worked in a factory making wooden crates, then wire, and then radios, for two decades. Ai-ming heard him humming fragments of music when he thought no one was listening. Eventually she came to understand that these fragments were all that remained of his own symphonies, quartets and other musical works. The written copies had been destroyed.

Ai-ming might wake hearing Shostakovich or Bach or Prokofiev; she knew them all, but their music didn't interest her. Beside the hump of her grandmother's snoring body, she fidgeted, hoping that Big Mother Knife would wake; half-asleep, she said things Ai-ming wasn't supposed to hear.

"I was a nuisance," Ai-ming told me. "To wake her up, I would loudly sing 'One's Young Life Is Like a Flower,' which was also illegal at the time. My grandmother taught it to me by accident and I could do a perfect imitation of her." At my request, Ai-ming demonstrated. Big Mother Knife, with her delicate hands and wrestler's shoulders, her brittle yet sonorous alto, her curled hair like a cotton ball, came to life before my eyes: *Ah, my beloved country, when will I fall into your embrace?*

Most nights, Big Mother woke, cursed her grand-daughter angrily and fell back asleep. But now and then, she softened.

"My stories are too old for you," she might say. "You don't have the brains to understand them."

"Maybe you don't tell them well."

"My stories are too vast. You haven't got the patience. Go play in the dirt instead."

"I have more patience than you."

"Belligerent child!"

In these moments, Ai-ming knew her father was eavesdropping. She could hear the muffled hiccups of his laughter. The smell of his tobacco slid over them, as if he was right on the other side of the wall.

"I assumed," Ai-ming told me, "that when Big Mother's stories finished, life would continue and I would go back to being myself. But it wasn't true. The stories got longer and longer, and I got smaller and smaller. When I told my grandmother this, she laughed her head off. She said, 'But that's how the world is, isn't it? Or did you think you were bigger than the world?'

"She would say, 'Are you ready? This next story will last so long you'll forget you were ever born.'

"'Hurry up, Big Mother!'

"'Listen now: one night, a young man with poems folded up in his pocket heard Swirl singing in the New World Teahouse. It was the first time he'd been there, and the poor soul fell in love with her. Well, who wouldn't fall in love with her?' Big Mother said. Why did her voice break like that? Was she crying? 'No one could help it. That was the world back then.'"

≡

WEN THE DREAMER, the aspiring poet, was born in the village of Bingpai to a prosperous family with a shaky history. Back in 1872, his grandfather had received a great honour: the Imperial court selected him to be one of 120 children sent to study in America. The family sold everything to help pay for the boy's journey. Fortune smiled on them for, after only ten years, that crackerjack son, now called Old West, sailed home, having lived next door to Mark Twain, studied at Yale and obtained his degree in civil engineering.

But after ten years at the Shanghai Armoury, Old West suddenly died of consumption, leaving behind a wife and baby daughter, and owing ten years' skilled labour to the Emperor. It was a calamity. Old West's father wept ten thousand tears and called destruction down upon himself. The four remaining sons, determined to prove their worth, banded together. Within a generation, the brothers acquired a dozen acres of land, including apple orchards and an enviable brick house, and were among the wealthiest men in Bingpai.

Meanwhile, Old West's daughter grew up terrified of her father's books, as if they held a disease that could destroy a village. Little West packed the books into a container and buried the lot of them. Her only son, born long after she had given up hope of a child, was the apple of her eye, and she hoped he would grow up to be a proper landlord like his great-uncles. Instead the boy lost his head to poetry. The boy was a walking cartload of books, he sat at his desk, calligraphy brush in hand, gazing up at the ceiling as if waiting for words to swallow him. His bedroom appeared to float, disconnected, above the solid world of transactions, commerce and land. She called him, sometimes gently, sometimes roughly, Wen the Dreamer. He was an observant and sensitive teenager and when the war came, it broke him.

In 1949, when the fighting ended, Little West sent him to Shanghai, hoping it would restore his vigour. Books made all his pockets heavy. When acquaintances met him on the road, Wen said he couldn't stop to discuss the Communists or the Nationalists, Stalin, Truman or the weather, because he was composing a six-character eight-line regulated verse in his head, and any variation in his path would push the words out of order. It was a lie. In fact, he was empty of poetry and afraid of words. During the war, Bingpai had been ravaged by the worst famine in a century, but he himself had never known hunger. He had sat in his study memorizing ancient and modern verses while, outside, labourers ate nothing but tree bark, mothers sold their children and young boys died horrifying deaths on the front lines. Half the village of Bingpai starved to death, but the gentry, inheritors of seemingly limitless resources, survived. Now, the Shanghai literati were talking about a new kind of poetry, a revolutionary literature worthy of a reborn nation, and the idea of it both moved and troubled him. Could the avant-garde express the ideas that went unspoken, could it confront the hypocrisy of lives like theirs? He did not know. When his poems came back from one of the revolutionary journals, a thick brush had scrawled across the page: "Excellent calligraphy. But your poems still sleep in their pastoral prison. Moon this, wind that, and who cares about your bloody grandfather?! Wake up!!!"

He knew they were right. Wen kept the rejection letter and threw the poems away. He remembered Bertolt Brecht:

I would also like to be wise.
In the old books it says what wisdom is:
To shun the strife of the world and to live out

Your brief time without fear
All this I cannot do.

By chance, he wandered into the New World Teahouse. A young woman was singing and Wen the Dreamer, perplexed and enchanted, listened to her for five straight hours. Afterwards, he wanted to speak to her, to commend the harsh beauty of her music, but with what words? The young woman's music contained poetry and the written word, and yet it travelled far beyond them to a realm, a silence, he had believed inexpressible. Wen wanted to call out to her but instead he watched her disappear, alone, up a flight of stairs. Nothing had shifted, the world was still the same, and yet, walking home, Wen felt as if his life had snapped in two. He stood for a long time looking at the muddy, sleepless river, which in the darkness was only a sound, trying to understand what had changed.

On a muggy August night, a package arrived for Swirl in the quarters she shared with three widows. This package contained a single notebook: the shape of a miniature door, bound together by a length of walnut-coloured cotton string. There was no postmark, return address or explanatory letter: only her name written on the envelope in a square yet affecting calligraphy. She sat down to her dinner of salted turnips but the notebook, occupying the empty space beside her, beckoned. Swirl opened it to the first page and began to read. It was a story, handwritten in brush and ink. She hadn't read a story in years, and at first could make no sense of it.

Page by page, her cramped, lonely room dissolved; she breathed in the dusty air of an imaginary Beijing where the government was on its knees, the old beliefs were all corrupted, and two friends, Da-wei and May Fourth, once intimate in every way, had arrived at "the tenth word," the place where vows are broken and lives diverge. When the notebook ended just as it had begun—in mid-sentence—she retrieved the envelope and shook it mightily, hoping that another might fall out, but it was empty. She sat on her bed in the newly quiet room, consoling herself by setting a passage of the story to music. When she sang the words, they took on yet another life, and filled the room with possibility. Her neighbours, the widows, rapped on the walls and yelled at her to be quiet.

A few days later, a second chapter arrived. Why was someone harassing her with mail? The following week, she received a third and a fourth. The novel continued, following first Da-wei and then May Fourth, as they made their way across a China in ruins. The narrative leaped and turned, as if entire chapters or pages had been ripped out; but Swirl, too, had been uprooted by the war, and she had no trouble filling in the missing gaps. Bit by bit, her irritation gave way to recognition and, slowly, without her realizing it, attachment.

On its surface, the story was a simple epic chronicling the fall of empire, but the people trapped inside the book reminded her of people she tried not to remember: her brothers and parents, her lost husband and son. People who, against their will, had been pushed by war to the cliff's edge. She read the fourth, ninth and twelfth notebooks as if reading would keep these characters anchored to the pages. Of course she was only a spectator; one by one, they spilled into the sea and were swept away. There were moments so piteous, she wanted to slam the book shut and close her eyes against its images, yet the novel insistently pulled her forward, as if its very survival depended on leaving the past and the dead behind. But what if the novel was written by someone she knew? Her family had all been singers, performers and storytellers. What if they had somehow lived, or lived long enough to write this fictional world? These irrational thoughts frightened her, as if she was being tempted backwards into a grief larger than the world or reality itself. What if the notebooks came from her dead husband, a Nationalist soldier killed at the start of the war, letters misplaced in the chaos and only now arriving? Swirl had heard of such a thing happening, a bag of mail lost in northwest China in the fourth century, preserved by the desert air. Thirteen hundred years later, an Hungarian explorer discovered them in a collapsed watchtower. But such things were as good as fairy tales. She chided herself for her delusions.

The parcels arrived on Sunday or Thursday evenings, when she was occupied in the teahouse downstairs, performing *The Dream of the West Chamber*. Could the writer be someone in the audience, or did he or she simply take the opportunity to slip in unnoticed, leaving the parcel at her door? Sleepless, she burned candles she couldn't afford to waste and reread the notebooks, searching for clues. Something else had caught Swirl's attention. The writer was playing with the names of Da-wei and May Fourth. In the first notebook, for instance, wèi had been written 位 which means place or location. In the third, wèi 卫, an ancient kingdom in Henan or Hebei Province. And in the sixth notebook, wēi 危, another name for Taiwan, as if the writer's location was coded into the book itself.

The day she received the twenty-fifth notebook, she met her sister in Fuxing Park. "I can't shake the feeling that I know this person," Swirl said. "But why such an elaborate game and why am I the recipient? I'm just a widow with no literary taste whatsoever."

"You mean those packages are still arriving?" Big Mother said, incredulous. "You should have told me sooner. It could be a criminal gang or a political trap!"

Swirl could only laugh.

"And please don't give me this nonsense about literary taste," her sister continued. "That kind of talk is just camel's lips and horse's mouth. Speaking of which, when will you stop living with those miserable widows and come stay with me?"

The next time they met, Swirl didn't mention the novel at all. Big Mother brought it up, saying that such fictions were a false world in which her younger sister, if she was not careful, would lose her corporeal being and become only air and longing.

But Swirl was only half-listening. She was thinking of the novel's characters: Da-wei, the adventurer, and May Fourth, the scholar. Their great fear was not death, but the brevity of an insufficient life. She recognized in them desires which, until now, had gone unexpressed in her. She smiled at her sister, unable to mask her sadness. "Big Mother," she said, "don't take it so seriously. It's only a book after all."

After the thirty-first notebook, she waited as usual. But day after day, and then week after week, no more deliveries came.

As time passed, the cold loneliness of Swirl's life reasserted itself. She ate her dinners and the notebooks piled up across from her, like a friend gone quiet.

Downstairs, rumours abounded.

The manager was worried that, with Chairman Mao in power, teahouses would be denounced as bourgeois frivolities, singers would be assigned to work units, and the lyrics of every song monitored. Bread Crumb fretted that the government would ban all games, especially and including chess. Not for the first time, Swirl wondered if it was time to leave Shanghai; passage to Hong Kong was getting more expensive by the day. But down at the train ticket office, she ran into the owner of the Library of the Gods, who was out taking the air with his cockatoo. In her distraction, she mentioned the mysterious notebooks. The bookseller teased her and said she had a twin in this district—a failed poet known as Wen the Dreamer was going from place to place, seeking a copy of the very same book.

"Try the Old Cat at the Perilous Heights bookstore. Suzhou Creek Road," he said. "Third lane down. She's got her whiskers in everything."

Swirl thanked him. She took the tram to the bookshop, thinking she would buy the rest of the novel and take it with her to Hong Kong. The Perilous Heights Bookstore was housed in one wing of a stout courtyard house, and the books were three-deep from floor to ceiling. In the literature section, she climbed a sliding ladder and began scanning shelves. But with neither title nor author, the search was futile. Meanwhile a steady stream of patrons arrived, young men and women who gazed all around, from north to south, as if looking for something they had dropped. One approached the bookseller and began whispering urgently. He was pushed aside by a grandfather wearing a Western jacket over a dark blue gown.

"Is it ready?" he said, between dry coughs. The Old Cat, who didn't look all that old, handed him a mimeographed sheaf of papers. From her vantage point, Swirl could see it was a copy of Guo Moruo's translation of Dr. *Faustus*.

The Grandfather's lips began to tremble. "But what about Part 2!"

"This is not a factory," the Old Cat said, slapping a lozenge on the counter. "Come back next week."

Others wanted foreign novels, works by philosophers, economists and nuclear physicists. As she fielded questions the Old Cat barely looked up. She herself was copying endless pages in her flowing script. Apparently the mimeograph was in need of a part that might never be replaced.

When Swirl climbed down from her ladder and inquired after Da-wei and May Fourth, the bookseller muttered, "Not again."

Every morning, Swirl would go to the bookstore; it was calm inside and the shelves were full of treasures. Surely another story could serve the same purpose, and lift her out of her solitude. She lost herself in travel books about Paris and New York, imagining a journey that would bring her to the far west.

Behind her table, the Old Cat rarely lifted her eyes; the only movement came from her ballpoint pen which slid efficiently up and down the page, so that the pen seemed to be the one delivering advice, information and succour. A bestseller, *Poor Persons Take Up Guns to Revolution*, kept the papers from flying away.

Several weeks into her new routine, Swirl saw another tower of paper settle on the desk, as if the first stack had drawn an admirer. Then, her eyes lifting, she took in a clean grey coat with cloth buttons, a pocket filled with papers, and finally, smooth, ink-stained hands. She looked again and saw a young man with wavy hair looking at her with embarrassed recognition in his eyes.

"Wen the Dreamer," she said.

"Miss Swirl," he answered.

"Took long enough," the Old Cat said. Her pen bobbed against the sea of the page.

The young man's manuscript threatened to fall, and he steadied the pages with the fingertips of his right hand. Swirl climbed down from the ladder and stared unashamedly at the top sheet, studying the neat columns of words, the calmly passionate calligraphy that had described the impossible love affair between May Fourth and Da-wei. She wanted to scoop the manuscript up, to rejoin May Fourth in the train to Hohhot, *peering through the dust-caked windows to see her beloved smoking on the platform; he would still be there in a week, a month, a lifetime, if she asked him to. It is not in me, she realized, to fall in love with someone who would wait. I can never settle for half a freedom.*

"May I?" she said, nodding at the manuscript.

The young man's fingertips refused to lift from the pages.

"I'm afraid," he said, "unfortunately, due to my negligence . . ."

He was not at all like her husband. So this was the writer, the mysterious sender of packages. Wen the Dreamer was wispy and pale, while her husband's Nationalist uniform had barely seemed to contain him. She blushed.

"Forgive me," he said, beginning again. "I'm afraid this manuscript is a different story. A different writer."

"It's yours, though."

"Yes," he said. "No. Well, you understand, the *writing* is mine." She had inched nearer to him. Almost there.

"Quit cowering in the bushes," the Old Cat said. The pen lifted its head and pointed its nib at Swirl. "If you, Little Miss, are looking for Da-wei's creator, good luck! I'll be the first to congratulate you when you find him, and to offer him, of course, a generous remittance, excellent terms, etc. But the author's whereabouts are as big a mystery to you as they are to poor Wen here. That said, if you need someone to *copy* your letters or write out your correspondence, well! There's no finer hand or gentler soul than his."

"I've looked everywhere for the rest of the novel," Wen the Dreamer said. "There must be, at least, another five hundred pages. Maybe more. I think it's called the Book of Records."

"But you—" Swirl began. She kept her gaze on the manuscript, which seemed solid and unimpeachable.

"I made a copy of the book for you, because I hoped . . . I wanted . . ."

Swirl knew she should end the conversation. Yet she could not bring herself to move away from the table.

"I wanted the story to bring you pleasure. What the Old Cat says is true, the words are not mine." His slender hands came together and clasped themselves. "I sent the first chapters before I finished copying the manuscript. When I realized what had happened, that the book ended, literally, in mid-sentence, I tried to write my own chapters. I tried to finish the story but I . . ."

"You did not have the talent," the Old Cat said.

His wispiness grew sorrowful now. But still he did not falter or retreat, he stayed very still and would not stop looking at her.

"Perhaps one day."

"Pardon me," Swirl said, stepping backwards. She felt ashamed but could not fathom why she should feel this way, if the emotion belonged to him or to her. She turned and walked to the door and managed to twist it open. Fresh air filled her lungs and she heard pages fluttering on every side.

"You'd be amazed at how few people can tell a story," the Old Cat was saying. The sound of her voice was as rough and reassuring as pebbles rolling together. "Yet still these new emperors want to ban them, burn them, cross them all out. Don't they know how hard it is to come by pleasure? Or perhaps they do know. The sly goats."

"Might I have the honour of walking you home?" Wen the Dreamer said.

The wind seemed to push her backwards and spin her around. But once she was facing him, once she saw his observant, hopeful eyes, words failed her. She opened her mouth and then closed it again.

"Heavens, the suspense!" the Old Cat said.

Finally, as if it were also the wind's doing, Swirl nodded in answer to Wen. "If you must."

Wen the Dreamer was at her side, he was holding the door, and she walked out.

Leaves were falling everywhere. Soon winter would come with its padded coats and knitted mittens and, at the arrival of the first frost, Wen the Dreamer would bring her scarves and woollen socks, jars of honey, and novels that he had copied by hand in his contained yet passionate script.

Winter was kind to Wen. His wispiness became a delicate kind of hardiness. Young girls and their mothers hung their washing across the alleyways and admired the elongated question mark of his body as he loped down the slippery walks, towards the teahouse where Swirl sang. "Don't go too fast," his neighbours called. "Your words will get scrambled!" He still didn't know how to talk about the new political order, the different factions and all his ideals; lines of poetry occupied his thoughts, he wrote them down and threw them out. He wrote and wrote and burned the pages. He waited.

"Carrier pigeon!" they called him.

And, still, out of an insistent curiosity, Swirl began approaching strangers reading in teahouses to enquire if they were acquainted with Da-wei, if they had perhaps journeyed to the Taklamakan desert and been impressed by his ingenuity in sending private messages to his lover over the radio broadcast, even while tens of thousands of people listened? "Hiding in plain sight," a well-dressed lady answered. "But, no, I've never heard of this devil." "Are you certain it's a local writer?" a poet asked.

"Everyone here is worthless. It must be a translation of a foreign work." A university student was convinced it was plagiarized from a novel by She Lao, another thought it sounded like a modern retelling of *Record of Heretofore Lost Works* or maybe Li Mengchu's *Slap the Table in Amazement*. "Anyway, don't waste your time on novels," someone told her. "The one to read right now is that upstart gun collector poet from Chengdu. Though, in general, anything universally praised is usually preposterous rubbish."

One night she returned to the old notebooks, reading them all over again from the beginning. As her candle flickered, she became certain that the writer had gone into exile or perhaps met with some tragedy. Perhaps she was one of the war wounded, she had been torn from her former existence, and the novel was now no more than a dream disturbed. Or, perhaps, like Swirl's husband, the writer had been killed in the fighting, and the last chapters could only be recovered in the next world. Wen had told her that it was not he but the author who had written the names of the major character—Da-wei and May Fourth—with different ideograms. Wen, too, believed, that the names were part of a code, a trail that someone could follow. But to what end? Swirl wrapped the notebooks carefully in brown paper; she must be vigilant. After all, the Book of Records was just a distraction from the realities of modern life. It was only a book, so why couldn't she let it go? She opened her trunk and saw objects from her past, a vanished time and a former self. If she let her guard down, she could almost see her son crawling towards her. He was pulling on her dress, on her fingertips, his delight like a string around her heart. Swirl had given birth to him when she was just fourteen years old. On the night he died, it had been too dark, too windy, for a child to travel to the netherworld on his own. She had wanted to follow him over the cliff edge, into the sea, but Big Mother had wept and begged Swirl not to leave her.

She could not sleep and lay awake until morning.

A dull light framed the curtains. Swirl heard an infant weeping, went to the window and when she looked down, she saw a couple trying to fit their baby into his winter coat, adjusting arms then legs then head as the baby lolled and weakly fought, then scrunched up his face and wailed, and still the outerwear refused to fasten. Wen the Dreamer came along the avenue, a block of pages sticking out of his pocket. He leaned towards the weeping child like a comma in a line so that, momentarily, the child, confused, suspended his wailing, the outerwear was fastened, and the little family went on their tremulous way.

Later that morning, when she stood with Wen on Huaihai Road, when he venerated her missing parents and older brothers, her lost husband and beloved son, when he wished for the blessing of her older sister, Swirl had a pure memory of her little boy. He had lost his footing and fallen backwards from the tram onto the concrete. Not even a scratch on him. He had laughed and asked if he could do it again, and then he had reached out his frail hand and snatched the bread out of Sparrow's mouth. Sparrow's lips had closed over air, bewilderment flooding his little face.

On Huaihai Road, Wen was asking her to be his wife.

Swirl remembered the quiet of the bed when she had woken suddenly. She had picked up her son's perfect hand, and a grey sadness seemed to move from his chest into hers, and in that moment, when she knew her child was dead, she lost her parents, her brothers and her husband all over again. Unable to stop crying, she had refused to let go of the child's body. But he grew rigid and cold in death. Only Big Mother had finally managed to lift the body from her arms.

"Miss Swirl," Wen said now, as shoppers with empty bags wandered past, "I promise you that for all our life together, I will seek worlds that we might never have encountered in our singularity and our solitude. I will shelter our family. I will share your tears. I will bind my happiness to yours. Our country is about to be born. Let us, too, have the chance to begin again."

"Yes," Swirl said, as if his words were a prayer. "Let us."

3

ONCE, AI-MING SAID TO ME, "Ma-li, I'm sure I've disappeared. Have I? Can you *really* see me?" She lifted her right hand and then her left, ever so slowly. Unsure if she was teasing or not, I echoed her movements, imagining I was at the mercy of the wind, pushed forward, turned sideways, only by forces unseen. "I'm invisible, too, Ai-ming. See?" I pulled her into the bathroom where we stared at our reflections as if they, and thus we, ourselves, were a mirage. It's only now, in hindsight, that I think she saw her own disappearance as a quality to be desired. That perhaps she needed, finally, to live unobserved.

It was 1991, mid-March, and Ai-ming had been with us for three months. Ma was working all the time now, and had taken an extra job to cover expenses for Ai-ming, for the future. I decided to use my Chinese New Year money, my lucky money, to treat Ai-ming to dinner. My plan was to take her to my father's favourite restaurant. The night we set out, the weather was mild, and we held hands as we walked beside the shrubs on 18th Avenue, past sagging houses and unkempt lawns, beneath cherry blossoms that perfumed even the saddest-looking blocks.

At Main Street, we turned north. I remember that an old grey cat lay in the middle of the pavement and didn't move as we approached, she only stretched one foot further away, and swiped her tail from side to side. The restaurant seemed to step out from the shadows wearing a vest of lights. It was a Polish place called Mazurka. It was warm inside and a quarter full, and there were white napkins and heavy utensils, and tea lights in miniature glasses. With Ai-ming, I felt grown-up and worldly, a true sophisticate. She, after all, came from Beijing, a city that, in 1991, had eleven million people. Ai-ming had explained to me the law of large numbers (LLN), and the various methods of constructing a mathematical proof, including the "proof without words" which used only visual images. I marvelled at statements like

If we know x, we also know y, because . . . or

If p then q . . .

In the summer of 1989, while still in Beijing, Ai-ming had sat the national university entrance examinations. Shortly after, she had been offered a place in the newly established computer science department at Tsinghua University, the most prestigious scientific university in China.

"I should have gone," she told me. "But how could I?"

Her decision not to attend Tsinghua, a principled but reckless choice, astonishes me now. But when I was eleven years old, I told her it all made sense.

Over cabbage rolls and perogies, Ai-ming told me that she was grateful for my mother's generosity but she felt unworthy. She felt vulnerable in the daytime, afraid to be seen, but she needed to be courageous and start her life again. Ai-ming told me that solitude can reshape your life. "Like a river that gets cut off from the sea," she said. "You think it's moving somewhere, but it's not. You can drown inside yourself. That's how I feel. Do you understand, Ma-li?"

I remembered a night before Ai-ming came to live with us, when I had submerged my face under the bath water and imagined what it would be like to stop breathing, to stop time, as Ba had done. I said I understood. How I yearned to understand everything.

The candlelight grazed all the objects of the room. The waiter spoke to us kindly, as if we had come from very far away, from a place where words waited for their echo. I feared my childhood would pass before he finished a sentence. And even when I answered him in my impeccable Canadian accent, he continued with the slowness of the ages, until I, too, felt my pulse slow, and time became relative, as the physicists had proved it was, so perhaps Ai-ming and I are still seated there, in a corner of the restaurant, waiting for our meal to come, for a sentence to end, for this intermission to run its course.

By then, Ai-ming had decided that she would attempt to enter the United States. The amnesty for Chinese students arriving after the Tiananmen demonstrations had ended, but, in March, a school friend of her mother's wrote to say that the U.S. Congress was considering a new immigration bill, similar to the 1986 blanket amnesty that had pardoned 2.8 million illegal aliens and granted them permanent residence. The stipulation then had been that the applicant had to have been residing in the United States for at least four years; no one knew what the new restrictions might be. The friend, who lived in San Francisco, offered Ai-ming a place to live temporarily; she said that to delay was foolish.

My mother had already obtained a forged passport for Ai-ming and other related papers. Neither of us wanted her to leave, but the decision was not ours. My mother's low income meant that we did not qualify to sponsor Ai-ming's immigration to Canada.

Ai-ming felt sure that one day, later in our lives, I would visit her in the United States. She would boast that she knew me because, by then, I would be well known. "An actor," she guessed. I shook my head. "A painter?" "No way." "A magician!" "Ai-ming!" I groaned, aghast. She smiled and said, "A writer? Sentences are equations, too." "Maybe." "An expert in substituting numbers for numbers." I had no idea what that was but I smiled anyway and said, "Sure." Only later did I find out it was the Chinese term for algebraic number theory. She told me I possessed what every great mathematician required, an excellent memory and a sense of poetry. I felt she saw into me, past every facade and flourish, and that the more she knew me, the more she loved me. I was too young, then, to know how lasting this kind of love is, how rarely it comes into one's life, how difficult it is to accept oneself, let alone another. I carried this security–Ai-ming's love, the love of an older sister–out of my childhood and into my adult life.

Or perhaps it could be that I have taken all our remaining conversations, all the half-finished and barely begun ones, and put each word into this particular night, that I have projected back in time some explanation for the inexplicable, and the reasons that I loved her and waited eagerly for each and every letter until the day arrived when no more letters came. Did she try to return to Shanghai and to her mother? Did she make a success of herself in the United States? Had there been an accident? Despite my efforts, I still do not know. It could be that I am misremembering everything. I had only a small understanding of the things that had happened in her country, my father's country, in 1989, at the end of spring and the beginning of summer, the events that had necessitated her leaving. Here, inside my father's favourite restaurant, I asked the question I had been longing to speak aloud, to ask if she been part of the demonstrations in Tiananmen Square.

Ai-ming hesitated for a long time before answering. Finally, she told me about days and nights when more than a million people had come to the Square. Students had begun a hunger strike that lasted seven days and Ai-ming herself had spent nights on the concrete, sleeping beside her best friend, Yiwen. They sat in the open, with almost nothing to shelter them from the sun or rain. During those six weeks of demonstrations, she had felt at home in China; she had understood, for the first time, what it felt like to look at her country through her own eyes and her own history, to come awake alongside millions of others. She didn't want to be her own still river, she wished to be part of the ocean. But she would never go back now, she said. When her father died, she had been dispossessed. She, too, had passed away.

Ai-ming told me that I would always be family to her, I would always be her little sister, Ma-li, Marie, Girl. With my many names, I felt like a tree with crowns of branches. She sang snippets of songs Big Mother had taught her and we laughed all the way home. When we arrived, I felt that, little by little, our arms disappeared, the shape of our bodies ceased to exist, even our faces, so that inside we were well and truly hidden, erased from the world. But this did not seem a loss; we embraced the possibility of being part of something larger than ourselves.

Back in our apartment, Ai-ming had not turned the lights on. She made tea and we lay in the darkness and stared out the windows, into the courtyard and the neighbouring, mysterious homes. Ai-ming continued to tell me the story of the Book of Records, which was not, after all, a recapitulation of those thirty-one notebooks, but about a life much closer to my own. A story that contained my history and would contain my future.

WHEN SWIRL AND Wen the Dreamer married in Bingpai in 1951, the singers and booksellers of Shanghai arrived bristling with musical instruments and hand-copied books. Wen's uncles slapped his back, sucked the ends of their long pipes and shouted, "Your wife is a treasure. Old West is smiling down on you!" They played cards and smoked so heavily, the resulting thick fog washed out into the road and confused passing bicyclists. The Old Cat, in a three-piece suit, danced with such elegance that even Ba Lute, itchy in his peasant clothes, wept as he played. Afterwards, the Old Cat proposed a toast to "that infamous explorer, that giant among men, Da-wei!" Everyone drank, most thinking this must be the scoundrel who had broken her heart. The party seemed to expand beyond its limits, twirling forward like a well-known song with extra verses.

Sparrow had written a piece of music, a truncated sonata with main theme and development, and he hummed it to Wen the Dreamer as the sun rose into the fog on the second day. In the echoing hum after he had finished, Wen said, "You are, of course, an acolyte of the illustrious Herr Bach?"

Sparrow didn't understand four of the words in that sentence but he nodded just in case.

"In that case, I have something for you," Wen said. He presented him with three precious records, imported from America.

Finally, on the third day, as the afternoon drew to a close, Swirl and Big Mother Knife sang a duet, and in their singing bade farewell to one another, to the narrow beds and the childhood fears they had shared, and the open roads that had marked this passage from one breath of life to the next. "I have fulfilled my duty to our parents," Big Mother told herself. Swirl would live here, in the village of Bingpai, in Wen the Dreamer's family home. She clutched her sister one more time, before turning away.

Everything passes, Big Mother thought, as she sat in the low bunk of the train returning home.

Dry shells of sunflower seeds cracked like kindling beneath her shoes. Ba Lute had met old friends from Headquarters and gone to play cards in their private compartment; Sparrow was reading a discarded copy of *Literary and Artistic Issues in the Soviet Union*. The landscape passed in waves of green and yellow as if the country were an endless unharvested sea. West of Suzhou the train stopped and goods were hustled out by a long line of porters. Big Mother stared out the window and saw a woman her age standing on the opposite platform, a small child in front of her. The little girl seemed lost in thought. The mother's hands rested protectively on the child's shoulders. Big Mother closed her bad eye and pressed the other to the glass.

The woman, on closer inspection, was crying freely. Tears slipped unchecked down her cheeks. Soldiers from the People's Liberation Army moved behind her, circling the mother and child with a sly friendliness. The whistle sounded and the doors of the train slammed closed. Still the woman didn't move.

The train pulled away and the mother, child and soldiers vanished from sight.

Ba Lute returned, half-drunk, his limbs clumsy. He tried to fold himself into the space beside her, only partly succeeding. "Despite your meanness, you're the one I come back to," he mumbled, eyes closed. "Home from the tiresome world." Big Mother wanted to insult him but she restrained herself. Her husband's lips were thin with sadness and his face had aged. Even his grey stubble looked desolate. Outside the window, the landscape hurried past as if it to erase everything that had come before.

A year passed, and then four or five, in which Big Mother Knife rarely saw her sister. Swirl and Wen now had a daughter, Zhuli, who had been born a ten-pound juggernaut before stretching into a lithe and sweet-natured child. "The girl," wrote Swirl, "sings all the time. This child is the mystery at the centre of my life."

Big Mother wrote back, "They turn into wretches."

It was 1956 and Big Mother's family had been in Shanghai for almost a decade. In quick succession, she had given birth to two more fluffy-haired boys with soft, triangular eyebrows. Ba Lute had insisted on naming them Da Shan (Big Mountain) and Fei Xiong (Flying Bear). What next, Big Mother had shouted at him, Tasty Mutton? The walls of the alleyway house had begun to press in on her like a jacket grown too tight. This morning, for instance, Da Shan was jabbing all ten fingers into his younger brother's screaming face. Meanwhile, Sparrow was deaf to everything but the records he had borrowed from the Conservatory. Her oldest son was about to graduate with a double major in piano and composition but, night after night, he sat with his foolish forehead pressed to the gramophone, as if the machine was his mother. He was transcribing Bach's *Goldberg Variations* into jianpu and the bourgeois music fluttered through the house, on and on, until Big Mother heard it even when the rooms were silent. Meanwhile, her hero husband was busy leading another land reform campaign, he was always away, overthrowing a landlord's family, repossessing fields of mung beans, flax and millet, and maybe the air itself, on behalf of the People. And if it wasn't land reform, it was song and dance troupes, political study sessions, Party meetings, or private flute lessons for yet another influential cadre. Did he even teach at the Conservatory anymore? At home he was petulant and insufferable, and looked at Big Mother and the boys as if at a very dirty window. She ignored him. It wasn't difficult. The insults that should have pricked her heart were as harmless as porridge.

Still, those pretty piano notes were mocking all the movements she made. They dripped from the kitchen to the bedroom to the parlour, seeping like rainwater over the persimmons on the table, the winter coats of her family, and the placid softness of Chairman Mao's face in the grey portrait framed on the wall. She thought he looked doughy, not at all like the handsome, intrepid fighter he had once been. Regret crawled through her heart and limbs; did it crawl through Chairman Mao's? Despite her best efforts, loneliness was encroaching upon Big Mother Knife.

Around noon, after the boys had left for school, Ba Lute unexpectedly arrived home. Her husband carried his army bag over his shoulders, and grinned as if he'd just won a nasty brawl. His padded coat was the same oyster-shell blue as the winter sky, except for a streak of what looked like blood, and it saddened Big Mother that the outside world, with all its hatreds, both petty and historical, had come inside her home.

"Stupid me," she said. "I thought the war ended in 1949."

Ba Lute had been gone for six weeks and, at the thought of seeing his family again, had broken into a run as soon as he entered the laneway. His wife's indifference made him feel like a beggar. Big Mother was still in her nightdress and her curly hair stood up on her head like cotton batting. He couldn't decide whether to scold her or comfort her.

He threw down his copy of *Jiefang Daily* and a pack of Front Gate cigarettes. "The Party has launched another bold campaign. Aren't you interested? And why aren't you dressed?"

"Oh, good. A new campaign. As Chairman Mao says, 'After the enemies with guns have been wiped out, there will still be the enemies without guns.'"

He ignored her tone. "Haven't you been reading the papers?"

"They closed our office because the pipes froze," Big Mother said. "Everything flooded. We're a unit of more than two hundred people and the committee has to find a new space for us. So I've been liberated."

"That's no excuse to stay indoors and feel sorry for yourself!"

Big Mother eyed her husband.

He sighed and tried to soften his tone. "Isn't there anything to eat?" He took off his coat and went to the water basin, drinking straight from the dipper. Underneath all the padding, she saw that Ba Lute's clothes seemed far too large, as if he had halved in size. Perhaps he had donated his flesh to the peasants. She got up, smashed around and finally slapped some food down in front of him. Ba Lute acted as if hadn't eaten in a week. After polishing off a mountain of rice and a leg of chicken, their entire meat ration for the week, Ba Lute conceded he had missed her.

She sniffed. "Is it so bad out there?"

"The usual." He found a clean cloth and wiped his mouth, then his whole face, pressing down on his eyes. Ba Lute had always been too round and cocky for his own good. This new thinness gave him a vulnerable, starved look, which confused her. He ran the cloth over the back of his neck. "Our land reform policy is glorious, but the People are in disarray. Still, it's necessary work we're doing. No one can say otherwise." Without seeming to realize he was doing it, he started humming "Weeds Cannot Be Wiped Out."

"You and land reform," she said. "You'd think your mother gave birth to the idea."

Ba Lute was so startled that he laughed. He checked himself and said abruptly, "Go to the devil, how can you joke like that? You're going to get yourself killed." As he put the cloth down, his hands shook. "Big Mother, you've got to learn to hold your tongue."

She looked at the bone on his plate. Picked clean. "You're home for awhile, are you?"

"I am."

"Good. Because I'm going to Bingpai to see my sister."

"Eh?" he said. His eyebrows lifted so high she thought they would fly away. "But what about your husband?"

She picked up the bone and chewed on the end. "He'll survive."

Ba Lute smiled but then, thinking over what she said, frowned. He slapped his hand on the table, working himself up into a grand annoyance. "Big Mother, listen here. Don't you know we're right in the middle of a life-and-death campaign? Please! Don't look at me like that. I'm telling you, there's a war going on in the countryside."

"It's always a war with you people."

"There you go again! Now just hold on and think it through."

Once Ba Lute got going, she couldn't stop him. She stared hungrily at his empty plate.

"Some of these peasants, these desperate people," he continued, "have to be forced to remember every humiliation. Forced! They have to be driven nearly out of their minds with grief before they can find the courage to pick up their knives and drive the landlords out. Of course they're afraid. In the whole history of the world, what peasant revolution has ever made a lasting change?" He rubbed his bald head again. "I know what I'm talking about, don't think I don't. Anyway, it was all calming down but the new campaign stirred everyone up again. Encouraging the masses to criticize the Party! And now they've done it. . . ."

"My work unit has already issued me a travel permit."

"Your husband forbids it."

"Chairman Mao says women hold up half the sky." She took his plate, picked up the chicken bone and flung it towards the scraps bucket. She missed. The bone hit the wall and stuck there. "Be a model father," she said, "and look after your sons."

"Do you always have to be so stubborn?" he yelled. Ba Lute slumped forward over the table. "You weren't so pigheaded when I married you." He was like that. He exploded and then settled right down again. Like a trumpet.

For the first time in two months, Big Mother felt slightly better. "It's true," she nodded. "I wasn't."

The journey from Shanghai to the village of Bingpai was nineteen hours by train and minibus. By the end of her journey, Big Mother Knife felt like someone had broken both her legs. In Bingpai, she stumbled from the bus into the drizzle and found herself in an empty field. The village, which she remembered as prosperous, looked bedraggled and ugly.

When at last she trudged up the mountain path to Wen the Dreamer's family house, she was in a foul mood. At his gate, she thought her eyes were playing tricks on her. Surely the driver was a crook, and the fool had let her off at the wrong village or even the wrong county. Yet . . . there was no denying that the flagstones looked familiar. The courtyard was missing its gate, it had plain disappeared. Seeing lamplight, she marched through the inner courtyard and into the south wing. There was junk everywhere, as if the fine house was about to be torn down. Entering, she saw a half-dozen wraiths crawling on the ground. In her fright, she nearly dropped her soul (her father's expression), but then Big Mother Knife realized these were not wraiths but people. People who were busily removing the tiles and digging up the floors.

"Greetings, Sister Comrades!" she said.

A wraith stopped its digging motion and peered at her.

Big Mother pressed on. "I see you are busy with reconstruction work? Each one of us must build the new China! But can you tell me, where I should go to find the family that resides here?"

The woman who was staring at her said, "Thrown out. Executed like criminals."

"Travelling–like criminals?" Big Mother said. Her instinct was to laugh. She thought she had mistakenly heard xíng lù "executed" (刑 戮) rather than xíng lù "traveller" (行 路).

Another woman made a gun with her hand, shot at her own head, and broke into a chilling smile. "Firstly the man," she said. "Secondly," she shot again, "the woman."

"They buried silver coins under the floor," another said. "That money belongs to the village, they know it does, and we'll uncover it all."

Big Mother reached her hand out but the wall was too far away.

"Who are you, anyway?" the woman with the make-believe gun said. "You look familiar."

"I would like to know who gave you permission to be here," Big Mother said. To her fury, she could detect a trembling in her voice.

"Permission!" the woman hooted.

"Permission," the others echoed. They smiled at her as if she was the wraith.

Big Mother turned and walked outside. She went slowly through the inner courtyard, all the way to the front of the house. Here she lost momentum and sat down on a low brick wall a hundred yards from the entrance. Nobody had followed her and the kerosene lamp continued to flicker from inside. Now she heard the thwack of their shovels. That bus driver was the grandson of a turtle! He'd certainly dropped her at the wrong place. Ba Lute's warnings were getting under her skin. She pulled on her hair and tried to wake herself, she pressed her hands violently to her face, but no matter what she did, her eyes refused to open and the dream would not end. She stared all around and saw the absurdity of her travelling bag, the muddy ground, the grey house and tiny night stars coming out. She would have to go back into the house and straighten things out. Yes, she would go back inside. It was a strange, windy night and she could hear a shrill cry echoing over the hillside. What ghosts were visiting this place? She could hear shouts now, coming nearer, and the ringing of a gong. A funeral, she thought numbly, but still Big Mother did not stand up or withdraw.

A crowd was coming along the road, swaying and heaving in a procession. Big Mother pushed herself onto her frozen feet. She had no idea how long she'd been sitting here, but the women with the shovels had gone home. In the fog, and in their excitement, they had not even seen her as they passed.

As the parade approached, Big Mother could hear their voices more distinctly. Although there was indeed a gong, bells and the occasional burst of singing, it was not a funeral. Certain words were repeated, "stand up," "have courage," "devil," but the shouting was oddly disjointed, as if opposing leaders were battling for control of the slogans.

At the head of the procession, Wen the Dreamer walked with his body crookedly bent. A woman walked behind him. Swirl's hair fell loose and wild. She was completely tipped forward, as if she carried a piece of furniture on her back, but there was none. The distance between them halved and then halved again. Frenzied faces closed in on Big Mother, crying and groaning. She could not make out all the words but she heard:

"Honour the Chairman!"

"Kill the demons!"

"Long live our glorious land reform!"

I have crossed into death itself, Big Mother thought. Now she saw that her sister's arms were roped together behind her, in a position that forced her two elbows up into the air. Everyone seemed fuelled by exhaustion, as if they had recently been shaken from sleep. The cavalcade stretched along the road, but they were so absorbed by their own noise that they, too, did not notice

Big Mother. The very last person, a small boy struggling to keep up, glanced in her direction but his eyes did not fix on her. He hurried along.

Big Mother stood up and, leaving a wide gap, followed them. The procession continued for at least another hour. Finally, just before the tree line, the shouting faded and the people drained away like rivulets of water. By the time Big Mother reached the end point, her sister and Wen had been untied and were standing, incongruously, by themselves. They were cautiously testing their backs, slowly stretching out their arms. They were carrying their own ropes, as if the ropes were only props.

"Is is really you, my sister?" Big Mother said.

Swirl turned, peering into the darkness.

"Little Swirl," Big Mother said again, afraid to touch the woman. "Is that you?"

Big Mother did not hear the entire story that night or in the nights that immediately followed. All her sister would say was that these parades, "struggle sessions," she called them, had been going on for the past three months.

"Most of the time, it's harmless," Swirl said. "They take us to the schoolyard and denounce us as landlords. We have to kneel, but all they want is a thorough self-criticism. Occasionally, like tonight, we're paraded through the village."

Big Mother could not contain her fury. "And the rest of the time?"

Swirl glanced at Zhuli, who was folded into her father's lap, and said nothing.

Everyone spoke in whispers, as if afraid to wake the gods of destiny, or even Chairman Mao himself. The hut, with its mud walls and straw roof, was meant for animals, that much was abundantly clear. Big Mother wondered where the evicted pigs and cows had gone.

"We're not suffering," her sister said.

"It was inevitable," Wen the Dreamer told her, his voice barely louder than the steam from his tea. "Justice had to be done eventually."

In this way, two days and two nights passed in a silence that cut deeply into Big Mother. She did not need a lengthy explanation, it was clear what had taken place. But in Shanghai, she had not witnessed the land reform campaign. In the cities, people from all corners of life and with every political affiliation had been reassigned to new quarters. People who had lost their homes were given new ones. It had been part of the war recovery.

On the third night, Big Mother lay on the kang beside her sister and the child, Zhuli, who was already five years old. The child snored vigorously. The kang, heated from below by a charcoal stove, looked like a relic from somebody's tomb. To make space, Wen's elderly mother had gone to stay with a relation.

Despite the relative warmth of the heated bed, her sister was shivering.

"Tell me something," Swirl said suddenly. "Just a few words to distract me from this place."

Big Mother swallowed several times to alleviate the dryness in her throat. Outside, Wen was smoking; the thin walls might as well be cloth. She told her sister about Sparrow and his brothers, about the jianpu music that ran from page to page. Sparrow never stopped composing. He didn't breathe, she thought, he only emitted music. "My boys are energetic and have more hidden thoughts than a cartload of books. A mother never knows her children as well as she imagines."

"How true, how true," her sister breathed.

Big Mother said she'd been back to an old teahouse where they used to sing, the Purple Mountain Teahouse. "They've changed the name," she said. "It's now the Red Mountain People's Refreshment House." Swirl giggled. "The rooms are closed and all they serve is tea and melon seeds. But, still, the usual crowd comes to chatter, drink a little or fill their canisters. There are even singers who perform the new repertoire, 'The East Is Red,' 'Song of the Guerrillas,' and all that. It's stirring, who can argue! Even I want to overthrow something when I hear it. But revolutionary music hurts the ears after awhile. There's no nostalgia in it, no place for people to share their sorrows. Of course," Big Mother continued hurriedly, "in the New China such sorrows as we knew are long gone." She went on to describe a few of the patrons, including the ones who still came with their orioles and thrushes, and the storytellers and balladeers who now told the epic of Chairman Mao's Long March, in fifty dogged episodes.

"Do you remember that book I told you about," Swirl asked. "The thirty-one notebooks? The Book of Records." Her voice barely reached Big Mother, even though they were curled together on the narrow kang.

"You burned it, I hope? Anything that inspires such devotion is surely banned."

"Burn the Book of Records?" her sister asked. A flash in her voice. Indignation. "How could I?"

"To save yourself," Big Mother said.

"To save myself, I couldn't."

The book was still in its hiding place inside the family home. Tucked into the pages were all the letters Wen the Dreamer had written to Swirl. When those hungry spirits found no silver coins, they would open the walls. Nothing hidden would remain unseen. Swirl described the coded names, how the ideograms used for Da-wei and May Fourth changed, and seemed to refer to compass points on a map. Big Mother felt a terrible chill. The love letters would be bad enough but what was in that book anyway? What if it turned out to be written by a Nationalist traitor? They would all be screwed to the eighteenth generation.

"I need to go back to the house," Swirl said. "I have to get those notebooks back."

"Don't be a fool."

The words were spoken harshly but Swirl didn't seem to hear.

"Wen's grandfather was a copyist, too, did you know? There are books hidden in the ground that have been preserved for centuries, all the books that Old West brought from America." She pulled the cover up to her chin so that only her eyes and the bridge of her nose were visible. "Everything on this earth has its lifespan and then, it must be natural, we have to make it disappear. As if the new didn't come from the old. As if the old didn't grow from the new."

Big Mother hesitated and then she asked softly, "But what is this upheaval?"

"Haven't you seen it? I thought the land reform campaign had reached everywhere. During the war . . . I'll never forget the cruelties we saw. I understand why nothing can stay the same."

"Of course, but . . ."

"Once everything is broken, they can build society once more."

How many times had her sister spoken these words? "They," Big Mother said. "The revolutionary committees? The Communist Party?"

"They say it's the wheel of history. I'm not afraid. You know how it is, one hand can't stop the flood from destroying the bank. Only . . . I worry about Zhuli. She's been born into the wrong class, she's the daughter of Wen the Dreamer. The daughter of a land-lord. Nothing I do can change that. What if I can't protect her?"

"Come with me to Shanghai. My no-good husband can arrange it."

"It's the wheel of history," Swirl said. There were no tears in her voice, just the cut glass of pragmatism. "The Party says only the guilty try to escape punishment. If we run away, not even Ba Lute will be able to intervene. We can't risk it. I have to protect Zhuli, but how?"

Much later, in the years after Swirl had been released from the desert labour camps, when Zhuli had already grown into a young woman, Big Mother pieced the story together.

The Party men had arrived in Bingpai on the day Wen and his uncles were dragging ice off the mountain lake. It was arduous work, but worthwhile because, once covered in straw, the ice, ever useful, would keep for many months. The uncles used to have labourers but now preferred to do this kind of work themselves. The previous year, when land redistribution had reached Bingpai, the brothers had known better than to argue. There were far worse fates than having to give up a few acres of land. In the neighbouring county, a dozen people had been struggled against–a sort of large meeting where accusations were shouted, where the accused were beaten and sometimes tortured–and executed, but the dead had been, mostly, rich men infamous for their savagery. Last year, when delegates from the Bingpai peasants' association arrived at their gate, the brothers had not resisted and had relinquished the title deeds for all seventeen acres of the family holdings, which would be redivided among the village. True, Er Ge's wife had left him, but he still had the two grown children. And Ji Zi had talked of killing himself, but no one took him seriously. Meanwhile life continued: until land reform was finalized, the fields still had to be tilled and orchards tended. In fact, the harvest of sweet apples that year was the most bountiful in the brothers' memory.

As the cart complained its way through the gate, Wen and his uncles were surprised to see two strangers, as well as the village head and the chairman of the peasants' association, standing outside. Da Ge stepped out from behind the block of ice. He greeted the visitors and invited them inside to share a meal. The village head declined. It was all rather uncomfortable and Da Ge, who had always been impatient, said, "Well, if there's nothing urgent, we'll get back to work. The ice can't wait."

One of the strangers, who had yet to introduce himself, intervened. There was a meeting underway at the village school, he informed them, and the brothers were late.

The village head stepped forward. "These two teachers," he said, indicating the strangers, "have come all the way from the county Party committee. Of course, as your family is so prominent in Bingpai, how could we start the meeting without you?"

In the courtyard, the silence seemed to echo off the bricks and ice. Where was everyone anyway? Neither Da Ge nor his brothers had eaten in almost six hours. Still, he led his siblings and Wen through the gate and fell in line behind the strangers and the village head.

At the primary school, Swirl had been bundled off to the side with her daughter, where they knelt with twenty-odd others on the cold ground. Among them were the wives of Wen's uncles, who had been brought under guard and were now at centre stage. The crowd was already in the hundreds, yet more people kept arriving to take part in the meeting. Da Ge's wife was repeatedly slapped and kicked until she cried out for mercy. The fierce, no-nonsense woman, already in her mid-fifties, was hysterical. She was pawing at the ground as if trying to find a coin in the ice.

Zhuli had long stopped crying. She clutched her mother, completely silent. Swirl didn't dare try to comfort her. When I get home, she told herself, I will warm a little water, wet a cloth and wipe her frozen tears away. It's nothing. Nothing that a little warm water can't clean away.

Now the men came, the four brothers and her Wen. They were surrounded and quickly trussed up. Swirl could hear Da Ge shouting. Her daughter was weakly calling out, "Ba!" Swirl cupped her body around Zhuli, thinking that the child must not see, nothing must happen. But hands came and pulled at Zhuli. Voices shouted at the child to open her eyes, she had to learn. Swirl stumbled to her feet and tried to get her daughter back, but they moved decisively and brutally. When she looked up from the ground, she saw that Zhuli had been lifted onto a man's thin shoulders. The girl sat, unmoving, staring ahead of her.

The arrival of Wen the Dreamer and his uncles had brought renewed life to the freezing crowd. New accusations came to the fore. One spoke of the famine and how he'd sold his land to Da Ge for nothing. "Robbery!" someone shouted. "You used your good fortune to trample your neighbours into the mud. How else could you acquire over seventeen acres in so short a time?" The brother of Er Ge's wife accused Er Ge of mistreating her, beating her and even depriving her of food. Er Ge denied it, he tried to put up a fight but others came to knock him down. It was chaos. The strangers had dispersed through the crowd asking people, "Who beat you? Who humiliated your fathers and raped your daughters? Was it them?"

"It was . . . It was . . ."

"Who made their fortunes during the war?"

"These landowners think they can spit out a square of land. They think you should get down on your knees and bless them!"

"We must free ourselves!" There was revenge in their voices but also grief and weeping.

"Comrades, have the courage to stand together once and for all!"

"A life for a life!"

"Who humiliated you? Tell us. This is not your shame! Why should you carry it?"

A woman had rushed into the circle. She pointed at a man in a dark blue gown. "This man raped me when I was six years old," she said. "He covered my face with my mother's clothes and he . . ." She was cradling her stomach and began to sob. "That was only the beginning. He saw that my father was dead and I had no one to stand up for me. This monster, this animal! Every pain I suffered gave him pleasure." Someone pushed a shovel into her hands. At first her blows were weak, as if only grief, not rage, motivated her. But the chanting of the crowd drove her on and the shovel took on a new, determined rhythm. She continued to land the shovel even after it made no difference.

"Twenty years of war and for what? To be thrown back into the gutters of society again?"

"I worked myself to death to harvest five dàn of grain. Meanwhile you took four dàn in rent," a man said to Da Ge. "We ate the husks of rice, the husks of wheat, the husks of millet. My children have been hungry from the day they were born. But what are your tenants to you? Nothing but fertilizer!"

"I gave you fair terms," Da Ge began but he was immediately drowned out.

"Fair?" The man laughed bitterly.

"Pay your debts! Everyone must pay their debts!"

"If you don't settle with them now," one of the strangers said calmly, "these landowners will wait until we're gone, and then they will wipe you out one by one. You cannot make half a revolution."

Scorn and contempt were heaped on the landlords. The agitation increased. Another family was brought in and there were more crimes and more denunciations. Together, their stories made a claim that no one could deny.

"Aren't these your countrymen?" a man said, turning on Wen. "Isn't this your crime?"

"My crime," Wen said.

The man slapped him. "Is this your crime?"

"I admit it. I accept," he cried.

Wen's nose began to bleed. The man slapped him repeatedly, as if he were disciplining a child. The crowd was laughing and the laughter had a sharp, bleating sound. Two men on the stage were kicked until they no longer moved. Swirl thought she must be hallucinating when the guns were drawn and Da Ge and his wife were executed. Torches were lit and others demanded yet more killing. She saw Wen dragged forward. Her husband begged for mercy. The gun moved away from him, came back, moved away, came back. Her daughter was crying, struggling to free herself from the stranger's rigid arms. "Ba!" she screamed. "Ba!" Er Ge was shot in the chest and then in the face. Three more men were shot. One would not die and had to be beaten. Swirl felt herself losing consciousness. A deep silence seemed to come at her from every side.

"It's over," someone said. She lifted her face and searched the darkness. A woman was hovering over her. It was the wife of the deputy village head, a girl who sometimes came to sit with Swirl in the village school and share a few stories of the city, learn a few songs. "Go home," the girl whispered. "Tomorrow your house will be taken over by the peasants' association, but there are some empty shelters up on the hillside. They'll bring you there. They won't leave you without a roof over your head. They are better than the landlords of the past."

The girl's voice faded and her form merged into the shadows. Zhuli was pulling at Swirl's arms now, the child was filthy. When she finally looked up, she saw Wen crouched over the bodies of his two uncles, trying unsuccessfully to lift Da Ge's body into his twisted arms.

But all this would not be told to Big Mother Knife until much later. Swirl would not speak and neither would Wen. At the time, Big Mother did not fully comprehend that struggle sessions and denunciation meetings still continued. No one else had been executed. Instead Swirl saw that those who had lifted shovels, who had landed blows or pulled the triggers of the pistols, appeared ill at ease. When they met Wen on the village roads, they stared at him, afraid, as if it was Wen who had killed a man. And if he had not done it with his own two hands, then surely, without him, no violence would have been necessary. At this altitude, the fog was unrelenting. A person could hardly see his own shadow anymore.

On the fourth night of her stay, Big Mother lay awake. This entire mud hut, she thought, was smaller than the pantry in Wen the Dreamer's former house. The straw roof, of poor quality, needed to be replaced, it sounded like an ancestor shivering in the wind. She closed her eyes and a fragment of the famous poem that she had recited at Swirl's wedding came back to her:

> The marriage of a girl, away from her parents
> Is the launching of a little boat on a great river.
> You were very young when your mother died
> Which made me the more tender of you.
> Your elder sister has looked out for you,
> And now you are both crying and cannot part,
> Yet it is right that you should go on . . . .

The words came from an earlier version of this country, another dream. On the kang, Little Zhuli dug her heels into Big Mother's back as if to say, "There isn't enough heat to go around! Keep me warm, old lady, or go your own way." How could such a puny creature take up so much space? Fed up, Big Mother climbed out of bed. The little devil grunted in satisfaction, expanding into the warmth she had left behind.

Big Mother found her shoes. She shook them out ferociously. When she was satisfied no prickly creatures had nested there, she slipped them on. Overtop a second sweater, she buttoned her padded coat, pulled down her woollen hat and went out.

The winter air was not so terrible as she had feared. Big Mother pointed her good eye right then left, taking stock of her position. The moon was muffled by clouds and so she trusted the compass inside her own head, walking downhill until the trees fell away and she was surrounded by snow-draped land. A fallen branch sat on the crisp whiteness. She picked it up.

"But why am I awake," she asked herself, "and on whom will I use this weapon?"

Her heart, which earlier had been thumping, quieted. When she reached the elegant house, Big Mother did not hesitate. She lifted her stick, strode confidently through the gateless entrance and climbed the first staircase.

Bit by bit, her good eye adjusted to the pall. Here and there she could make out clumps of rubble but not a whiff of furniture.

This morning, she had asked Swirl, innocuously, if the item she wished to retrieve was difficult to reach. "Yes and no," Swirl had said. "Do you remember the steps in the east wing that go up to the alcove?" Instead of ascending all the way, her sister told her, the stairs served as a ladder to reach a high shelf, a very long, narrow ledge. "On the far side, there's a little opening below the roof. It's a headache to get to it, a person could slip and break their neck. The peasants' association will surely look in easier places first." Big Mother continued through the rooms. Now she found herself at the foot of the alcove steps. Putting aside her walking stick, she paused to offer a poem to the God of Literature because, after all, these mysterious notebooks belonged to his domain. She recited:

When the mind is exalted,
the body is lightened
and feels as if it could float in the wind.
This city is famed as a centre of letters;
and all you writers coming here
prove that the name of a great land
is made by better things than wealth.

She ascended.

The ledge, when she reached it, was indeed narrow, barely half a foot across and stretching far along the wall. The wraiths, however, had done her a favour because the shelf, stripped clean, was clear of obstacles.

Unwieldy as a pigeon, cursing the thick coat she wore, she stepped out onto the shelf. "I refuse," she told herself, "to end up a bag of bones on the floor for my sister to carry away." Big Mother inched along the ledge. She could feel her feet sweating inside her shoes. She cursed the God of Literature for not telling her to bring along Flying Bear. Her smallest son could be counted on to do stupid things like this. At last, the shelf ended. She groped blindly for the hiding place but could not find it. As she reached out once more, she lost her footing. Her hip jutted out, she flailed wildly for a handhold but grasped only air. One foot kicked out. Big Mother flung herself desperately to the right. She collided with the wall, her right hand shot wide and then, just as her thoughts slowed and she knew she was done for, her fingers caught on an opening. Big Mother held on for dear life, her fingers squeezing so hard she could feel the small bones scraping together. The room straightened. She was still standing, one leg up in the air.

She started to laugh, but thinking better of it, grew serious. In this opening, she found, just as Swirl had said, a cardboard box. Still, she wanted to be sure and so, with one hand, she undid the string, pushed off the lid, and slipped her hand into the opening. She had never held the notebooks before but their surfaces seemed utterly familiar to her, as if the Book of Records had touched her fingers a thousand times before.

"Old God," she said gleefully. "I shouldn't have cursed you. Look what I've found!"

With one arm cupped around the box, she waddled back along the beam, alighted on the platform, descended the stairs and took hold of her weapon once more.

Air swelled her lungs as she retraced her steps. The walking stick served her well, reminding her of the sighted child leading the blind musicians through the rubble of war and away from the obliterated town. It was a lifetime ago, and the child must be grown now. Big Mother hurried through a passage that led to the inner courtyard until she arrived, finally, gulping clean air, under the night sky. In their clarity, the stars seemed to exist within arm's reach. Was it this box in her arm that was pushing open so many doors in her memory? What kind of creature was this book? She thought of Swirl's little boy, the one who had died in 1942. He had been only a few years older than Sparrow but, unlike Sparrow, had never seemed afraid of gunshots, explosions, screams or fire. She remembered lifting his small body from her sister's arms, and how the tears Swirl wept had seemed to burn Big Mother's skin.

This house, she perceived, would one day decay to rubble. It would disappear from the face of the earth and leave no imprint, and all the books and pages that Wen the Dreamer and his mother, uncles and Old West had so carefully, or fearfully, preserved would be relegated to ash and dust. Except, perhaps, for this book, which would go on to another hiding place, to live a further existence.

That night, Sparrow woke in the darkness. Music was seeping from the walls, entering the room where he and his two younger brothers slept. Music was mixing with his brothers' uneven snoring, as if both children performed in unison from the same corner of the orchestra. The five-year-old, Flying Bear, was small, pretty and he snored like a tank. He must have been kicking at his brother because Da Shan was squeezed up against the wall, having relinquished both blanket and pillow. Already, at the age of seven, Da Shan was an ascetic, preferring hot water and steamed bread to all else; the boy was determined to join the People's Liberation Army at the earliest opportunity.

Sparrow had been dreaming. In the dream, he had been walking along the first floor of the Shanghai Conservatory, past a room where violinists were lined up like figurines in a shop window, past a stately chamber with a guzheng, pipa and dulcimer, arriving at last in a hall where seven grand pianos stood like mighty oaks. Through the shimmering windows, the nighttime sky was exhaling into morning. Old Bach himself had come to Shanghai, he was seated at the furthermost piano. The seventh canon of Bach's *Goldberg Variations* rolled towards Sparrow like a tide of sadness. Sparrow wanted to step out of the way but he was too slow and the notes collided into him. They ran up and down his spine, and seemed to dismantle him into a thousand pieces of the whole, where each part was more complete and more alive than his entire self had ever been.

As he lay in bed, Sparrow wondered if Herr Bach had ever dreamed of Shanghai. He pushed the covers aside and sat up. Seeing Flying Bear's annexation of the whole bed, Sparrow pulled him backwards; the boy bleated angrily. Da Shan, sensing open space around him, rolled back from the edge. Sparrow left the room.

There was music trickling through the house. He'd forgotten his slippers and the floor bit him with its coldness, but still he kept walking until he reached his father's study. The door was ajar, music escaped through the opening. Knowing that his father would be angry if he saw him, Sparrow made not a whisper of noise. So when Ba Lute called out to him, at first he could think of no response.

His father spoke again. "It's warm in here, Sparrow. Come in." Sparrow entered the room.

Ba Lute was sitting on a low chair before the record player. He was hunched over, almost wilted, and hardly looked himself. The apartment was hollow without Big Mother Knife, Sparrow concluded. Her discontent and foul mouth were as fundamental to their lives as the beams of the house, the food they ate, and his father's Communist Party membership.

"I've heard this piece of music a hundred times before," Ba Lute said. "But to hear it alone, in the night, is really something."

Thick smoke from his father's Flying Horse cigarettes made Sparrow's eyes water, but still he ventured further into the room, sitting down at his father's desk. Ba Lute did not object. The music went on, merging with the smoke, now quick and light, quarter notes blurring like a flash of wings, a tapering branch. Ba Lute had bowed his head. His eyes were half closed as if he was looking at something inside himself. When the second side ended, he turned the record over and set it playing again. The ninth variation caused Sparrow to rest his head upon the desk. All he wanted was to live inside these *Goldberg Variations*, to have them expand infinitely within him. He wanted to know them as well as he knew his own thoughts.

"But what if there's trouble?" Ba Lute said. "Does she think they're immune?"

Sparrow looked up. Who are they, he wondered.

Wanting to sound like the son of a Communist hero, Sparrow said, "We could go and rescue her."

His father didn't answer.

The music continued.

Sparrow walked out into the moonscape of the fifteenth variation, side by side with his father and yet separated from him. Glenn Gould played on, knowing that the music was written and the paths were ordained, but sounding each note and measure as if no one had ever heard it before. It was so distinguished and yet so real, that he sighed audibly thinking that, even if he composed music for a hundred thousand years, he would never attain such grace.

"There's no future in music," Ba Lute said. His voice held no reproach. He could have been saying that this room was square and the motherland had twenty-two provinces, one autonomous region, and a population of 528 million. Sparrow listened as if his father were speaking to some other individual, to the portraits of Chairman Mao, Premier Zhou Enlai and Vice-Premier Liu Shaoqi, for instance, that gazed at them intelligently from the wall. His father's face seemed to fall in line with the portraits. "When you were a child, fine, it was okay to be a dreamer. But you're a bit wiser now, aren't you? Isn't it time to start reading the papers and building your future? In a new world, one must learn new ways. You should be studying Marxist-Leninist-Mao Zedong thought with greater fervour! You should be applying yourself to revolutionary culture. Chairman Mao says, 'If you want knowledge, you must take part in the practice of changing reality. If you want to know the taste of a pear, you must change the pear by eating it yourself. If you want to know the theory and methods of revolution, you must take part in revolution.'"

The sixteenth variation came upon them majestically, a stately entrance garnished with trills. As the notes quickened, they seemed to carry Sparrow with them. He saw an immense square filled with sunshine.

"When you practically *live* in the Conservatory," his father was saying, "when you shut the door to that practice room, do you think no one hears you? Do you believe, truly, that no one notices that you have played Bach for seventy-nine consecutive days, and before that Busoni for thirty-one days! You refuse to trouble yourself with the erhu, pipa or sanxian. And I have done so much for the land reform campaign! I have been a model father, no one can say otherwise . . ." Ba Lute drank morosely and fell silent. "Why do you love this Bach and this Busoni? What does it have to do with you?"

His father stood up, circled the room until he came face to face with the portrait of Premier Zhou Enlai. "Of course Bach had his faith, too," Ba Lute conceded. "The poor son of a rabbit had more duties than our own Party Secretary: every week another mass, fugue, cantata, as if Bach was a factory not a human being. But look at my life, Sparrow." From the portrait, Premier Zhou seemed to nod in sympathy. "Every week, fifty performances in schools, factories, villages, meetings! I'm a machine for the Party and I'll perform on my deathbed if necessary. Old Bach understood that music serves a greater purpose, but don't I know this, too? Doesn't Chairman Mao? . . . In your heart, Sparrow, you think the foreigner is a brighter comrade than your own father." Ba Lute let out a heavy sigh. "What is it that he promises you? At some point, you must stop stealing Bach's chickens and get your own, isn't it so?"

Outside the world was dark and the young wutong tree in the courtyard seemed to hold the weight of the winter night upon its thin crown. Sparrow wished that he could turn the hands of the clock forward, wind it another year, and then another, to when his symphonies would be played in the Conservatory's auditorium. He imagined an immense orchestra of Mahlerian proportions, large enough to make the music inside him rattle the ceilings, vibrate the floor and realign the walls.

"My son has heard nothing," Ba Lute said. "He is deaf."

"I'm listening, Ba."

"To me," his father said, staring at the album cover. "I want you to listen *to me*." But he spoke as if his words were directed to Glenn Gould or to Bach himself. "Be practical, my son. Think of the future. Try to understand. There are many degrees and many roads of happiness."

When Big Mother Knife returned to the mud hut, Swirl and the little devil lay exactly as she had left them, joined together on the kang in exhausted sleep. Wen was cocooned in a blanket on the floor. Her sister's face in the moonlight was pale and lined, and Zhuli seemed to pull on her as children do, resilient and single-minded in her needs. Sitting in the corner, using her coat as a blanket, Big Mother watched moonlight creep beneath the door. It entered the room so piercingly that, when she looked down at her own fingers, she hardly recognized herself. She thought she saw the hands of Swirl. She thought her shoes were the very shoes of Wen the Dreamer, her knees were Ba Lute's, her arms belonged to Da Shan, her stomach to Flying Bear, her heart to Sparrow. She had a terrible premonition that, one by one, they would be broken off and taken away from her. Or was it she who would be the first to leave?

Big Mother's escapade with the God of Literature seemed ages ago and miles away.

The previous day, Big Mother had gone to town and purchased the plainest of practical items, heavy blankets, a thermos, padded coats, as well as rice, barley, cooking oil, salt and cigarettes. In a few months' time, Big Mother told herself, she would get permission to come and see her sister again. By then the spring planting would have begun, and she could assess their needs once more. Swirl had told her that the Party Secretary had promised her a position teaching in the primary school. Perhaps conditions were not so dire. But even as she considered this, a thick sadness filled her.

She looked up and saw that Zhuli had woken and was winking at her, one small hand covering her right eye.

"Good morning, little devil," Big Mother said.

The girl switched hands and covered her left eye.

Big Mother sucked her teeth. "Impudent monkey!"

"Father used to call me that," Swirl said. "I remember now." Her sister's hair tumbled over her shoulders as she sat up. "Why don't you come up here where it's warm?"

Big Mother slowly climbed to her feet. Everything ached. Her body was growing old and useless, the result, surely, of endless political meetings and study sessions. The Party propaganda was muffling her thoughts, wrapping her in a thick dough of imbecility.

"What is it?" Swirl asked. "Why are you crying?"

"For joy," Big Mother lied.

Her sister laughed. The girl tittered, too.

Winking at the girl, Big Mother picked up the cardboard box and set it on the kang beside her sister.

Swirl looked intently at it, as if the box reminded her of a person she had not seen in many years. Her fingers reached out, pulled the loop and the string curled down. Swirl lifted the lid and slid it aside. She stared down at the thirty-one notebooks, the only chapters Wen had been able to find, of the Book of Records.

"But–" She touched the corner of the box. "I know it isn't possible."

"Let us just say, the God of Literature summoned it home."

The following morning, in the bus on the way back to Shanghai, fate placed Big Mother beside a hardy young woman whose husband was deputy village head. "Far from home, hmm?" the young woman said, unfolding a red handkerchief, spreading it over her knees like a tablecloth, and depositing a great quantity of sunflower seeds on top of it.

"In this vast and glorious country," Big Mother said gently, "everywhere is home."

"Isn't it so!" the woman said, drawing her fingers through the seeds as if in search of a silver coin. The countryside flew past the windows, woken by the first light of morning. All around them, people were asleep in their seats or pretending to be. Patiently, the young woman attempted to extract the reason for Big Mother's visit to Bingpai ("Your sister is who, did you say? That young lady who used to sing in the teahouses?"), working like a needle beneath Big Mother's skin. Big Mother, contemplating the sunflower husks accumulating on the floor, and thinking, in general, of the greed that propelled wars and occupations, and of the bloody excesses of civil war, opened her thermos and poured a generous cup of tea for her companion. As often happened, Big Mother Knife decided, impulsively, to adjust her strategy.

"I was pleased," she began, "to witness the glories of land reform here in the countryside."

"Genius!" the young woman said weightily. "Devised–no, composed!–by the Chairman himself. A program of thought that has no equal in the history of all mankind, past, present, or futuristic."

"Indeed," Big Mother said. They sat in thoughtful silence for a moment and then she continued, "I, myself, welcome any sacrifice to emancipate our beloved countrymen from these heinous–"

"Oh, very heinous!" the young woman whispered.

"–feudal chains. No doubt your husband, the deputy village head, has done his duty with distinction." Big Mother reached into her coat pocket and withdrew a handful of White Rabbit candies.

"Wa!" the young woman said in astonishment.

"Please, try one. Try several. These delicacies were sent to us from the Shanghai propaganda chief himself. The flavour is delicate yet robust. Did I mention that my husband is a composer and a musician? They say his revolutionary operas have found favour with Chairman Mao himself."

"Ah, ah," the woman said softly.

Big Mother dropped her voice. The words seemed to come to her as if seeping out from the thirty-one notebooks in her bag, which Swirl had insisted she take to Shanghai; her sister would dispose of the love letters herself, or so Big Mother hoped. "But our Great Helmsman has always directed our affairs, in both grand and humble ways. Of course, my husband's more modest than the most bashful ox, but he journeyed alongside our nation's heroes all the way to Yan'an, ten thousand li! My husband played with such revolutionary fervour that his fingers were more calloused than his shoeless feet. Yes, every step he played the guqin. He had to re-string the bow with horsehairs."

"No hairs were more joyously volunteered!"

Big Mother allowed herself a smile. "I'm sure it is so."

The young woman accepted another handful of sweets. She slipped all the pieces except one into her shirt pocket. "Your husband is from where?"

"From Hunan Province, the very cradle of the Revolution," Big Mother said. The woman was nervously unwrapping her candy and Big Mother waited patiently for the crackling of the paper to subside. "His revolutionary name is Song of the People. He is, if you allow me, a big brute of a man. A true, modern spirit."

"I have heard his name," the woman said chewing daintily, the candy sticking her words together.

"The last time he came to your village was for my sister's wedding. Actually, Wen the Dreamer and my husband are as close as brothers."

Did she sense consternation? Had even the sunflower seeds suddenly turned cold?

"Our village would give your husband a great welcome," the hardy young woman said. "If you could just let us know in advance so that all the necessary preparations can be made—"

"Oh no," Big Mother said kindly. "He dislikes having a fuss made over him. As Chairman Mao so honourably says, 'We cadres in particular must advocate diligence and frugality!' But I'm certain he will visit, he has such great feeling for the people here, in particular, as I say, Comrade Wen the Dreamer. Please, have another candy."

As the bus heaved on, the two women took turns pouring each other tea, sharing their dried fruit, and paying poetic tribute to their husbands, fathers and great leaders. Fourteen hours later, when the bus arrived in Shanghai, Big Mother Knife had consumed so many sunflower seeds she felt as if she could beat her wings and fly away. The young woman clasped her hands and wished her longevity, prosperity and revolutionary glory, and they stood calling to one another like traffic directors, long after the bus had emptied and filled once more. Big Mother walked home from the bus station, through the rowdy twilit streets, and the novel in her bag gave her a pleasant, illusory calm, as if she were leaving a secret meeting and the documents she carried could bring down systems, countries, lies and corruption.

Perhaps it was not the papers themselves, their secrets, that were so explosive, but the names of the readers that must be protected. Courageous cliques, resistance fighters, spies and dreamers! She did not know why these thoughts came to her, but it was as if the very air shrouded the buildings in paranoia. How small yet heavy the notebooks felt. She began to wonder if Wen the Dreamer, during his hours of copying the Book of Records, had merged with the author or even the characters themselves, or perhaps he had transformed into something more expansive and intangible? When he finished copying, did he go back to being himself or were the very structures of his thoughts, their hue and rhythm, subtly changed? Past Beijing Road, she came to familiar streets, narrow laneways and finally the back door of their courtyard. Already she could hear a voice singing, a female colleague rehearsing with Ba Lute or perhaps just the radio, turned up wastefully high. When Big Mother entered the side wing of the house, her husband was hovering guiltily just inside the door, his shirt crookedly buttoned. He scratched his shiny head and looked at her in confused panic, blocking her entrance.

"Let me in, for heaven's sake!" she cried.

Deflating, he folded sideways. She saw that the room was dark, that the only residual light came from the lamps outside. She set her bag down. "Did you run out of kerosene?" she asked. And then she heard it: a low trickle of sound beneath the blaring radio. She looked to Ba Lute for an explanation but he only shrugged and smiled sheepishly.

Her heart fell to her knees. A tart. A singer so operatic she needed ten radios at maximum volume to cover her cries. Grabbing the broom, Big Mother followed the sound towards the bedrooms. At the first door, she peered inside and saw her two youngest sons asleep, almost on top of each other, as if fleeing from dreams on the northern side of the bed. She pressed on to Ba Lute's study. How did he dare? She would smash his nose, she would rip out his remaining hairs, she would . . . The door was closed but still the sound slid out, like water brimming from a glass. She turned the handle and pushed.

Two lamps glowed dimly on the far side of the room. She gazed in the direction of the light. Sparrow was sitting at his father's desk, his pen poised over a long sheet of paper. There was paper, in fact, everywhere, in the armchair, on the carpet, cascading across the desk, balled-up sheets and ink-stained pages. On the record player, a disc turned.

"Have the men in this house lost their minds?" she said finally, lowering the broom.

Her son looked down and stared expectantly at the strewn pages as if they might answer on his behalf.

"Shall I leave this madhouse and return to the sane, oh yes, the marvellously sane, countryside?"

"Oh," Sparrow said, when no one else answered. "No."

"We have a minor, which is to say, a small and unimportant, school project," Ba Lute said. That brute, that Song of the People, had come up behind her.

"A project! To exist in darkness like cavemen?" Big Mother asked. "To see how long it takes before state radio makes you deaf?"

Ba Lute pushed her gently into the room and shut the door behind them. "There's nothing to worry about," he said. "It's just that, some of our interests–a few musical interests–do not need to be broadcast."

She picked up a sheet of paper from the floor and held it up to her good eye. She studied the numbers that climbed up and down the page, the numbers one through seven, the lines and dots, the chords lifting like ladders. They were transcribing music into jianpu notation.

"A school project?" she said, doubtfully.

"Extracurricular," Sparrow said. There was ink on his face.

"But why?"

The music from the record player swirled faintly around them, adding its own thoughts to the conversation. The baroque constructions her son loved so much, Bach's *Goldberg Variations*. Sparrow, grown so tall, was standing beside her now. When had the child grown? Only yesterday he had been running beneath the tables of the teahouses, wearing the rough green hat she had knitted for him, the little flaps cupping his ears.

"For pleasure," her son said quietly.

"Yes," Ba Lute said, as if the word had dropped from the sky. "For pleasure!"

"But what use is this? If it's sheet music you want, why don't you just take your son to Old Zhang? Jianpu is for little children and teahouse singers, not Conservatory students." The record ran on, parsing its phrases into the air, and she saw that her husband and son were not listening to her, they were listening to it. "I'm tired," she said abruptly. "I'm going to bed. Don't bother me." She turned and left the room, just as the music trumpeted into a bouquet of sound, raining down on her like false applause. She closed the door behind her.

All night, beneath the blare of the radio, music trickled through the house. She heard it, faintly, when she lay on her left side and then on her right, when she lay face down, face up, or diagonally across the bed. Finally, she crept out of her room and into bed with her boys. Flying Bear slept heavily, his paws curled and toes pointing up, but her dear Da Shan crossed the bed to be with her. This one, too, had grown too quickly. He rolled awkwardly into her arms. "I'm glad you are home, Mama," he said, his voice drowsy with sleep. He clutched at her hand and held her, reminding Big Mother of Swirl and her little daughter, and that rough kang, and the quiet smoke from the cigarettes of Wen the Dreamer.

In the spring, Big Mother returned to Bingpai, and then twice more in the winter and following spring. Life had quieted in the village and although Swirl's family still lived in the mud hut, the family had slowly begun to thrive again. Wen had begun farming half an acre of irrigated land and Swirl was teaching in the schoolhouse.

In all this time, Big Mother had not opened the box containing the thirty-one notebooks. But halfway through 1958, the sight in her good eye began to deteriorate. She woke up one morning congested, feverish and half blind. Immediately she began cleaning the house, from top to bottom and from right to left. Curtains came down, and blankets and pillows were hurled from their sleeping mats. She polished ledges, scrubbed walls, emptied cabinets, sifted through the boys' room and discovered pencil drawings of herself and Ba Lute, she fat as a pomelo and her husband tall as a leek. Underneath, in Flying Bear's rangy writing were the words, yué qìn (moon guitar) and dí zi (flute). The little turds! They were already laughing at authority. She beat the quilts violently, thinking that Mencius himself would have pulled their ears, straightened their handwriting, and introduced some physical deprivation to their lives, but here she was, carrying the drawing in her pocket as if it were a treasured pack of Hatamen cigarettes. "Oh, Mother!" she cried, startling Sparrow who was bent over a sheaf of manuscript paper.

Sparrow watched her with increasing anxiety. He had noticed her bumping into things, favouring her good eye, turning her head this way and that like a pigeon. These last few years, she had grown round and soft, yet also more quick-tempered, like a potentate of former times. The apartment was in great disorder. "Oh, Father!" she sighed, setting a small cardboard box on the table. As if all the woes of the world hung from her shoulders, she collapsed into a chair. There was no string or tape and the box could be readily opened, but Big Mother Knife just stared at it, as if expecting the lid to stand up on its own.

"Shall I open your package for you, Mama?" he asked.

"Eh!" she said, turning her head ninety degrees to peer at him with her left eye. "Do I interrupt you? Do I smash into your thoughts like this?"

"Sorry, Mama."

"You . . . men!" she shouted, as Flying Bear padded by in his plastic slippers. "You must have had a brick for a mother. How else could you have grown into such misbehaving capitalist tyrants?" The boy gazed up at her. His mouth, which had been about to close around a piece of steamed bread, froze in indecision.

Sparrow watched covertly as his mother's attention returned to the battered box. She sat motionless, as if willing the contents to clear their throats and account for themselves. Perhaps it was empty, Sparrow thought. Big Mother reached her hand out for a cup of tea that wasn't there, and then she sighed and rubbed her forehead and continued looking at the box. When Sparrow poured a fresh cup of tea for her, setting it beside her disconsolate hand, she jumped and glared hatefully at him. He sat back down again. Flying Bear crammed the bread into his mouth and hustled away.

When he next looked up, he saw that she had inched the box nearer to her, opened it and removed a tidy stack of notebooks. She opened the first one and held it up to her good eye. She was looking at the page so hard he thought it might spontaneously combust. "Ma," he said, summoning his courage. Her good eye swivelled to face him. "Shall I read it to you?"

"Go away!"

He was so startled his pencil fell out of his hand. Hurriedly, Sparrow gathered his papers and left the table.

"Nosy interfering child!" she yelled after him.

Sparrow retreated to the bedroom, where he found Flying Bear giggling. He cuffed him lightly and the boy let himself roll away in a graceful somersault. Da Shan was standing incongruously in the middle of the room, bent over, touching his fingertips to his bare toes. Sparrow put his papers on the bed and sat in the last light by the window, waiting. When he heard his mother calling him back, he smiled and his brothers smiled back at him. Sparrow heaved himself up, returned to the kitchen, and saw his mother clenching her fists like a toddler. He sat down beside her. Bitterly, Big Mother handed him the first notebook. Without waiting for instructions, he began to read aloud.

The story began halfway through the lyrics of a song. He read,

How can you ignore this sharp awl
That pierces your heart?
If you yearn for things outside yourself
You will never obtain what you are seeking.

4

"MA-li, COME BACK. Wake up."

In my dreams, the Book of Records continued. As I came awake, I couldn't remember where I was or even who I might have been. I saw lights gliding across my bedroom ceiling, they captured all my attention, endlessly approaching, recurring yet unpredictable.

Outside, it was still dark. Ai-ming was sitting on the edge of my bed, wearing the coat that Ma had given her. Her face was fuller now, her hair was the sea, she looked so lovely sitting there. I stretched out my arms and held her tightly around the waist. Ai-ming scratched my head. She smelled good, like biscuits.

"One day, Ma-li, we'll go to Shanghai and I'll introduce you to Big Mother Knife."

"Big Mother!" I sighed. "She'll bite my head off."

"Only if she likes you. Hurry and get up, before I eat all the breakfast."

I heard the opening and closing of doors and the footsteps of Ma and Ai-ming as if they crossed effortlessly not only from room to room, but between my dreams and my present. What must it feel like, I wondered, to begin again? Would I still be the same person if I woke up in a different language and another existence? Rubbing my eyes, I climbed out of bed.

It was May 16, 1991. Ai-ming's suitcase, the same one with which she had arrived, waited beside the sofa. In a little while, she and Ma would drive the rental car to the border and they would cross into the United States. Once through, Ai-ming would board a bus to San Francisco, where her mother's friend was waiting to receive her.

At the dining table, Ma was setting out French toast. I mixed juice from frozen concentrate, readied three glasses, and served it as if it were champagne.

Ai-ming told us that, for the first time in many months she had not dreamed at all, and this morning, opening her eyes, she'd felt at peace, as if she were standing in the centre of Fuxing Park in Shanghai, in a deep pool of sunlight. Even the surrounding buildings, built in varied times and eras of the past, swayed as if they, too, were made of nothing more than leaves.

I said that I had dreamed of the border.

Ma sighed.

"Please take me with you," I said, even though I knew it was futile. "What if you get thrown in prison? How will you send me a message? They don't put children in jail. I'm the only one who can rescue you."

"Let's hope it won't come to that," Ma said.

Part of me understood that Ai-ming and Ma wished this leave-taking to be a hopeful one, and so I picked up my fork and went along with them. How I longed to be older, to be able to play a role. We lingered over breakfast, inventing a game that involved drawing words in the air. Ai-ming said that to arrive 来 is made up of the radical for tree 木 and the word not yet 未 : arrival is a tree that is still to come. Ma said that the word onion includes the character 洋 yáng (infinity, to contain multitudes), thus the onion as the root of infinity. I wanted to know why "infinity" consisted of 氵 (water) and 羊 (sheep), but no one could tell me.

If I pass over what follows, it is because, even now, more than twenty-five years later, I regret this parting. In Canada, no amnesty had been passed since 1983, and Ma didn't have the financial resources to help Ai-ming in the ways she needed. In America, we all wanted to believe, Ai-ming would have the best chance for a stable future.

Before she left, she hugged me for a long while. She had been with us so short a time but now that she was leaving, I saw how deeply, how effortlessly, she had altered us. I feared that Ma and I could not take care of one another on our own.

"There's no shame in crying," Ai-ming whispered. "No shame in remembering. Don't forget, Ma-li. Nothing's gone. Not yet."

Her arms released me. I opened my eyes. Because I loved her, I said goodbye. I held on to the character she had drawn for me, 未 (wèi), not yet, the future, a movement or a piece of music, a question still unanswered.

Afterwards, I lay on the sofa. I didn't cry. Poetry and memory, Ai-ming had said, were strong in me; I had been made for mathematics. I set myself to remembering everything she had told me, the beautiful, cruel and courageous acts, committed by her father and by mine, which bound our lives together.

BIG MOTHER KNIFE was ill. Exhaustion from her last visit to Bingpai, the nineteen-hour journey and an overdose of folded-egg pancakes, had all combined to wreck her bowels. When the worst had passed, she lay in bed, miserable. Even her eyelids felt overworked, they drooped and blocked the light.

Sparrow took his magazines and scores and stationed himself in his parents' bedroom, bringing his mother tea, peeling oranges for her, shifting the curtains according to the passage of the sun and his mother's whims, and waiting, always waiting, until she was lucid enough to ask him to come to her bedside, to bring the stack of notebooks she called the Book of Records and continue the story.

The desert setting of the early chapters became Sparrow's second home, until even the skin on his own hands felt patchy and rough. Sometimes he forgot that he was reading aloud. Instead, the words became his own; he was Da-wei himself, trapped in a radio station in the Gobi Desert, as war came like a tornado and tore the ground apart, until he feared he was the last person left in this overturned world. To comfort himself, Da-wei imagined listeners he couldn't see and never heard from, he made up letters and, day by day, embroidered their lives:

"Isn't it true, Mister Da-wei, that some are fated to disappear just as certain lakes evaporate in the driest season? Meanwhile, others must cross the ceiling of the world. Long live those fighting for our independence! May we spare one another and find peace, may we one day forgive our brothers because this war is both our illness and our hope. Mister Da-wei, I ask you to dedicate the third movement of Old Bei's Symphony No. 3 to my son, Harvest Wang. I wish to say: Big Harvest, stand tall and serve your country bravely. Happy birthday, my son."

Listeners followed Da-wei's voice through the twilight of their small rooms, into the chill of night and along the first seam of morning. People waited, crowded together or all alone, for the fighting to pass by, for the calm that came before the next storm, for the storm that would follow this small reprieve. *This next piece of music came to me by way of my grandfather,* Da-wei said. His voice was so intimate, it was as if he sat across from you in your warmest room. *He was taught to play it by a German musician in Qingdao, who played an instrument as tall as he was and twice as round, called a chai-lou. Have a listen.* And then, when the music was finished, *Wasn't it beautiful! Let's listen again. Once more, Old Bach and his suites for chai-lou.*

"Do I know this person," Big Mother said, turning a plum contemplatively in her hand. "Who is this devil writer?"

I've been alone in this radio station so long that I can recognize every record by its marks, as if each one is a face I know.

The story ran on and the afternoons disappeared. As spring of 1958 gave way to summer, Sparrow went back and reread earlier chapters, he crowded the open spaces of the novel with landscapes and wishes of his own so that he, too, could become an inseparable part of this new world where desires he had never acknowledged were, in these characters, given form and substance and freedom.

"Sparrow," his mother would call, after waking and turning her face towards the afternoon light. And he would rise, walk calmly to the chair beside her bed, and pick up the chapter that waited on the bedside table, as if going to meet his future.

Sparrow was caught up in Da-wei's desperate flight to the port of Shanghai when the rat-a-tat on the back gate sounded, and kept sounding as if the mechanism had jammed and the door was now destined to clap forever. His hands did not wish to release the notebook. Only his mother's cursing forced him to tuck it under his arm, leap up and run out to the courtyard. Da Shan had gotten into another fight, he thought, or Flying Bear was being bullied by the intimidating neighbour he had nicknamed Wind Factory. But when Sparrow opened the back gate, he saw no one. There was a beggar child, not more than six years old. He would have closed the door again except that she didn't say anything. She only stood there with a plastic bag in her hand. In the plastic bag he glimpsed clothes, a towel and, strangely, two records.

"You must have the wrong house, Little Miss."

"Aunt?" she said.

"This is not your aunt's house," Sparrow told her kindly.

"Please tell my Aunt Mother Knife that I'm here."

He knelt down to reach her height, and then he noticed that one of the albums was a foreign record. He looked into the little girl's face which seemed, somehow, obscured by dust. He knew the words on the album were in German, and he recognized the ones that mattered, J.S. Bach. Sparrow looked at her again, unwilling to believe he could recognize this grieving, destitute child.

"Tell my aunt," she said firmly.

But it was unnecessary because his mother had come out into the courtyard, a quilt thrown over her shoulders, and was now standing behind him. His mother cried out and pulled the child into her arms. "Zhuli!" she said. "Where's your Ma?" Panicking, she pushed past Sparrow into the laneway, staring all around.

"Swirl," Big Mother shouted, and kept shouting. The alley was empty, not a single person, nothing but rubbish and wind.

Sparrow flew down the lane, all the way to Beijing Road. But his Aunt Swirl and Wen the Dreamer were not there, not under the welcoming archway, and not on the street. Finally he used the few coins in his pocket to buy a half-dozen roasted sweet potatoes and a paper bag of steamed bread, then he stormed back across the intersection, dodging bicycles, leaping between pedestrians. Back home, he found Zhuli seated across the table from his mother. The child was wearing Flying Bear's clothes and the small, familiar shirt (it had once belonged to Sparrow) draped over her like a tent. When Sparrow set the food in front of her, she ate without looking up, breathing through her nose as she tried to shove as much as possible into her mouth. Big Mother watched in silence.

When Zhuli finished eating, she went, of her own accord, to the bedroom that Sparrow shared with his brothers. She found another shirt and pulled it on over the one she was already wearing. Then she climbed into the bed and asked Sparrow to lie down, too. Confused, he did as the child asked. Zhuli, who seemed to be growing smaller every moment, crept into his arms, closed her eyes and fell asleep.

—

Late that night, a sealed envelope was slipped through the front gate. It was addressed to "Mrs. Song of the People" and Mr. and Mrs. Ma had accidentally trampled it as they passed to the east wing. Mr. Ma gave it to Big Mother Knife who tore it open but, unable to make out the words with her good eye, thrust it at Ba Lute. The letter said that Swirl and Wen the Dreamer were guilty of counter-revolutionary crimes and sentenced to eight years of hard labour. They had already been transported to separate re-education camps in the Northwest. No matter how many times Big Mother heard the words, the letter made no sense. The letter continued: "The mother of Comrade Wen has died of illness. As there is no one in Bingpai with whom to entrust the child, I have taken the liberty of bringing her here. You will find the necessary paperwork and residence permits enclosed. Long live our motherland! Long live Chairman Mao!" There was a crushed, melted White Rabbit candy in the envelope.

"You know how it is," Ba Lute said at last. "Sometimes the local revolutionary committee gets carried away. I'll take care of it. A sentence like this won't get carried out immediately. Swirl and Wen must still be in Bingpai." But he wouldn't look her in the face, examining instead the empty cigarette pack in his hand.

All night, Ba Lute tossed and turned. The more Big Mother tried to see the room's outlines, the more the walls seemed to fold around her. Her husband cried out in his sleep, and she whacked his arm until he quieted. In Big Mother's own fevered dreams, her sister appeared, but Swirl was a small child again. They were fleeing Shanghai, trying to outrun the Japanese army.

When Big Mother next woke, Zhuli was asleep beside her.

They remained in bed while Ba Lute and the boys got up. They listened as schoolbags rustled open and closed, loudspeakers bellowed the national anthem, and bells and clappers rattled through the laneways. When Big Mother opened her eyes again, she was momentarily confused and thought that she and Swirl were lying in their parents' bed, her sister's gleaming hair flowing across the pillows. Her sister was the great love of her life. When their husbands had disappeared into the war, she and Swirl had survived together, and Big Mother had never let her sister down. She swiped at her tears, but she could not make them stop falling.

She had a vague sense, a disturbance, of people struggling up, people rushing over one another, and on and on these people climbed and fell and pulled each other down, in a large and sickening silence. But for what crime? In the re-education camps of the Northwest, her sister and Wen the Dreamer would undoubtedly be separated from one another. Surely they would be released soon, any crimes they had committed must certainly be small mistakes. But what was a small counter-revolutionary crime? Big Mother had never yet heard of one. The little girl sat up. As if her aunt's tears scalded her, Zhuli crawled out from under the covers and walked out of the room.

That night, Ba Lute boarded the bus for Bingpai. He drowsed, thinking of gamblers and the smoke at Swirl's wedding, of birds and music, and of the slow churning of Chairman Mao's newly formed wartime orchestra, and when he woke, the bus was tilting over a mountain pass, attacking a hairpin curve. He gripped the seat in front of him. It was miserable outside. Within and without, Ba Lute felt an enveloping sense of danger and deception. This foreboding was so strong that, when dawn came, he was taken aback to find the bus rolling across a delicate landscape. The green-gold fragility of the surrounding fields, the silvery bicycles and low lines of birds rising and lifting as one confused him. Banners proclaimed, "Serve the People!" and "Dare to think, dare to act!" The early summer had been unbearable, with bouts of thunder and unrelenting heat. His shirt felt glued permanently to his back.

Arriving in Bingpai, Ba Lute walked to the Party office, a meek little building with a very short door.

Inside, he was surprised to see an electric fan wobbling from the ceiling, funnelling the warm air down. The office had its own generator. Once Ba Lute had made himself known, he was welcomed by the village head with a very large piece of cake. Banishing his anxiety, he stretched himself out so that he was lordly and unassailable, and spoke in a bellowing voice. When Ba Lute mentioned Swirl and Wen the Dreamer's names, the grinning official in his over-warm jacket turned pink and damp. The fan pushed droplets of sweat across his bald head.

"One moment please, Comrade," the man said, and fled the room.

More cake appeared. A worker entered, singing, "Good day, Comrade!" He presented a cup of tea, wiped the already clean surface of the table and hobbled out. "Long live our Great Leader!"

"Well?" Ba Lute said, when the village head returned. "Where are they? I'm very eager to see them."

The dishevelled man looked as if he had been to Moscow and back. "Well, of course," he began, "they're registered here–"

"Yes, yes."

"–but, this morning, or, more accurately, at the present hour–"

"Comrade Wen is a greatly admired lyricist, a book of songs, as the saying goes. We can have no other for our concert. General Chen Yi himself insists!"

The man looked up, startled. "Respects to Chen Yi! A brave general and faithful servant to Chairman Mao himself. A twelve-barrel hero! Long may he–"

Ba Lute took a gulp of tea and slapped the cup on the table. "Comrade Wen and his wife must present themselves immediately. I'm ready to press on."

"Brother Comrade, life goes in unexpected spirals. That is to say, there are many unexpected places to which a man returns–"

"Your poetry confuses me, Comrade."

The man blushed. "Let me begin again. Elder brother, the truth of the matter is, they are not here." The man shifted uncomfortably.

"Speak freely, please."

The man poured tea and bade him drink.

Ba Lute waited. The fan turned faster now, as if trying to take flight.

"We do our utmost to keep order," the man said, "but as a leading light such as yourself knows, the People cannot move in half-steps: they would only fall down, wouldn't they? To traverse so great a divide, they must leap and sometimes overleap. And it could be that, in the case of Comrade Wen, they have, perhaps, overleapt. However, we live in a time in which the revolutionary dream must run its course, don't you agree?"

Ba Lute said nothing. The cake tasted old in his mouth.

"It appears," the man said, "that Comrade Wen and his wife had a hidden cellar on his family's ancestral land."

Ba Lute drank the remaining tea in his cup and looked thoughtfully at the pot. "That is no crime, Comrade."

The man waited and let silence stand in for contradiction. "Of course," he continued, "the contraband always surfaces. We confiscated everything. Books, records, some valuable heirlooms. He had the Book of Songs and the Book of History. He also possessed books from America. I am surprised," he said, allowing a brief pause, "that you did not know."

Ba Lute looked at the wall behind the man. There was no mistaking the sudden change in tone, all that confused poetry, that shiny sweat, suddenly vanishing like a mist.

"I did not know," Ba Lute said evenly.

"Mmmm."

The man stood up, reached up to a long string and stopped the fan. It slowed to a halt, and left the room confined and utterly still. "As cadres, we, of course, can only serve the People and follow the Party line. We turned him over to the revolutionary committee and they passed judgment. He was found to be a dangerous element."

Big Lute's throat was dry, but no more tea was offered.

"Re-education through hard labour," the man continued, sitting down again. "This was the conclusion and he was duly taken away."

"And his wife, Comrade Swirl?"

"Convicted rightist and shameless bourgeois element. The same punishment." The man seemed to thrive in the heat now. He looked pink and golden. "This hidden library may have been built by Comrade Wen's mother during one war or another, to hide these rare books from invaders. She died last year so how can we know? Perhaps you've heard of her father, Old West? A reactionary element, very close to the Imperialist regime in his day. Of course, Old West was once a celebrated scholar sent abroad to serve his country and such hiding places were once common . . . Well, who am I to judge? We are only a small village. We are still learning the correct line." The man smiled at Ba Lute. How strange this smile was, part pity, part warning. "The revolutionary committee operates under Chen Yi, does it not?" the man said smoothly. "I imagine that Chen Yi might have informed you of the sentence that was handed out."

"Tell me," Ba Lute said, ignoring the man's insinuation, "how was the library discovered?"

"Comrade Wen and his wife were in the fields as usual. Their daughter climbed down into the opening. It was she who discovered it. The melting ice must have dislodged the entrance." He poured the last of his tea into a potted plant on the floor, then he replaced the cup soundlessly on the table. "It was warm down there. More comfortable, in fact, than where they were living. One of the villagers was crossing the field, and he saw Comrade Zhuli disappearing, as if swallowed up by the earth."

The village head studied him openly. Ba Lute stared back, unrepentant. Behind the laboured elegance, the cloaked eyes, and the man's soft, sweating nose, his unwavering expression was familiar. The silence between them grew thoughtful. Ba Lute closed his eyes and then looked at the village head again. He felt as if he had exited the office and then re-entered through a different door. "I knew you at Headquarters. Back in '46. Didn't I?"

The man's face lit up with pleasure.

Ba Lute continued. "You were recruited for the orchestra. Maybe it was '44, could it be?" He could see these eyes now, that shiny bald head, behind an oboe. The orchestra leader had gone to the villages to recruit youngsters, and his friend, Li Delun, had taught them how to play. "These kids have never even seen an instrument in their dreams!" Delun had said. Even the way the new recruits held their oboes and trumpets was humorous, walking with them as if with a brand new girlfriend. "Ah, ah, ah, ah," Ba Lute said, trying to clear his thoughts.

"Wasn't it a memorable time?" the man said. "Learning to play the oboe in the middle of the Japanese invasion, reforming our thoughts and holding ballroom dances every Saturday night. The great leaders like to waltz. This surprised me."

"There is no music ensemble here," Ba Lute said.

"No, not here."

"Do you still have your oboe?"

Silence. The man hesitated, unsure if a joke was being made at his expense. "Yes," he admitted.

"Old One-two," Ba Lute said, suddenly remembering the man's name. They had all taken part in the same self-criticism sessions, which in reality were open attacks on one another. This man had been strict but he had not been a sadist like some of the others. "We nicknamed you One-two, because you could never count inside your head."

The man laughed. The sound was so unexpected, Ba Lute started and knocked over his empty cup. The man quickly righted it. "You're right. The trombonist gave me that name," he said. "It stuck."

Ba Lute was so thirsty even his eyes felt dry. An image came to him of this room and all the past rooms he had known, he tried to see how all the doorways and entrances fit together, but none of the corners would hold still. "Tell me your requirements," he said finally.

"My friend, you misunderstand me."

"I would like permission to visit them. Are they being detained nearby?"

"Comrade," the man said, "that is not possible." He blinked rapidly as if his feelings had been injured. "They were sentenced to labour in the Northwest. In the meantime, the revolutionary committee had no choice but to demolish their hut."

So the letter had not exaggerated, Ba Lute thought. They were gone.

One-two stood up from the desk. "You must know how things are. You are justly celebrated! A champion of the land reform campaign, a triumphant musical foot soldier. We hardened ourselves at Headquarters, didn't we? We were the first to be reformed through struggle. As Chairman Mao says, true rebellion is not organized or beautiful. Heroes like you built the road. I'm only following the path."

How could such flattering words feel like mockery? The office was terribly clean, terribly bright.

"More tea?" the man asked.

"No. Thank you."

"Is there something else I might assist you with?"

Ba Lute stood, raising himself up to his full height. The village head shifted uncomfortably. "Thank you, Comrade," Ba Lute said. "You've been very helpful. I'm sure we'll have the chance to speak again."

"Now I remember," the man said, though of course he had never forgotten. "The wife of my deputy met your wife on the bus and, though the journey was only a day, they formed a bond together. Since then, she has kept a watchful eye on Zhuli. Delivering her to safety."

Ba Lute felt the walls shifting once again.

"One should be careful of the sun," the man said, as if talking to himself. He reached out, pulled the string, and the fan started up once more. "One should learn to practise in the shade."

The cold forced its way in. Even though Swirl had emptied her suitcase and wore every piece of clothing she owned, there was no way to defeat it. Just now at the tap, she had watched, mesmerized, as her hands submerged in water and she had failed to register any sensation. It was as if the hands belonged to someone else. She had yanked them out, frightened, nonsensically, that the fingers would shatter. Nothing around her was what it seemed. The air, thick blue, appeared like paper.

She shared a single long bed with a district leader, a doctor, an economist, a public security officer, a schoolteacher, a tax lawyer and a translator of Russian literature. She, herself, was known as the wife. The first week, she had identified them by their sleeping habits: how they tossed, shouted and snored, how often they got up at night, how violently they squeezed back in, or if they slept as motionless as death. This morning, the district leader, convinced she had committed no crime, was speculating about her release date. "Perhaps today," she said. "This month, certainly."

"Comrade! Don't you see this very idea makes you a perfect candidate for re-education?" The economist, who had been here the longest, was convinced no one would ever leave.

"I committed myself to the party when I was eleven years old! Without people like me, there would be no Revolution."

"Hush. You're the only one who still thinks of yourself as a revolutionary."

The other women tittered but the district leader was unbothered. "I don't expect a criminal like you to understand. The Party is my family and I would rather die than betray it."

After roll call, they filed into the canteen. So many feet made a storm in the dust; it coloured the air, caked the floors and was the salt to everything that touched their lips. Swirl and the translator ate side by side. The translator chewed with her eyes tightly closed, making noises of gratitude as if, in her mind, she was relishing a succulent leg of duck.

Yesterday, Swirl had been handed a notice from the Bingpai revolutionary committee stating that Zhuli was now registered to live in Shanghai. The news had taken such a weight from Swirl that she, who never cried, had surprised everyone by weeping continuously. She had no news of Wen, only rumours that in the men's camp not far away, no one survived. The corpses were left in the desert, unburied. Swirl would not allow herself to believe it.

Outside, beneath a sky that had turned from blue to paper white, they got in line to rinse their bowls. The colour of purity, Swirl thought. The ancients had imagined white as the colour of funerals, of fulfillment, loss and completion and now the white sky seemed ready to erase the earth. She hoisted up a basket and spade and joined her group. Try as she might, she couldn't understand how she had walked to the cliff edge and found herself here. At the work site, several kilometres away, they were digging a channel. The soil, dry and easily eroded, fell apart under minimal pressure. She worked without thoughts; by midday, the sand glowed like a coin.

Night after night, stories were passed across the long bed. Months ticked by until at last she knew the intricate histories of all the women she slept beside, and they knew hers. A line of women who, one by one, had fallen through a rip in a dream and woken here. A lifetime ago, Swirl had gone to the ticketing office in Shanghai, ready to buy passage to Hong Kong, but she had been distracted by a novel, the Book of Records. It embarrassed her now, the way she burned candles so unthinkingly, gazing at words that seemed to hide ideas, or ideas inexpressible in words, how the sentences had carried her forward like a river or a piece of music. And yet how close the truth had seemed back then. She had been twenty-four years old and she had fallen in love.

Each day, the darkness fell fast. Black was the colour of the northern sky and therefore the heavens, the colour of the oceans, of everything profound and necessary, and so it must contain the life she was trying to reach. Her hands trembled all the time. On upholding her sentence, the head of the Bingpai revolutionary committee had assessed her coldly. He had concluded, "Deep in your heart you oppose the Communist Party." Swirl had denied the accusation, but if hadn't been true then, surely it was true now. Maybe her crime had been as simple as the inability to believe. In truth, since the age of fourteen, and until she met Wen, she had believed in almost nothing.

The life of a prisoner is one of endless motion. She was moved here and there, like a sack of goods. Dig ditches, mill flour, tend the pigs, grow vegetables, reform your thoughts, love the Party, collect firewood, denounce others, wash the grain, sing a song. The district leader, so sure she would be resurrected back to society, eventually committed suicide. The economist, adamant that the universe had forgotten them, was the first to be released. Day followed night, until Swirl suspected the Party itself no longer knew her whereabouts. No letters arrived and no word from Wen; she remembered sitting at the teahouse, waiting for instalments that would never come. The doctor told them of a camp not far away where a woman, who had been pregnant when she was sentenced, had given birth and the little boy had become the joy of the women's dormitory; the story seemed impossible. How could a mother and infant survive in these conditions? Swirl dreamed of Big Mother and for days, consoled herself with childhood. In a dream, she sat beside her lost son, her parents, Wen, Zhuli. They talked about everything and then, when time ran out, they returned her to the dormitory, fitting her back like a book on a shelf.

Her one friend was the translator of Russian literature, and Swirl loved her. She would have given her the last fen in her pocket, the last piece of bread. The friend, quite famous, was the premier translator of the works of Dostoevsky.

On the long bed, the Translator had been the first to volunteer her story.

"It was during the Hundred Flowers Campaign. They told us to criticize the Party, the university, each other, even the quality of our lunches and the functioning of the toilets." The Translator turned over and so did all the women, one after another, like waves against the shore. "So I, the idiot, stepped forward and said that my request for permission to travel to Leningrad had been denied fourteen times, and that a scholar of my standing must engage with her contemporaries. While I carried on, everyone else ran for higher ground.

"What I later wondered," the Translator said, laying an index finger gently on her own nose, "was how I could have studied Dostoevsky so keenly and not realized I was digging my own grave?" The word, Dostoevsky, made up of eight different ideograms, made them all murmur in admiration. "My old mother thinks I've been assigned to a university in Harbin. She'll fall to heaven's gate if she learns the truth." The Translator thumped the bed with her hand, as if to chase away a ghost.

"We must not lose hope! Chairman Mao is a good man. He knows our qualities and he will rescue us." The Translator pressed one hand to her heart as if to keep it from breaking. An echo of agreement rolled from woman to woman. "How can it be otherwise?"

There came a period of time when there was no food. These were months of desperation. Even labour was halted. The camp director agreed that energy would be better spent seeking wild grasses or roots. Famine was devastating the province; to give a single grain of millet to convicts would surely be a counter-revolutionary crime. Swirl had the sensation of pages fluttering before her eyes. It was the Translator, fanning her. She had the sensation of being rolled down a hallway. It was the Translator massaging her arms and legs. She dreamed she was eating a succulent duck leg.

It was the Translator, who had stolen a handful of beans from the kitchen of the camp director, cooked them illicitly and fed them to her. She listened as someone read aloud from the Book of Records. It wasn't real. It was the Translator holding her hand. Confused, Swirl asked, "Who will come to rescue us?"

The Translator said, with a small smile, "No one. So be it."

At the end of the famine, there were only three left on their long bed: the Translator, the tax lawyer and Swirl. They slept curled together for warmth. The rest—the doctor, public security officer, schoolteacher and district leader—had gone, as the saying went, into the pure white sky, into the western heavens.

In 1963, the tax lawyer was released and Swirl and the Translator were transferred to a camp called Farm 835. For the first time, they were allowed to receive mail. Swirl was greeted with two envelopes of letters—from Big Mother and family, and from Zhuli—packets so thick they took up half her sleeping mat. She savoured one each day, as if each was a bowl of rice. The translator, alone in the world, had received nothing.

One day, they were preparing the Translator's coat for winter, sewing layers of cotton batting into the lining. The Translator was sitting with her eyes closed. She had a washcloth resting on her feet in place of shoes.

A voice called out to them.

Swirl glanced up to see one of the guards beside a stranger, a visitor from an alien world. The stranger, a city person, wore blue slacks and a blue coat filmed in dust. The longer she looked at him, the more he seemed like a sign on the road, blurred and far away, difficult to read. He was tall and slender, handsome, perhaps in his early twenties.

"Aunt Swirl—"

She stared. The guard looked at her curiously. He said something to the young man, then turned and walked away, leaving the young man by himself.

"You know me, don't you, Aunt Swirl?"

Her voice didn't work. She tried again, but the words came out strangely. "Little Sparrow."

The Translator opened her eyes. "A handsome gentleman, to be sure. But Comrade Swirl, this bird is not so little."

He was standing before them now. Setting aside the coat and batting, Swirl got to her feet. She had to hold the Translator's shoulder for support.

"Sparrow," she said. "How strange it is to see you. This . . ." She shook her head to clear it. "This is my friend, the Lady Dostoevsky."

"A pleasure to know you, Comrade!"

"Isn't it though! Well, come nearer and let us have a look at you . . ."

Swirl wanted to reassure him but all the words within reach seemed too thin, too airy.

The high dome of the air swallowed their voices. "How did you arrive? There's no transport for miles."

"By train and bus. After Lanzhou, a donkey cart picked me up. For the last two days, we saw no one."

The boy, but he was no longer a boy, looked overwhelmed. It was her, Swirl realized suddenly. She must be quite unrecognizable, and her appearance had upset him. She felt ashamed even though she knew that it had nothing to do with shame, only time and circumstances, and her powerlessness to change them. She was touched that he made light of the considerable journey from Shanghai, five full days of travel at least.

Sparrow began unpacking cartons of cigarettes, biscuits, rice, dried fish, salt, preserved vegetables, and box after box of soft sorghum candy.

The abundance was so unnerving, the Translator let out a soft curse. She leaned sideways. "So this is the nephew, eh? The composer destined to become the Beethoven of the Huangpu River? Are you sure that's what he does?"

Perhaps out of embarrassment or panic Sparrow tried to surround them with words. He said everyone was well, that Zhuli

was thriving. He said he was writing music, that his Symphony
No. 2 was inspired by their journey across China during the war
years, the tea houses and blind musicians . . . He'd been thinking
about the quality of sunshine, that is, how daylight wipes away
the stars and the planets, making them invisible to human eyes.
If one needed the darkness in order to see the heavens, might
daylight be a form of blindness? Could it be that sound was also
be a form of deafness? If so, what was silence?

His eyes had filled with tears, perhaps due to the dryness of
the high plateau. She and the Translator gazed at him as if at an
apparition. To their astonishment he withdrew a book from his
bag, *The Rain on Mount Ba*, a classic novel.

"Zhuli asked me to give this to you, her favourite book."

Swirl took it in her hands, confused. "But how can Zhuli be
reading it already?"

"She's eleven now," Sparrow said, as if confused himself. With
the rucksack emptied and hanging uselessly in his hand, he
looked forlorn. He wanted to keep bringing things out, she
thought, as if he could fill the desert with flowers.

The Translator lit cigarettes for each of them, and for a long
time they simply sat in contemplative silence, smoking. Swirl
tried to see the sky and the dormitories and the camp office
though Sparrow's eyes, but all she could do was glance at him,
as if in a dream, and follow the smoke that curled out of his
fingers.

"My mother is petitioning to have your conviction overturned," he said. "She's applied for permission to visit you and
should be able to come within the month. Ba Lute says you
mustn't go back to Bingpai, you'll live with us in Shanghai.
Zhuli is such a gifted violinist, she never stops practising, the
Conservatory will do anything to keep her."

"But Sparrow . . ."

"My parents are still looking for Uncle Wen. I feel certain we'll
have news of him soon."

"Sparrow," Swirl said, taking his hand for the first time. She steadied her voice. "You must tell Big Mother that, when you found me, my only sadness was missing my family, my husband, my daughter. Nothing else. No suffering. You must thank them for me. You must tell Zhuli my life is good, the Party is re-educating me and I'll succeed in correcting my mistakes. Make sure she thinks only of her future. She must not be troubled."

"Of course, aunt."

Sparrow suddenly remembered something in his pocket. He took out a photograph of Zhuli with her violin, and gave it to her. She had not seen her daughter's face in more than four years. She stared at the image, as if into an unknown world.

"What is the famous poem?" the Translator said. "*Destined to arrive in a swirl of dust / and to rise inexorably like mist on the river.* Your daughter looks like you. My dear Swirl, the child has your face."

Why do I weep, she thought, trembling. I should be overjoyed. Her daughter had seemed forever lost to her, and yet here she was, so near and close at hand. Perhaps her husband existed like her, still accused of being a traitor and an enemy, and yet their destinies had merged a long time ago.

That afternoon, at the camp office, Swirl waited in the doorway, sheltered from the scorching sun, with Sparrow. The oil truck arrived, her nephew climbed up into the back and, as if it had always been so easy, he left Farm 835. He held firmly to one of the oil drums, gazing back as the distance between them grew, and she knew there was something he wished to say but couldn't. She tried to imagine his departure: the camp office diminishing in size, and then other buildings that would arrive and also vanish, until Sparrow came to the rail line, the endless trains and faces in the windows. Daylight drained into the ground. She knew that, one day soon, without warning, the conviction against her would be overturned. Like thousands of other surviving counter-revolutionaries, she would be informed, after years of prison labour, that she had never been a criminal.

Would she weep? Would she feel joy? She should feel grateful for the chance to return to life. Yet even as Swirl imagined Shanghai, she feared that only the wide open desert and the sky seemed to know her, that it would sharpen and forever expand.

5

ALL THAT AFTERNOON, AFTER Ai-ming and Ma drove away, I sat at the window reading Ma's copy of *David Copperfield*. Again and again, I returned to the opening lines: "Whether I shall turn out to be the hero of my own life, or whether that station will be held by anybody else, these pages must show."

Around seven at night, Ma finally came home. I watched her walk across the inner courtyard and ascend the stairs, moving slowly as if the stairs grew invisibly steeper. Her green coat, delicate as a summer leaf, was so familiar to me, she'd had it since before I was born. I watched it rise through the stairwell, as if against the flow of time. Seeing me through the glass, she smiled and began to move faster. She was carrying a parcel in her hands, a small, white bakery box.

I ran to the door and opened it, pulling Ma inside.

I had prepared a meal of rice, cucumbers and hardboiled eggs; as we ate, Ma filled the silence by describing, in detail, how the day had unfolded. The border guard, yawning, had waved them through. On the outskirts of Seattle, they'd run into morning traffic. They'd stopped for hamburgers. Ai-ming had bought my favourite sponge cake, and sent it home with Ma in the white bakery box. Ma had waited until Ai-ming boarded the Greyhound, she'd watched the bus pull away and disappear.

After dinner, Ma telephoned Shanghai, speaking for over an hour with Ai-ming's mother. I sat beside her on the sofa, near enough that her voice covered me.

In bed that night, I concentrated with all my strength, hoping I could hear my father's voice if only I listened hard enough. Light and shadow slid across the ceiling, now here, now gone, and as I thought about the reasons Ba had left this world, sadness overwhelmed me. Yet the wind sounded against the windows and in the next room, Ma still breathed and changed and dreamed. I wanted to go to her, I wanted to find a way to protect her. Ai-ming had left me a letter which I picked up again:

> "We told each other secretly in the quiet midnight world / That we wished to fly in heaven, two birds joined wingtip to wingtip / And to grow together on the earth, two branches of one tree. / Earth endures, heaven endures, even though both shall end."

Ai-ming was the link between us, my father and hers, my mother and me. Until we knew she was safe, how could we possibly let her go? At that time, I thought I never would.

"In the fall of 1965," I told the windows, the room, the photograph of my father on the desk, "on the night before Sparrow's twenty-fourth birthday, a young man, wearing an overcoat far too big for his skinny body, arrived in the night."

≡

THE HOUSEHOLD—BA LUTE, Big Mother and the two boys, Zhuli and Swirl (newly released, within days of her friend, the Translator)—was fast asleep, but Sparrow was still writing. Outside, a shadow appeared in the laneway. As Sparrow worked on his Symphony No. 3, he could hear the scratching of their steps, back and forth, around and back. The noise crept into his music: a low bassoon interfering with the bass line, now here, now gone.

Irritated, Sparrow set down his pencil. He picked up the lamp, descended the stairs and exited into the courtyard, listening: no sound at all. He flung open the back gate.

The stranger cried out, making them both fall sideways.

Embarrassed, Sparrow shook the lamp. "Speak, Comrade!" he said, as gruffly as he could. "How can I assist you!"

At first, only the wind replied. And then the stranger said, his voice no louder than a sigh, "I'm looking for Young Sparrow."

He was very slight, very short and surely no one to be afraid of, but still the lamp in Sparrow's hand trembled. "Young Sparrow? What do you want with him?"

In the stranger's hand, a crumpled envelope appeared. Even in the low light, Sparrow knew the handwriting immediately. It was the very same calligraphy he had gazed at ever since he was a teenager: square yet full of ardour, telling the story of Da-wei and May Fourth. The stranger shivered miserably and yanked his hand back. He was nervous, but not in the smug, twitchy way of a spy or a jailer. Rather, the young man seemed horrified by the width of the alleyway.

"I am he. That is, I'm Sparrow. What do you need, Comrade?" The stranger shook his head.

"Is that a letter for me?"

"I have what you would call . . . news."

"Quickly, come inside." The stranger shook his head. Sparrow had to prevent himself from dragging him bodily into the house. "Have you eaten yet? Come. No one will harm you."

The young man glanced past him. The shadows were not kind to him; everything about him was meagre and crushed. "I will not come in," he said softly, as if counselling himself. "No, no. I will not! Absolutely, definitely not."

Sparrow reached into his pocket. Last night, an official in the Central Commission for Discipline Inspection had paid him twenty yuan for private lessons–the official wanted to learn Beethoven's "Moonlight" Sonata–and the large bills were still on him. "Comrade, if you cannot stay and join me for a meal, please accept this small, inconsequential gift." He had intended to pull out just one bill, but all four came out.

The young man blinked, stunned.

Sparrow hesitated. Then, firmly, as a father might, he took the letter from the stranger's hands and put the money there instead. Now that it was leaving him, Sparrow felt a pang of confusion and remorse; he did not have another fen in his pocket. Still, he held the young man's gaze. "Accept the money or come inside."

The stranger opened his hand and stared at the miraculous bills. "I would not take anything from the family of Brother Wen," he whispered. "But my circumstances . . . well, it's obvious, isn't it?" He looked at Sparrow directly, and it was clear that the stranger was no more than eleven or twelve years old. A child.

And then the boy, his destitution and Sparrow's money vanished down the laneway. Except for the envelope in Sparrow's hands, it was as if the child had never been.

He shut the door and retraced his steps through the inner courtyard. Upstairs, from the balcony, he looked out in the direction the boy had run. Dawn had begun to crease the sky, and already the ration line on Beijing Road was forming, growing longer by the moment, but the child was long gone.

The envelope was addressed, not to his parents, not to Aunt Swirl or Zhuli, but to "Young Sparrow." He crouched down with the lamp, opened the envelope, slid out the single sheet of paper and began to read.

At dawn, Zhuli came out onto the balcony. She called down to Mrs. Ma who was waiting her turn at the water spigot, wished her good morning, grinned at Sparrow, took his empty teacup away and returned with it full and steaming. She sat on a broken chair and said, "Love letter?"

He grunted.

"Dear cousin," she whispered, "Happy birthday! May this be the year your thrilling Symphony no. 3 is performed in the concert hall before Chairman Mao himself and our devoted Premier Zhou Enlai! Before President He Luting and all the grand musicians of the Shanghai Conservatory! May the bouquets at your feet be fragrant and plentiful, and may the soloist of your next piano concerto be a certain elegant boy from Changsha–"

"Zhuli, if you don't hurry, that boy from Changsha will have reserved the best practice room. You'll have to play your violin in the street."

"You're right! Jiang Kai practises more than anyone in the Conservatory. Except me. But you know," she said, her voice dropping even lower, "the piano in Room 103 is *ancient* and all the pianists avoid it. For a violinist, there's so much space it's practically a villa." She shoved him on the knee. "But, *really*, who is the letter from?"

He had turned the envelope over before she recognized her father's handwriting. "Premier Zhou Enlai, inviting me to perform at his grand reception where–"

"The envelope is too plain."

"Herr Bach, asking me to–"

"The envelope is too new."

"The neighbourhood grandma, asking why I compose for the degenerate piano rather than the glorious guqin."

She nodded. "I see. Cousin," she said, after a moment, "this morning I found the bag of dried peas that went missing. They were in the sleeve of my mother's coat."

"What did you do?"

"I left them there! She thinks she's such a skilful thief!"

"She's an excellent thief, only there's nowhere to hide anything."

"The other day," Zhuli continued, "I tried to throw out a sock that had eight holes in it but Ma fished it out of the garbage, washed it, mended it and put it back in my drawer. It's like wearing a fishing net. I've been mending it for the last three years! She goes through the trash looking for things, she actually . . . Last night, she wrapped the quilt twice around herself, even though it was boiling hot. And then she asked me to sleep very close and keep the draft away. I tried to do what she wanted, but there was no draft! Still she shook and shivered!"

His cousin was a joyful and free creature, she seemed to have no relation to any of them. "Aunt Swirl went to the end of the world and came back. Give her time."

"Speaking of time!" She leaped up, grabbing her violin case. "I'll come to your office at noon! Let me treat you to a birthday lunch."

Sparrow slipped the envelope away so that he was nearly sitting on it. "Cousin, about the Ravel. Your technique is excellent of course, but yesterday the phrasing sounded pinched to me, especially the pizzicato. It's a matter of finding the simple in the complex, rather than the complex in the complex, do you understand what I mean? Work on the bowing today, won't you?"

"My serious Sparrow, what would I do without you? Come to Room 103 at lunchtime, and I'll make Ravel himself proud."

Alone once more, Sparrow picked up the envelope again. It was true, there was nowhere to hide anything in this house, or even this neighbourhood, not even a bag of peas or a guilty thought. He reread Wen the Dreamer's letter, then he took the box of matches from the window ledge, held the letter over the cigarette tin and set it alight. Wen's handwriting became distorted and round, long and thin, until every sentence was the same: nothing but residue. But Sparrow remembered every word as if the brief letter was a poem or Bach partita. He could stand up and deliver it now, word for word, note for note.

—

All morning, the words floated through Sparrow's thoughts and would not leave him, even when Flying Bear dropped his breakfast on the floor and Da Shan walked barefoot into porcelain shards. The letter continued even as Sparrow washed blood, pottery and breakfast out of Da Shan's foot.

"Should we go to the clinic? Probably I need stitches?"

"I don't think so. Antiseptic should do."

"Of course." His voice a disappointed trombone.

Meanwhile, Swirl cleaned the floor, Ba Lute dished out another bowl of food, his mother yelled at everyone, and Flying Bear pretended to spear his brother in the back.

The letter sat in his mind and brought unexpected tears to Sparrow's eyes.

Da Shan leaned forward, wiped the tears away with his delicate fingers and said nothing.

My dear friend, I trust this letter finds you well and that you remember me, your dreaming friend who treasures you like his own son. Today I am neither in the east nor the west. One day I will tell you all the vagaries, cliff-hangers and digressions of the story. But, in short: I escaped from H– camp and have gone into hiding. I cannot describe conditions to you, little bird. The camp was the very end of the earth. I am no counter-revolutionary and neither were those exiled with me. In my heart, I believe that it is this age and our leaders who one day will have to account for their crimes. For the last month, I have been searching for a safe house. Last week, fate brought me to Shanghai and I saw my family. They did not see me and I did not dare make myself known. The authorities closed in and I left the city headed for G– Province. Little bird, please do all you can to prevent my family from searching for me. I must close this letter. A book could not hold all I wish to say.

Your friend,

Comrade "Bach"

P.S. I have found a further chapter of our Book of Records.

It came into my hands in the most unlikely of places, after my transfer from J–.

P.P.S. If ever the chance presents itself, seek out Comrade Glass Eye in the Village of Cats and do present a copy of the Book of Records to him. He was my companion at J– and his preferred composer is Schönberg. Tell him you are well acquainted with his childhood friends, the adventurer, Da-wei, and the fearless May Fourth.

Three days passed before officers from the Public Security Bureau showed up at the door. Like the destitute stranger, the officers came early in the morning, before breakfast was even on the table. Unlike him, they banged on the laneway gate and bullied their way in. They said that the "counter-revolutionary, criminal, rightist, political pollutant" . . . and here they had to pause and search through their papers . . . "Comrade Wen!" . . . had escaped, critically injuring two army officers. They accused Ba Lute of harbouring an enemy of the state.

Ba Lute listened calmly, but when the two officers announced that Swirl and Zhuli must come immediately for questioning, he leaped forward, flinging down the draft of Sparrow's Symphony No. 3 that happened to be in his hands. "How dare you shame me in my own house!" he shouted. He began rampaging through the rooms. "Come over here! Is Comrade Wen under the bed? Is he in the closet? Did we use his corpse to fuel the stove? Check the garbage pail, shit house and laundry bag!" He hurled objects across the room as the security officers, pale and unconditioned, knocked each other down in their haste to escape the careening objects of Ba Lute. Sparrow's father was taller than ever but only half as round, and therefore twice as intimidating. "Comrade Wen has the aggression of a falling leaf! How did he injure two officers? The way a drop of rain injures the pavement? Who's selling potatoes here?"

"Uncle–" Zhuli said.

"Have you lost your mind?" Big Mother Knife said calmly.

"I've had enough!" Ba Lute shouted. "You've wrongly imprisoned his wife! That's right! Look at you quivering like a bag of fresh tofu! Check the records yourselves, she's been resurrected! She's working for the Party now and she's probably ranked higher than you are! You little shits have stained our Revolution and one day I'm going to haul you before Chen Yi himself and have him whip your balls. Donkeys! Do you have any clue who I am?"

Mrs. Ma was summoned and she sternly informed the officers that she was the head of the residential committee, and there were absolutely no escaped rightists in her jurisdiction. The very thought, she murmured, was appalling. Everyone here had their papers and household registration in order, they could be sure of that. She tossed her sleek head and offered to escort the officers outside.

Beside the door, Sparrow said nothing. The pages of his symphony, flung aside by Ba Lute, had shoe prints on them. He went to gather them up.

Only when the officers were gone did Swirl turn to Big Mother. "Did they say that Wen escaped?"

"Yes," she said. Her better eye moistened and she turned away to gauge the destruction that had befallen her house.

"But how?" Swirl said, sitting down. "Where could he go?"

Ba Lute blustered back into the room, yelling, "Fuck! Fuck, fuck, fuck, fuck, fuck, what have I done?" Sparrow hustled his younger brothers into the kitchen, distracting them with little sugar pyramids and a quick game of Watching the Tiger, and then he went to the balcony and peered into the can that held the ashes of Wen the Dreamer's letter. There were a dozen ends of cigarettes, a thick wad of tobacco but not a trace of the page, the writing or the words. Sparrow looked over the railing. In the laneway, the two officers were deep in agitated conversation. Mrs. Ma was firmly shaking her head. Waste water from the gutter circled their feet.

The letter had disappeared for good, Sparrow thought. It had dissolved into the air itself, escaped to where no officer, spy or committee chairman could ever retrieve it. At the first opportunity, when no one else was around, he would tell Aunt Swirl what Wen the Dreamer had written.

Sparrow left with Zhuli, his cousin clutching her violin case in both arms, walking with one foot narrowly in front of the other as if she regretted every inch of space she inhabited. Against the grey-blue wave of oncoming pedestrians, Sparrow wanted to clear a path for her and so he walked with his chest out and his slender arms swinging, deluding himself that he was a tank and not a paper boat. But nobody, not even schoolchildren, moved aside for him. Bicycles whizzed so close their handlebars clipped his elbows. How unlike Ba Lute he was. Given his father's heft, Sparrow felt soft, flimsy and inessential.

The tram arrived. Zhuli turned and smiled distractedly back at him before the rippling blue of her dress disappeared among the other passengers. They did not meet up again until the gates of the Conservatory, where she called down to him from above. Zhuli was balanced gracefully on a concrete ledge, one hand hooked around the iron fence, the rest of her body tipped to the side. Her hair, gathered into a long braid, sat on her shoulder and the ends seemed alive in the breeze. Inside the gates, the pianist Yin Chai, the brightest star of the Conservatory and admittedly appealing in army-style shirt and trousers, was sitting on a bench. He had returned from Moscow after taking second place in the Tchaikovsky competition and everywhere he went, or so it seemed to Sparrow, a flood of stage lights followed him.

"What do you think, cousin?" Zhuli said, making a soft landing beside him.

The chatter of the students drummed at him like a headache. He smiled to hide his envy and fell back on a cliché, "'Can the sparrow and swallow know the will of the great swan?' Yin Chai is a national treasure."

"I prefer your compositions to his melodrama."

"Do you?" Sparrow said, unable to believe it. Yet when his cousin played his work, it was as if she sifted the dust away, lost the notes and found the music.

He told Zhuli he would come find her in Room 103, her preferred practice room, and then dodged the crowd and climbed the imposing staircase. On the ground floor, all five hundred of the Conservatory's pianos seemed to be singing and feuding together. He skirted Room 204 with its gongs and cymbals, 313 with its many-stringed zithers, and the violin-making workshops of 320. On the fourth floor, he glanced past an open door and saw the President of the Conservatory, He Luting, deep in conversation with a cadre Sparrow didn't recognize. "That's your decision," He Luting was saying, "but exactly what constitutes a crime these days?" President He was famously blunt. Occasionally he invited Sparrow to his home to drink lemonade, listen to records and read over his compositions. The whole Conservatory knew that, when He Luting was a child, his elder brother had owned a French music text, and the book so enthralled Comrade He that, at night, he would sneak downstairs and copy it out by hand. Fascinated by the construction of Western music, he taught himself staff notation. When he finally became a Conservatory student in the 1920s, he was famous for falling out of bed with his hands still moving in the air. Sparrow longed to know what He Luting had been playing in his dreams. Had he been performing or composing? Had he been dreaming of his teacher, Huang Zi, who had himself studied under Paul Hindemith? Could dreams shed light on the architecture of the music in his head? Sparrow, too, dreamed all the time of things he had not written. Each morning when he woke, he heard these pieces like a vanishing noise in the street, and he wanted to weep over the music he had lost.

"No need to waste time. Just put your threats in *Liberation Daily* and see what else I say–" He Luting's glasses had slipped far down his nose. In response, the stranger wore a complacent smile. Sparrow hurried on.

Further along the corridor, he arrived at the office he shared with Old Wu, a prodigy who played the erhu as if it were no more strenuous than clipping his toenails. He hadn't seen Old Wu in weeks.

On Sparrow's desk was a note written in the margins of a scrap of newspaper: "Teacher Sparrow, thank you for lending me your copy of *Musical Life of the Germans*. I read it in a single sitting and couldn't sleep all night. Shall I come by your office today, around one? Respectfully yours, Jiang Kai." Sparrow reread the letter. At one this afternoon, Yin Chai would be performing Tchaikovsky in the auditorium to oceanic waves of applause. Kai must have forgotten.

Sparrow slipped the note into his desk. The four ivory walls of the little room seemed to angle towards the window's opening. He took out his Symphony No. 3, shoeprints and all, and laid the first movement across his desk. Try as he might, he could not smooth out the crumpled pages. He took up his pencil anyway.

Time itself, the hours, minutes and seconds, the things they counted and the way they counted them, had sped up in the New China. He wanted to express this change, to write a symphony that inhabited both the modern and the old: the not yet and the nearly gone. The ticking in the first measures was a quote from Prokofiev's whirring machines in Symphony No. 7, and in the foreground was a dance, allegro risoluto, quickening until the bars were rickety with steps, twisting free at last like a gunshot to the sky. A free fall into the second movement, a scherzo, a trio of violins that did not sound like themselves, withdrawing as winds and brass began a slow march. A sound gone just as it was learning to be heard.

From the opposite wall, Chairman Mao gazed at him with a knowing smile. What have you ever written, Chairman Mao said chidingly, that is original? What can you possibly say that is worthy? Time passed and the paper grew warm in its patch of morning light. Three-quarters of Sparrow's time was spent meeting quotas for the latest political campaign, and the other quarter teaching composition music theory. His own Symphony No. 1

had been performed, and well reviewed, only to be criticized by the Union of Composers. The symphony, they said, suffered from formalism and useless experimentation; the solemnity of the third movement did nothing to elevate the People; and the meaning, overall, was not immediately clear. If it hadn't been for He Luting's protection, the criticisms would have been far worse. Symphony No. 2, which he knew to be a work of great beauty, languished in his desk drawer, having never even been submitted for approval. Last month, he had set six poems of Wang Wei and Bertolt Brecht to music but these, Sparrow knew, were better left unheard. His students wanted revolutionary accessibility and his superiors tried to educate him on the correct political line, but what line could this be? As soon as he contained it in his hand, it opened its wings and filled the sky. What musical idea stayed fixed for a year or a lifetime, let alone a revolutionary age?

He squeaked open his desk drawer and looked again at Kai's confident handwriting. Like He Luting, Kai had come from the remote countryside, he was playful and virtuosic, possessed an extraordinary memory, and loved music as mysteriously, as confusedly, as Sparrow himself. But Kai was prepared to succeed. To be a renowned musician, one surely had to be already successful in one's own mind; only musicians with this nature could rise above the others. Life, Sparrow felt, would have no choice but to be generous to Kai.

He tried not to think of his own diminishing opportunities. He erased the last twenty measures he had written. For a long time, he sat, thinking, until the room itself became another room. On the empty page, a line came to him. The line moved forward along a steepening curve. He followed it, no longer conscious of the act of writing.

The morning passed. Sparrow was thinking of the letter from Wen the Dreamer and the mysterious Comrade Glass Eye when the door jumped open and Zhuli appeared, pale as an unlit candle.

She was holding a green thermos, her violin case and a paper bag. "Cousin," she said, "isn't your stomach rumbling? I waited for you in Room 103, but you never came!"

He had forgotten. She waved his apology away and grinned. In her old blue dress, Zhuli looked tired but also energized, older than her fourteen years. He got up and went to the little table laid with cups and dishes, picked out two that were the least tea-stained, and examined the package of pear syrup candies that Old Wu had received from an admirer, a girl nicknamed Biscuit. Old Wu had sampled one and abandoned the remainder.

He poured tea and scattered a few candies on a plate. Zhuli was looking intently at the pages on his desk. She was humming the melody now. Lost in thought, she unlatched her violin case, lifted her violin and began to experiment with the phrasing.

"Not yet, Zhuli."

She lowered her arm. "But Sparrow, listen to this. I can already hear how–"

"The second movement isn't even finished. I've barely begun it."

"Barely begun it? You've exhausted yourself on this symphony! Cousin, can't you see it's the most sublime thing you've ever written? I think you should show it to Conductor Lu right away. You trust him, don't you?"

There was a boisterous knock and the door opened again. Here was Kai, looking as if he had woken only minutes ago and run from Changsha to reach them. He was wearing a knock-off army cap and a rumpled shirt that was, comically, grass-stained. After greeting them, he immediately crossed the room. "What are you playing, Comrade Zhuli?"

She frowned at him and smoothed her dress.

"It's nothing," Sparrow said. "Just a few lazy thoughts of mine." He gathered the sheets, Kai's note and an essay he had been consulting, and cleared everything away. "Kai," he said "if you hurry, you can still make it to Yin Chai's recital. You won't even be late."

"But aren't we meeting? I left you a note." His face, even his handsome cap, seemed to fall. Sparrow felt as if he had accidentally closed a piano lid on the young man's fingers.

"Teacher Sparrow is composing," Zhuli said solemnly. "Have you eaten, Kai? Take these."

Sparrow watched the paper bag leap from one hand to the other. He felt old when he said, "Please don't leave crumbs on Wu Li's sofa."

Kai looked hungrily into the paper bag. "Old Wu? He'll send his mother to clean them. Or maybe his grandmother."

His cousin let a laugh escape.

They were so lighthearted, these two. Zhuli's arms were bare but she seemed not to feel the breeze of the open window.

Kai looked at him with a direct, unsettling frankness. "It would be good to go outside, stroll in the park and listen to the music of the People." The sun warmed Sparrow's hands. "Come, Teacher. You've been at work since dawn. And wasn't it your birthday?"

"He never celebrates," Zhuli said. "He starves himself of joy. Luckily, joy seeps into all his compositions."

"Don't either of you have lessons?" Sparrow said, trying to maintain his dignity.

"All the pianists are downstairs, writing self-criticisms. I stayed up all night reading the book you lent me, and then I came at two in the morning to work on Mozart's Concerto No. 9. It was just me and the stray dogs and the wind. Even the the most stubborn old grandmas weren't out lining up for meat."

"Up since 2 a.m.!" Zhuli said, clearly impressed.

Sparrow tried to think of an escape route. He wanted to be alone with the window, the papers on his desk, and the freedom of his thoughts.

"An hour," Zhuli said. "Steal an hour from your life and give it to us."

She smiled at him, a smile as big and openhearted as Aunt Swirl's when he was a child, and so he did.

—

In the park, Zhuli and the pianist walked on either side of him, as if afraid Sparrow would make a run for it. What do the sparrow and the swallow know, he thought again, of the ways of swans? There was a swan, as it happened, in the shade of the pond, fluffing her grey-white wings, trying to appear larger and more deadly than she was. He heard the softness of her trilling.

"The room I live in," the pianist was saying, "is the size of one and a half men lying down. I have just enough space to turn over and back again."

Zhuli's violin case swung as she walked. "How come you don't board at the Conservatory? Maybe you prefer sleeping in a cave."

"I had to pull all sorts of strings to get this terrible room, but it's near my stepfather. He was ill last year . . . anyway, the mice are good company."

Zhuli ducked under a low branch. "Be careful or the mice will multiply and take over the cat's room."

When Kai laughed, his hair stood upright in the wind.

Without Sparrow's noticing the transition, Zhuli was telling the pianist about Ba Lute and the confrontation with the public security officers this morning. The pianist's walk slowed. "What camp was your father at again?" he said.

"I don't know. But it's in Gansu Province, isn't it, cousin?"

"I'm not sure, Zhuli."

She tensed. Faint perspiration gleamed on her forehead and her cheeks. She looked as if she could take on any campaign, criticism or family member, and leave them battered on the floor.

"You don't have to worry about me, cousin," she said, her voice low. "I know when to keep my mouth shut. If only you could hear me in our political study class. I think I've memorized more slogans than the Premier himself." She lifted her chin defiantly. Her recklessness, her casualness with words, stunned him. His cousin had been this way ever since Swirl's return.

But perhaps, he thought, this bravado was not for him but for Kai.

The sun touched everything now. They attempted to find refuge on a bench under a flowering pear tree. They sat as if they were alone and self-contained, the joy of only a few minutes ago dissolving. Perhaps it was the heat that made them quiet. Nobody stood nearby yet Sparrow felt the weight of someone, or some attentive presence. There was shouting in the distance, or maybe laughing.

"This morning," Kai said, his voice barely audible, "the President of the Conservatory was in the newspapers. Did you read it? *Liberation Daily* has a full page on him. *Wen Hui Bao*, too. They say He Luting is anti-Party and anti-socialist, and that the most damaging accusations are coming from inside the Conservatory."

"I thought you were practising all morning," Zhuli said.

Kai paused. "I think that half my life might be spent running from one position to another until I trip and make a fatal mistake."

"Have you been to Wuhan?" Sparrow asked, wanting to change the subject. He knew He Luting was under investigation, of course, but Kai's words still chilled him.

"Forgive me, Teacher. I'm only a student and yet I feel that I can be very free with you. What did you ask me?"

"Would you like to go to Wuhan?"

"With you," the pianist said.

"Yes. If you have time to spare during the break. The journey and my research would need three or four days, perhaps longer. I'm looking for an assistant, I've been commissioned by the Conservatory to gather—"

"Yes," the pianist said.

"But I haven't told you why."

"I'll go."

Zhuli was hugging her violin case to her chest as if it concealed her. She refused to be a child and demand to go with them. She had her mother to think of, too. One day soon, she thought, she would play for her father, whose face she no longer recalled, but who used to sing, "Little girl, where are you going? Tell your father and he will take you. Tell your father and he will find a map, bring the tea, make the sun lift, and string the trees along the road." Was it a poem, a story, or something he had composed? "Zhuli," he would say, "little dreamer." She let go of his voice and heard Ravel, the song itself, and her shoes scratching the pebbles each time she shifted her weight. She could see the light and the park and her cousin and Kai, but these pictures were only tenuously connected to the sound of the violin in her head. She heard it on waking and she knew it continued relentlessly through her sleeping hours; she, herself, came and went, not truly real, but the music had no beginning, it persisted, whether she was there or not, awake or not, aware or sleeping. She had accepted it all her life, but lately, she had begun to wonder what purpose it served. Prokofiev, Bach and Old Bei occupied the space that the Party, the nation and Chairman Mao occupied for others. Why was this? How had she had been made differently? After her parents had been taken away from Bingpai, she had been cut into an entirely different person.

There was a man limping across the park, one hand holding a rip in his shirt, as if this unsightliness bothered him more than the blood that ran down his face. People stared as he passed but no one spoke. Instead, a cold ring of quiet seemed to expand around this injured stranger, like water filling a plastic bag.

Zhuli walked back to the Conservatory alone. Her cousin and Jiang Kai had gone ahead, the two of them serious as Soviet spies, leaning towards one another, the pianist's hand on the small of Sparrow's back, the place, she knew, Sparrow had sustained an injury. He worked on his compositions for eighteen hours a day. Often, she came home from the Conservatory to find him lying on the floor of his closet room, in terrible pain. She would massage the spasms in his back and scold him for working too hard. It was as if Sparrow feared all the music inside him would be shut off, like a tap gone dry. But, honestly, who had ever heard of a Sparrow without music?

Ahead of her, Kai turned, lifted one eyebrow and grinned at her. The pianist had the same open, honest smile as Premier Zhou Enlai. She imagined the coffin-sized room he lived in, the rough floors and rodents, and wondered how Kai had ever managed to learn piano if he had grown up in a destitute village outside of Changsha. What kind of strings could a village boy pull? The pianist was a bag of tricks, she concluded. He wore his rural background well, like a penny novel wrapped inside an elegant cover. When not smiling, though, he had a face that could only be described as vigilant.

Her violin case swung with the rhythm of her steps. A procession of carts passed, each one weighed down with oil drums, the drivers sweating ferociously as if they were pedalling up Mount Ba itself. At the corner of Huaihai Road, she saw Conservatory students fluttering around Yin Chai, who had the glazed expression of someone who had withstood hours of adoration. The prettiest one, Biscuit, carried a trophy of flowers. Empress Biscuit detached herself from the group, came over, and overwhelmed Zhuli with revolutionary slogans, inside of which was posed, like a bee sting, the line, I saw you leaving with handsome Jiang Kai! Zhuli blinked and said, "The sun of Mao Zedong gives new fervour to my music!" and clutched her violin to her chest. Biscuit looked at her knowingly. The beauty queen would never be a great violinist, Zhuli thought, side-stepping Biscuit's velvety hair which curled in long arabesques against the wind. She hid the moon and shamed the flowers, as the poets said, but she played Beethoven as if he had never been alive.

She decided not to practise after all and ran abruptly into the road, hopping into a passing tram decorated with a banner that said, "Protect Chairman Mao!" It was so crowded, it squeezed even her envy out, so that when she entered the laneway off Beijing Road, she felt fine and light. Arriving home, she crossed the inner courtyard and entered the kitchen so unassertively that she caught her mother in the act of pocketing a spoon. Startled, Swirl turned. A handful of dried mung beans showered to the ground. Zhuli went to the table, clapped a mosquito between her hands and pretended she had witnessed nothing.

"Ma," she said, turning back, "I'm perfecting Ravel's *Tzigane*. It's incredibly difficult."

"Ravel," her mother said, pleased.

"Shall I play it for you soon?"

"Yes, my girl." Her mother smiled and a few more beans clicked and clacked on the tiled floor.

Five years of hard labour, Sparrow always reminded her, watching people who had done no wrong disappear, could not be wiped away so quickly, yet still Zhuli wanted to shake her mother, drag her mind back from the camps and make her present. What mattered was the here and now and not the life before, what mattered were the changeable things of today and tomorrow and not the ever, infinitely, unbearably unchanging yesterday. She got a broom and quickly swept up the beans, rinsed them in the sink, and spread them to dry on a clean cloth.

"Ma," she said, but her mother was now at the kitchen table. Zhuli went to her, wanting to ask forgiveness for the disrespectful thoughts in her head, but then she noticed the two travelling bags on the floor, and the papers, maps and notebooks on the table.

Zhuli picked up one of the notebooks, opened it and began to read. Her mother's handwriting covered page after page: persistent, balanced, sharp. Zhuli recognized the story right away, Da-wei's radio station in the desert, May Fourth's journey into the western borderlands, and the great revolution that had overtaken their lives. The tantalizing, epic Book of Records.

"You're making a new copy," Zhuli said. "Ma?"

"I finally finished it this morning."

Her mother drew a widening circle on the biggest map. "Your father's camp was here," Swirl said, "but if he returned to Gansu Province I think he would avoid this region . . ."

Zhuli could not follow her mother's trajectories. They criss-crossed and overran one another like the interlacing of a bird's nest.

"So I should begin my search here," her mother concluded. And her fingertip came to rest on an open place.

Zhuli wanted to take her mother's frail hand, lift it off the map, and hide it in her own. She wanted to take the map and burn it in the stove. "How would you do that?" she said quietly.

"Your aunt and I will go together. We travelled the length of this country when we were young."

"It's not the same as it was."

"True. Back then, there was the war against Japan, famine, and then the Nationalists bombed the Yellow River and terrible flooding came . . ."

"That's not what I meant," Zhuli said. "The neighbourhood grandmas will talk and the public security men will break down the door again. They'll say you're siding with a convicted rightist. And then what?" She wanted to say, but did not, How can you even think of leaving me again? Don't I matter? Isn't there any part of you for me and not for him?

"Big Mother will be teaching a new model opera in Gansu Province," Swirl said. "Since she's leader of the Song and Dance Troupe, she arranged for me to accompany her. She already told the neighbours she's going to handle my resurrection back into society. She told them that once I had lived in a Gansu mud hut for a few weeks, I would overcome the wrongs I committed and the idiocies of my youth."

Her mother reached out, hesitantly, to touch the long ends of Zhuli's hair. Her eyes were forthright and calm. "Foolish girl," she said softly, teasingly. "I've already been to the sea and back. This is only a small journey." Her mother's grey shirt and pants were ironed and clean, proper and unassuming, but there was a look in her mother's eyes that had nothing to do with propriety and obedience. There was no resignation, only a sharp knife in a pool of water. Her mother, she thought, had all the attributes of the famous proverb: one who thrives in calamity but perishes in soft living.

"Ma," Zhuli said, "please let me go with you." Even as she said it, she knew she didn't want to leave. "Big Mother can arrange it, can't she?"

Her mother said nothing as if the thought itself was not worth hearing.

Instead, Swirl picked up the copy she had made of Chapter 17 of the Da-wei novel and began to ramble like the evening news-reader. She would make further copies of all the chapters, she said, each one bound into a separate notebook, thirty-one notebooks in all. But in each one, the text would be marginally altered, and the date of copying added. They would use the same code as the origi-nal author, folding locations and information into the names of Da-wei and May Fourth, clues meant only for Zhuli's father, changes he would recognize immediately as not belonging to the original Book of Records.

"But what location?" Zhuli asked. "It's too dangerous for him to come here."

Her mother had thought of everything. The location belonged to a third party, the Lady Dostoevsky, who had been resurrected by the Party and was now living in Gansu Province, working for a plant and flower clinic.

"She has given the clinic a wondrous name," her mother said. "She calls it Notes from the Underground. The idea suddenly came to me. I remembered how Da-wei sent messages to his lover over the radio broadcasts, through the public airwaves. Hiding in plain sight. Big Mother and I will keep making copies as we go, and we'll scatter them all over the Northwest. She's already used the Conservatory's machine to make a dozen copies of Chapter 17, your father's favou-rite chapter. Wen might go without food for five days, but he can't resist the literature section of the bookshops. We added the date, you see? As soon as your father sees it, he'll know the message wasn't left by the author. The message could only have come from us."

Zhuli put her arms around her mother. Her mother hugged her back but her arms were light as wings.

"When do you leave, Ma?" she asked.

"Tomorrow morning."

She gripped her mother tighter. She remembered the little house they'd had in Bingpai, and the hidden, underground cavern, filled with books and musical instruments. She had climbed down into it as if into a magic kingdom and, in doing so, altered her parents' lives forever. Did such caverns still exist, she wondered. If she found another, would she enter it again?

Her mother's eyes flashed an unnerving light, part anger, part madness, part love. "Zhuli, be careful what you say and whom you trust. No one is immune. Everyone thinks that with one betrayal they can save themselves and everyone they love." She looked down at the map again as if it, and not this room, this city, was the real world. "Think only of your studies. Don't write to me, don't be distracted. Promise me you won't take any risks. Concentrate on your music."

As Zhuli was on her way out again, Big Mother Knife was in the midst of winnowing through clothes, dried fruit, sewing needles, sleeping mats, various washcloths, a cooking pot and a collection of knives, trying to fit them into Ba Lute's army rucksacks. "I'd rather have this cleaver than this pair of trousers," Big Mother said thoughtfully, holding both items up for display.

"I'd rather you had the trousers," Swirl said. "Come, tuck the cleaver into my quilt . . ."

Big Mother started singing a verse from "How the North Wind Blows," interspersing bawdy words, and Swirl laughed and said, "Cover your ears, Zhuli!"

"Or add your own verse!" her aunt said, and the two sisters giggled and folded the clothing into smaller and smaller squares.

Da Shan had come home from school and was lying on the sofa with Chairman Mao's guerrilla warfare essays on his stomach. "Take me with you," he said. "I'll be your pack horse."

"If I gave you two grapes," his mother said scornfully, "it would break your back."

Da Shan sighed. "Why so hard, Mama?" he said and Big Mother turned, the trousers dangling from her fingertips. Her face softened and Da Shan sat up, took the trousers, folded them and rolled them up and handed them back to her. "You'll need these, Mama," he said, and smiled.

Zhuli clutched her violin and turned in the direction of the Conservatory. The spring sky was a haze of pink and grey. She walked slowly, listening to the scores in her bag rustling like kept creatures, wondering if Kai would come to see her in Room 103, or if instead she would find Yin Chai and Her Royal Biscuit huddled indecently together. Apparently Biscuit and Old Wu had broken up. But maybe, if she was lucky, the practice rooms would be completely still. Once or twice now, she'd had nightmares of standing up on stage before a thousand people, the eternally sleepless faces of Chairman Mao, Zhou Enlai and Liu Shaoqi gazing down on her from the walls, but when she set bow to strings, the first notes of *Tzigane* refused to sound. The audience grew restless. They laughed as she tried to restring her violin, jeered as she replaced her bow, deafened her with abuse, but no matter what she did, her violin would not play.

"Stage fright," Sparrow had told her. "It's normal to feel anxiety." The Conservatory had set the date for Zhuli's next solo concert, mid-October, a few days after her fifteenth birthday. She had wanted to play Bach or her beloved Prokofiev, but Teacher Tan would not hear of it. He wanted her to aim for the next Tchaikovsky Competition, four years away. "The Ravel is a better preparation, unless you prefer Paganini's *Caprice No. 24*."

"I'm the daughter of a convicted rightist, Teacher. I won't be allowed to compete abroad."

His eyes gave nothing away. "We must have faith in the Party. And you, too, must do your part."

But two nights ago, Kai had told her that some, if not all, of these opportunities–competitions, scholarships–would be withdrawn. The Conservatory had been unusually quiet that night. It had been so hot, perhaps everyone had fled. "One day soon," Kai joked, "we'll arrive at the exits but all the doors will be locked." His next solo concert had also been scheduled for October.

"If it weren't for Ba Lute, they would never have accepted me into the Conservatory at all," she said. "I fully expect to be transferred to an agricultural college in Shandong Province."

"All the more reason to try to go abroad."

She played a few measures of the Ravel. "Your father is a Party member, of course."

"A pure seed of the earth. A peasant who played the bamboo flute and joined the Revolution so early, even our Great Helmsman didn't know there was one."

He liked to shock her. She refused to laugh. "I don't believe anything you say, Kai."

He took her hand and held it. "I'm glad, Zhuli. Never trust me." He leaned forward and pressed his mouth to her cheek and then to her lips. The warmth of his mouth humiliated her, she turned her face but he kept holding on to her hand, the heat of his breath against her ear. Just at the moment when she wanted to give in, to kiss him fiercely, he had released her fingers. "Do what the old violinist says," Kai told her. He continued as if nothing unusual had occurred. "Play the Ravel. I can do the accompaniment, if you wish."

"Fine," she said. She was trembling. He had switched gears as smoothly as a bird circling, as unequivocally as a madman. "Since you like it so much."

When he left, she had picked up her violin again. How had he dared? But a giddy, shameful pleasure had swelled inside her. Why had she allowed him?

Now she reached the stone gates of the Conservatory where hundreds of students were milling about the courtyard, reminding her of a fire crackling. Zhuli went straight to her political study class, she was nearly an hour early but still she was the last to take her seat. One of her classmates, wearing a crimson armband, made a show of taking down her name. The girl, also a violinist, was sincerely single-minded. Last summer, she had been one of the students sent out to the countryside. He Luting had refused to stop classes, and so only a limited number, the children of cadres, had been permitted to go. Most of them, including Kai, had lived in the barest shelters. Some of them had clearly never touched dirt before but, still, they came back as heroes.

Back at the Conservatory, they showed their newfound knowledge by continuously questioning their teachers, their parents and music itself. "We must take responsibility for our minds!" this girl had proclaimed. "To change our consciousness, we must change our conditions!" The teacher was barred from the room. Zhuli and her classmates wrote essays on discarded newspapers and butcher paper and pasted them up on the north wall. "Are we gifted?" the essays asked. "If so, who cares?" "What good is this music, these empty enchantments, that only entrench the bourgeoisie and isolate the poor?" "If it is beauty against ugliness, then choose ugliness!" "Comrades, the Revolution depends on us!"

Now the class turned their attention to the playwright, Wu, and the poet, Guo. Both men, once celebrated, had been discovered to be enemies of the People.

"Guo claims he hasn't studied Mao Zedong thought properly, he says we should burn all his books, he claims he is reformed but we know him, Comrades, don't we? The snake lies. How long has he been a Party member? How long has he been a hidden traitor?"

"And yet the authorities do nothing!"

"We women must be at the forefront of violent class struggle, we must make it our nature. Nobody can struggle for you. Nobody can wash your face for you! Revolution is not just writing an essay or playing 'Song of the Guerrillas' . . ."

"Exactly, the older generation used the Revolution to protect their status. They've betrayed us."

The students began offering criticisms of themselves and each other, and the girl next to her, an erhu major, mocked Zhuli for favouring music in the "negative" and "pessimistic" key of E-flat minor, and continuing to play sonatas by revisionist Soviet composers, including the disgraced formalist, Prokofiev. Zhuli rebuked herself fiercely, vowed to embrace the optimism of the C and G major keys, and ended her self-criticism with, "Long live the Great Revolution to create a proletarian culture, long live the Republic, long live Chairman Mao!" Had she been critical enough, too critical? Their faces, their gestures, their eyes were cold. They knew that, in the moment of speaking, she believed what she said, but as soon as class ended, clarity fell apart. All her thoughts kept intruding on each other.

By the end of the study session, her hands sat on her knees like stones. Standing, she could feel her dress glued with sweat to her back and legs. Embarrassed, she sat down again, dropped her eyes and busied herself with her books.

After the class had disbanded, she wandered up one hallway and down the other, arriving at Room 103 as if at the home of a confidant. She found Kai there with her cousin. Sparrow was leaning against the far wall and when he lifted his rapt face and smiled at her, she thought his eyes had the saddest light. Kai grinned at her. She closed the door behind her and felt as if she had stepped into outer space. Bach's *Goldberg Variation* No. 21 gave way to a joyous, bold and imperious No. 22. Kai played as if he were juggling a dozen silver knives, and all the edges flickered and shone.

Kai, she thought, you are as lost as I am. You have no idea where this beauty comes from and you know better than to think that such clarity could come from your own heart. Maybe, like Sparrow, Kai was terrified that one day the sound would shut off, his mind would go mute, and all the notes would disappear. Dear Kai. Ah, she thought, quickly correcting herself, the word "dear" was stupid with sentimentality and had been struck from permissible usage. What should she call him then? Her eyes threatened to fill. Jiang Kai was so much like her and yet . . . in the dramatic flashing of his hands, he played every note as if it belonged to him alone. He was all capriciousness and beauty and sophisticated performance; she thought he would be better suited to the hot-headed genius of Beethoven or Rachmaninoff or even the modernist high-rises of Stravinsky. Bach, she'd always thought, was a coded man, a strange fish, a composer who loved God and devoted himself to the numeric order of the world, but whose heart was fragmented. He existed outside of time. One day, Kai would play Bach with all the ardour that the composer called forth, but not yet. Kai was still too young, too certain.

At her insistence, Sparrow played the first movement of his unfinished Symphony No. 3 while she and Kai leaned against the wall. The opening slid from the key of E-flat major to an unexpectedly luminous B minor. She heard atonality etched into a falsely harmonious surface, she heard brittle ruptures and time speeding up like a wheel spinning ever faster. For all her talent, and for all of Kai's, it was Sparrow, she knew, who had the truest gift. His music made her turn away from the never-possible and the almost-here, away from an unmade, untested future. The present, Sparrow seemed to say, is all we have, yet it is the one thing we will never learn to hold in our hands.

While others in the Conservatory gave poetic names to their work ("Young Soldier's Joy" or "Thirty Miles to the Courier Station") Sparrow, as usual, gave only a number. Yet Zhuli imagined she could hear her father's presence in the music just as clearly as if Wen the Dreamer's name was written on the page. Could his name be written there in secret? Bach, for instance, had encrypted the four letters of his name into a single motif. These four notes, where in the German system B is B-flat and H is B-natural, served as his signature, surfacing through the music. And hadn't Schumann encoded the town where his lover was born? It would be just like her cousin to speak without speaking. Zhuli's left hand was playing an invisible violin, and when she noticed herself doing this, she abruptly stopped. Still, she heard a recurring pattern inside Sparrow's new work, as if they were the very footsteps of Wen the Dreamer. At night, her father walked across her own dreams, too. Since escaping the camp, where could he possibly hide? Last month, Zhuli had overheard her mother saying that the bodies of those who died in the desert camps were left to decompose in the sand dunes. Scientists and teachers, longtime Party members, doctors, soldiers, paper-pushers and engineers, more than enough to build a better China in the underworld.

"Careful. Even ghosts are illegal here," Big Mother had said.

"The lie is too big. I can't pretend, I don't wish to."

Big Mother Knife said that another purge was coming, there were rumours in her unit.

"I'm a stupid fool," Swirl said. "I was a fool."

In what way had she been a fool, Zhuli wondered. What did she mean?

Big Mother had dissolved the melancholy with a long, rumbling burp. "If you can't pretend to be a Communist, the only answer is—"

Abruptly, Sparrow stopped playing. "It's unfinished," he said. "I can't go on."

"But it's extraordinary," Kai exclaimed. "It's your masterpiece."

Blushing, Sparrow handed Zhuli her violin. "It's nothing," he said.

To banish the awkwardness in the room, she chose Ysaye's sonata in the dubious E minor key. She envied the composer's intellect, the observant compassion that Sparrow possessed, and wished to cultivate it within herself, but it was impossible. She was a performer, a transparent glass giving shape to water, nothing more than a glass. When the sonata ended, Kai leaped up and rushed from the room. "Some people really don't like E minor," Zhuli murmured.

"Perhaps he has an assignation."

It was late, almost midnight. "I don't think that our pianist has a lover."

Sparrow looked faint.

To bring the colour back to his face, she reminded him that his mother and hers were packing their bags, they were leaving for the hinterlands of Gansu. "It's better for Aunt Swirl. Shanghai is uneasy right now," he said.

"Why?"

He didn't answer. Zhuli wanted to ask him about fear because this unease inside of her, it too was a kind of desertification, a kind of hunger, and where would it end? It was cutting a fault line, running all the way to her hands.

But at that moment, Kai returned. "The Professor brought food for us," Kai said, holding up three helpings of noodles, three wheat buns and, stunningly, a small jar of wine. Zhuli had no idea who the Professor was but decided it didn't matter. Her stomach was rumbling. The melancholy in her cousin's eyes vanished as if it had never been.

Kai said some students had returned from demonstrating, but the streets were calm. Calm for you, Zhuli thought. Both Kai and her cousin had unassailable class backgrounds, they were Sons of the Soil, Sons of Revolutionary Heroes, Sons of . . . she laughed and drank the wine. Her cousin's face was hazy with joy.

She and Kai squeezed together on the bench. The alcohol made her thoughts light and immodest and she decided to climb up on the bench and salute her cousin. Kai wrapped an arm around her legs to prevent her from toppling over, and the pressure of his hands made Zhuli want to push him away and yet also collapse into his arms. "Cousin Sparrow!" she proclaimed. "Twice my age—"

"So old?" he protested.

"—but my best friend in all the world! I shall stand beside you when the flood comes!"

"May the flood bypass us all, sweet Zhuli," Sparrow said.

"May the flood lift us to better shores," Kai said.

Zhuli was the first to give in to exhaustion. She left them. Outside the practice room, she stood listening for a few moments, waiting for the music or voices to start up again, but there was nothing.

And yet, early the next morning, when the Conservatory was still quiet, here he was, just as he had promised: dear Kai, that exhausted performer, half draped over the piano as if over the arm of an old friend.

"You're late, Comrade Zhuli," he said.

"Did you sleep here?"

"With my eyes open and a pen in my hand."

"Writing self-criticisms, I'm sure."

He smiled. How tired he looked, and yet electrified, as if he had just emerged from a ten-hour seminar with Glenn Gould himself. "The truth is," he said, "I'd never even heard Tzigane. I came early in order to practise it. I feared you would drop me from your concert and perform with Yin Chai instead."

"So you've mastered it."

There it was again: the proud shine in his eyes. "Of course."

After playing it through once, they sat facing one another cross-legged on the floor. "Did you listen to the Oistrakh recording?" she asked him.

"A dozen times. I found it eerie and couldn't stop . . . I also listened to Heifetz and Neveu."

"Professor Tan told me to think about it alongside Gounod's Faust," Zhuli said. "You know, 'All that you desire, I can give you.' Selling your soul to the evil spirits. The usual thing." Tan had said that the violin score of Tzigane was devilishly difficult. Perfect, she had thought.

Kai nodded and made illegible, floating marks on his score. "The piano part is mysterious, isn't it?" He turned a few pages. "First, it enters late. Second, I find it cold. See how it never loses control and is never out of breath? And yet I feel there's a great hunger here. It wants to control things. To push the violin closer to the edge, maybe."

It was true. In the last third, the violin spun in faster and faster, nearly impossible, circles. She said aloud, without thinking, "Not love then, but something like it."

She and Kai played the piece again and the incompatibility between the two instruments heightened, like a dance between two lovers who had long since ruined one another and yet moved forward in the same maddening steps. It doesn't end well, thought Zhuli, reaching for the notes, her back pinched, her neck aching. She was the devil playing. The walls of Room 103 danced sideways and seemed to give way to her, as if she had become the rain and torrent.

The music ended. She sat down at the piano and stared at the keys. Kai took up her hands which were hot and damp. She hated it when people touched her hands, they were sensitive and in constant pain, and she'd had dreams in which they were crushed or cut open. As if he could read her thoughts, he let them go, picked up his pencil and tapped the score. "You see more in each measure than any violinist at the Conservatory."

"The Conservatory is a tiny corner of the world." She took the pencil from him, flipped to the meno vivo and said: "Here is where I stumbled. Fatally. Let's go back once more."

His hand floated down her back.

She moved to stand up, but his hand was around her waist.

"Zhuli." His voice was too near to her, his mouth pressed against her hair. "Don't be afraid," he said.

She wasn't afraid. Only, she thought, letting his mouth find hers, there are too many people, too many words, too many things that I wish for. I have the feeling there is too little time. They kissed. She didn't know that she was still upright, she felt as if she had lain down on the floor of the room.

She pulled away and stood up and went to her violin as if

nothing had happened, proud that she could be as uncaring as him, and tested the first bars of *Tzigane*. Her mind felt resolute and numb, but her heart was exhilarated. Kai was smiling at her. What did he feel, she wondered. Deep down, in that secret part of him, was there anyone he really trusted? She willed herself to disappear into Ravel. She let herself go, into the walls and into sound itself.

6

Without our realizing it, the weeks follow-ing Ai-ming's departure became months, and the months years.

On May 18, 1996, I was watching television and attempting to solve a hard problem ("Let D be a positive integer that is not a per-fect square. Prove that the continued fraction of $\sqrt{D}$ is periodic") when the telephone rang. Ai-ming's voice was miraculously clear, as if all that was required of me was to reach out my hand and pull her into the room. I was overjoyed. It had been a month since her last letter and Ma and I were expecting good news: after five long years, the rumoured amnesty had finally materialized and Ai-ming, along with nearly half a million others, had submitted her application for permanent residence in the United States.

"Ma-li," she said, "I called to wish you happy birthday."

I had just turned seventeen. Ai-ming rained questions on me–about Ma, math camp, my plans for university, our lives–but I ignored her. "What happened to your application? Did they schedule your interview?"

"No . . . nothing yet."

I told her to give me her number, to hang up so that I could call her back.

"Oh no, don't bother," Ai-ming said. "These phone cards are so cheap. Just a penny a minute."

She had a hint of New York in her English now, a tension that hadn't been there before. In both San Francisco and New York, she'd been working different jobs–waitress, house cleaner, nanny, tutor. At first, in the newness of America, her letters had glimmered with observations, jokes and stories. Ma and I had visited her twice in San Francisco where, despite everything, she had seemed happy. But after she moved to New York in 1993 we didn't see her anymore. Ai-ming always said it wasn't the right time–she was living in a dormitory and couldn't receive visitors; her hours were erratic; she was working night shifts. Still, her letters arrived like clockwork. Ai-ming didn't write about the present anymore, but about things she remembered from Beijing or from her childhood.

In 1995, when Congress passed Section 245(i) of the Immigration and Nationality Act, we thought she would gain legal status within the year.

On the phone now, I didn't know what to say. There was static now, all of a sudden. "Ai-ming, how are things, really?"

"Marie, my English has improved so much. They won't be able to turn me down." Her laugh seemed to come from someone else. "As soon as I have my papers, I'm going home. My mother . . . It's nothing, only . . ." Behind her I heard a machine rattling. "You'll come to New York soon, won't you?"

"Of course!" But even as I said the words, I had no idea how such a trip would be possible. Ma and I were as broke as we had ever been.

"You're seventeen already. If we crossed on the street, maybe I wouldn't recognize you."

"I'm just the same, only taller. . . . Ai-ming, I have a new joke: What did the Buddhist birthday card say?" She was already giggling. "It said, 'Not thinking of you.'"

"Ma-li, how many Buddhists does it take to screw in the light bulb?"

"Zero! They are the light bulb."

The machinery behind her seemed to laugh in counterpoint. "Could you . . ." She coughed and took a breath. She said, "Do you still have that handwritten copy of Chapter 17? It was your father's copy . . ."

I should have persisted, I should have asked her what she wanted to tell me, but Ai-ming seemed so fragile. It was as if I had become the older sister, and she the younger. I told her, "Of course, it's right here on the bookshelf, beside the set we photocopied in San Francisco. Remember? I can see it from where I'm standing . . . This summer we'll come to New York, I promise."

"I miss your voices. Sometimes I'm on the subway for hours each day, I feel like a child in the underworld, and I imagine all kinds of things . . . The netherworld is a kingdom of its own, with its own prefectures, magistrates and government, it's supposed to be another city entirely . . . *I am lovesick for some lost paradise / I would rise free and journey far away.* Do you know this poem?"

Her words frightened me. "Ai-ming, don't lose hope now, not when you've worked so hard."

"Oh, Ma-li, it's not that I'm unhappy. Far from it. I just want to take another step. I want to live."

Before saying goodbye, I had written down her new telephone number on the same page as my solution for the continued fraction of $\sqrt{D}$. But when Ma tried to reach Ai-ming that night, the line was disconnected. I feared that I had misheard or made an error transcribing it, yet her voice had been so precisely, perfectly clear. When Ma tried to reach Ai-ming's mother, the line rang, but no one answered.

Two weeks later, a letter arrived. Ai-ming said that her mother's health had suddenly deteriorated and she was going home. She told us not to worry about her, that very soon she would be able to visit us in Canada. I had wanted to give Ai-ming my e-mail address–marie.jiang1979@pegasusmail.com. We had just set up the internet at home and this was the first address I'd ever had; I knew it meant we would never lose touch, we would be able to communicate almost instantaneously. Each afternoon, when I arrived home from school, I was convinced there would be a letter or a voice mail, but there was only quiet, a qù that became a friction in the air.

When summer came, we flew to New York and took the subway to Ai-ming's last known address. One of her roommates, Ida, an older woman, said that she had warned Ai-ming not to go. If the INS found out she'd left the country, Ai-ming's application would be thrown out. Worse, if she was caught re-entering, she'd be barred from the United States for a decade. Ida, herself, had just been granted amnesty under the same program. She gave us directions to the plastic flower factory where Ai-ming had been working, but when we arrived, no one in the office would speak to us. Finally, just as we were leaving, a teenaged girl ran out. She spoke to us in Cantonese. She said that Ai-ming had been expected back weeks ago but had never turned up.

Not knowing what else to do, Ma and I wandered through Chinatown, carrying a photograph of Ai-ming from restaurant to restaurant. One after another, people studied the picture and shook their heads.

Neither of us had ever been to New York before, and I felt like a blade of grass in a world of fish. Every vehicle, it seemed, was in disguise, dressed up as a yellow cab. Ma, dazed, barely seemed to notice the city. As if in a dream, we walked across the Brooklyn Bridge, above the rippling water.

That night, Ma used her credit card so that we could attend a concert in Carnegie Hall; in the foyer and the main hall, I studied every face, row after row, up the steep balcony until everything disappeared into shadow. A poem from the Book of Records lodged in my thoughts, *Family members wander, scattered on the road, attached to shadows / Longing for home, five landscapes merge into a single city.* The music, Beethoven's "Emperor" Concerto, which my father had performed decades ago with China's Central Philharmonic, made Ma weep. I sat in the dark, grown up now. I felt too wide, too full of feeling, for the small space I inhabited.

On the plane home, I told Ma it was only a matter of time before Ai-ming contacted us. All we could do was wait.

After Ma's diagnosis in 1998, everything changed. We no longer fit into the hours, days and weeks of the regular world. She began to speak of the future not as an open and undetermined place, but as a fixed measure of time; a year, maybe two, if she was lucky. Her pragmatism hurt me. I was only nineteen years old, and needed to believe she would be the one to defy the numbers. When her chemotherapy began, I had been at university, a mathematics major at last, and I could think of all sorts of statistical reasons why she should not die. I spent many hours brooding over just this problem, as if Ma's life and death were a simple question of numbers and probabilities. To my surprise, but probably not to Ma's, all the anger I had stored up since my father's death returned. When I looked at my university classmates, I heard in their voices and saw in their lives a freedom I felt had been unfairly taken from me. How oblivious they seemed of their good fortune. I compensated by studying harder, by trying to outdo everyone, to defy–what? I didn't know. It's no wonder that I became such a solitary young woman. I was irrationally upset with Ma and angry all over again with Ba. I saw that I might lose my mother no matter what the numbers said, no matter how many things she still had left to experience.

As usual, Ma let me think what I wanted.

In the meantime, she altered her diet and dealt with the unending bureaucracy of sick leave, sick pay, health and life insurance, the web of paperwork and medication that quickly encircled her life, so that the measurement of time became divorced from the rising and the falling of the sun, and became instead about the intervals between treatment regimens, hospital stays, meal times, rest and recovery. She made a will and left a sum of money to Ai-ming, which to this day has not been claimed; neither I nor my mother's lawyer have been able to locate her. That year, I published a paper in a prestigious mathematics journal and I am glad that Ma lived to see this small success, this glimpse of a future stability.

During those long hours at the hospital, I willed myself to understand everything there was to know about algebraic geometry; somehow, the impossibility of my task saved me. I wrote my papers and tried to find my mother's strength within myself. In the last two years of her life, I changed. Ma's diagnosis was an end but also a beginning, a period of time intensely lived. We were lucky because, finally, we had time to talk, to go back to subjects we might not have raised in a lifetime of reserve, of quiet. In those two years, I knew only two constants: mathematics and Ma. I learned a great deal about the tenacity of love and also the terrible pain of letting it go. The brevity of my parents' lives has shaped me.

In 1999, Ma asked me to find Ai-ming. "You're the only one who knows," she said.

What did I know, I wondered, what had I truly understood back then? "I'll try, Ma."

"I couldn't find her. I tried so hard but I couldn't do it. There's no more time."

But what if there had been an accident? What if Ai-ming had passed away? I wanted to say these things but could not imagine speaking the words aloud.

The painkillers made her words slow and heavy. "She went back to Beijing. Maybe Shanghai. I'm sure of it."

"I'll look, Ma."

"I wrote a letter to Ai-ming."

"How?"

"I sent it to her mother in Shanghai. But it was returned, her mother had moved. There was no forwarding address. I called that number so many times." Ma's eyes filled with tears. "I promised her mother that I would take care of Ai-ming. I gave her my word. They were family to us."

"Please don't be upset," I said. "Please. I'll find them."

"Look straight ahead and don't turn back. Don't follow illusions, don't forget to come home." It was as if she could see into the future, she knew I would take on my father's regret and guilt. "You're listening to me, aren't you, Marie? Li-ling . . ."

"You don't have to worry about anything, Ma. I promise."

Not once did she ask for my father, yet I believe that somehow it was the same, that to hope for Ai-ming was also to hope for his return.

Before she passed away, Ma gave me a photograph Ai-ming had left us. The picture was a duplicate of one Ai-ming carried, which had belonged to her father. It showed Sparrow, Kai and Zhuli. On the back, my mother had written *Shanghai Conservatory of Music, 1966.*

My mother died fifteen years ago but I have been thinking about her more than ever, the way it felt when she put her arms around me, about her qualities, especially her loyalty, pragmatism and quickness to laughter. She wanted to give me a different example of how to live my life and how to let hers go. And so, at the end, her words were contradictory. Look forward or look back? How could I find Ai-ming and also turn away from my father? Or did she think both acts were the same thing? It's taken me years to begin searching, to realize that the days are not linear, that time does not simply move forward but spirals closer and closer to a shifting centre. How much did Ma know? How will I know when to stop looking? I think it's possible to build a house of facts, but the truth at the centre might be another realm entirely.

It's possible that I have lost track of the dates, the time, the chapters and permutations of the story. That afterwards, I reconstructed what I could about Ai-ming's family and mine. Years later, certain images persisted in my memory–a vast desert, a poet who courted beautiful Swirl with a story not his own, music that made not a sound—and I returned to them with greater frequency. I wanted to find her again, to let her know what I remembered, and to return something of what she had given me.

Even now, I send letters to all the last known addresses.

When I walk through our old neighbourhood, Ai-ming's voice comes back, as does my mother's. I wish to describe lives that no longer have a physical counterpart in this world; or perhaps, more accurately, lives that might continue if only I had the eyes to see them. Even now, certain memories are only growing clearer. "Once more, Sparrow recited the letter he had received from Wen the Dreamer. It had its own cadence now, the pulse of a libretto: My dear friend / I trust this letter finds you well! / And that you remember me / your dreaming friend. . . ."

THE PREVIOUS NIGHT, Sparrow had told Swirl and Big Mother about the letter, reciting it by heart. Big Mother had punched her knee joyfully, and then punched the other one. "The puny bird picks up all the news!"

"So it's true," Swirl said. "I knew it was true." For a moment she appeared as Sparrow remembered her, long before the camps, a teenaged girl outrunning the war. "If he contacts you again, tell him to go to the plant and flower clinic of the Lady Dostoevsky, Notes from the Underground. Lanzhou City, Gansu Province."

"Notes from the Underground," Sparrow repeated. "Lanzhou City."

"You'll take care of Zhuli, won't you?"

"Between Ba Lute and me, Zhuli will want for nothing. I promise."

"Be vigilant and keep your wits about you," Big Mother said. "Shanghai is full of walking sticks." She meant informers and spies. Beside her, the rucksacks, packed and waiting, hunched together like conspirators.

"I will."

Light from the moon slid through the window, gathering in Big Mother's water basin. Slapping her belly like a drum, she recited,

> "Moonlight in front of my bed
> I took it for frost on the ground
> I lift my head, gaze at the mountain moon
> Lower it, and think of home."

To Sparrow, she said roughly: "Watch over your father. He has no clue how to live without me." Her eyes reddened.

"Be careful, Ma."

Big Mother laughed, a cackling that sliced across moon and water.

Perhaps one day in the future, Sparrow thought now, as he lay in bed, he would write an opera about the life of Wen the Dreamer. And now the messenger sets out to Hubei Province to find the mysterious Comrade Glass Eye, bringing a copy of a copy of a copy of the Book of Records. The opera would open with a flourish, with the bravado of Shostakovich, before modulating towards the aligned, careful beauty of Kurt Weill, a libretto from Mayakovsky:

> The streets our brushes
> the squares our palettes
> The thousand-paged book of time
> says nothing about the days of revolution.
> Futurists, dreamers, poets
> come out into the street

and Li He:

Yellow dust, clear water under three mountains
the change of a thousand years is rapid as a galloping horse.
In the distance China is nine wisps of smoke
and in a single cup of water the ocean churns.

Could such an opera be more than an idea, a counterfeit, an imitation? Could he sit down and write an original work, a story about the possible future rather than the disputed past?

How difficult would it be to track down Comrade Glass Eye? Surely in the Village of Cats, outside of Wuhan, he would be easy to find.

Two days later, he told Ba Lute that he had accepted the Conservatory's commission to collect folk songs in Hebei Province. His composition student, Jiang Kai, would accompany him during the six-day trip, and serve as research assistant. Sparrow even showed his father the steel wire recorder and wire reels he had borrowed from the Conservatory. Ba Lute nearly levitated with pride. He unpacked crumbling maps and expired train schedules; he weighed Sparrow down with letters for long-lost comrades from Headquarters until Flying Bear giggled and said, "He doesn't work for China Post, Ba!"

Da Shan said morosely, "Who knows if your friends are still alive?"

Ba Lute gaped at him. Sparrow gathered up the letters and said, "Don't worry, Ba, I'll deliver them all."

Zhuli tapped her fingers on the cracker in her hand, swept her long hair over her shoulders and said, "Careful with the ruffian."

He smiled and resumed packing and she slowly ate her cracker. She whispered to him, "I'm not going anywhere until my mother gets back. She and Big Mother must be halfway to the desert by now. You'd like me to go with you and Jiang Kai . . . wouldn't you?"

He kept packing.

Zhuli continued. "I would love to but . . . what if there's a visitor or a message from my father?" And she stared at him with her searching eyes.

"Yes," Sparrow said. "Good idea."

Then he told her: "Think only of your concert, Zhuli. Practise every moment, don't let this opportunity slip away. Think what it will mean to your parents if the Party allows you to study overseas."

She blinked away sudden tears. "I won't let them down, cousin."

He met Kai at the bus station early the next morning. Beside the squat buildings, the ration lineups shifted in blurred congestion, winding around corners and disappearing into the horizon. The streets felt tense and watchful. When their bus flapped open its doors, they managed to find two seats near the back, over the tire. Kai insisted on carrying the wire recorder. Meanwhile Sparrow held his erhu against his chest and tried not to be crushed. More and more people shouldered on and the bus seemed to expand and contract like a lung, and then only contract. A supremely old lady folded herself onto Sparrow's seat, and he found himself squeezed against Kai's shoulder. As the bus bounced onto Jintang Road, Sparrow saw the city change, the concrete blocks giving way to open spaces, patches of light gliding into the flatlands of the outskirts. Kai's unruly hair shuddered in the breeze. Sparrow began to sweat. The bus laboured on.

At some point, he must have fallen asleep. He woke up to find Kai's arm around him, protecting him and the erhu from the old lady who had the concentrated heft of a bowling ball. Inch by inch, she was appropriating the seat, and at the same time cracking sunflower seeds in her teeth. Sparrow tried to return to the dream he'd just awoken from, which involved Herr Bach seated before a comically small pianoforte, playing No. 13 of the *Goldberg Variations* in order to demonstrate a particular subtlety of strict counterpoint. The composer's name brought together the words bā (longing) and hè (awe). Bach's face was as solemn as the moon. In the sticky, sweaty rocking of the bus, music rippled in his memory as he walked on stepping stones marked bā, hè, bā, hè, Sparrow fell asleep again.

Kai woke him in Suzhou. They alighted, as if drunk, from the bus. Inside Sparrow's rucksack, the thirty-one notebooks of the Book of Records (all mimeographed except for the hand-copied Chapter 17) elbowed against his back, as if he were carrying Da-wei and May Fourth on his shoulders. They sprinted to catch the bus to Nanjing, which had just begun to pull away. The bus groaned forward and the ticket taker waved them up to the roof to find a space among the chickens, the students and the baggage.

Kai climbed up first, then turned, reached down and grabbed Sparrow's arm just as the bus was picking up speed. When Sparrow looked dizzily up, all he saw was the pianist's earnest face against the white sky, and then, panicking and holding on for dear life, he was hoisted up beside Kai. The students on the roof made space for the bewitching Kai, who naturally took centre stage. The pianist could speak with both the quickstep of the city and the balladry of the countryside, he was a one-man Book of Songs and Book of History. Kai told a sly joke that made the boys howl and the girls smile knowingly. The grip of Kai's hand on his had left a bruise on Sparrow's skin and it ached to the teetering of the bus. "Teacher," the pianist said, touching his arm briefly, "won't you play a song to light our way?" A teasing affection gleamed in Kai's eyes and made the girls draw closer. "This comrade," he told them, "is our nation's most celebrated young composer! Believe me, you'll remember this day for the rest of your lives."

Sparrow ignored him, tuned his erhu and swept them into "Fine Horses Galloping," which got the boys whooping and the girls singing. A red-cheeked beauty with sparkling eyes somehow ended up at his knee. When he finished she asked him to play it all over again, which he did before segueing into "The Night of Shanghai." As he played, he remembered standing on the round tables of the teahouses, singing "Jasmine" to the rattling of coins and the offerings of tea and melon seeds, his mother and Aunt Swirl harmonizing with him, back when he first imagined that all the world was a song, a performance or a dream, that music was survival and could fill an empty stomach and chase the war away.

The students sang and shouted, and the driver thundered at them to keep it down, and the passengers below yelled cào dàn (Satan) and sent other furious epithets up at them, but these only dissipated harmlessly away. Kai suggested Sparrow play "Bird's Eye View," which was apt and also full of melancholy. He did, and Kai sang, and by the end of the tune, the affectionate girl at Sparrow's side had tears in her velvety eyes, and he thought he could hear old people sobbing down in the belly of the bus.

The afternoon passed and twilight descended, slowly at first, then ever more quickly. Along the motorway, towns jumbled out into smaller and smaller buildings until finally the land won out, ever vast and golden and infinite. Now and then, a handful of passengers would leap off and someone else would climb up. In the fading light, he saw Kai watching him, and he felt the pianist's hand on his shoulder, then the back of his neck, then along the thinness of his spine. The girl was pressed against Sparrow's other arm and the clean sweetness of her hair radiated up a pensive fragrance, hopeful as a bouquet of winter flowers. The Party said that desire, like intellect and skill, was a tool for struggle. But love, if it served the smaller self before the greater one, the individual before the People, was a betrayal of revolutionary ideals, of love itself.

He watched the lowlands disappear, giving way to higher altitudes and drier winds. Quilts were unrolled, thermoses opened and wisps of steam plaited together and curled into the night sky. Sparrow slept under the protection of stars and a half moon, hidden by a cover he shared with Kai, in the warmth of the pianist's arms.

They passed small rivers and one-lane overpasses and finally descended into a mid-sized town that looked exactly like other mid-sized towns. Layers of dust had covered them both and turned them mirroring shades of mahogany. It was early morning. While they waited on a concrete bench for the next bus, Kai told him stories of his village outside of Changsha. "My hometown is nearby, only a few hours away by bicycle. But if you visited, Teacher Sparrow, you'd think you'd gone back a hundred years or more. The same faces appear and reappear, they return with every generation. An old farmer might be reborn as his neighbour's infant, a wealthy landowner might come back as an indentured farmer. In villages like mine, individuals pass away, but generations and routines cycle on forever."

The pianist shifted his rucksack, looked out into the steady traffic of bicycles and wobbling trucks, and a storm of swallows that had gathered on the opposite bench.

"But one day, when my father himself was a child," Kai continued, "a new school opened in the next town. The school was run by a trio of former shopkeepers who had been converted to Christianity by Jesuit missionaries. These three oiled their hair and wore black cassocks so long they swept the ground. They were pious men and also entrepreneurs. As soon as they arrived in town, they took over two shops and converted them into a church and a school. Instead of tuition fees, they asked the farmers to pay them in vegetables and grain, in labour to maintain the buildings and harvest the land, and in faith to their god, who seemed to be a well-fed baby from Tianjin, carried in the arms of an empress, and swaddled in celebratory clothes. People admired the baby because he was a cheerful god of prosperity. And every week, the three priests would gather the faithful in their church and play music on a small piano that, they said, had come to China two hundred years ago on a ship brought by Italians who had floated up the Yangtze River. But how this musical instrument went from the Italians to the three priests, no one knew.

"My father," Kai added, "was a village schoolteacher himself who farmed a few acres of land. He sent me to the priests when I was very small because he wanted to find out more about this piano. Actually, we were believers in a way. We had complete faith in the things the priests provided: food, loans, education and medicine.

"And so I went and studied with all my heart," Kai said. "I wasn't the cleverest child in my class, but I was sensitive. So desperately did I want to escape my village that I even felt sorry for the grass that grew in that blighted place. I assumed that every village on earth must look like this, and so I fantasized about going far away, to the moon or another planet. The three priests, meanwhile, mistook my desire to change my life for authentic faith, that is, a child's pure longing for the sacred. They embraced me as one of their own. When I was six years old, they began to give me lessons on the piano. I don't know how they really acquired these instruments, but they had enough to form a chamber ensemble. They also had a good library. I learned to play a little bit of everything, violin and viola, organ, flute, even the horn, but I always went back to the piano. The keys felt like a part of my body. The piano, I thought, came from that outer, better world, from the sky and not from the dirt.

"My practice was so unruly that my fingers went numb and I even bruised my fingertips. Anyway, I sang and learned solfège and counterpoint, and the priests told us that music would free us from the discontent of our lives, that we need no longer be reborn as rats or serfs or even rich men, because we are all part of the same design, all children of the same heaven. So when Chairman Mao came with his liberating army, when the land restitution corps arrived, when the landlords were rounded up and dispossessed, when some were buried alive, when the peasants were raised up to Party secretaries, we were already prepared and willing to accept this new state of affairs. As Mencius says, a benevolent man cannot be rich. We had already been told that we were equal, and that the gates were open to us and we need only choose to walk through. The three priests were convinced that Communism was God's design." Kai smiled ambiguously. "Still, despite the great Revolution that I witnessed, I felt my destiny was to leave this village."

"But, after land reform, what happened to the school, the priests and the piano?" Sparrow asked.

Kai shrugged. He seemed irreconcilably separate from the scene he was describing. "The school is still there and the priests continue to teach. In fact, during the land reform campaign, the head priest, Father Ignatius, became Party secretary for the commune. He took the lead in repossessing land on behalf of the town, he condemned every landlord even though the church was a landlord itself. The priests gave up their holdings and proclaimed Chairman Mao the second coming of their liberator. So even after revolution, people's lives continue in cycles and not straight lines. I go home, every Spring Festival, to play for them, and they ask me, quietly, if I have been true to God. In my heart, I take God to mean the Party, the country and my family, and I say yes.

"When the famine began in 1959, the priests showed they were only men after all and had no idea how to multiply fish or loaves. My mother, father and two sisters all died that winter. Even Father Ignatius starved to death." He shifted his bag and rested it on his knees, partially blocking his face. "I watched them starve. I was the youngest and the only son, and they did everything to protect me. Our village cadres blocked letters to distant family. Anyone caught trying to leave the village was arrested. The punishment was severe. If you've never been hungry, you can't imagine ... When I first came to Shanghai, I saw that it might as well be a different planet. People had not ... they knew nothing about the famine or the ruin. When I was young, I was determined to fit into this new world, to save myself, because Shanghai was a paradise."

They were silent. Finally, Sparrow said, "To come to Shanghai at all, to go from your village to the city, is like crossing the ocean."

Kai nodded. "After my parents died, one of the music teachers saved me. Because of my ability, he sent me to live with a friend of the family, a learned man, a professor of literature here at Jiaotong University. He was the first from our village to go to university. He has been like a father to me since I was ten years old.

"Imagine!" Kai's laugh was sharp and sad. "A stuttering, know-nothing child, suddenly clean and tidy in a professor's salon. Six years later, I still call him 'Professor'! I like to think that, if he had sons of his own, they would address him in the same way. You'll understand when you meet him. I sat like a turnip while his students and colleagues debated and shouted. Sometimes I felt like an animal brought in from the forest. I know that I reminded the Professor of himself, long ago. But I could play. I could play Bach and Mozart even while my education, my language, was rudimentary. I was determined to rise to a new position in life, I had to learn to emulate the Professor and his circle—in every way, in their clothing, their habits and their language. Outside, in the streets, the Party might proclaim a new order, an end to feudalism, an uprising against the old class prejudices, but in the Professor's salon," Kai's voice dropped to almost a whisper, "the old order was still preserved.

"I don't blame him. A child of the countryside, you see, doesn't easily glorify the countryside. But because of the Professor's friends, my thinking has changed. Shanghai, I've come to realize, is not big enough for me and will never satisfy all the questions of my soul. I have split into too many people. I blame the priests, who instilled in me the idea of a better world, and the faith that I was destined for greater things. I blame the Professor, too, who once opened my mind but is now limited by nostalgia for the past. I want to make my parents and my sisters proud. I want to rise higher still. Do you feel as I do, Teacher? Your music has meant everything to me, it showed me . . . I ask myself why your symphonies are never performed, and I think it's because they make us feel so much, they make us question not only who we are, but who we aim to be. Fou Ts'ong has married the daughter of Yehudi Menuhin, he plays the piano from London to Berlin, and yet his parents are criticized as bourgeois elements. We pianists are not to follow his example despite everything he has accomplished. But surely we would better serve the People if we were part of the greater world. Why shouldn't your music be celebrated in Moscow or Paris or New York?"

The young man spoke with complete confidence, a childlike determination that seemed to Sparrow like a residue from another time. And yet, like some of the other students Kai's age, he also spoke as if there was no distinction between teacher and student, father and son, no formality. They had been born only ten years apart, Sparrow thought, but it was as if they had grown up in different centuries.

"My music . . ." Sparrow said finally. "When I was young, all I wanted was to write my music. Nothing more. And that is still what I feel."

"I hear something else in your compositions. I hear a gap between what you say and what you desire. The music is asking for something more . . . I'm certain we are the same." He turned and looked directly into Sparrow's eyes. "I no longer wish to live with restraints, Teacher. I wish to cast off the ordinary. The Professor has come to fear the Revolution. I do not. I wish the awakening of our times to waken me as well. We can't simply learn from Western art and music, we also need to examine and criticize our daily experience and our own thought. We shouldn't be afraid of our own voices. The time has come to speak what's really in our minds."

The bus came at that moment and Sparrow was saved from having to respond.

They spent the first two days in the villages outside Wuhan collecting music and two days in Wuhan City itself, including an afternoon at the gong and cymbal factory. Each time Sparrow delicately mentioned the name Comrade Glass Eye, his inquiry was met with confusion or curiosity, but mostly indifference. On the fifth day, however, a stranger approached them as they sat in the Red Opera Teahouse.

He was a compact man in his late sixties with a big, shiny

head and the cloaked eyes of a gambler. "Comrades," he said, "we were on the same bus from Nanjing. What a pleasure it is to meet you again! Tell me, how long will you stay in Wuhan?"

"At least another day and night," Sparrow said.

"I'm glad to hear it, and by the way, Long live Chairman Mao! Long live the incomparable Communist Party!" His throat crackled when he said the words and he had to stop and cough in between. "Last night, my little niece told me she heard Shanghai musicians performing at the Small Peach Garden and I knew it must be you." He flicked open his fan as if snapping open a knife. "Hot, isn't it? Wuhan, you know, the furnace of the South." As he waved the fan in slow, brutal strokes, he recounted how, before the war, he had lived in Shanghai and studied the violin briefly with Tan Hong. "By the way, my name is Old Huang, but please address me as Jian, as my friends do. Not the jiān that means 'flounder' but jiān as in the mythical bird with one eye and one wing." He pulled his chair closer towards them and whispered, full of emotion, "Please tell me about my dear friend Tan Hong. Does he still teach at the Shanghai Conservatory?"

They spent half the morning eating melon seeds and discussing the state of music.

Jian invited them to stay with him. "It's a simple room," he said, lifting his right arm and fanning the top of his head. "Hardly fit for two celebrated musicians such as yourselves, but the garden has fine acoustics. When I heard you on the bus, I realized that it's been far too long since I heard anyone play the erhu with such articulated feeling. And if I may be frank, Comrade Sparrow, I feel I already know you. Last year at the Wuhan Cultural Palace, visiting musicians performed your String Quintet in C Major. It is an understatement of unforgivable proportions to say that your compositions enraptured me. Truly, such intricate counterpoint and depth of feeling is unusual in these times. Please honour me with your presence!"

Sparrow accepted on their behalf.

In Jian's dwelling, after a lunch of fiery noodles, they sat in the shade of a parasol tree and smoked. Sparrow felt grateful for the sun touching the top of his head and the tops of his knees, for the pale yet bitter tea and the fragrant sponge cake that Jian had divided into two large pieces, with one tiny sliver for himself. His thoughts turned inward and he settled on the composition lecture he wanted to give on revolutionary expressionism, Schönberg's *Treatise on Harmony*, and Tcherepnin's essay on folk music's eternal line. "Developing variation," he would begin, quoting Schönberg, "means that we begin with a basic unit, and from this unit elaborate the idea of a piece. As composers, keep in mind fluency, contrast, variety, logic and unity, on the one hand, and character, mood, expression on the other. . . ."

Just then, Jian slapped his head as if he had forgotten to put out the brazier. He ran out and, when he returned, he carried a very old, astonishingly beautiful violin. He offered it to Kai who in turn handed it to Sparrow, who accepted it with solemnity. Under the elderly man's watchful gaze, Sparrow tuned the instrument. He felt the thinness of the strings and the fragility of the violin's body. What music would best suit an instrument of this pedigree and seniority, he wondered. He wiped the strings down and considered the possibilities. Finally, he lifted the instrument and played the opening aria from Handel's *Xerxes*, and then Mendelssohn's "Song without Words." The violin was worldly-wise and expressive. Sparrow glanced at Jian. Their host sat in the shadows and remembered and smiled and seemed to grow young again.

When Sparrow finished, he offered the violin back to its owner.

"Now that we are familiar as brothers," Jian said, accepting it, "may I ask what brings you to Wuhan? I assume it is not just to see the renowned Guqin Terrace." His broad forehead caught the afternoon light in a melancholic way.

"Comrade Kai and I are collecting folk songs from Hebei Province." After a moment, he added, "And, if circumstances allow, I'm looking for a friend of my family."

Jian nodded. He allowed Sparrow's trust to rest in the air for a moment before answering. "Tell me the friend's name and perhaps I can assist you. You see, I work in the town planning office, and keep track of all the permits, births, deaths, promotions, demotions and rehabilitations. I am the keeper of all the numbers in this town, and know them horizontally, vertically and upside down. Our world is made of numbers," the old man said and smiled sadly, "and long may the fires of Revolution burn."

"I know this friend only as Comrade Glass Eye."

Jian took up the violin, thinking. He played an echo of Handel's *Xerxes*, and then held a low E / D-sharp while leaning forward in his chair. "I have a friend who suits that description but does not normally carry that name. You look surprised," Jian said, smiling, "but this is not so surprising because, as you know, I'm called Jian, after the one-eyed bird. This left eye, you see, is made of glass, and I have worn a prosthetic eye ever since I was a teenager." Jian half turned his face so that he looked first at Sparrow, then at Kai, with his glass eye. Sparrow leaned towards it, mesmerized. "My friend's name is Teacher Ai Di Sheng and he has made my glass eye ever since I lost the original. But then, in 1958, during the Hundred Flowers Campaign, he was labelled a rightist and sent to a reform-through-labour camp in the North-west. A year after he was detained, my only glass eye was stolen! I was devastated. I preferred to starve and die rather than to show my empty eye cavity in this town. For many years, I wore a scarf to hide the wound. There is no eye left behind, you see."

As Sparrow stared, the eye shone with a disconcerting light.

"When Teacher Ai Di Sheng was resurrected and came home, I felt as if I, myself, had been released from the edge of the world. Without the prosthetic, I knew this society would never accept me or see me as one of its own. I had heard labour camp conditions were miserable, and so I brought him a basket of food, the best I could find under the circumstances, and some food coupons I had been saving. It wasn't much but gifts like this were extremely rare back then. He had to make the new eye three times because he hadn't held a glass tube or a paintbrush in ten years, and his hands shook continuously. I was the first to visit him, but eventually his patients began arriving from across the province. Truly, he is famous in these parts."

Carefully, Jian lifted the violin that was resting on his knee like a beloved cat and set it inside its battered case. A moment later, Sparrow felt a light rain beginning to fall.

"I'll pay him a visit this evening," Jian said. "If he agrees, we can go and see him tomorrow. Your timing is perfect because he's been on my mind recently. Teacher Ai is not a young man and he lives all alone."

He began to gather the tea things. When they stood to help him, he smiled and laughed again, and he seemed a young man, younger than they, as if his eye would never grow old and it carried him along, subtly renewed.

Sparrow woke before dawn. In the small room, shapes swam out of the darkness: a writing table and the spindly leaves of a spider plant, peeling wallpaper and a cloth cap hunched over a hook on the door. Kai's breathing seemed to come from the bed itself: from the long pillow they shared and a quilt rumpled around them. Sparrow felt aware of every creak of the bed and the window frames, of the nearness of the wall and of Kai. He heard the low splash of water falling into a bucket followed by silence, and wondered if the gentleman violinist was this very moment slipping the glass eye into its orbit. He recalled how the prosthetic had not stayed still but had moved minutely as Jian spoke. It shifted more slowly than the other eye as if it had a mind of its own. Kai was awake now. He turned onto his side and lightly touched Sparrow's jaw and neck, above the curve of Sparrow's collarbone. This near to one another, it was impossible to hide. All his life, he had slept on mats and narrow cots beside his brothers and his classmates, but for the first time he felt the intimacy of what it meant to lie beside another person. The sudden heat in Sparrow's skin grew shameful and humiliating but Kai did not turn away. He left his hand where it was, and then he laid his palm flat against Sparrow's chest as if to hold him where he was, always at a remove yet always near. Desire, or something so small as love, was subservient to revolution; this truth he knew, but the truth Sparrow felt led to another life entirely. He knew, or feared, they could not be reconciled. Outside, they heard the old man humming to himself. Kai drew back, pushed the cover aside and got out of the bed.

The sun was still low and the town misty when the three of them climbed onto Jian's moped, a vehicle allocated to him by the town planning office. They flew along a paved road that gradually broke down into stone, then gravel, then white dust, as if they were moving through time, to an age before stones and cities, or perhaps to an era in the future. Or this is how Sparrow felt with Kai seated behind him, the pianist's hands on Sparrow's waist, holding on against the force of their speed.

Initially, he worried that Jian would not see vehicles, plough animals or bicycles approaching from the left, and he committed himself to keeping watch, but as the town shrank and the sky brightened, he began to feel as if nothing bad could happen to them. Jian was wearing a cap with furred earflaps, one of which was pinned up, the other flapping freely in the wind, so he seemed truly one-winged and folkloric. At length, Jian turned onto a narrow road heading east and navigated them towards daybreak, past a string of houses, down a mangy dirt lane, arriving finally at a mud brick house with asymmetrical gables. They came to a stop.

A wiry man of indiscernible age, wearing ill-fitting clothing and holding a watering can, was standing inside a patch of dust-covered vegetables. He set the can down and came forward to meet them. Jian hailed him with, "Long live Chairman Mao!" and introduced Sparrow and Kai as the celebrated musicians they had discussed the previous night. The wiry man nodded. "You've suddenly materialized," said Comrade Glass Eye, "like the travelling musical troupes who visited in the first years of our great Republic." Even his voice was thin, as if his vocal cords were made of reeds. He studied them with both lightness and wariness.

Sparrow reached into his bag and withdrew a bulky package. He presented their host with a carton of Front Gate cigarettes, a bottle of cognac and a bag of White Rabbit sweets, which Ba Lute had given him to ease his journey through the province, calling them the new currency of the Republic.

"Gifts for Comrade Glass Eye," Sparrow said, trying not to drop the bottle which was sliding out from between his fingertips.

The man's head bobbed as he graciously accepted the gifts. "Very few people know me by that name," he said. "Locally, I'm called Ai Di Sheng, after Thomas Edison, of course, because of my experiments with electricity. The villagers mean it as a joke, but a friendly joke. Sometimes the children and the drunkards call me Teacher Suiren, the fabled creator of fire. I guess I have been called many things. My workshop is just over here. Come in, please."

He turned and began walking quickly towards the door beneath the second gable, the gifts rustling against his oversized shirt. Sparrow had to jog to keep up. Quietly, Comrade Glass Eye said to him, "Who instructed you to search for me by that name?"

"My uncle, known as Wen the Dreamer."

The man showed no expression but kept on walking, balancing his gifts.

A wooden door opened without a creak or complaint and then a lamp hissed on although the man had touched nothing. Sparrow, Kai and Jian followed him inside. They dodged an enormous glass fishing buoy, climbed three steps, and entered a room with a single long table and a wall of shelves. Wires of light began to gleam, as if awoken by their movements. Comrade Glass Eye put his gifts down. He gestured towards the full yet uncluttered room and said, "You are welcome to look around."

"Teacher," Kai said, "is your main interest light?"

"It was," the man said. "But when I returned from re-education, I discovered that my supply of copper wires was gone. During the Great Leap Forward, people broke down my door and carried away all the metal. You remember the slogan, 'Struggle to produce 10.7 million tonnes of steel.' When Chairman Mao instructed the villages to industrialize, my neighbours discovered all my bits and pieces, even my voltage meter, my collection of batteries, pinhole cameras and metal coils, not to mention my cooking pots and metal spoons, and fed them to the smelter that you'll see if you walk fifty paces to the east of here. They managed to produce a surprising quantity of steel but, sadly, none of it was useable." He shrugged and one of the electric lights fizzled, dimmed and then gleamed brightly again. "Upon my release, my neighbours all came and said, 'Isn't it a shame, Teacher Edison, you weren't here to help us fulfill our steel quota?' And then I was glad that I hadn't been present to hand over all my spatulas and wires, as well as my mother's wedding ring and the German stein my father brought from Düsseldorf many years ago, as well as my bicycle. Sometimes it is better not to say goodbye."

The man paused for breath and to consider the long table, which held only a few items. "Come and look at my eyes," he said.

He lifted out a cabinet, set it before them, and slid open a drawer that curved to the side like a hidden wing. Laid out on a notched paper surface, in even rows of eight, were eyes. Another light crackled on automatically. The eyes were ordered in a spectrum from black to chestnut irises, each with a subtle interweaving of lines, fissures and depths. They were hollow half-spheres made to fit, the man said, over the non-working eye, or over a sphere which had been implanted in the socket.

"These are for the right side," he said. He slid open the second drawer which extended in the opposite direction. Forty further glass eyes appeared. "And these are for the left. Each one is paired to another, but I prefer to store them separately."

Sparrow inched closer, hypnotized by the play of colours and the unreal, discomfitting feeling of the eyes moving over him.

"It seems like yesterday," said Jian, who had been silent until now, "that I first met Teacher Ai Di Sheng, in this very room. I had lost my eye when my best friend, in a regrettable moment, punched me in the face. How could I lose my eye over something so inconsequential? Afterward, I couldn't eat or sleep properly, and when I looked at my reflection all I saw was the empty socket, as if my entire self was being funnelled into that small, ugly opening. All night I would sit in my dark room and play my violin and its voice was the only thing that comforted me. Only music could express my pure feeling. I was broken by the loss of that eye.

"My best friend, who had hit me unintentionally and who also felt shame when he looked at my face, discovered Teacher Edison. So, one day, I found my way here. We sat at this table, face to face, and we spoke about vision, one-sidedness and the double nature of life. He asked me whether a glass eye would be for myself or for my best friend; in other words, did I yearn for a new eye as a window to the outside world, or for the world to look in on me? Well, I was very depressed and both perspectives struck me as equally valid. After all, when I remember my past, I see myself as if from the outside, I perceive myself as another person might. So we came to the conclusion that eyes are not one-sided. Teacher Edison lectured me for a long time. He said that a glass eye could not be a replacement for the lost one, but rather a new addition, neither a blindfold nor a seeing eye, but a painted mirror . . . 'Please!' I said, 'I don't care what it is . . . if you can help me you must! I feel as if I've been cut in two.' And so, over many days, he painted my first prosthetic. It was chestnut brown with flecks of orange and a hint of gold, which he said was the nature of my seeing eye. One day, on a sunny morning just like today, we put it in for the first time. After the long wait and my impatience, I refused to look in the mirror. I was afraid of the devil I might see! What if my reflection turned out to be a monster, a new self even more hideous than before? But he ignored my tears and fixed the eye in place."

Jian closed both eyes and seemed to hold his breath, then he opened them, looking directly at Sparrow. "When I finally looked into the mirror, I saw myself, as if for the first time, as a human being like any other. It is just an eye, such a small thing, but . . ." He turned towards the very thin man. "I think it's almost time for a new eye, Comrade."

Comrade Glass Eye assessed the violinist's face. "As we get older," he said, "the colour of the iris fades. So perhaps you are right, and the colour could come down a degree."

"So you see," said Jian, "we two are like brothers."

On the long table, Sparrow took in a delicate set of glass tubes, a Bunsen burner, miniature jars of paint and slender paintbrushes that seemed to have only a single hair.

"I have a spare room," Comrade Glass Eye said, "just through here, if you, my friends, wish to stay a few nights with me. It is a simple but welcoming place." Under the electric lamps, both of the man's eyes seemed like painted objects, peculiar, shining with a mystery of their own. Before Sparrow could answer, Kai said, "We would be glad to, Teacher." The thin man clapped his hands, making them all jump. "And you, Old Jian? Come and keep an old fool company."

"I brought my violin," Jian said. "And young Sparrow plays the erhu."

"Then you must come and see my musical instruments. If you follow me this way . . ."

That night, it stormed. As Sparrow played for them, the tap-tap of rain needles percolated into the music, interfering with the notes, muffling some and enlarging others, as if the downpour had a mind of its own and conducted the entire field of sound within and without the two-gabled house. Comrade Glass Eye served a muddy, sweetened coffee that he said came from the Buddhist lands of the southern seas, followed by a rice wine Jian said came from the western borders of Turkmenistan. In the corner of the room was a small harpsichord, so thin and earth-toned that Sparrow had not even realized it was there. He lifted the cover, revealing a Latin inscription.

"Music," Comrade Glass Eye translated, "is a solace of great labours. So, young man," he said, turning to Kai, "won't you play for us? Teacher Sparrow has told us that you are a divine pianist."

Kai tried to say he was merely ordinary but they would not hear of it. Finally, he sat down on the rickety wooden bench. He began to play a Bach cantata transcribed for keyboard, the "Actus Tragicus." Sparrow had the feeling of descending a sunlit staircase. The libretto rose up to meet him: "Ah, Lord! Teach us to think that we might die so that we might become wise. *Put your house in order, my child, for you will die and no longer remain among the living.*"

The priests in Kai's village must have owned a harpsichord, for the pianist played it as if it were his own. He ingeniously folded the music in half and then half again, emerging at the third movement with a chorus unexpectedly rapt with joy: *Today, today, you will be with me in Paradise.* And from this height, a place best described as kǔ lè, a state containing both joy and sorrow, the music began to tumble down, suddenly blending into Sparrow's own unfinished Symphony No. 3. Kai had only heard it the one time but now he played it from memory. The transition astonished Sparrow. The notes simultaneously faltered and climbed, faltered and lifted. The music seemed cast in an unknown and unimagined hue, so that Sparrow felt as if he were hearing his own composition for the first time.

When the movement ended, Comrade Glass Eye shook his head. "But what music is this, that reminds me of things I once knew?" He began, drunkenly, to remember the camps of the Northwest. "Was it so much to ask," he said, "to be allowed to live one's own life, honouring one's parents and raising one's children to the best of one's ability? Why is so simple a life the most difficult to obtain?" The portraits of Mao Zedong, Zhou Enlai and Lin Biao assessed them like busybody neighbours. "Poor Teacher Edison!" cried Jian, leaping to his feet. Sparrow feared the walls were listening and he wanted to say it was only music but could not bring himself to voice words so patently untrue. Kai paused to let the audience settle. The pianist gulped down a full glass of the Turkmenistan wine, and caught Sparrow's eye with a sad, helpless smile. He began playing again as the rain fell harder, sweeping them all away from Wuhan, from the county, the province and even the earth itself until everything swayed including the tremor of Kai's music. They focused exclusively on the sixth and seventh bottles, and Sparrow experienced a delirious freedom of thought and freedom of movement. The doors exhaled and covers of beds swept open to welcome them and Sparrow listened to the deluge while Kai held him clumsily in his arms. "How could you play my symphony so perfectly?" he asked. Kai answered, "How could you think I would forget it?" They fell asleep this way, touching without fully touching, near and far away, satiated and yet full of yearning.

Sparrow was the first to wake. He heard the rattle of a truck on the broken road outside and became aware of Kai slowly falling off the narrow bed. Gently, he pulled the unconscious pianist back onto the mat and covered him. The young man murmured in his sleep and said, "Dear Sparrow," and Sparrow felt, for the first time, how the purest joy could be a heaviness. He lay quietly, the wine now aching in his head, and listened to a noise from outside, the sharp note of a spade tapping stone. He pulled on his clothes and went out. In the dusty garden patch, Comrade Glass Eye was on his knees, occupied by something just emerging from the ground.

"He arrives," Comrade Glass Eye said, addressing the plants, "the nephew of Wen the Dreamer. A renowned composer as if from another time and age." Aided by Sparrow, he slowly got to his feet. "Let me show you the furnace our village built during the Great Leap Forward. A model of ingenuity," he said frowning.

They began to walk away from the house, sloping down a hill towards a line of softly whistling trees. Sparrow saw the smelter Comrade Glass Eye had spoken of, a misshapen black hat rising up from the dirt, abandoned.

"There it is! May it stand for eternity!" Comrade Glass Eye said, nearly shouting. Then his voice dropped low. "A rumour says that Wen the Dreamer is no longer at the camp."

Sparrow nodded.

"If you've come all this way to inquire after him," the older man said, "I know nothing of his whereabouts. I am very sorry."

They were not moving quickly. Comrade Glass Eye favoured the right side of his body, and his forehead shone with the effort of hiding his physical pain. It seemed clear to Sparrow that the inventor was gravely ill.

"Teacher, let's stop here to rest."

"No need, no need." And then, even more softly: "I'll feel better away from the house. There are spies everywhere. I'm afraid I was rather foolish with my words last night."

Sparrow nodded. He turned to look back, half expecting the doors and windows to have tottered after them.

"Wen the Dreamer had a suitcase," Comrade Glass Eye said, after they had been walking for some time. "A very important suitcase. It held a clean set of clothes, a picture of his wife and their little girl, what was her name . . ."

"Zhuli," Sparrow said.

"Of course. Zhuli."

"I received a letter from him."

The old man seemed not to hear. His eyes were glassy in the sun, and then they were suddenly wet. Tears fell and mixed with the man's sweat, and only then did Sparrow know that Comrade Glass Eye had understood. "Our friend is not only a fine calligrapher," the man whispered, "but an escape artist of the highest rank. Where does a person hide in the desert? It's like a fish trying to hide in a tree!" He stopped to turn away, lifting his hands to his face. He said, from behind this shelter, "I've seen men leave this world midway through a sentence. If I tell you what we lived through, would you believe me?" His hands descended. "If I told you that, all through the bitter winter, we lived inside caves, what would you say? That good men, educated and honest men, had to copy the ways of animals in order to survive the climate, but we were not animals! We were missing sharp teeth and pointed ears and thick fur coats! We and all our men starved . . . Comrade Sparrow, I'm going to tell you the truth about these camps. I'm a very old man and if it turns out you're a spy, I've nothing to lose but myself. I can't betray Wen because I've no idea where he's gone. I only hope he took the suitcase with him."

"I promise you," Sparrow said. "I'll keep all our secrets."

The old man nodded. He was already half-submerged in his own memories.

"The year I met Wen the Dreamer," Comrade Glass Eye said, "there was famine everywhere. In 1958, during the Great Leap Forward, the true face of our Revolution was revealed. Why did our leaders dream that every farmer could be reborn as a steel-maker? How did they imagine that a boy who had studied the fields all his life could make iron ore out of nothing? I think it is much more serious than ideology, production and material needs. We had to become only what they proclaimed us to be, we existed to be forged and re-forged by the Party. Here in this village, the communal kitchen was shut down for lack of food. The ground and the trees were stripped bare. Nobody had a pot to cook their soup in, let alone soup itself. In six months, half the people starved, first the children and the old, and then the rest.

"It is a pitiful death, this useless wasting away, and it was a silent famine because few in the city knew what was happening in the countryside. All they knew was that food enough was coming in through the proper channels. All the grain had been requisitioned, you see, they took it away and left the countryside with nothing." He nodded his head, and turned his face to the undulating line of land and air, to the grey mountains in the distance. "In the Northwest, our own famine was a catastrophe. We had no ceremonies. What can the Party say at the funeral of a convicted rightist? To them, he had already died long ago.

"But I was fortunate in my gifts. If I may say so, hunger inspired my most ingenious creations! Over time, your uncle became my tall and trusted assistant. Wen the Dreamer and I made pulleys and tools out of nothing more than the desert wind. Every storehouse can be broken into—every camp administrator's private quarters, every cook's kitchen—if you have the right hands and the right tools. Dreaming Wen could reach the highest windows, he could stretch like an expanding ladder. We had a motto, Brother Wen and I, not to waste anything in the wastelands. We ingested compost, animal feed, we welcomed any nutrient under the sun. From the Party to our stomachs! From the sun of Chairman Mao to our lips! We promised ourselves that we would seek out the last edible crumb on this empty plate and find a way to eat the plate itself, if necessary. There would be no slow death for us, only a slow regeneration. Every day we woke up and cursed our leaders, the Revolution and history, and we worshipped life, learning and the future.

"Do you know why I was sentenced to re-education through labour, Young Sparrow?" He smiled, as if he was about to tell a long and satisfying joke. "Let me digress and offer you this tale within a tale. Well, my crime begins with my mother. During the civil war, she left my father and ran away with a Nationalist soldier, a fighter for Chiang Kai-shek. My father, it must be said, was not the easiest man. He used to fall asleep wearing his own shorts on his head to keep out the cold, and when he woke in the morning, he would forget they were there, and go out into the village just as he had gone to sleep. My mother, meanwhile, was the brightest star in the village, intelligent, kind and lovely, and twenty years younger than him. Her Nationalist lover was, in fact, a childhood friend. Just as the civil war was breathing its last, he crept back to the village under cover of night. They disappeared together. Chairman Mao was all but leader by then. My father feared my mother would be caught, charged with sedition and executed. He couldn't sleep and became so worried that he wasted away, as if he, himself, was on the run. But, one morning, a letter arrived from my mother. She told us she had followed her lover and General Chiang Kai-shek out of the country and into exile in Taiwan. And so, she was gone forever.

"I knew my mother loved me as much as she loved her sweetheart; thus she would never be happy separated from him or me. One thing I have learned, dear Sparrow, is that light is never still and solid and so it is with love. Light can be split into many directions. Its nature is to break apart. My mother only wrote to me the once; I never heard from her again. But I kept that letter all my teenaged years and I felt her suffering and believed that she felt mine. We were connected, as surely as this blade of grass is attached to the soil below.

"My father's love for her, meanwhile, was set to flow evermore towards her, no matter where she went or what she did, and it burned brightly until the end of his brief and patient life.

"Anyhow, by 1955 I was a bachelor and an orphan, and the Chairman chose this moment to launch his brightest campaign. 'Let a hundred flowers bloom,' he told us. 'Let a hundred schools of thought contend!' We were told we must question ourselves, our superiors, and the state of our nation so as to make a country that was both unified and just. Young Sparrow, I had spent too long in my workshop, alone with my crystal radios, homemade batteries and amplifiers, in a closed room where inanimate objects listened to me and to one another. So I came forward with my mother's letter in my hand and I asked that her crimes be forgiven and forgotten. I thought that if she was rehabilitated, she would be allowed to come out of exile and return to China, and I could see her once more. Love is a revolutionary act, I argued. My mother had broken with the Old Ways, with the suffocating hierarchies of Confucianism, and she had embraced her destiny.

"What a mistake. I should better have argued that Emperor Hirohito and Chiang Kai-shek deserved a villa in France, paid for by the Communist Party of China. I should have heeded the wise saying, *no flower can bloom for a hundred days*. Every joke ends! At first, they listened to me and were compassionate. 'Brave Edison,' they said, 'it is right that you show this fidelity to your lost mother. You are a faithful son of the Revolution!' The Hundred Flowers Movement was still a spring bouquet and anything could be said. It was an exciting time, my friend. All of us, young and old, were awakening towards freedom. I felt a deep pride in my country and I know I wasn't the only one. So of course, I didn't stop there. I went on about the waste in the village bureaucracy, the favours and bribes that bankrupted the poor, the laughable quality of our scientific education, even the quality of our trains. 'With all the gifts of our homeland,' I proclaimed, 'we should be the flowering tree of modernity!'

"The Anti-Rightist Campaign began. Everyone with something to lose, from our Great Helmsman to the local village brute, had heard enough. They summoned me to a meeting in town. I was convinced that my mother had finally arrived and I would see her again! I spent a fortune on a new set of clothes and a jade necklace for her. A very bourgeois thing to do, I admit. When I arrived at the hall, there were hundreds of people already there. I searched every face for hers. A dozen times I thought I saw her.

"I heard my name echoing on the loudspeaker. It was as if I was underwater and my name was breaking apart in the current. Two cadres pushed me up onto the stage where a man stood, holding my mother's letter. I was ecstatic. I looked all around, convinced she waited behind the curtains. The man waved the letter in my face to get my attention. I tried to focus. The man accused me of bourgeois familial tendencies and gross sympathy for the enemy. 'What enemy?' I asked, confused. He slapped my face. Enraged, I tried to grab the letter from his hands but it ripped. I had to get away, I thought, so that I could find her. She was somewhere in this room. 'Ma,' I called. 'I am here. Where have they put you?' The two cadres tied my arms with ropes as if I was a beast. The crowd began to shout my name and curse me. I thought it was a dream. Someone was bleeding but it couldn't be me. Someone was being beaten for the edification of the crowd, but surely it wasn't me. I imagined that the letter expanded and covered me and hid me and everything became dark. I woke up when they emptied a bucket of water on me, and then I shouted in rage and called them betrayers, monsters and ghosts. My words touched no one; instead, they were recorded in a file. This is how I know what was said: because the words have been repeated back to me so many times since then.

"I was carted away to Jiabangou. For months I simply refused to believe that I was there. Men whose only crime was honest criticism were digging ditches and wasting away. Meanwhile, back home, their families lived in ignominy, their kids were hounded in schools or kicked out altogether, their houses were confiscated, their possessions trashed, their wives forced to beg on the streets, empty the public toilets and denounce their own husbands. We could protest all we wanted but it made no difference. The guards told us we were lucky that, not only had we been spared execution, but we had a roof over our heads and shoes on our feet.

"There are many stages to hunger. By 1959, they were burying us by the truckload. The cold, young Sparrow, was metallic, bitter, and had appetites of its own. The cold crawls into your body and destroys you from the inside. Even the camp leaders told us not to waste our last days on this earth digging ditches. So we were free: free to wander the desert in search of something to eat. Wen the Dreamer used to say it was like searching an empty pocket for coins. Still, we persevered. There were times when the only thing we carried back, after an entire day of scavenging, was each other. Nothing in our stomachs but an echo. Wen weighed no more than a ten-year-old child. Often we didn't have the energy to return to the caves and so we slept, unsheltered, in the open.

"When he was weak, we sat so close our heads touched. He would pick up the story he'd been telling me as if he'd just set it down a moment ago, as if he had only to close his eyes and find the right page. His chest had caved in, his eyes had grown frighteningly large, and his bones were knives, but I think Wen was most afraid of silence. Again and again, he told me that his daughter was the light of his days and his wife was the centre of his world. I couldn't help but fall in love with her, too. Every lovely thing in the air was his beloved Swirl: the turquoise sky, sand that shimmered like stars, the sunlight that touched our rough skins. He spoke to her at night as if she was seated beside us; when he had a fever, he would crawl out of the cave determined to find food for her. Once I saw him washing grains of sand in a pot of water, convinced that he was cleaning the rice for his suffering Swirl. But even mad, he could tell stories. Maybe he told them better than in saner days, I wouldn't know. We swore never to leave one another because the worst fate would be to feel abandoned in this frozen and beautiful world. It is one thing to suffer, another thing to be forgotten.

"Later on, he rarely spoke his wife's name. Instead, he occupied himself by telling a story that had no beginning and no end, and that was born of the Revolution. One of the characters, May Fourth, reminded me very much of my own mother. May Fourth leaves her life and disappears into the wilderness; meanwhile, Da-wei searches for his family across the ocean and the desert. Wen could divide their lives into pieces and distribute them over a hundred days or over a thousand.

"One day, I recognized myself in the story: there was suddenly a young man who made glass eyes for a living and felt most at ease, most himself, among the partially sighted and the blind. I also began to recognize the lives of our fellow inmates in Jiabangou. I heard the echo of their star-crossed loves and youthful dreams. In the end, I never knew how much Wen the Dreamer made up, or how much was part of the original book he had memorized. Perhaps no one knows but the author himself; even Wen has lost track of where he begins and where the story joins him. He has become far more than a skilled calligrapher.

"The Year of the Rat arrived. It was 1960. Strings were pulled by a childhood friend of my mother who had heard of my case and worked discreetly to have me freed. I was unexpectedly resurrected. I was literally brought back to life because, in a few months' time, there would be almost no 'rightists' left. Professors, thinkers and scientists, leaders who had taken part in the Long March, grandfathers who had spilled blood for the Party, good men, weak men, honest and conniving men, bachelor men and men with a dozen desperate children: they were no more. Our great Communist community turned away as these human beings were ground to dust.

"I had to leave, even if it meant breaking my promise and abandoning Wen. The last time I saw him, your uncle told me that he had made a plan of escape. I actually laughed. Getting out was impossible. He might as well have made a plan to turn Mao Zedong into Charlie Chaplin. I told him his ragged clothes weighed more than he did. Worse, there was nowhere to go. The Party guarded the train station as if it were a storehouse of gold.

"'But I am not gold,' he said.

"'Then what are you, my friend?'

"'Just a copy of a copy. A migrating soul.'

"He was mad, I thought, and soon would leave this world. This was the only escape open to him. I hid my grief and I said to him, 'One day the Anti-Rightist Campaign and Jiabangou will be common knowledge, the way the Boxer Rebellion and the Long March are written into our books and our memories. My brother, we will not be abandoned by history.'

"Wen said to me, 'That will not happen in our lifetimes, nor the lifetime of this stone beneath my foot.' Then he looked down at the ground on which there were no visible stones, only dry grass and splintered branches. Who was right? It's too soon to say.

"There was no one around us, there was not even a breeze. There was no one to overhear me but I had gotten into the habit of whispering. But what could I say that was honest and true? What had I learned in these three terrible years? Did I know more about living or dying? 'Wen,' I said, 'this country exists in fear. I am a rationalist and a scientific man. I believe the rules of life become ever more intricate, there are unseen wires from each to each that we cannot see, not yet. We are here to learn and not to forget, here to question and not to answer. You are a man of questions. Of all the destinies of the world, this is a heroic one, and yet it carries suffering for it is hard to live with so little certainty. Why were we sent here to Jiabangou? Whose purpose did it serve? For I believe it must serve some purpose: we are the builders of the Revolution and also its scapegoats.'

"'Escape is the only answer,' Wen said.

"'Escape is death.'

"Wen smiled. He had wasted away. If he lay down to rest his head, I feared he might never rise again. He said, 'I would never walk knowingly to my death.'

"He showed me his suitcase. Written on the inside of the lining were the names of all the men who had died, and the dates of their falling. It is, I believe, the only accurate record that exists. He told me he had a plan to do something more. He would take the names of the dead and hide them, one by one, in the Book of Records, alongside May Fourth and Da-wei. He would populate this fictional world with true names and true deeds. They would live on, as dangerous as revolutionaries but as intangible as ghosts. What new movement could the Party proclaim that would bring these dead souls into line? What crackdown could erase something that was hidden in plain sight?

"'This is my fate,' Wen the Dreamer told me. 'To escape and continue this story, to make infinite copies, to let these stories permeate the soil, invisible and undeniable.'

"And so he escaped," Comrade Glass Eye said. "With the suitcase, I am sure, and convinced of his destiny." He wiped his eyes. "I am glad Wen the Dreamer sent you to me, but I wonder which story he wanted you to hear. You know how it is: pull one thread, and the whole curtain unravels."

"He wanted me to hear just the story you told," Sparrow said. "I am sure of it."

"There is the engineer we called Geiger, and also the former soldier, Paper Gun." He waved at the air as if the two men were standing beside him. "I was given the name Comrade Glass Eye. Perhaps that is the lesson the Party wanted us to learn: in our basic needs—air, water, food, and shelter—nothing separates the doctor from the flea, the educated from the ignorant. So, in fact, I was re-educated after all. I learned this lesson all too well."

Across the clear morning, Sparrow could see Kai bringing water to the garden, ladling it out with a small container.

"If you had to guess, where do you think my uncle might have gone?"

"Wen the Dreamer has no identity papers and he has, therefore, little room to manoeuvre." The old man shook his head. "He is a refugee in his own country. There are two routes that I can see: either the northern journey of May Fourth into the desert, or across the ocean like Da-wei. Which would your uncle choose?"

"Neither. He will not leave my Aunt Swirl or Zhuli."

"Agreed. Regardless of his trajectory, you will hear from him."

"Yes," Sparrow said. "He can't prevent himself from putting pen to paper."

The old man laughed. He seemed to emit light for a moment and then the light wavered and dimmed.

"Come," Comrade Glass Eye said. "I think your friend has recovered from last night's festivities. He is ready to continue playing music for us and I'm ready to rest my feet and close my eyes, bend my head, and listen attentively. I remember now that Wen the Dreamer always began his stories with the greeting, 'Kàn guān. Dear listener.'"

That same day, while practising Prokofiev's Violin Sonata No. 2, Zhuli could not stop thinking about her parents. Had Swirl and Big Mother Knife reached Gansu Province? What was the probability that her father would come across an altered copy of the Book of Records? It was as likely, Zhuli thought, as her being invited to play Prokofiev before Chairman Mao and the villagers of Bingpai.

She had been just a child then, only six years old, when she discovered the underground library. Sitting alone, frozen by the winter sun, she had seen a stranger emerging from the soil. His head had seemed to lift from the ground as if he were crawling out of his own grave. The stranger turned north, his long, baggy body melting into the trees. Zhuli had stood, peering after him. Was he an escaped convict or just a stranger passing through? Maybe it was the ghost of her great-grandfather, Old West.

Zhuli went to investigate. After the land reform had been achieved, after they had been assigned the mud brick house, Zhuli had been expelled from the village school. The child of a disgraced landlord, the peasants' association decided, should study the textbook of the fields and the equations of the sky. Besides, she already knew how to read and should no longer take up precious space. With nowhere to go and no one to play with, Zhuli had tried to stay with her parents in the fields, but she got in the way of the plough and cut her feet on the sharp rice stalks. Her mother, exasperated, yelled at her to go home. She obeyed but inside the hut, the loneliness became unbearable.

Zhuli decided to investigate the spot where the old man had emerged. Crouching in the shade of a gnarled tree, she saw a clean, dark stone and, beneath it, flattened grass and a branch worn smooth: it was a handle. She lifted the trap door. There was a rope with knots. She was small and, even in her bulky, padded coat, climbed down easily.

In some ways, this hidden space was more comfortable than the bare room in which she lived with her parents. It was just below ground, as if a very large and well-made wooden box, a shipping container, had been buried with a living room inside it, like an afterlife for Old West. There was a cushioned chair large enough for six Zhulis, an imported kerosene lamp and a full case of oil, stacks and stacks of books, and a soft, woven mat on the floor. She lit one of the lamps and, pulling shut the trap door, glimpsed two musical instruments, a qin and an erhu, though she hadn't known their names at the time. When she set it on her lap, the qin was heavy and cold. It had a creaking roughness and, at first, she simply sat with it and stared at the room which, in comparison to the mud house, seemed modern and strange. The crumbling books were from another age, they were literally from another continent, but the heavy qin felt alive. On her lap it seemed to breathe in and out, like the great-grandfather to whom it must have belonged.

Zhuli went down almost every day, even if only for an hour. Over an entire season, she tested the range of the qin's five, battered strings. She did not know how to tune the instrument but quickly settled on a harmony that seemed to suit both the strings and herself. Later on, she learned that the classical guqin was associated with elderly scholars and erudite books ("With snakes, conservatives and reactionaries," her classmates said) and it was true, Old West's qin had made her feel part of a floating darkness. The sounds it made were otherworldly, and had more in common with punctuation than with words. At night, Zhuli slept curled up beside her mother, longing to be in the underground library. She needed to make sure the instrument was still breathing. Truly, it felt as if the old qin was her stronger, braver twin.

Spring was late that year and all the farmers and the hungry people were anxiously watching the ground. An otherwise kind boy named Lu saw her emerge from the soil, just as she had glimpsed the old man. That very day, the container was dug up and all the objects carted off. The books, the soft carpets and the cushioned chair were confiscated, proof that Old West's descendants were biding their time and continued to conceal their wealth. Neighbours whom Zhuli knew, who always greeted her on the paths and sometimes gave her something small to eat, came and plastered the mud brick house with hastily written denunciations, the words so large they could be read from the road. She knew only a handful of characters, but she recognized the ones for girl/daughter 女 and sky 天, which had been linked together to form a single word, witch 妖 (yāo).

That evening, the little hut was very quiet. Zhuli asked her mother why the word yāo was written on their house. Her mother combed Zhuli's hair and said it was nothing, a small disagreement with the neighbours and, anyway, what an odd word to recognize. Swirl did something she never did, she mixed a paste of herbs and eucalyptus oil and rubbed the mixture over Zhuli's arms and legs, gently massaging her arms, legs, feet, fingers and even her toes. With every circular motion of her mother's fingers, Zhuli disappeared piece by piece. She remembered the soothing warmth of the kang and her father's suitcase with its dulled fabric and brass clasps, and a keyhole the size of her pinky. Once she had asked for the key but he said it didn't exist.

Night fell. Into the silence a true demon came. It shouted and raged as if to topple the hut. All at once there were people everywhere, some holding ropes and even singing, then hands shoving her aside as she tried to reach her mother, who had been forced to her knees. Swirl was saying, "Pity . . . pity." There was a loud clap and her mother cried out. Wen the Dreamer's voice shook as if it was coming from the foundations of the little house itself. Zhuli cried and cried. Was it her screaming that frightened all the demons away? She imagined she was the daughter and sky twisted up, demonic, and all the neighbours were afraid of her now. The men left, half carrying, half dragging her parents with them, as if they, too, were objects retrieved from underground. And then the room, in shambles, was silent. She climbed up onto the kang even though its warmth had dulled. She was afraid to feed coal into its mouth and heat the bed again, so she pulled all the quilts around herself, lay down and closed her eyes. She asked herself how the underground room could harm anyone, and why knowing of its existence was enough to bring forth demons. No answers came to her. Events were like dreams, she concluded, and thus could not be real. When she awoke from this dream, she told herself, the bed would be warm and her parents would be here and it would be morning. This time she would be very careful when she climbed into Old West's buried library, she would smuggle the qin out and hide it here. Was it still breathing? A day passed and then another. There was nothing to eat but she stole a few leaves from the young plants in the communal garden, and her dreams grew lengthy and warm and elastic. Was it then that she saw the excavation and the hole in the ground? Perhaps other events occurred as well but she no longer recalled them. She drummed her fingers on the cold bed and hummed to herself, and the music comforted her.

When she woke after the third night, a young woman was sitting in her father's chair with a bag of White Rabbit sweets in her lap. Zhuli stared at the woman but could not remember who she was. Nevertheless, she said politely, "Good morning, older sister."

"Pack your things," the woman said firmly. Her words were oddly accented because the candy had made her teeth sticky. Zhuli took the five objects that were nearest to her, which included a dress, a washcloth, and two of her father's records.

They walked under the village gates and towards the next town. Zhuli knew she had been to town before but she could not remember why. Nothing looked familiar. They came to a round-about with a half-dozen soot-covered minibuses. The White Rabbit muttered that her parents were lucky not to have their heads chopped off, they were fortunate that the worst excesses were a thing of the past. "They've been sent for re-education, that's all," she said. "Since you've never been educated at all, it seemed pointless to send you along with them."

Inside the bus, the rim of the windowsill overflowed with the husks of sunflower seeds. Every time Zhuli moved, the plastic bag with her belongings crackled like a witch laughing.

The countryside appeared to be breaking up into a rubble of shapes, tilting huts, splattered concrete and blocks of ash. People appeared from every road, moving and running to keep up with something she couldn't see. The White Rabbit talked a lot but her voice seemed to pass over Zhuli's head and out the window. She looked down at her feet and saw that her cloth shoes were muddy and that she had violet bruise on her left knee. The more she stared at it, the bluer and deeper it seemed to grow. She must have fallen asleep because when she woke there was a big moon outside the bus, and also a patter of electric lights, but everything else was darkness. The bus seemed to turn around in many circles before finally stopping and everyone suddenly leaped into action, pulling down bags and birds and chickens. A dog ran onto the bus and people ran off. The woman smelled of the sweets she had been eating all evening. They walked. There were many people on the sidewalks and Zhuli's bag scratched against their legs. The White Rabbit is taking me to my mother, she thought. Zhuli quickened her steps and, as the woman hurried along, too, Zhuli feared that she might snap, lift with happiness and break apart as soon as her mother took her in her arms. The bag cackled and snickered beside her, *To my mother, to my mother! To Ma, to Ma!*

They came to an archway, a lane and then an alleyway. She followed the woman along the rows of doors, so similar they all seemed to be children of one another. The White Rabbit chose one and stopped. "These are your relatives. Knock here and ask for your aunt." The lady knelt down and gave her one last candy and an envelope with red letterhead. She touched Zhuli's knee and the big, round bruise, which Zhuli had forgotten about, shot pain up her leg all the way to her eyes. "Good luck, Zhuli," the woman said and then she, too, disappeared. Zhuli faced the door, listening to the echoing sound of the woman's footsteps. She waited for the pain in her knee to subside, and she slipped the candy into the envelope. After waiting what seemed a long time, she lifted her hand and knocked.

The eerie creaking of the door made her shiver. A teenaged boy appeared. He had uncombed hair and nice eyebrows.

"I'm looking for my aunt," Zhuli cried.

His eyebrows lifted. He saw the two records angling out of her plastic bag.

"Bā Hè," she said. Bach. The teenager's eyes and the door opened wider. "You should tell my aunt that I am here," she said firmly. She shoved the paper with red letterhead against his stomach.

Late that night, she woke up, alert, and saw moonlight on her exposed feet. There were monsters beside her on the bed–her cousins, she later learned, Flying Bear and Da Shan. She crawled away from them and out of the room, towards a light waving at her in the distance. *To mother, to mother.* Zhuli was pulled forward until she reached that room. Two candles were lit and their fire swayed like unsteady feet. She saw Sparrow's teacup first, and then his hand, and then his arm connected to his shoulder, and so on, until she reached his eyes. He was not surprised to see her.

She wanted to cry but she climbed onto a chair beside him as if waiting to have her fortune read.

Her cousin was doing his homework and she picked up a pencil thinking that she could do something for him. Sparrow got up and gave her a cup of tea. She requested a task and he thought for a moment, then gave her some paper and a list of words which he instructed her to copy. She could not read all of them but reading seemed secondary; Ba had taught her how to copy neatly. All she wanted was the paper and the pencil and something to do. The list of words must have come from Flying Bear's homework, some kind of vocabulary lesson around the word shū 书 (book). For years, she kept this sheet of paper written in her child's hand:

Qin shū (a story that is sung), jìn shū (a banned book), tīng shū (to listen to a performance of storytelling), shī shū (the Book of *Songs* and the Book of *History*), mò shū (to write from memory), chuán shū gē (carrier pigeon), huǐ guò shū (a written repentance), niǎo chóng shū (bird writing, a style of calligraphy), jiǎn tǎo shū (self-criticism).

After her pencil was dull and her teacup twice emptied, Sparrow lifted her up and returned her to the shared bed. She asked him where the plastic bag had gone away to. He said nothing. She told him that she had wanted to keep the old qin but it was too late. What had they done to it? Had her devotion to the qin caused her parents suffering? Perhaps she was not speaking aloud because he still didn't answer. I did this, Zhuli thought. How did I do this? Because of me, Old West's treasures have all been taken away. Her parents came back to her in a rush of images. Was she powerless or powerful? Had Zhuli, herself, opened the door to the demons who barged in? Her parents had been roped together as if they were oxen. Why had her mother wept for pity? How had the men known, Zhuli thought, that she was part girl and part sky, a yāo who had been seduced by wood and strings that were not alive. But the qin *was* alive, she thought, fighting sleep. She and it were the very same thing.

The next day, Sparrow sat her down in front of the record player and played all the music he could find. Her cousin listened with his eyes closed and Zhuli copied him and did the same. Inside her head, the music built columns and arches, it cleared a space within and without, a new consciousness. So there *were* worlds buried inside other worlds but first you had to find the opening and the entryway. Sparrow showed her how to remove the record from its paper sleeve, how to set it on the turntable, how to place the needle in its groove. Everything in Big Mother Knife's house was careful and considered; a world away from the bullying she had recently endured. Everything in Ba Lute's home made music. Zhuli watched them all playing their instruments, she watched their hands and bodies, she let the music write itself into her memory. She felt, as with the qin, that she had always known this music. That they recognized one another.

There was a small violin that belonged to Flying Bear, which he shunned. One day she sat beside it for several hours and finally, she placed it on her lap like the old qin and tentatively plucked the strings. She did this day after day but her cousin told her: "It's not a zither and, in any case, you are too young to learn the violin." She continued for nearly a week and finally Sparrow took the violin from her, lifted Flying Bear's bow and began to play. It was too small for him, and his body folded around the instrument as if to prevent its voice from escaping. Zhuli recognized that voice, she felt she had known it longer than she had known life. Sparrow became her first violin teacher. Later, when she was eight, he passed her on to Professor Tan at the Conservatory. She accepted every word, gesture and criticism; her teacher was blunt and, during his tantrums, Zhuli feared he would smash her violin on the floor or break it on her head. But it was all drama. Professor Tan recognized that, in each piece that she played, she heard more and more music. But what was music? Every note could only be understood by its relation to those around it. Merged, they made new sounds, new colours, a new resonance or dissonance, a stability or rupture. Inside the pure tone of C was a ladder of rich overtones as well as the echoes of other Cs, like a man wearing many suits of clothes, or a grandmother carrying all her memories inside her. Was this what music was, was it time itself containing fractions of seconds, minutes, hours, and all the ages, all the generations? What was chronology and how did she fit into it? How had her father and mother escaped from time, and how could they ever come back?

When Ma finally returned home after six years in the desert camps, Zhuli wondered what words she could possibly say to her. There were no words adequate to the feeling between them. One night, Zhuli played the opening of Handel's *Xerxes* for her mother. It was the simplest of songs, romantic, maybe even deadly with bourgeois sentiment, of course it was no Stravinsky, and yet in the middle of the aria, Zhuli felt as if her arms and her body were disappearing. She felt the only reality was this wire of tension between herself and Ma: it was the one true, unfinished movement of her life. In this room, there was only the act of listening, there was only Swirl, a counting down and a counting up, the beginning that could never be a real beginning. Her mother stared at her as if she did not recognize her daughter.

"Ma," Zhuli had wanted to say, "it was my fault. I found this opening in the ground. . . . I should have been sent away, not you. But don't you see how long I waited for you, don't you see how much I have tried to improve myself. I only exist now, I only . . ." If she put the violin down, would the real Zhuli, the one they had left behind, appear as surely as night after day? If there was no me, she thought, Great-grandfather West's container would never have been discovered. Her parents would not have been condemned. These notes would not sound. An insignificant soul like hers could break the world but never remake it. What was the world becoming? Her mother was sickly pale and the hollows in her face reminded Zhuli of the grave itself. One blunt motion and Swirl would fold. And yet, Zhuli thought, we are alive now. I am alive. My mother is alive. It is a new age, a new beginning, and we are here.

7

I N THE SPRING OF 2000, after my mother passed away, I gave myself entirely to my studies. The logic of mathematics—its methods of induction and deduction, its power to describe abstract shapes that have no counterpart in the real world—sustained me. I moved out of the apartment that my mother had been renting ever since she and Ba first came to Canada, and in which I had grown up. Desperate to leave it behind, I cobbled together every penny I had and bought a dilapidated apartment on Alexander Street. The windows looked straight out into the port of Vancouver and, at night, the endless arrivals and departures of multi-coloured shipping containers, what they held, what they divulged, comforted me.

I kept my parents' papers in the bedroom closet and a Cantor quote taped to the wall: "The essence of mathematics lies in its freedom," and, like a child, I distracted myself by imagining numbers so immense, so limitless, they far exceeded all the atoms in the universe. Numbers, real and imaginary, were a language inside me, equations were branchings of substance and shadow, relationships and interrelationships, randomness and pattern, the fractional, incomplete yet consistently ordered world we live in. I listened to my father's records but thought only of intervals, frequency and temperament, of the expression of numbers in an audible world.

By the time I turned twenty-five I had finished my Ph.D. and, thanks to a well-received paper I had published in *Inventiones Mathematicae*, I was offered teaching positions in Canada, the United States, Korea and Germany. To the surprise of my professors, I chose to stay in Vancouver. A year later, I was teaching Galois theory, calculus and number theory, as well as a seminar on the symmetry and combinatorial structure of Bach's *Goldberg Variations*. I had a small, but close, circle of friends. In and out of my research time, I continued to be preoccupied by Ma's death and by the statistical improbability of finding Ai-ming. My mind was full of numbers; I was not lonely.

Yet I understood, even then, that my life was strange, shaped by questions that seemed to have multiple and conflicting answers.

In 2006, the year I turned twenty-seven, I made my first visit to Hong Kong.

For the next ten days, I disappeared into the crowds, nightclubs and bars of Mong Kok, returning to my rented room at 7 a.m. and sleeping until mid-afternoon. Ever since Ma's death, work had been my entire existence; I had become, without knowing it, the perfect caricature of a reclusive professor, or as G.H. Hardy described mathematics, "the most austere and the most remote." In the concentrated work of trying to prove a theorem, social life fell by the wayside. But, here, in Hong Kong's neon lights and perpetual noise, I let myself be someone else entirely. Walking home as the city woke, miles from sober, I felt happy for the first time in many years.

Finally, the day before I was due to fly home, I willed myself to find the dwelling in which Ba had been living—the last one, since he had moved several times during the final months of his life. The address, 9F, Alhambra Building, 202 San Tin Dei, was known to me from police and coroner reports, which concluded: "The deceased, Jiang Kai, burdened by gambling debts, suffering from acute depression, committed suicide by jumping from his ninth-floor window."

Sixteen years later, the building was still there, and I wondered how much it had changed, if at all, since 1989. There was no lobby, there was not even a door, just a grey staircase that led up from the street. I went up, passing room after room; metal grates or small altars, offering oranges to the ancestors, were all that separated each dwelling from the stairwell. The apartments were minuscule, with barely enough space for a bed. I saw windows the size of a sheet of paper. I climbed higher and higher. The door to 9F was closed and though I stood before it for a full half hour, I could not bring myself to knock. I had an irrational fear that Ba would open the door, that I would face the window he had climbed through. I turned around and descended. After leaving the building, I took a taxi to the district office of the Hong Kong Police where I requested a copy of my father's file. An officer helped me fill out an application for access to information, telling me that I would receive a reply, by post, within thirty days. I left the police station and wandered aimlessly. Standing on an overpass that crossed a six-lane thoroughfare, and despite the noise of traffic and the vibration of the entire structure, I could hear nothing. My life felt entirely out of order.

I took the subway almost all the way to the Chinese border, switched to a bus and then walked up a paved road. My father's only request had been to be buried at this cemetery, a place whose name brings together the characters 和 (harmony) and 合 (to close, to be reunited). But I did not know, and had never known, exactly where his ashes lay. In the cemetery office, I was surprised to find they had no record of him at all. The young man at the desk asked, bored but apologetic, if it was possible that my mother had scattered his ashes in the Garden of Remembrance. "It's possible," I said. "She never told me." The man returned to his paperwork and I went outside. All the graves were set on narrow terraces, rising upwards along concrete steps. After walking for several hours in the heat, I was drenched in sweat and could barely see. Crickets cried unceasingly and the butterflies were delicate yet large as handkerchiefs. Above me, cotton balls that seemed to come from nowhere glided through the air.

I came by chance to a small columbarium where, inside, four tiny tea cups and four pairs of red chopsticks lay waiting on a sheet of newspaper. Square niches, for holding urns and ashes, were mounted on the walls. But some squares were empty: these had only cardboard covers with two characters written in red marker, 吉 (fortunate) and 玉 (jade). What this meant, I could not fathom. The room was soft with spiderwebs, and the teacups and chopsticks appeared to have been left behind by ghosts. Desperate to find him, but afraid, too, I studied all the pictures one by one. His picture was not there. I left the columbarium and walked between the graves, but still Ba could not be found. At last I sat down on the steps of a long walkway. A worker, clothed in blue, passed by, with a white towel tucked into the collar of his uniform. He wanted to help but I could not communicate what it was that I wished for, and finally he left me where I was, under the sun, thinking of my parents.

Four weeks later, a small box arrived at my office at the university. Inside were a number of documents, police and autopsy reports, some of which my mother had already received. There were a dozen photographs of my father's body, his clothes and few possessions. There were also letters I had never seen before, eight from my mother, and five from Sparrow. One of Sparrow's letters contained a composition, 31 pages long, the pages taped together: a sonata for piano and violin called *The Sun Shines on the People's Square.* At the top, Sparrow had written: "For Jiang Kai." The pages, copied by hand, were dated May 27, 1989. A one-page report stapled to it took me many minutes to decipher. Finally, I understood that these pages had been accidentally misfiled and the error had only come to light in 1997 during the digitization of all police files. Because so many years had passed and the file was now closed, they were releasing the original documents to me, the only surviving family member. I was looking at letters that even my mother had never seen—not when she went to Hong Kong to bury my father and not later on, when she, too, requested the file.

I took everything home. That night, I read through the pages slowly, once, twice, three times. I woke up in the night and reread it. The photographs of my father's body, the cold detachment of the report and the details of the inquiry opened up emotions I could not stand to feel.

Finally, I put the papers back into the box, and the box under my desk. I went on with my life, returning to the world of numbers. Their possibilities, their language and structure, filled me. They were as beloved, alive and universal as music.

Not long after, I met a colleague who was also a professional musician, a violinist. His name was Yasunari, and he became my closest friend. One night, I gave Sparrow's manuscript to him, confiding its origins. Yasunari said he would arrange everything.

A few weeks later, I went to his apartment. We opened a bottle of wine, toasted the composer, and then I sat on the sofa and listened. I had never heard Sparrow's music before, but as the violin and piano began, I felt a strange humming, as if I'd heard this music in my childhood. Perhaps it was an echo of Bach's Sonata No. 4, an echo of that recording of Glenn Gould and Yehudi Menuhin I would later chance upon in Chinatown: it was as if I knew this person, and had always known him. In that piece of music, I imagined I heard three voices—piano, violin and composer—and in their separateness, they carried sorrow, yes, but also . . . how can I describe it? Inside *The Sun Shines on the People's Square*, I heard an unbroken space protecting all three, and also a limitlessness, an ever-expanding room like the desert. All of my unanswerable questions seemed to circle within the notes, at the intersection of piano and violin, between the music and the pauses, the rests. How did a composer live his life unheard? Could music record a time that otherwise left no trace?

I walked home. Lights on the ski hills gleamed faintly behind the clouds, leaving a blue wash in an otherwise darkened sky. I thought about my father, about his love for Sparrow and Zhuli.

How many notes are there in Bach's *Goldberg Variations*? In Shostakovich's Fifth Symphony? How many words are each of us granted over the course of a lifetime? That night, I began writing down my memories of Ai-ming. I wrote slowly at first, and then the story quickened. I hoped that writing would allow me, finally, to keep the promise I had made to Ma. I wanted, as Ai-ming did, to move forward, to take a further step.

A few months later, Yasunari asked me to marry him and I did. I was twenty-eight years old, but still far too young and unsettled in myself. Indeed I might go so far as to say that I was hostile to myself; I was, in so many ways, my father's daughter. I broke Yasunari's heart when, after only a short time, I abandoned our marriage, and I felt as if I had torn my own future into pieces. My father's death consumed me, a rift had opened between my thoughts and my emotions, and one day I woke with the sensation that I was falling through that rift and would fall forever. I was drawn to suicide.

Time passed. My emotional life was, as Big Mother Knife would say, as firm as a stack of eggs.

And yet, during this time, my research flourished. Blindly, I followed the first principle of pure mathematics, the hunger for beauty; in number theory we say that beauty exists in the machinery. Unexpectedly, my work on elliptic curves won a French number theory award and the revered journal, *Annals of Mathematics*, published one of my papers. My name was put forward for a Meadows Prize. I wondered at the absurdity of things. I had no explanation, except perhaps that I fell asleep as one person and woke as another. The surface of my life confounded me. Yet, in the world of numbers, everything felt possible: numbers had no substance and were made entirely of thought.

My mother's voice returned to me. *If you're trapped in a room and nobody is coming to save you, what can you do? You have to bang on the walls and break the windows. Li-ling, you have to climb out by yourself.* Month after month, my father's copy of Sparrow's sonata sat in a drawer, waiting. I woke one morning unable to deny this truth, that the love I carried for Ba had survived undimmed.

In 2010, I travelled, for the first time, to mainland China.

I was attending a number theory conference in Hangzhou, but it was Weibo and QQ, Chinese social media sites, that absorbed me. As many as 700 million Chinese, more than 50 percent of the population, regularly access the internet; until recently, 60 percent of internet users did not use their real names (as of 2013, anonymity became illegal). The Great Firewall, as it is commonly known, routinely deletes 16 percent of all Chinese internet conversations. Looking for Ai-ming in cyberspace was like trying to pluck a needle from the sea, but I saw, too, that the internet was a series of doors: all I had to do was create the door she could open. I began posting scanned copies of Chapter 17 of the Book of Records; I also posted jokes I knew Ai-ming would love. For instance, "The Yoda embedding, contravariant it is." Or, "Q: How do you tell an extroverted mathematician from an introverted one? A: An extroverted mathematician stares at your shoes when talking to you." Every post was a letter to the possible.

From Hangzhou I took the train to Shanghai, where I visited the Conservatory. I found nothing on Kai, Zhuli or Sparrow; it was as if they had never been.

That night in Shanghai, I fell asleep to the clamour of radios, a profusion of opera, disco, Beethoven, shouting and speech. When I woke, nothing stirred. It was as if my bed had fallen into outer space. In English, consciousness and unconsciousness are part of a vertical plane, so that we wake up ↑ and we fall ↓ asleep and we sink ↓ into a coma. Chinese uses the horizontal line, so that to wake is to cross a border towards consciousness → and to faint is to go back ← . Meanwhile, time itself is vertical so that last year is "the year above" ↑ and next year is "the year below" ↓ . The day before yesterday (前 天) is the day "in front" ↑ and the day after tomorrow (後天) is the day "behind" ↓ . This means that future generations are not the generations ahead, but the ones behind (後代). Therefore, to look into the future one must turn around, a mirroring echo of Walter Benjamin's famous evocation of the angel of history, "The storm irresistibly propels him into the future to which his back is turned, while the pile of debris before him grows skyward." How we map time, how it becomes lived and three-dimensional to us, how time is bent and elastic and repeated, has informed all my research, proofs and equations.

When I was a child, I would continuously pester Ai-ming. "Don't stop!" "What happened to Swirl and Big Mother Knife?" Or: "What happened to Zhuli? Don't let it finish!" She had come into my life at the crux of her own. She was a sister to me; from the beginning we were joined, two halves of the world Sparrow and Kai had left behind. Long after she departed, Ai-ming's voice tugged away at my thoughts, returning me again and again to the same ever-expanding, ever-contracting piece of music. Could I awake now and cross towards her? Near the end, she seemed almost to forget that I was there and it was as if the story came from the room itself: a conversation overheard, a piece of music still circling the air.

ZHULI WAS IN ROOM 103, following the magisterial Prokofiev up his porcelain staircases, when Kai entered without knocking. She ignored him: Prokofiev required all her concentration. Every measure brought her closer to the disgraced Russian, who had been accused by Stalin of formalism, his major compositions banned; yet in this room, Prokofiev was becoming flesh and blood while Zhuli herself was vanishing. From eighths to sixteenths then three times as fast, the notes chipped into one another, every note had to touch the air, make its singular gesture, and elaborate this unending melody.

And then, the music stopped. Her bow stopped. It was as if she could hear nothing, or had forgotten everything, or had been pushed underwater. Trembling, she lowered her violin. Kai and Sparrow had only just returned from Wuhan the previous day. She had heard Sparrow coming in after midnight.

Kai was still watching her.

"What do you want?" She hadn't meant to say it so brusquely, but the expression on his face, the pity, enraged her. "I reserved this room until eleven o'clock! And, as you know, the piano is in terrible condition anyway."

"Will you come upstairs with me?"

Ah, she thought, looking back at her violin, glimpsing her own reflection. Who was real and who was false?

"Comrade Zhuli," he said. "Something has happened."

She wiped the strings of her bow, latched her violin case and followed him out of the room. At the staircase, he took hold of her hand briefly. All the way to the fourth floor, her hand prickled with heat and discomfort. She heard yelling above them. The staircase became chaotic. Zhuli was separated from Kai and pushed down the corridor. On both sides, the walls were covered with dà zì bào, big character posters, the same as had appeared in Bingpai long ago. She glimpsed the word yāo, which seemed to crawl from sheet to sheet. Someone, or something, was being denounced. The language of these attacks was copied from newspaper editorials, these were the same words that spilled endlessly from Party cadres and shouting loudspeakers,

WE MUST SWEEP AWAY THE HORDE OF DEMONS
WHO HAVE ENTRENCHED THEMSELVES
IN CULTURAL INSTITUTIONS

she stopped and students pushed roughly past her, laughing.

BREAK THE BOURGEOIS "SPECIALISTS," "SCHOLARS,"
"AUTHORITIES" AND "VENERABLE MASTERS"
AND TRAMPLE EVERY BIT OF THEIR PRESTIGE
INTO THE DUST.

Without realizing it, she had reached the office of He Luting, the President of the Conservatory, and she heard, absurdly, music. Could Professor He truly be practising inside his quarters? Yet there was no piano in his office and so the music, Debussy's *Petite Suite*, with its uneasy mixture of triviality and sorrow, must be coming from a recording. Zhuli fought a hysterical wave of laughter. She had not heard Debussy for months, not since the composer had been targeted in *Wen Hui Bao* and the Beijing papers, his music labelled decadent, and the long-dead Frenchman a composer whose "elaborate impressionist cookery" was an insult to the hardships of the poor. Sparrow had confiscated all her Debussy scores and put them who-knows-where.

"But 'La plus que lente' is inside my mind," she had said, handing the music over. "Can you erase the Impressionist cookery in my mind?"

The longest, most vitriolic poster had been affixed to Professor He's door. The sheet, torn from butcher paper, was as tall as she was and the calligraphy, very square, was oddly beautiful. It was surrounded by other smaller posters. Zhuli stepped closer, the words wavering. The ink looked so freshly black, she thought she could wipe the malicious words off with her hands.

She had almost touched the word yāo when Kai came up beside her. She turned to him, her hand outstretched and, out of nervousness, smiled. Her attention was caught by the dozens of posters continuing down the hallway. The words jeered and seemed to move, to come loose and slide along the walls. She saw a long essay, written in ungainly calligraphy, filled with names, and this list of "scholars" and "specialists" included Sparrow, Ba

Lute, Professor Tan and a dozen more teachers and musicians. Stunned, she went closer. *Petite Suite* trickled and teased through the walls. It was the piano, not the names, that made her shudder. The music came to her as if she were watching a dozen points of glass falling towards them.

"There are more posters," Kai said. "In the courtyard and on the gates."

"But who is targeting them?" she said. She should have lowered her voice but she did not. "Why are they denouncing my uncle?"

Kai was already pushing back into the crush of people, some chanting, some grinning like opera-goers. Here were Biscuit and her Page-Turners, as Zhuli called them, and here was the string class as if they always travelled ensemble.

Zhuli said, "Ba Lute performed for Chairman Mao."

Nobody seemed to hear her except Biscuit, who looked at Zhuli with unexpected kindness.

"My uncle was a hero at Headquarters," Zhuli told her. "He led a battalion of the New Fourth Route Army."

Biscuit blinked nervously and looked away.

Kai took her hand and pulled her behind him. At the end of the corridor, the noise lessened. How hot it was, how desperately humid, yet Kai's hand was cool and dry. She clutched the handle of her violin case, stood very still and listened with all her strength, but under the bursts of contemptuous laughter she no longer heard the Debussy.

Outside, the posters were more precise and prescriptive. When Zhuli had arrived this morning, just before 6 a.m., the walls had been bare, so the posters must have been pasted up in broad daylight, with the approval of the class committees or even . . . Zhuli's thoughts became confused. Big Mother Knife had been right. A new campaign was underway.

STAND UP AND REBEL!
KILL THOSE WHO WOULD SABOTAGE OUR REVOLUTION.
STAND UP AND BE FREE.

"It's not just here," Kai said as he led her through the east gate. "This morning there are denunciations at Jiaotong University, and even at the Beijing universities, at Tsinghua and Beida. They all say the same thing."

On Fenyang Road, people flowed to work, talking, complaining, pulling children, weighed down by bags, water drums, instruments, birds, chairs, unidentifiable metal objects, pushed forward by hunger, routine, necessity, even joy. The air was sticky. Zhuli wanted to crouch down with her throbbing hands over her ears and block out the sun and the noise. No, she decided suddenly, her thoughts clearing. Those denunciations, those posters, could not be real.

"How was your trip to Wuhan?" She spoke the words casually, as if they had just now met on the street. "Sparrow looked exhausted when he got up this morning. And yet here you are, already hard at work!"

He looked at her steadily, as if trying to hear between the words. "I slept on the bus."

"And did you and my cousin come home with recordings full of music?"

Kai still said nothing. He reminded her of a cat with one paw raised, about to touch the ground, momentarily confused.

"That was your mission, wasn't it?" she reminded him. "To traverse the countryside, to record and preserve the folk songs of our motherland." Whose words was she using, she wondered. She forced herself to look him in the eye.

"Oh," he said, one hand shading his face from the sun. "We came back with three reels."

She wanted to beg him to come away with her, to come and play for a few hours. Or to go to the music library and browse the old recordings, there was a Shostakovich string quartet she longed to hear. Instead she said carelessly, "I have to go. I left my scores in Room 103."

"Forget them. Go home, Zhuli."

"I'm no prodigy like you," she said. "I don't improve by merely wishing it."

"This is the start of a new campaign. Don't you understand?" The sincerity in his eyes brought both hope and fury to her. He said, "The Red Guards can turn your life to ashes. They will."

Before I met you, Zhuli thought, *I had no one to please but myself. Jiang Kai, you are as real and unreal as the shadow of an airplane.* She wanted to ask Kai if he loved Sparrow for who he was, or if it was his talent that was the true attraction. Didn't he understand that a gift like Sparrow's could not be bought or borrowed, it could not be stolen? Did Kai love the person, or did he love what Sparrow's music made him feel? Her own thoughts surprised and upset her. She nodded brightly. "Until they do, I can only practise."

He smiled at her, in the way that Ba Lute sometimes smiled thinly at Flying Bear. Kai reached into his satchel and withdrew a sheaf of music. "Don't be stubborn," he said. "Take these." She stared down. He had placed in her hands familiar pieces by the deceased composer Xian Xinghai, a hero of the Revolution.

In her bewilderment, she felt entirely alone. The concrete buildings, crowded roads and all the passersby seemed to move inside a light that didn't reach her. "Jiang Kai," she said spitefully, "now I understand. I'll forget Prokofiev. I'll play the 'March of the Volunteers' and 'The Internationale' for all eternity. *The old world shall be destroyed. Arise, slaves, arise! Do not say that we have nothing.* That should win me the Tchaikovsky Competition and please everyone, you most of all."

There was his patronizing half-smile again. "Comrade Zhuli, don't make the silly mistake of thinking your talent is enough."

"My talent doesn't concern me," she said. "What I need to know is, will Sparrow's talent protect him? That's what you and I care the most about, isn't it?"

Instead of speaking, he painstakingly tied up his bag, which was patched in both corners and on the strap. He should conduct, Zhuli thought, all his movements have the illusion of expressing so much.

She wanted to ask him how he could acquiesce on the surface and not be compromised inside. You could not play revolutionary music, truly revolutionary music, if you were a coward in your heart. You could not play if your hands, your wrists, your arms were not free. Every note would be abject, weak, a lie. Every note would reveal you. Or perhaps she was wrong and Kai was right. Maybe, no matter his or her convictions, a great musician, a true genius, could play any piece and be believed.

She wanted to put all these thoughts into questions but by the time she had recovered herself, Kai had turned and walked away.

The movement in the street rustled and shamed her; no one else had a moment to rest, to think, to be afraid. Yet here she was, with time on her hands. She looked down at the music he had given her, which she saw now had been transcribed for violin and copied out by hand. Midway through, the notes wobbled and tilted, as if running into the wind. It must have taken him hours. But why would Jiang Kai do such a thing for her? When did he have time?

She began walking, directionless, fearful that the posters trailed behind her like mud stuck to her shoes. The words: counter-revolutionary, monsters, blind feeling, false love, *witch*. Inside her head, Ravel's *Tzigane* refused to be quiet. It billowed on and revealed itself as the composition of a madman. To escape, she rushed between the bicycles to Xiangyang Park. The grain and oil lineups snaked past her, and a line of grandmothers stood in studied silence, clutching their ration coupons. The sun was high now and the heat intolerable, but everyone seemed blank and unsweating. Of course, I will go back and find Kai and apologize, Zhuli thought, even though she kept walking. How many self-criticisms had she written? A thousand pages, two thousand? Yes, she was selfish and plagued by immoderate desires and yes, her love for music was a weakness. She had confessed these faults since she was eight years old, but she had stubbornly refused to purify her heart. Chairman Mao said, "To be aware of one's own mistakes and yet make no attempt to correct them means taking a liberal attitude to oneself. These people talk Marxism but practise liberalism. Yes, this is how the minds of certain people work and they are extremely harmful to the revolutionary collective." The park came like a sip of water. There was a shaded bamboo bench and she sat down, her violin case on her lap.

In the grass, a boy, no more than five or six years old, was curled up on the ground while his mother stood a few feet away. She wore a grey suit and a grey cap made of wool, a furnace in this humidity. The mother had a ball which she nudged towards her son, but the boy ignored her. Even the ball was grey. She retrieved it, turned and kicked it back to him. Still her son did not move. He lay motionless in the grass like an injured animal. Minutes passed. The boy leaped up as if suddenly awakened.

The boy went to the ball and faced his mother. But, unexpectedly, he turned and kicked the ball in the opposite direction. A thump echoed in the grove.

The boy waited.

The mother ran gracefully past her son and caught up with the ball. Undeterred, she returned it to him. Once again, he made as if to return it, but then, at the last moment, gave it a hard kick in the opposite direction. Once more, the mother chased it down. Again and again this scene repeated itself, the boy nastily kicking the ball away, the mother patiently retrieving it, the boy standing idly.

Zhuli closed her eyes.

When she opened them again, she saw that the torment had ended and that the boy and his mother were playing. They dodged one another, feinted, floated the ball towards an imagined net.

Zhuli slid sideways on the bench, opened her violin case and stared at the instrument. She had a lunatic desire to smash it on the ground. Beyond the park, she heard what sounded like an encroaching sea but was only Red Guards. "Down with Wu Bei!" the students shouted. "Kill the traitor, destroy the criminal gang, down with Wu Bei, down with Wu Bei!"

The boy, who moments ago had been laughing in delight, inexplicably grew weary. His mother passed the ball to him and he abruptly turned and walked away. The ball rolled past him, into the trees. He sat down. His mother ran after the ball, tapped it back to her son and waited. When nothing happened, she pecked it forward again but the boy was now prone in the grass. Still his mother circled him, the ball creeping ahead of her. They seemed oblivious to the shouting of the Red Guards at the out-skirts of the park. She had never seen a child and a mother act in this manner; it was as if the world had fallen on its side and the child had been shaken into irritable old age. The mother hovered in her shapeless grey suit. What was love to this child? It could be rescinded as easily as a command.

"The more ruthless we are to enemies, the more we love the People!" "What will you sacrifice, what will you sacrifice?" "Stand up and serve the Revolution!"

Something is coming for me, Zhuli thought. "The more ruth-less we are . . ." But an ocean, she thought, overcome suddenly by inappropriate laughter, only an ocean would destroy her. She closed the violin case and set it in carefully in the grass. Ravel's *Tzigane* slid over the shouting and covered her thoughts. Note by note, the music began again, it sounded so fiercely that her arms strained from hallucinatory exertion, her shoulders ached, and yet the music in her thoughts played on lavishly. Music was pour-ing into the ground. Far away, the voices of the students sounded like weeping, "We must remake ourselves and change the world! We must serve the People with our hearts and minds! From the Red East there rises a sun, in China there appears a Mao Zedong!"

Time, the park, the slogans, the mother and child: she pushed them all away.

Time, the pressure of the strings against her fingers, the weightlessness of the bow, would not leave.

When the last note ended, she awoke into the quiet. The demonstration had moved on. The grove was empty and the mother and the boy had vanished as if they had never been. Even the patch of shadow in which they had stood was gone.

There was someone watching her. The haze in the air and her own distraction had made her careless, and she had not noticed this other person. He stood up now and came towards her. Zhuli finally recognized him. Tofu Liu, her classmates called him mockingly. He was a soft-hearted, soft-spoken violinist. He was almost camouflaged; both his trousers and shirt were the same shade of army green.

"Long live Chairman Mao," he said, "and long live our glorious Revolution!"

"Long may it flourish. Long live the great Communist Party of China."

"Comrade Zhuli," he said. "I didn't mean to follow you. Actually, as it happens, I wanted to ask you . . . it's nothing really. So." He remained standing, as if hoping some campaign would sweep him away. When it didn't, he shifted his violin case to the other hand and continued. "Well, Professor Tan says that *Tzigane* is one of the most impossible pieces to learn, yet you play it effortlessly." The smile that touched his lips was swift and sad. "There's a Prokofiev for two violins I'm eager to learn and Professor Tan had an idea that you . . . Of course you have your own concert to prepare for. I believe this piece might suit you perfectly. Really, it isn't boring at all. The Prokofiev for two violins, I mean. Not boring. Say yes only if this would interest you. Or if it might please you . . . Well, do you want to?"

How would he survive? Zhuli wondered. He was as firm as a beaten egg. "I like Prokofiev."

Liu smiled. His eyes were too bright, too kind. "I'll copy the score and bring it for you tomorrow."

"Okay," she said. To her own surprise, she asked him, "Little Liu, what is happening now? What is happening to us?"

He hadn't moved but it felt as if he had taken a step closer to her. "It's what happens to every generation."

She didn't understand. The very trees seemed to bend and hold them.

"Don't you recognize it, Zhuli?" he asked. "I think history is not so different from music, all the different eras, like when the Baroque ended and Classical began, when one kind of understanding transformed into another . . . Our parents used to blame a person's suffering on destiny, but when traditional beliefs fell away, we began to understand the deeper reasons for society's inequalities." He was speaking nervously, as if unwinding a breathless Tchaikovsky descent. "Chairman Mao says we must defend the Revolution by identifying everyone and everything that is counter-revolutionary. We students have so many fights and arguments because we are still developing our political understanding. We're teaching ourselves to think in an entirely new way, uncorrupted by the old consciousness. But the youth are capable, aren't they? Truly, I think we are more selfless than the generation before us. My father was a rightist like yours . . . Maybe we can become . . . But it is difficult because we must struggle *against ourselves*, really question our motivations and ask on whose behalf we're building a more just society." He was timid but there was no shame in his eyes. "If some people say what is in their hearts and other people say what glides easily off the tongue, how we can talk to one another? We will never find common purpose. I believe in the Party, of course, and I don't want to lose faith. I will never lose faith . . ."

"Yes," Zhuli said. "I agree with you." Here it was again, welling up inside her, laughter and fear.

"I've always known I can speak openly to you, Zhuli. You're not like the others. We saw what our fathers went through. So . . ." He looked at her and nodded. "See you tomorrow."

Liu was already walking backwards, his violin case smashing against his right knee. He turned and his green clothes faded into the sunshine. Zhuli watched him go and felt a painful hammering in her heart. Why did he trust her? Whom should she trust? Her hands had no sensation, as if they were made of wood. But the notes filled her thoughts as if she were still in Room 103, as if her mind had not noticed that her hands no longer moved.

Up until the instant he entered Kai's room, Sparrow had convinced himself he was not going. The meeting, or as Kai called it, the study group, was not meant for someone like him. Yet, for nearly forty minutes, Sparrow pedalled his bicycle east, turning left at Henan Middle Road, right at Haining and finally into a kaleidoscope of smaller streets. He dismounted and walked in circles until he discovered the alleyway and a staircase into the concrete block building.

On the third floor, he knocked at number 32. Kai appeared, windy-haired even though he probably hadn't left his room. Pleasure flooded his face the moment he saw Sparrow. "I was afraid you wouldn't find it." Sparrow smiled as if he, himself, had never doubted.

How small it was, and dark. A radio was placed up against the door, the volume deafening. There were shapes that could be people or could be objects, but no fan and the room was stifling. A young woman, despite moving aside to make room for Sparrow, was still so close that he was submerged in the almond scent of her hair. Someone demanded Sparrow's ID card, others laughed, and a young man said, "Too puny to stand up to the wind. Definitely not public security." "Were you followed?" And then a grandmother's prickly voice: "He probably followed *you*, San Li." Laughter. Sparrow was trembling, he could smell his own sweat. "Just relax," the almond-scented girl said impatiently. "Are you really the great composer that Kai goes on and on about?" Before he could answer, they began talking about a book he hadn't read: he hadn't even heard of it. They mentioned a book he did know, Kang Youwei's *Book of the Great Community*, but the moment he silently congratulated himself, the conversation rumbled on.

In the corner, Kai had not spoken. He was at least a decade younger than the men and women in this room.

"Old Cat, what did you bring? Where are you?" "In your lap." This was the grandmother speaking now. "San Li, pay attention to what's in your lap for once!"

The grandmother reached into a cloth bag and pulled out a small stack of books. "A few odds and ends. *Essays in Skepticism*–"

"Delightful," the almond-scented girl, whom they called Ling, purred.

"And Xi Li, *On the Aesthetic Education of Man*, Shen Congwen, and what else . . ."

Another candle was lit. Ling picked up Xi Li, or Friedrich Schiller, searching for the place they had left off the previous week. Sparrow knew Schiller only as the German writer beloved by Verdi, whose poem Brahms had used in a funeral song:

Even the beautiful must die!
See! The gods weep, all the goddesses weep
Because the beautiful perishes, because perfection dies
Even to be a song of lament on a loved ones' lips is glorious . . .

San Li said, "Hurry up, the spy is dozing off!"

"A birch tree, a spruce, a poplar is beautiful," Ling began, "when it climbs slenderly aloft; an oak, when it grows crooked; the reason is, because the latter, left to itself, loves the crooked, the former, on the contrary, loves the direct course. . . . Which tree will the painter like most to seek out, in order to use it in a landscape? Certainly that one, which makes use of the freedom, that even, with some boldness, ventures something, steps out of order, even if it must here cause a breach, and there disarrange something through its stormy interference."

She read for thirty, forty minutes, and every word was distinct. When she closed the book, the grandmother asked if she would be willing to take it away and mimeograph a new copy.

"I'm already copying *My Education* and the department is suspicious. Give it to San Li."

General merriment followed. "Last time, he stuck all the pages together with syrup–" "Ling found a fishbone, didn't she?" "Chicken bone." "I like to leave a little something for you lot." "It's the Permanent Revolution of San Li's dinner."

When the laughter faded and the Schiller remained unspoken for, Sparrow raised his voice. "I will do it."

"Well, well," Ling said. "A bookish spy! Kai was right to be intrigued."

"Have it ready by next week," the Old Cat told him over the scattered giggling. "And don't eat with it."

"Take this one, too," San Li said. "*Dmitri Shostakovich*. Translated from Russian. It's too technical for us."

Sparrow accepted.

In the darkness, the radio announcer was repeating familiar words, *Those representatives of the bourgeoisie who have sneaked into the Party, the government, the army, and various spheres of culture are a group of counter-revolutionary revisionists . . .*

Bowls of peanuts and a jug of rice wine were passed from hand to hand. The older gentleman proposed a toast to "Lakes of wine and forests of meat!" and when everyone raised their cups, the lone candle went out. Ling started humming a song he couldn't place.

"My boy," the older man said, turning to Kai, "it's been weeks since I saw you. The piano in my house grows dusty, and Ling says you never visit anymore."

"Why, I saw her yesterday," Kai said laughing, "but I'll come tomorrow, Professor."

The wine had permeated all of Sparrow's limbs, and the Professor appeared round as a floating balloon as he scooted over.

Some of them we have already seen through, the radio shouted, *others we have not! Some are still trusted by us and are being trained as our successors . . .*

Tipsily, the Professor turned to Sparrow. "I've heard so much about you, Comrade. If I may say so, your String Octet is one of my favourite pieces of music. Such an honour to finally make your acquaintance." Around them, conversation was breaking into smaller pieces. The Professor hummed a song, "Jasmine," that took Sparrow back to the teahouses of his youth. Sparrow confided that he had travelled the length of the country singing that very song.

"In my youth," the Professor said, "I, too, travelled. I was conscripted by the Kuomintang. Fortunately, I managed to slip away and cross over to the Communist army. It was horror. The fighting, I mean. But we made this country." He paused, thumped his knee twice softly and said, "Afterwards, I arrived at the victory celebration in my hometown, only to be told . . . when the Japanese entered the town, my wife disappeared. I said to myself, many people were displaced during the aggression. If the gods are watching, I'll surely find her again." The Professor had gone to Shanghai to teach history and Western philosophy at Jiaotong University. "Our books are full of stories of mistaken identity, star-crossed love, years of separation. Do you know the classic song, 'The Faraway Place,' well, you must, of course. I can't hear it without thinking that my beloved has finally returned. It's been twenty years since I last saw her, but in my mind she's the same."

"Tell him how I came to live with you," Kai said. His voice was soft. In the darkness, it was unexpectedly near.

"Ah," the Professor said. "Well, in 1960, I learned that my wife's nephew had a gift for music. I arranged admission for him to the preparatory school of the Shanghai Conservatory–"

"You moved heaven and earth," Kai said.

"Well. I had fought bravely in the war. As I said, people bent their ears to me back then. In any case, that is how Jiang Kai arrived in Shanghai. He was eleven years old, it was just after the Three Years of Catastrophe . . . I tell you, this was my first indication of the disaster that was happening there. We had shortages in Shanghai, of course, but nothing like the countryside . . ." The Professor motioned towards the window. "Kai came to live with me and, in my home, there was suddenly music. I was tutoring Ling at the time, and he used to follow her everywhere she went. They were inseparable."

He took the erhu and held it as if the instrument could answer a confusion in his mind. The old Professor played the opening notes of "The Faraway Place," then smiled regretfully at Sparrow. He set the bow down.

In the room, conversation had turned inward. Ling was saying, "But who loves the Revolution more than we do? Who would die for it? I would. So why can't I criticize policies and still be considered a reformer within the Party? Why does the Party persist in believing that criticism only comes from class enemies?"

"But the cultural revolution, the new campaign, is about questioning the old ways of doing things," Kai said. "Renewing ourselves–"

San Li was peremptory. "Don't be naive. It's criticism along acceptable and correct lines–"

Ling intervened. "Every work unit has to turn over a set percentage of rightists, but that's crazy, isn't it? Or maybe it's genius. Either way, it's entirely systematic."

The talk murmured on, never finding a way through or an idea they could all agree on.

Loosened by the wine, Sparrow's thoughts drifted. Underneath the radio and the voices, he felt concealed, as if he really were a spy. Tomorrow he would arrive at his office at the Conservatory and continue his symphony. The four white walls, the plain desk and open space in his mind, could so spare a life be called freedom? He had been listening to Bach again. How had this composer from the West turned away from the linear and found his voice in the cyclical, in canons and fugues, in what Bach referred to as God's time and in what the ancient Song and Tang scholars saw as the continual reiterations of the past, the turning of the wheel of history? Campaigns, revolutions themselves, arrived in waves, ending only to start again. Could Bach's limitations create another kind of freedom? Could an absence of freedom reveal the borders of their lives, their mortality, their fate? What if life and fate turned out to be the same thing? He shook the thought away. The wine was making him soft. He would have to stand up soon, find his bicycle and pedal home, and it would be up to his feet and legs to turn in circles. This room, he told himself, was an anomaly, perhaps one of many: corners of the city that had not yet been polished smooth. Zhuli would have understood, instinctively, what troubled him, she would have seen how the Professor and his friends were willing to leave their allotted space and march to the centre of the stage. But all Sparrow wanted was time to sit in his room and write, he wanted to set down this music that came, unstoppable, unending, from his thoughts.

The Old Cat picked up the remaining book, opened it almost halfway and began to read grumpily. Her voice reminded him, with a pang, of his mother. The story was familiar to Sparrow even though he had never encountered this book before.

She read, "Grandfather smiled sympathetically, but did not tell Cuicui what had gone on the night before. He thought to himself: 'If only you could dream on forever. Some people become the prime minister in their dreams.'"

The glasses were emptied and the books packed away. So as not to attract attention, they left at intervals: the Old Cat and Ling, followed by San Li, Sparrow and finally the Professor. Kai, who was leaning against the wall by the door, touched Sparrow's arm lightly as he passed through. In the hallway, Sparrow stood listening, but instead of the Professor or Kai, all he heard was the belligerent clamouring of the radio, of all the radios in the building. The entire city, he realized, would soon be deaf, and that would be the end of his musical career.

He wished that a week had already passed, and that he was, at this very moment, returning up the concrete stairs to Kai's room. If only he were just now lifting his hand to knock, waiting to be allowed inside. Instead of leaving he might, at this moment, be arriving.

Early the next morning, when Zhuli entered Room 103, *Tzigane* became the only Shanghai. Hours later, she emerged humbled and electrified. The sky was blue-grey as if it had swallowed all the Mao coats in the city. She heard Ravel (*Tzigane*), Prokofiev (Sonata for Solo Violin No. 4) and Bach (Partita for Solo Violin No. 2), each on a separate channel as if she were standing between three concert halls. On Julu Road, cyclists seemed to branch out from the music itself; they disappeared in the fog of July sunshine. She walked east on Changde Road and west again. A line of tricycle carts, weighed down by oil drums, creaked north and commuters parted around them like shoals of fish, their trousers fluttering. Time slowed.

A woman shouted at her to get out of the way and a flatbed truck, crusted in mud, nearly knocked her down as it rushed by. "Are you deaf?" a little boy shouted. He was holding a stick for no reason. He ran away with his weapon. "Capitalist Miss!" a woman spat at her, but when Zhuli turned to look back, the woman was gone. On and on she walked until she found herself back at the Conservatory once more. The courtyard and the building were deserted, as if it were Spring Festival and all the musicians had gone home for the holidays.

Her footsteps echoed nervously in the empty hallways. She went up to Sparrow's office, but when she knocked, no one answered.

On the third floor, her class, the orchestral class, appeared to be cancelled. Out of some fifty students, only six were present. Nobody looked up when she came in. The Professor, known as Go Slow, was missing. Eventually the other five students wandered off. The now empty room seemed to close in around her. An aimless inspection of her schoolbag revealed a copy of Beethoven's "Emperor" Concerto, which she had borrowed from the library days ago and had been carrying in her schoolbag without realizing. Zhuli opened it across six desks. The copy was dirty, smudged by pencil marks and eraser dust. Beethoven, she knew, had never intended for this concerto to have so feudal a name as "Emperor." The name had attached itself long after his death. She followed the solo piano through its ascents and tumbling falls, and into the second movement, a B major dream and sorrow extending like a paper accordion.

If there was indeed an emperor in this concerto, she concluded, he was not a king at all, but a man with ambitions of greatness, an emperor in his own mind, a child who once imagined a different life but had come to see the disconnection between what he aspired to be and what he was capable of being. In 1811, when Beethoven was almost fully deaf, he performed this piano concerto, but the music that the composer heard in his mind failed to move his listeners. The performance was a disaster and, until his death, Beethoven rarely performed again. But what had mattered most in that moment, Zhuli wondered: the concerto in his mind or the concerto of his audience? What mattered most in this moment: the words on the posters or the lives—of her parents, of Ba Lute and Sparrow—in suspension, the promise of Mao Zedong thought or the day-to-day reality of New China? Which would win out, the Shanghai of utopia, or the city of the real?

She heard shouting. "Down! Down! Down!" they chanted. Footsteps thundered into the classrooms and stairwells. Furniture crashed above her head. Zhuli heard the strange dislocation of piano notes, she heard hammering and laughing and then, unmistakably, the smell of fire. She tucked the score in her bag, went out of the side door and into the courtyard, and hurried home.

That night, Ba Lute told her that she should cut her hair, that the long braid that slid against the small of her back was a symbol of vanity. "Cut it right to your chin," her uncle said. "Why can't you wear it like the other girls?" Zhuli felt a shiver of fear, but she agreed. "Here, I'll do it for you," he said anxiously. A rusty pair of scissors, normally used to cut chicken, already lay on the table. "No, uncle," she said. "It's too much trouble. I'll ask my mother to cut it."

"Your mother! But where is she? I've no idea where those two have gone! There hasn't been a single letter or message."

"Then I will wait."

"Today, little Zhuli. We must do it today."

He had lost weight and seemed to stand crookedly. His straw shoes made a weak, scraping noise against the floor.

"I will, uncle."

When he had retreated, she saw her mother's copy of the Book of Records on a chair beside the kindling, as if Ba Lute meant to burn it. Zhuli picked up the cardboard box and took it to her room. On the bed, she lifted the lid. She could not stop herself from withdrawing a notebook at random and opening it. Wen the Dreamer's refined yet passionate script moved her all over again. Her parents seemed to rest in her hands, as if the novel had never been a mirror of the past, but of the present. What if Da-wei and May Fourth, separated for so many years, still wandered as exiles, and this was the reason the novel could not be finished? Missing her parents, Zhuli followed her father's handwriting down the page. In the story, Da-wei lay awake in his New York dormitory as jazz and German lullabies crowded through the rooms, men argued and women laboured, a child wept in its newfound English, new to Da-wei as well, and he marvelled at everything he might one day understand. Month after month, he worked odd jobs. He repeatedly mended his cap and padded coat, thinking that soon, tomorrow, his life would be reinvented. Lonely and bored, he copied pages from *The Travels of Lao Can*, the only book he had carried from China until, on a desolate spring day, he ran out of paper. He sat staring at the iron beauty of the Hudson River, remembering a passage from a famous Lu Xun essay:

"What's the use of copying those?" a friend had asked Lu Xun.
"There's no use."
"In that case, what's your reason for copying them?"
"There's no reason."

What was the purpose, Da-wei finally asked himself, of copying a life but erasing himself?

When Zhuli woke, she was alone and in Shanghai once more. It was morning but still dark and she felt an extraordinary peace, a calm willingness to give in to the destiny of her life. Prokofiev's *Violin Sonata No. 2* rang in her head as if she had been practising in her sleep. She returned Chapter 16 to the Book of Records, and hid the cardboard box beneath her bed. In the kitchen, she saw the chicken scissors on the table and she put them in her bag. Outside, the air was wonderfully cool. She felt that everyone was awake but no one spoke; the shutters were closed, but all the neighbours watched. The scissors made her feel strong and prepared for all eventualities. She passed a wall that was covered in meticulously flowing calligraphy:

IF THE FATHER IS A HERO, SO IS THE SON! IF THE FATHER IS A COUNTER-REVOLUTIONARY, THE SON MUST BE A SON OF A BITCH! DIG OUT THE CHILDREN OF RIGHTISTS, CAPITALIST ROADERS, AND COUNTER-REVOLUTIONARIES, DIG OUT THE SNAKES OF THE OLD REGIME! LONG LIVE CHAIRMAN MAO, LONG LIVE THE DICTATORSHIP OF THE PROLETARIAT, LONG LIVE THE GREAT PROLETARIAN CULTURAL REVOLUTION!

Prokofiev continued, the third movement now, with its poetic sweep, the violin teetering on discordant notes while the orchestra carried on, oblivious. Prokofiev was a world-weary, cantankerous grandfather shuffling ahead of her, a celebrated pianist whose sonatas sang as if they had been written for the violin. After his return from a tour in 1938, his passport was confiscated. In the campaigns that followed, his music was denounced by the Politburo as formalist, bourgeois and counter-revolutionary and he never composed again. Sparrow had told her that when Prokofiev died, in 1953, there were no flowers to be had because all the city's flowers had been rounded up for Stalin's death, which had occurred a few days earlier. People had made do with paper flowers instead. Sparrow had heard it from the conductor, Li Delun, who had been studying in Moscow at the time. Because of the grandeur of Stalin's funeral, no musicians were available to play for Prokofiev, and so his family played a recording of the funeral march from *Romeo and Juliet*. The first 115 pages of the newspaper carried tributes to Stalin; on page 116, there was a small notice on the death of the great composer.

Her long braid touched the small of her back, a pressure like her mother's hand guiding her through the invisible, ever-watching crowds.

Just before dawn, Sparrow looked up to see a figure standing in the doorway of his office. He put down his pencil. Kai stepped into the light and yet, in the same moment, seemed to disappear. In just two weeks, since their return to the city, he had lost weight. There was a confusion in his eyes, and he appeared much older than his seventeen years. "Am I disturbing you, Teacher?"

"Come in."

Kai turned and looked over his shoulder. He retraced his steps, reached the door and shut it, and the click of the lock sent a chill down Sparrow's spine. He stood up and busied himself with the thermos. The teacups clinked mildly against the table and Kai sat down in Old Wu's chair. Old Wu had not shown up in the office for at least a month and his desk was covered in a film of dust.

"You didn't come to class yesterday," Sparrow said.

"Did anybody come?"

He lifted the cups and turned back to Kai. "Two students."

"Let me guess," Kai said, smiling in an off-putting way. "Was it—"

"No, don't. It isn't important. Tell me how you are. I haven't seen you since . . . well, since a few nights ago."

"I'm fine," Kai said. "Don't I look it?" He smiled again but this time it was warmer, meant for Sparrow. "Teacher," he said. Then, beginning again, "Comrade, you must be the only one in the building. Do you never rest?"

"Isn't Zhuli here?"

"What time is it?" he said distractedly, standing up and coming to where Sparrow was. "Around four, I imagine."

"The best time for composing. It's like another world."

Kai took the tea and peered out the window.

When Sparrow followed his gaze, he saw only the darkness. I'm a teacher, the eldest son of a revolutionary hero, Sparrow told himself, and there's no reason for me to be afraid. "Is something worrying you?" he asked.

"No," Kai said. And then, more credibly, "No, I don't think so. It's quiet tonight." He shifted and Sparrow noticed the armband on the pianist's sleeve.

"Have you joined the Red Guards then," he said touching the red cloth.

"Joined?" Kai said, his hand resting overtop of Sparrow's. His voice was lightness itself. "People like me don't join anymore. We are Red Guards, that's all."

We, Kai meant, as in those with revolutionary class backgrounds. Uneasy with the subject, he searched for another but could think only of Kai's adoptive father and his dream of a great musical community. "How is Professor Fen?" he said, pulling his hand back.

"The same," Kai said. "Superior and forgiving as always, even though his students at Jiaotong have begun denouncing him. He's convinced this campaign is a little jolt, nothing more. A few denunciations and it will all blow over. He applauds their revolutionary fervour." Kai sipped his tea and set the cup down noiselessly. "Maybe he's right. He usually is."

"This new campaign is just beginning," Sparrow said.

"The Professor thinks it's still 1919 and the era of New Culture," Kai said bitterly, as if he had not heard him. "He really thinks that he can have these open discussions just as they did back then, that everything and anything is up for debate. His position has made him naive! The worst is that he's dragging San Li and Ling down with him. They're devoted followers. They mistakenly believe he has the ear of the Party. If something happens to Ling, I'll never forgive him."

The only light in the room was a candle flickering unevenly. There must be a draft, Sparrow thought, looking up into the darkened corners.

"I nearly had an exit visa," Kai said, "but yesterday . . . everything fell apart. The Professor arranged for me to study in Leipzig, he had arranged it through a contact in the Premier's office. But it's all gone. I didn't tell you because . . . it's not that I don't want to stay and serve the Revolution . . . I was waiting until I had the exit visa in my pocket. It was only a matter of days. The visa was already approved, the last steps were formalities. But now . . . this morning, the cadre who signed my papers was denounced. They say he's going to be expelled from the Party . . . Teacher, what if suspicion filters down to the Professor and to me? The Professor tells me not to worry. He says his brothers and his wife died at the hands of the Kuomintang and the Japanese, they died as revolutionary heroes and therefore he is untouchable. It is his right, his right, he says, to criticize the Party and its policies because of his family's status. He sees nothing, hears nothing! My whole life was about to be transformed but now . . . if I can't get out, what will happen to me?"

The pianist caught himself. He put his hands around his elbows and stood very still. "I have to leave," he said, more calmly now. "I want the same overseas ticket that Fou Ts'ong got by sheer will and talent. It is the only thing I have ever wanted."

How much like Zhuli the young pianist was, Sparrow thought

numbly. How strange he had never noticed it before. They believed they could attain what the Party had put beyond their reach, that they could strive and strive and go unpunished for their longings. From where had this blind ambition come?

"You must take precautions," Sparrow said. His own words surprised him. Had it always come so naturally, he wondered, to speak words that didn't suit him?

"Yes," Kai nodded, relieved. "I must."

"Perhaps," Sparrow continued, "you should go down to your home village for a few days. In any case, classes have been suspended. Didn't you say there was a piano there? You could continue to practise. There's your concert, after all, in just a few months."

"Yes," Kai said again. And then, absent-mindedly, "I'll play Beethoven, of course. Concerto No. 1 or, well, I don't know, No. 5. I've always preferred the later works. But do you think No. 5 is too full of sentiment? The second movement worries me." He hummed a few bars and stopped, contemplating. Kai had cut his hair, it was close-cropped now, accentuating the graceful line of his neck. Sparrow glanced out the window again, fearful that someone was watching them. There was nothing.

"I've interrupted you," Kai said, shifting closer. His eyes seemed perilously bright. "I've come with all my problems as usual and here you are, always working. You're the only one I know whose attachment to music is completely pure. You're the one who deserves to go abroad."

"No," Sparrow said. He didn't know how to answer. "It's no interruption. Actually, I was thinking of you." His Symphony No. 3 lay on his desk, the first three movements taped roughly together, beside a copy of Chapter 17 of the Book of Records. His pencil had rolled off the table and now lay on the floor. Sparrow picked it up and placed it carefully across the pages.

"Teacher Sparrow, we rely on each other, don't we? Even though we don't judge things the same way, we understand one another. I don't know when I began to trust you. I know we're the same."

Sparrow had stepped to the side, opening a distance between them. He kept turning away, out of shyness and confusion.

"I know I must sound selfish to you," Kai said. "I'm honestly worried about the Professor. So many people have come and gone from his study groups and everyone knows his views, he takes no pains to hide them, he says things that could be misunderstood and he's blind to the consequences . . ."

On the desk, the pencil was rolling from side to side as if in the gutter of the sidewalk. Sparrow put his hand down to still it. "I'd like to hear those pieces you mentioned," he said. "It's been so long since I properly listened to them." He went to Old Wu's record player and picked out Beethoven's Piano Concerto No. 5.

He knelt down, lifted the plastic lid, and shifted the record from its cover. The disc, a recording made by Glenn Gould, conducted by Leopold Stokowski, was in near perfect condition. He had not listened to it in some time.

Kai had picked up Chapter 17 and was reading the first page.

Sparrow set the needle down as carefully if he were setting it in the palm of a child's hand. At a very early age, Sparrow thought, his mind rambling, he had known that he would not be a performer, he did not have the genius of interpretation, even if he played well enough. Sparrow's gifts were of a different temperament. There was music inside him, it was as simple, inexplicable and exhilarating as that. Music overflowed from everything he saw. If it ended, he would have no idea how to make sense of the world. The record began to spin and the first sound was the sound of air. This was a room in America, he thought, perhaps a studio or a concert hall. Perhaps, he thought, technology was what had made Zhuli and Kai both naive and ambitious, they had grown up kneeling before record players and radios, they had been lulled into believing there were no barriers between themselves and the sound itself. The ubiquity of recording had made them all equal: they heard the same recording that Gould himself listened to when he placed the record on a turntable, they heard what an American or a

Frenchman or a German heard. Geography, ethnicity or nationality were not the determining factors; the degree of your listening was what set your experience apart, your intimacy with music was all that mattered, your attentiveness and your desire. But was it true? What if true understanding was something innate, something they could never attain? The music began, the first heroic chords.

There were days in my life, he thought, that I passed over as though they were nothing and there are moments, seconds, when everything comes into focus.

Kai was sitting beside him now, still holding the notebook. Sparrow distracted himself by thinking about Bach. Between the thousands of pieces the composer left behind, had Bach ever known silence? Surely never. How was it possible for Bach to feel so much and not to shy away from it? But in my life, Sparrow thought, I think there is a quiet coming now. He felt so certain of it that a sharp pain spread across his chest. A deep silence was about to arrive. How could he live with it?

"Chairman Mao is right," Kai was saying. "Somewhere along the way, the ideas of the older generation became corrupted. People like the Professor started off wanting to build a just society but then they got comfortable. They became decadent and felt they'd given up enough, and the rules applied to everyone but them. So what are we supposed to do? Everything they've taught me contradicts itself. Maybe they told more lies than truth."

"What the Party wants is always changing," Sparrow said quietly.

"I don't agree. Either we accept the old world where we as a nation are weak and humiliated or we try again and make a better country. I know how unjust it was. Sometimes I think I have no right to be here. I ask myself why I alone among my family was saved... What about my sisters, my parents? Weren't they equal citizens? ... When justice shifts, nobody can be left as they were. Isn't that so? Hasn't Chairman Mao always seen much further than we are able to?"

They were sitting as near to one another as possible without touching. The music filled the space between them, its motifs turning over as if the composer had no conclusion, only movements that came around in a spiral, rising each time to a new beginning but an old place.

"Is this a novel?" Kai said, returning Chapter 17 to him.

"It's a story that's been in my family for many years." The notebook was so worn, and the weight utterly familiar in Sparrow's hand.

"Do you think I could read it one day?"

Sparrow nodded.

Kai continued as if speaking to himself. "Not now but one day. That's what I hope for. I wasn't trying to flatter you, Sparrow. A talent like yours comes along only once in a generation. You must finish your Symphony No. 3, no matter what happens."

At some point they fell asleep on the floor. He woke to the heaviness of Kai's arm over him. It was hot, and sometime in the night, Kai had taken off his shirt and now lay, half undressed, beside him. How thin he had grown. Kai held him tightly, his mouth against Sparrow's neck, his breathing calm and undisturbed, but he was not asleep. Sparrow lay on his back and let his hand drift down to cover Kai's. The pianist caressed him, tentatively at first and then with greater confidence. Sparrow's hand followed Kai's hand and an unbearable heat settled deep into his body. They lay together, frightened, half wishing sleep would come and take them, and release them from this aching, intolerable yearning. They drifted and woke and held one another, and in the fitfulness of Kai's touch, he felt as loved as he had ever felt. The first wash of dawn arrived without his noticing.

That evening, the study group met in the Old Cat's apartment, located in a twisting lane on the northwest side of the city. Sparrow had been pleased when, in the afternoon, Kai came to the laneway house to remind him of the meeting. He had been surprised when Kai invited Zhuli as well, though not as surprised as his cousin. Zhuli, blushing, had agreed.

They were the last to arrive. Just as before, the group assessed his clothing ("Did you trip and fall into the Huangpu River?") and manner ("Nervous. As if he has thorns in his shoes.") To Zhuli, on the other hand, they were welcoming, even familial. "Welcome, welcome!" the Old Cat shouted. "No need to be so formal. Just call me Old Cat, everyone does." Kai greeted them both, but his eyes stayed fixed on Zhuli, who seemed oblivious of him. He had removed the armband of the Red Guards.

"I used to own the Perilous Heights bookshop on Suzhou Creek Road," the Old Cat said, splashing tea into a bowl and slapping it down in front of Zhuli. "But during the Anti-Rightist Campaign, the government was banning titles left and right. There was so much overthrowing go on, I couldn't take it. Hell, I'm fifty years old. A relic! Overthrow me too hard and I won't get up. So in 1955 I closed the shop and moved everything here."

"But to keep so many books . . ." Zhuli said. "Aren't you worried about busybodies?"

"What can I do? The pages are absorbent. I need them to soundproof my walls."

A tray of cigarettes was passed around. As smoke floated through the air, conversation stilled. They began to concentrate.

The Professor read aloud from the most battered book Sparrow had ever seen. The book turned out to be a play, Part 1 of Guo Moruo's translation of *Faust*. Time dissolved. Sparrow, who knew only Gounod's opera, at first felt in familiar territory, but then he realized he had never met this Faust at all. The German Faust chafes against his condition. This Faust was seeking a freedom within the mind that would expand his spirit as well as his intellect, so that both could attain their most divine state. But what if the truths of the mind and the soul were not merely different, but incompatible? "In me there are two souls, alas, and their / Division tears my life in two."

Zhuli leaned towards the Professor's voice as if towards the sound of a flute.

When the reading ended, Ling stretched her lovely arms up into the air and said, "I prefer *The Sorrows of Young Werther*."

"That's because you're a hopeless romantic," said the Old Cat.

"Or because Young Werther is like a German San Li," said San Li.

"In that case, I take it back." Ling glared at him and then at Kai who grinned at Sparrow who blushed and looked at the teapot. Out of the corner of his eye, Sparrow saw Zhuli bow her head and smile widely into a tower of books.

The Old Cat tapped a manuscript that lay beside the Professor's sandalled foot. "When this translation first came out, even Chairman Mao praised it. But the Party has turned on Guo . . ."

"I wonder if Zhuli is right," Kai said, addressing the Old Cat. "Maybe it's time to get rid of these books. They're saying it's the Anti-Rightist Campaign all over again—"

"What do you know about '55? You were just a doorstep then."

"As of this month," Ling said, "Khrushchev is a 'phoney Communist,' the Soviets are 'revisionist Big Brothers,' and all the Russian composers are out. Are you getting rid of all your Fifth Symphonies and your This-and-that-ovskys? "

Kai blushed. "I never keep music. I memorize the scores and get rid of them."

"Shit," San Li said, "I can't even remember how to get home."

Sparrow laughed and tumbled a stack of books onto Zhuli's lap. He tried to catch the avalanche and caused another.

The Old Cat peered into the ruins. "Look at that!" she said. "A-Fan's *Weeping over His Daughter by the Sea*! I've been looking for those poems for thirty years." Zhuli plucked it from the pile and handed it to her.

"And what about you," Ling said, eyeing Sparrow. "Don't tell me you memorize everything, too."

"I don't . . . I prefer, well, I transcribe the incorrect work into jianpu." He had done this for the disgraced works of Debussy,

Schönberg and Bartok. Manuscripts written in jianpu notation, with its easy-to-read numbers, were considered backwards and rudimentary. They aroused no suspicion.

Zhuli interrupted. "But afterwards, he really does destroy them. He burns them and leaves the ashes in a little bucket."

"This is a skill we perfect from an early age," the Professor said lightly. "How to grind ideas into a fine cloud of dust."

San Li interrupted. "For months this study group has been reading Schiller, Goethe and Shen Congwen. I'm not complaining. Really, Professor, I'm grateful because the other entertainment on offer stinks. But maybe it's time to start reading what's right in front of us."

The Old Cat coughed. "Surely not!"

"There's a new campaign," he continued. "Or are we so taken with all the Germans who died a hundred years ago that no one notices?" He held up a copy of *Beijing Review*. "For instance, why don't we study this slop bucket written by the philosophy students at Beijing University?"

"San Li," the Professor interrupted, "enough."

Sparrow saw Zhuli gripping her violin case. She looked as if she wished to leave but was prevented from doing so by the books that had fallen into her lap.

"No, let's analyze this," San Li persisted. He read:

All revolutionary intellectuals, now is the time to go into battle! Resolutely, thoroughly, totally and completely wipe out all the ghosts and monsters. The leaders of Beijing University shout about "strengthening the leadership" but this only exposes who they really are: saboteurs of the Cultural Revolution. We must tell you, a spider cannot stop the wheel of a cart! We will carry socialist revolution through to the end!

"I would fail this kid. *Resolutely, thoroughly, totally*? Is she writing a thesaurus? But instead of this student being sent to remedial composition, the President of the University gets beaten up. I mean, he's an old guy and these kids really wipe the floor with him. Now the whole university is under the boot of the Red Guards, and this manifesto is the Voice of the Revolution."

"No need to read it aloud," the Old Cat said. "We can hear it anytime we wish on the loudspeakers."

"And now the Conservatory students are going around smashing violins." San Li laughed. "What kind of person breaks a *violin*?"

"The young aren't wrong," Kai said. There was an aggressive and unfamiliar despair in his eyes. "They say we need to change, remove obstacles and purge ourselves. Land reform brought equality but ten years later, it's already slipping away. It's obvious things aren't well in society."

"Purge ourselves of what?" the Professor asked.

"Individualism, privilege. The greed that is corrupting our Revolution."

"The Politburo leaders haven't managed to become socialists," San Li said. "Why should we?"

There was a murmur of nervous laughter which seemed, to Sparrow, to rise from the books themselves.

Kai blushed and stood up. "Comrade," he said to the Old Cat, "thank you for your hospitality. I can no longer listen to this conversation. Please excuse me."

The Old Cat and Ling had been talking to one another, and now paused, confused. The Professor stared, amazed. "Kai, my boy! Sit down, sit down. What's got into you? San Li, didn't I tell you to hold your tongue?"

"I say what's on my mind."

Kai's voice was calm. "You've never fought for anything, San Li. You have no idea what life is like outside Shanghai, and yet you dare to lecture us."

"In the Conservatory, you know better?"

Ling interrupted. "Be quiet, San Li. Kai, Sit down. There's no need to take all this to heart. After all, we only come together to think differently, don't we? You're a brother to me, I know you're upset but come–"

But Kai had already turned on the Professor. "You've already ruined me, and now you're endangering everyone in this room. For you, political struggle is just a game. It's taken me years to see you clearly."

The room was silent.

The Professor finally spoke. "Since when did the desire to know oneself, to better oneself, become a traitorous act in this country? Should this not frighten you, Kai? My son, you forget that I, too, lost my entire family in the Revolution."

Kai flushed. He swung his bag over shoulder and walked out of the room.

"Sparrow," the Professor said. "Go with him. He's very disappointed. He doesn't mean what he says. . . ."

Sparrow didn't move.

"I'll take Zhuli home," Ling said. "You live near Beijing Road, don't you? So do I."

How calm Zhuli appeared, Sparrow thought, as if it were she who had brought him here. Had she? What had they done?

"Can't you hurry up?" Ling said. There was a tremor of fear in her voice.

Sparrow got up, wished everyone well and left.

The Professor and San Li exited together, mumbling apologies, and so it was only Zhuli, the Old Cat and Ling who remained. Nobody mentioned Kai or what had happened; it was as if the argument had dissolved, having never been. So the educated class is not so different after all, Zhuli thought. In these times, we all rely on silence.

Ling told Zhuli that she was a student at Jiaotong University. "In fact," she said, "I study utilitarianism, Mencius and the art of couplets, so I qualify as one of San Li's 'slop bucket' philosophy students."

The Old Cat was reorganizing the books around her. "Maybe you need a copy of this," she said, tossing a thin book to Zhuli. "Fou Lei's translation of *Jean-Christophe*. You know it of course?"

"I'm embarrassed to say that I haven't read it yet."

"Ha, why apologize?" The Old Cat lifted her soft shoulders and then, from this great height, let them fall like a landslide. "I only suggest it because they say Rolland modelled his Jean-Christophe on Beethoven. A Beethoven for the times we live in. However, not every page is exciting. There you go. And this, Hu Shih's essay on Wu Dao-zi. A book outlawed, reviled by the government and, consequently, very popular." When the Old Cat sat beside her, Zhuli could smell crumbling paper, ink stone and a whiff of sugarcane.

"Miss Zhuli," Ling said, "do you carry your violin with you everywhere you go?"

The case in her lap was as cool as stone on an autumn night. Zhuli nodded.

"A bit strange, don't you think?" Ling said.

The Old Cat sniffed. "As strange as you carrying paper and pen in your pocket! You're a student after all, and she's a violinist."

"Then San Li might as well carry a sabre. It seems he majors in provocation."

"If you told him to stop carrying on, he might listen," the Old Cat said.

"Please! San Li would never perform for an audience of one."

Zhuli wanted to ask them about Kai. Instead she opened the Hu Shih essay and began to read the first lines. She flipped forward, read further. The text had been copied out by hand, in a square yet beautifully bold script. She turned more pages. This was the same hand that had copied the Book of Records. This was her own father's handwriting and she would know it anywhere.

The Old Cat peered at her. "Quite a clever essay, isn't it?" she said.

Was it Zhuli's imagination, or was there a question folded attentively inside this question? "I'm sure it must be, but I find myself interested in the calligrapher." To throw the Old Cat off the scent, she said, "Did you make this copy yourself?"

"Ai!" The Old Cat slapped her round knees with her round hands. "I've an enviable gift but not so divine as that. No, the calligrapher is a scholar from Shanghai, a poet in fact. But alas, he is not a poet anymore. He fell under the wheels of the Party and they sent him for re-education. I haven't seen him for years, he disappeared. For a musician, you have a good eye for calligraphy."

"It's because my own handwriting is so poor," Zhuli said. When my mother comes home, she thought, the first thing I'll do is bring her here. That is the proper way to do things.

"On that note, I have something for you to decipher." The Old Cat creaked herself upright, swayed past Ling and stopped at a desk. Zhuli had not even realized the desk was there, so camouflaged was it by papers. The Old Cat shuffled through a stack of folders before plucking out a single sheet. She handed it to Zhuli.

"Well, grandmother!" Zhuli said, after a moment. In her hand was the aria of the *Goldberg Variations*, transcribed into the numbers, dots and lines of jianpu notation. "You've gone and dropped a bag of books on me! I had no idea you studied Western classical music."

"I don't. Someone left this at my door, when, a month ago?" She looked to Ling, who nodded in confirmation. "Sure I can read jianpu but I have no clue what this music is."

Zhuli told her it was Bach.

"Oh, him." The Old Cat sounded disappointed. "I was hoping it might be that handsome firecracker, Old Bei. My niece and I have been inserting this piece of music into traditional song books." Ling smiled mischievously. Aunt and niece, Zhuli thought, so this is why I felt so comfortable with them. "We throw it in at random just to cause a little frisson. I added the words of Chairman Mao as a libretto: 'On a blank sheet of paper free from any mark, the freshest and most beautiful pictures can be painted.'"

"But who is the mysterious sender?" Zhuli asked.

"Who knows? There was a note which said that even banned music should be assessed on its own merits, that songs as well as novels could serve as samizdat, passed from person to person. Some foolish idealist. One of your kind, I'm sure."

"Someone from the Conservatory?" Zhuli said.

"At first we thought it was the Professor or Kai," Ling said. "But they both swore it wasn't them. In fact, Kai told us turn it in to the authorities. I swear, the boy is afraid of his own feet."

"But isn't Kai right to be cautious?" Zhuli asked. She thought Ling and her aunt were perversely unaware, as if they had never attended a political study session or encountered a blackboard newspaper.

"Ha, I know what you're thinking," the Old Cat said. "But, child, when you've seen as much as I have, you realize the die is cast. The so-called 'enemies of the People' are the ones whose luck has run out, nothing more. One day the traitor is Shen Congwen, the next Guo Moruo. If they want to come for you, they will come, and it doesn't matter what you read or what you failed to read. The books on your shelves, the music you cherish, the past lives you've lived, all these details are just an excuse. In the old days, spite and jealousy drove the eunuchs in all their power struggles. Perhaps we live in a new age, but people don't change overnight."

"But why give the authorities an excuse?" Zhuli asked. "If the neighbourhood can turn in one family of counter-revolutionaries, the whole block might be saved. People are just trying to get by." A voice in her head scolded her: *Why do you persist in playing music that is outrageously formalist? Why did you react disdainfully when Kai brought you the correct music? Are you too idiotic to realize that the very existence of a violin soloist is counter to the times?*

"Because, Zhuli," the Old Cat said, "these books were bequeathed to me by my beloved father. At some point, a person must decide whether they belong to the people who loved them, or whether they belong to the emperors. The truth is, my ancestry is long and my past is complex because this country is old. Ah, our

country is old! How can the Party convince me otherwise? I know
who I am and I know what old means. If the Party knows it too,
well, good for them. I must meet the destiny that was written out
by my lineage. If they want to hurry me into the next life, okay.
I'm old, I'll go. I would only miss my little Ling.

"The things you experience," she continued, "are written on
your cells as memories and patterns, which are reprinted again
on the next generation. And even if you never lift a shovel or
plant a cabbage, every day of your life something is written upon
you. And when you die, the entirety of that written record
returns to the earth. All we have on this earth, all we are, is a
record. Maybe the only things that persist are not the evildoers
and demons (though, admittedly, they do have a certain longevity) but copies of things. The original has long since passed away
from this universe, but on and on we copy. I have devoted my
minuscule life to the act of copying."

"Don't listen to her," Ling said. "When the authorities come,
she's soft as porridge. She knows how to ply them with old-woman
words."

The Old Cat grunted. "Sure. That, too."

"Still," Zhuli said, "in these times, we should take precautions."

"Ah, child. Sometimes an old woman simply gets set in her
ways. She's like a pain you can't dislodge."

Ling, San Li, Kai, the Old Cat, they must all come from exemplary class backgrounds, Zhuli realized. They had never been targeted and so, deep in their bones, did not believe they could be.
They were free because, in their minds, they persisted in believing they were. Maybe they were right but Zhuli felt as if she were
watching an oil drum that was about to explode.

She began to shift the books off her lap so that she could get
to her feet.

Still seated, Ling reached out to gather the empty cups. The
Old Cat was humming to herself, and the resemblance between
the Old Cat and Ling made Zhuli feel as if she were standing

between two arias. Maybe these volumes of books acted as a kind of sponge, shielding the Old Cat from the muck of the city outside her door.

The violin case knocked against Zhuli's knee. She was glad they had not asked her to play for them. Each time she lifted her bow to perform, she felt as if parts of herself were being peeled away.

"It was fate that you found us," the Old Cat said. "Or, to put it another way, fate that I found you again."

"What do you mean?" Zhuli asked. She was holding her father's book in her hands.

"Oh," the Old Cat said. The smile on her lips tried to hide a lasting pain. "Ignore my rambling. My thoughts wander from time to time. I get lost in the things that were."

Sparrow pedalled his bicycle behind Kai. There was no moon, only haphazard lighting, a low wattage bulb in a window, the glow from the oil lamp in an outdoor kitchen. At last the pianist coasted to a stop. "Forgive me, Sparrow," he said, turning. He was shivering as if he were ill. "I had to do it, I have to draw a clear line. Please, let me go. I have to . . . There's no choice. Can you understand? I have to do it for my parents, my sisters. I am the only one left. I'm sorry, I'm truly sorry . . ." They were sheltered by a willow so heavy with leaves its branches swept the ground. Kai looked at him with a beseeching air. "Let me go. There's nothing else to do. We must trust the Party in everything. Everything." He turned and began pedalling away. After a moment, Sparrow, too, began pedalling again, but slower now. Other travellers drifted between them and up ahead, Kai merged into the darkness and slowly disappeared. Sparrow rode for what seemed a long time, but the boulevard continued, endless. The wind picked up and he heard a hollow banging on the air. Everyone began pedalling faster, hoping to get home before the downpour, but it was already too late. Lightning broke the sky apart. Rain smacked the concrete so hard it ricocheted up, hard as pellets. He was instantly drenched. In a single moment, the rain had swept everyone off the road, towards shelter, and only a single car pushed on, oblivious. Sparrow turned into a laneway and dismounted. All he could think about was his desire to be with Kai, to pass another night with him, the desire was sharp and undeniable. *I care for him, yes, and what difference does it make, how and to what degree? To whom does it matter?* He stood gripping the handlebars, bewildered by his own self-delusion. To love as he did was, if not a counter-revolutionary crime, foolhardy and dangerous. Such love could only lead to ruin. Behind him voices called out, but the words were only gusts of air. A child reached out and firmly pulled him sideways, under the shelter of a tree. All Sparrow saw was the sudden disappearance of a city full of people.

At last, the rain ebbed. The road was silver with water. People came into the road anyway, their legs disappearing, sometimes up to their knees.

He climbed back onto his bicycle. Almost immediately he sank down as the front tire gave out. He must have hit a nail or a shard of glass. Sparrow was aware, suddenly, of the cold weight of his wet clothes and the water that dripped down from his hair, down his neck and back. He began pushing the bicycle beside him. Already the clean rainwater smelled of mud, he saw a dead chicken floating towards him beside a head of cabbage. An eddy came, sucked the chicken down and pushed it back up again. A little girl came running towards it, her long hair pasted alarmingly to her face.

As he walked, the water slowly drained away. Sparrow saw the cuffs of his trousers, then his ankles and his shoes. He had the numbing fear that the Shanghai that existed only moments ago was gone, it had been washed away and replaced.

Sparrow kept pushing his bicycle. Up ahead, at the intersection, people had gathered around a haze of lights. Sparrow barely noticed them, the air was humid once more. A musical idea had appeared in his thoughts, a wedge of notes. He must hurry home to write the phrases down. Chords opened, they made a bright uneasiness in his ears. He was suddenly engulfed by the crowd at the intersection and tried, stubbornly, to hear only the unfolding music. People became a series of figurations: girls wearing red scarves, a taunting voice, dissonant bursts of light. The very loudness of the crowd seemed to make it silent. Was it rage, he slowly realized, that was spilling back and forth, from one cluster of people to another? There was a fire, Sparrow now realized, his vision sharpening. He tried to pass through the mass but his bicycle made it impossible.

In the centre, an old man was standing on a chair. The crowd swayed around him, pressing closer. Sparrow saw a young woman, Zhuli's age, holding a broom by its handle, waving it before the old man. Sparrow thought the man on the chair would take the handle and begin a speech to the crowd, but then he realized the old man, soaked from the rain, was shaking with cold, he was weeping and trying to avert his eyes from the young woman and her taunting gestures. "Down with Wu Bei!" The ferocity of the chanting finally broke through Sparrow's thoughts. The old man was begging for mercy but none of his words were audible. For a fleeting moment, Sparrow thought he should step forward and push these children back, some of them were no more than nine or ten years old, but there were many bystanders, people of all ages, pressing in with a growing euphoria. He tried to go backwards but it was impossible, the crowd was surging forward once more. Scattered words were flung up, *reactionary, counter-revolutionary, traitor, demon*, until the chant started up again, "Down with Wu Bei!" The girl with the broom handle was accusing him of teaching literary works that mocked the reality of every man and woman standing before him. "You thought you could trample those beneath you," she said. She had a disconcertingly melodic voice. "You thought your high standing should make us small, but we are the ones with open hearts and clear minds. The monster is waking, Teacher! You have stepped on its head countless times but now the monster is crawling out of the mud. It is ugly and unmannered, free from your disdain and supe-riority. Yes, the monster is the seed of truth that you tried to lock away. We are free, even though you tried to warp our minds! Even though you corrupted our desires." She began to beat him, slow hits with the length of the broom, against his back, his thighs and chest, as if he were an animal she was punishing. The old man tottered and fell. He was picked up and forced roughly back on the chair, even though he could barely stand. "Fall down and we will only slap you harder," the young woman said sweetly. "What a small punishment this is for your crimes, but don't fear! Every weakness will be attended to. This is only the beginning."

Someone came and pulled up another chair, and a boy pushed a long, white, pointed, paper hat onto the old man's head. The crowd erupted in derisive laughter, pointing and shouting. The old man had turned so pale, it looked as if he would pass out. Scrawled on the dunce cap were the words, "I am an enemy of the People, a spreader of lies! I am a demon!"

Arms were lifted, the feverish chanting began again, drowning out the young woman who was still speaking. Sparrow could not move. Each chant seemed to hit the man's body like a physical blow. Another person came and affixed a long sheet of paper to the man's chest. The words read, "I teach shit, I eat shit, I am shit." Howls of laughter rang out, and the young man who had affixed the poster was overcome by hilarity. "Wu Bei," he cried, "we can smell your shit across Shanghai! You silly boy! Why don't you clean yourself up?" The old man, who once had stood before a lectern and tried to unravel the codes of literature, just as he, Sparrow, tried to understand the shape of music, wept in fear and humiliation. He would suffer less, Sparrow thought, if they tied him up and beat him unconscious. But the crowd only continued to taunt him.

"I am an enemy of the People," he was saying now.

They forced him to repeat line after line.

"I have corrupted the thoughts of the students entrusted to me."

"I have fed foreign shit into their bright and beautiful minds."

"I am a traitor to my country."

"I deserve death."

And then his own whimpering, "Have mercy, have mercy."

A gap opened up beside Sparrow and he slipped through it, the knot of the crowd quickly closing behind him. Gap by gap, he pushed his way forward. "In a hurry?" someone asked him. He was shoved but did not shove back. "What's your name and work unit?" the same voice asked. "I'm only trying to get closer," Sparrow said, terrified. The person laughed, disbelieving. "Look at the monster, the monster!" someone else said. "Soon we shall be at every window, inside every home!" The fire had grown and the laughter grew louder and louder. The man's personal papers were being displayed like trophies of war. Someone was reading the titles of books and each one was greeted with guffaws and insults. Words were hurled at him, *bourgeois, capitalist, imperialist, wolf,* and the young woman continued her rhythmic alternation between hitting him viciously and berating him. When it seemed as if she might tire, a young man took her place, and the chants escalated again. "There are no kings," the young man said, "no aristocrats, no landowners, no *teachers*, no natural ruling class. There are only locusts like you, thieves and pestilence!" "Set him on fire," the crowd begged. "Feed poison to the snake!" They threw ever more books and papers onto the fire, and even furniture and clothing. A child's silk dress was found and paraded through the crowd. The young woman came back with a large bottle of ink. She climbed up onto the chair beside the old man, pulled off the paper hat, and emptied the bottle onto his hair. The man tried to pull away but the ink poured into his eyes, ran down his nose and mouth and slid in hideous shapes down his body. As the old man tried desperately to wipe the thick liquid from his eyes and mouth, the crowd screamed in hysterical laughter. "Write something!" they shouted. "Wu Bei, enlighten us with your sophisticated thoughts! Compose a profound essay!" "Please, we beg you! Tell us what to think!" The young woman said, "Wu Bei, you've made a mess again!" "Stupid, dirty child," the young man said, raising the stick menacingly. The old man cowered and wept. "Don't move, don't move!" the young woman said. "You're ruining my elegant calligraphy!"

Sparrow moved backwards, step by tiny step, the metal frame of the front wheel scratching against the ground. Wu Bei's humiliation was a game that kept intensifying. Each person wanted to think up the next salvo. The crowd was giddy, even the moon above and the ragged summer trees seemed to shudder with elation. Wu Bei was completely alone, balanced clownishly on his wooden chair. Another young man had stepped forward with a razor in his hand and was proposing that he shave the old man's head. "He thinks his white hair makes him respectable," the young man said. "Shall we clip the butterfly's wings?" "Melt the autumn frost," another voice shouted. "Rip off his wings! Cut off his hair!" A wave of nausea overcame Sparrow. There was no more oxygen to breathe. "Why stop at his hair?" the man with the dull razor said. "Why should we allow His Excellency to belittle us?"

Sparrow forced himself to turn casually away from the crowd, bending forward as if to check the bicycle's tire. He glanced towards the edge of the road where a dozen plane trees stood aligned. There, under the nearest one, he saw Zhuli, standing by herself, lost in thought. She stood out because she was the only motionless person in this crowd. Zhuli held her violin tightly in her arms and was listening to the chanting as if to an excessively complicated piece of music. They had taken the razor to Wu Bei. "Can't you even find a decent barber, Wu Bei?" "You're ready for the dance now! Put on your three-piece suit and wait for the orchestra!" "Come and waltz with me, Wu Bei! Don't be shy . . ." Broken, the old man let out a howl of grief and the crowd erupted in jeering victory.

Sparrow walked calmly towards his cousin. Wu Bei slipped from his mind. Zhuli should not be here with her violin. He must get her home.

He walked towards her, lengthening his gait to appear confident and tall. "Cousin," he said when he reached her. She turned and looked at him with keen eyes. For a moment, he faltered and then he repeated, more sternly, "Cousin." She hardly seemed to breathe. He began walking Zhuli away, his bicycle beside them.

More people were coming to join the frenzy. They carried bottles of ink and rolls of paper, and they wore red armbands that, in the dim light, glowed against their arms.

"No," Zhuli said, turning back towards the noise. "Not this way. I'm going to the Conservatory."

"Ling was supposed to see you home," he said. He had to fight to keep his voice calm. "I never would have left you otherwise."

"She did take me home, but I came out again, after the rain. I reserved the practice room, you see," she said. "I must go. Room 103. It's the best room, you know. Because the piano is very old, nobody plays it. But I told you that once, didn't I? And I have my concert coming so soon, it's less than three months away. I don't know what's wrong with me. I can't seem to memorize the Ravel."

"Come, Zhuli," he said. "Let's go home together. I'll help you, I promise."

She was looking at him now. She sighed and followed behind him. "Where are we going, cousin?"

He did not answer.

After a moment, she said again, "But where are we going?"

"Home. Give me your violin."

She would not. They walked in the shadows.

Red Guards careening recklessly along the path barely noticed them. When one or two stared, Sparrow called out to them, "They're bringing down that traitor Wu Bei! The coward has already pissed himself." The Red Guards collapsed in laughter. They shouted, "Long live the Revolution!" and hurried on, afraid they had missed the show.

Behind them, the crowd had reached the crescendo of a poem by Chairman Mao, their voices ringing: "We wash away insects, and are strong."

Sparrow and Zhuli arrived home, in the laneway. His brothers were in bed but Ba Lute was sitting at the window, in the darkness. He started when they entered.

"Ba," Sparrow said.

"Door by door," Ba Lute said softly. "They are going to every house."

Zhuli had moved halfway into the cold room. "But, uncle, you're a Party member . . ."

Sparrow almost said, "So is Wu Bei," but when he saw his father's face he said nothing.

"If it comes to unending revolution," Ba Lute said, "even Party members and heroes must take their turn." He smiled and seemed to laugh and Sparrow felt a trickle of fear running down his spine.

"Father, why don't you go to bed? I'll stay awake."

"In bed or here or in the road, I won't be able to sleep."

"You must," Sparrow said firmly.

"And where is your mother!" Ba Lute said in despair. "Off endangering herself and all of us. Pretending she can rescue poor Wen! Who does she think she is? Does she have the ear of our Great Leader? Is she so invulnerable?"

"I'm sure she's written to us. Only the post has been so chaotic these past few weeks."

"No, no," Ba Lute said, speaking to himself. "It was not supposed to be like this. I criticized all the others at Headquarters. 'Give up your feudal allegiances,' I told them. 'Give up everything for the Party! Lenient treatment for those who confess, severe punishment for those who refuse! But a reward, yes, a reward, for those willing to surrender others.' They believed me and I believed myself. It is so much easier to believe than to disbelieve."

"Father," Sparrow said, but Ba Lute wasn't listening to him.

"After all, what good can come from disbelief? What grows, what changes, what improves? Isn't it always better for your country, your family, for yourself, to believe in something? Doubt can only lead to confusion and complications. And, in any case, our lives were better. We didn't mean to grow complacent, surely we weren't complacent, the struggle isn't finished, and yet . . ."

Ba Lute got up. His great hulk seemed absurdly small. He walked slowly from the room, shaking his head and saying, "In everything, I trust the Party. I trust Chairman Mao. But no, no. I never wanted this."

After Ba Lute had left the room, Sparrow sat with Zhuli in uneasy quiet. The curtains were closed but they could hear the vibration in the streets, waves of chanting and jubilation.

"This campaign is beginning very fiercely," Zhuli said. She said it lightly as if she were discussing a new piece of music. "Actually, someone denounced you, Sparrow. I saw it myself."

"The entire faculty was denounced. They can't shoot us all."

When she didn't answer, he joked that he would welcome the change. Time in the desert, away from his ambitious students, would be a reprieve. Finally some time to focus on his own work.

Zhuli wasn't listening. "I've hardly seen you in the last few days. Where have you been, what have you been doing?"

"Thinking."

"Have you finished the new symphony?"

"Ah," Sparrow said. "It's barely a symphony."

Zhuli smiled, but her face in the darkness looked very pale and thin. In another couple of months, she would turn fifteen but she did not look it; she appeared frail, as if her childhood sturdiness had abandoned her and left her with nothing to replace it. "If you're looking for compliments, I won't oblige. I know how much you hate them. But Sparrow, this symphony of yours, it helps me remember what music is. This symphony is the most honest thing you've ever written and it makes me afraid for you."

"Cousin, you must be exhausted. Why don't you rest?"

She smiled. "I'm not exhausted. In fact, I feel as if all my life I've been sleeping but now . . . finally, I'm coming awake."

"In what way have you been asleep?"

"I see now," she said, "that all the hours of practising, all the commitment, the ambition and the fantasizing, it's all coming to a climax." She was silent for a moment. "I'm moving too slowly.

What was it that Professor Tan taught me? About *Tzigane*. The one who plays too slowly will be swallowed by time."

"Nonsense."

"Yesterday," she continued, "when I left the Conservatory, I walked into the courtyard and, out of nowhere, I was surrounded by my classmates. They said that I must now come down to their level. They tried to grab my violin. I kept saying, 'I'm a patriot, I want to serve my country,' but they just laughed and said, 'The butterfly belongs to no country.' 'The rightist bitch needs a lesson.'" She paused, folding her hands together with an earnestness that seemed to take over her entire body. "A few others came running from inside and there was an argument. It turned into a fight but Tofu Liu and I managed to get away. If Tofu hadn't been there, I might have been in real trouble." She was laughing. "We ran away! And I thought, how strange it is that I am the one running, because they are the ones afraid of a world they can't control. Last night they went to Tofu Liu's house. You know him, don't you? So gentle he can hardly turn a page. They went through his house, beat his parents, smashed the furniture. All the musical instruments . . . his father is a rightist. Accused in 1958, the same year as my father."

"Why did you agree to go the study group?" Sparrow heard the change in his voice, as if he was accusing her, and was appalled by himself. "Why didn't you tell me?"

"Because when Kai came this morning, I saw that you were happy. I was glad to see you joyful. And Kai is our friend, isn't he? Because I *know*, of course I see things too. I think . . . there is nothing to say."

"You are not to practise in the Conservatory. I'm sure everything will return to normal but . . . you mustn't do anything to attract their attention."

"Do?" she said. "What should I do? Sparrow, do you know that Kai is a Red Guard now? I heard . . . he led the attack on Tofu Liu's parents—"

"You imagined it."

She stared at him, stunned. "How could I imagine something like that?"

"Kai was with me last night," Sparrow said.

"Was he with you all evening?"

He lied to her, he did it without thinking. "Yes."

She shook her head. "Tofu Liu *saw* him. And Kai was there at the Conservatory, when my classmates surrounded me."

"No, it's impossible."

"Well," she said. Disappointment surfaced in her eyes and then was pushed away. "If it's impossible, then I must be mistaken."

Did Sparrow believe that she would make things up? Had she ever done such a thing before? Zhuli's thoughts twisted uselessly. Yesterday afternoon, her classmates had stared at her with contempt, as if she were a traitor. The change had seemed to happen in a moment. Or maybe, she thought, the feeling had been inside them all along, but she had not understood it until she saw it in Kai's expression.

Beside her, Sparrow said nothing.

The children of class enemies are the enemies of the People! This daughter of a rightist is a dirty whore! Two months ago she knew she might have been swayed to denounce her own mother, she might have done anything to protect her place at the Conservatory. If they took music away from her, she would die. Yes, that was how perfidious the children of class enemies were! Her parents, meanwhile, the convicted traitors, had never implicated or denounced anyone. What did it mean? The People should come first, above family and self, above petty concerns like attachment and music and love. No more Prokofiev, no more Ravel, no more of the world instilled in her by Bach, no more Western music meant to be passively received. What were the words that Prokofiev had set to music? "Believe, comrades, and it will come to pass." We must struggle, Chairman Mao had said. We are heirs to a better world. Equality will protect us. Equality will make us powerful.

She broke the silence. "I am not well, Sparrow. Something is wrong in my head. I must have imagined everything."

"Dear Zhuli, go and rest. I'll wake you if something happens."

Dear, she thought. How brave he was, to use such nostalgic language. If she truly wanted to protect her family, shouldn't she turn herself in? But for what crime? Her thoughts frightened her, they made no sense.

The shouting had decreased in volume. The students had turned towards another street.

"These are professors' lodgings," Zhuli said. "Even if they don't come here tonight, we're like eggs in a nest."

Sparrow could not help but notice how Zhuli clutched her violin. He had an image of Wen the Dreamer, holding the battered suitcase, names sliding out like bits of clothing. He tried to clear his thoughts. Zhuli was only a child and children would not be harmed. Children, the Chairman said, carried the seeds of revolution.

In the pre-dawn darkness, Zhuli went to the Conservatory to return the score of Beethoven's "Emperor." The library was locked and she found herself inside Room 103, a room she had never entered before without her violin. There was no one around. She closed the door, sat down on the floor and rested for a long time. She had a desire to stop time moving so quickly. The previous night, Zhuli had stayed awake rereading Chairman Mao's talk on art and literature, but each time she felt a truth might be appearing, it muddied and broke away. The Chairman's words were elegant, perfectly sharp, but when they touched her thoughts, they became crooked. Unable to sleep, she had written a long self-criticism, but it was not the kind that the Party demanded. Instead, the same reactionary words kept rising to the surface and dirtying the page.

"Who am I at the base of things?"

"Do I have the ability to change?"

Say all you know, the Chairman had written, *and say it without reserve.*

"But there is more and more that I question! I'm afraid to hear what I think. I know that the Party is right in all things. I say it is right but even the simplest truths don't seem like truths at all."

We can learn what we did not know. We are not only good at destroying the old world, we are also good at building the new.

"What if the new is nothing but a virus of the same sickness? And what about devotion, what about duty and filial love? Must everything that is old be contemptible? Weren't we also something before?"

Why are you defending a musical culture that is not your own?

She pinched her hands and the pain shot all the way to her neck. "Enough of these thoughts! They're all useless because at the base somewhere I know what the Party says is right. Only I'm so selfish, so selfish . . ."

She heard scuffling nearby. Zhuli stood. A low moaning was coming from the cellars in the basement. Had someone been down there this entire time? Her body began to tremble. No, she told herself, her mind was troubled, she'd hardly slept. Still, she heard someone moaning in pain. Room 103 struck her, for the first time, as an echo of the underground library. Zhuli left the room, rushed up the stairs and out into the warm air. It was still early, still dark outside, as if the counting of time had paused and was only now being restarted again.

She had the family's oil and grain coupons in her pocket and she walked in a daze, her hand over the opening, hiding them and protecting them. Since Big Mother and Swirl's departure, it had been her responsibility to pick up the rations.

The queue for oil had already reached Julu Road. When she saw how long the line would take, her distraction turned into guilt. She should have come here first thing. It had been a mistake to go to the Conservatory, she had known better and yet, once again, she had followed stupidity and selfishness. She took her place at the end of the line, behind a girl who wore nothing on her feet and whose eyes were squeezed shut. The cut of her hair was as blunt as an anvil. Nobody spoke. Every building was shrouded in red banners. A broken chair lay in the road beside a length of rope caked in what looked like ink. Three phrases swung together in her thoughts: Party-mindedness, people-mindedness, ideological content. It is my thinking, Zhuli thought. Everything correct becomes something poisoned. If only I could quiet my thoughts. She felt as if she hadn't closed her eyes in days.

Distribution wouldn't begin for another hour. Perhaps, if she was lucky, she would reach the front of the line by noon. If they ran out of oil, she would come again the next day. She would give in, she would forget the Conservatory and walk away. A weight lifted from her shoulders at this thought. "Yes," she said, startling the girl beside her. She was addressing these thoughts to Kai, but the thoughts no longer seemed like hers. "There is always tomorrow and the day after and the day after. It is not too late to reform and grow."

Around her, people, buildings, objects all appeared disproportionately large, not only their substance but their shadows too. Had there ever been such a light-filled July? She saw now that she was standing beside a wall covered in posters. "Denounce the . . ." "Destroy the . . ." "Rise up and . . . eradicate . . . shame." The words, written in colossal characters of red ink, buzzed in her thoughts. "Bombard the headquarters!" It sounded like a game that Flying Bear and Da Shan had invented. How odd it must feel to write violent words in such orderly calligraphy. Zhuli shook the thought away. Dissonance required as precise a technique as beauty. In her mind, Prokofiev's libretto kept repeating: *The philosophers have tried in different ways to explain the world; the point is to change it.* Prokofiev quoted Marx, the Red Guards quoted Chairman Mao, everyone shouted borrowed ideas, her classmates memorized the Chairman's slogans and adopted his poetry as their own. So we are not so different from one another after all, Zhuli thought, except that I speak in the language of Bach and the musical ideas of Prokofiev but still, none of us knows the true nature of our voices, no matter the cause, none of us speaks with our own words. At the core, is there only desire but no justice? All we've learned since the fall of the old dynasties is how to amplify the noise.

This noise was splitting inside her now. She heard Sparrow's *Symphony No. 3*, as if from the air itself. Her own voice wept, "There is always tomorrow and the day after. It must not be too late."

The line nudged forward.

Zhuli had nearly reached the head of the line. Each time she saw another person leaving, their full quota of rations in their exultant hands, she felt increasingly giddy. She allowed herself to count the people in front of her. Eighteen. It was midday, the shade had long retreated and, in the glare, the buildings were dissolving into watery reflections. She stepped to the side and peered ahead. Seventeen. The pavement had a dulled to grainy whiteness. There was a growing disturbance behind but Zhuli, focused only on obtaining the rations, didn't turn. Voices chafed, followed by a woman's fearful answer, a sagging E minor tone. She was easily drowned out by taunts. Still, Zhuli wouldn't turn. Ahead of her the queue had begun to shift and in her exhausted thoughts, she saw the line as if from above, a millipede straining its tiny head forward. Zhuli was up against the barefoot girl in front of her, and when the girl turned, Zhuli turned as well, as if they were joined. She saw a woman being pulled from the lineup. The woman was her mother's age. A Red Guard, a tall, spindly girl, was pushing down on the back of the woman's neck as if the woman were an ox.

The woman was wearing a pale blouse and a navy skirt that fell below her knees. It must be her clothing, Zhuli thought dully, that had attracted the fury of the Red Guards. "Comrades, look at this trash!" the tall girl shouted, dragging the woman along the line. The girl was yelling so loudly her pink mouth seemed to swallow her face. Zhuli fought the urge to giggle, to dissolve in skittishness, to turn away and hide her shock, but just at that moment the girl pushed the woman straight towards her. "Slap her insolent face!" the girl screamed. Zhuli froze. "Slap her!" the girl shouted. Someone next to Zhuli reached out and gave the woman a stinging slap. The sound, or was it the echo, was soft and drawn out. The woman's face was hidden by her dark hair which had come loose from its elastic, and then her head was yanked back and Zhuli saw blood on the woman's mouth, both full and delicate. The woman, she thought dully, was being punished because of the desire, the degeneracy, inside her. "You, Comrade!" the girl cried. Zhuli lifted her eyes. "Teach this whore a lesson!" Someone very near, a man, was speaking in her ear, "Go ahead, don't be afraid. We all have lessons to learn, don't hesitate!" The woman was so close to Zhuli she could see the trembling of her eyelids and new droplets of blood starting to form. The girl was screaming words that made no sense. "Where have I put the ration coupons?" Zhuli thought, perplexed. "Has the line moved? I don't want to lose my place. I've been waiting such a very, very long time." She lifted her right hand but nothing happened. "Go on," the man urged. Softly, so softly: "What's wrong? Don't hesitate!" More and more people pressed towards them. The woman was suddenly yanked away. Zhuli's hand remained open, as if she was waiting to catch something in the air. "Little capitalist spy," the girl was saying. "Stinking whore!" The line was running forward. Someone appeared in the corner of her eye with an unthinkably large bag of flour. Young people were ransacking the distribution warehouse, even pulling out the workers. Zhuli closed her eyes. "Unmask them!" "Bourgeois rats!" "Drag them out!" The shouting had a merry, dancing quality, a French pierrot two-step. "Cleanly, quickly, cut off their heads!" From where had this crowd appeared? She heard a rupture like a plane coming down to land, but it was only this electrified, heaving mass of people. Time was slipping away. Soon it would be too late.

"Just shout the slogans," the girl beside her whispered. "Quickly! They're watching you. Oh, why are you so afraid?"

Was it the little girl with no shoes? But when she turned, she saw only a press of bodies and no sympathetic face. The queue no longer existed and had been reshaped by the crowd. Where were her ration coupons? Had somebody pulled them from her hand? No, they were still here, tucked in the pocket of her shirt. She felt nauseated and knew she would vomit. Where was the woman? What hideous flaw had they seen inside her? The crowd seemed to swell and hide her, separating her from the hysterical Red Guards, the mob was both a terror and safety. In its frenzy it was evolving from hundreds of bystanders into a single entity, a snake with a thousand eyes twisting this way and that, searching with ever greater intensity, magnifying every speck of dirt within it. The snake wound its long neck around and around. When it found her, it lifted her right up and forced her through the crowd. "Don't be afraid," she thought, "this is not real." She found herself standing in another line. Was that her voice crying out? There were a dozen people with her, old women, mothers and even girls, staring in shock. Red Guards swaggered around them, pushing them to their knees. Zhuli felt a shock of pain as she hit the concrete. Momentarily she became dissociated, she was watching from a few steps away, she was a part of the crowd and could see the targets and also herself. A girl, a different girl, was coming with scissors. She was yanking the heads back one by one and cutting off great clumps of hair. "Disgusting bitches," the girl repeated. Zhuli re-entered herself and felt the blinding snap of the scissors and then an alien lightness as a swath of hair fell. "It's nothing," she thought, "only I must not lose the ration coupons. Ba Lute will be very angry if I let them fall from my pocket." Other things began to happen. Someone said, "Oh, this is the violinist. The stuck-up bitch whose father is a counter-revolutionary." They pulled her bag from her, turned it upside down and the Beethoven score slid out in a wild flutter of pages. She heard crying and begging, the rough splitting of clothing, but Zhuli focused on the papers. "I know this filth. Her mother is a rightist dog!" They were laughing at it, stomping on it, pretending to sing from it. People had arrived with dripping buckets and she saw streaks of black cutting through the air. They threw ink, or was it paint, on all the kneeling bodies. Zhuli bowed her head and it was as if the jeering and the spitting had broken the surface, everything was coming inside. The first three, five, seven slaps made her cry out in pain and anger but after that, there was a numbness as she began to lose feeling. Time expanded, just as it had in Bingpai when she was a child, and her father was kneeling in the centre of the room. She had wondered, then, why her father had not stood up. Why would they not let him rise? She thought of Ma and what passed from mother to daughter, from husband to wife, from one beloved to another, a bloodline, a touch, a virus. "I was the one who opened Old West's library," Zhuli thought, beginning to lose consciousness. "It was my mistake and it is destroying my parents' lives. Every slap, kick and humiliation that I receive is one less for my mother. What am I inside? What is it they finally see?"

"I'm talking to you, you little slut!" They kept shouting. Her head was pulled back again. "How did this dirty whore slip through?" "Confess who you are!" They were screaming through their loudspeakers right into her ears as if they wanted to deafen her. They slapped the side of her head over and over. Is it a crime to be myself? Is it a crime to disbelieve? She wanted to weep at her own slowness, her own naïveté. The ink drying on her face made the skin tight and painful. All the other women were confessing to something. Zhuli seemed to be the only one still kneeling. She knew she was guilty but she could not confess. Around her, the crowd gave the impression of expanding and rising in exultation. "Open your mouth, you demon!" More slaps, and now they kicked her, pulled her upright again, and now they tied her arms behind her so that her wrists were high up, above her shoulders, and her head was nearly on the ground. "Hours of practice," Zhuli thought deliriously. "I have practised and practised. I have memorized thousands of hours of music, and what will this be? A tiny pearl of time soon to be dissolved." Zhuli could not hear. She saw faces all around her, she was aware of movement without noise. They seemed to think she was useless, an imbecile, and they turned their attention to the woman beside her who was crying so hard she could no longer hold herself up. Pity overwhelmed Zhuli and she saw darkness behind the woman. That is the place I must get to, she thought. But paint, or was it ink, and sweat had gotten into her eyes and she could not wipe them clean. It was unbearably hot. They would be back for her but she could hear only murmuring, a quiet, and it protected her. "I am ready now," she thought, "to bring all these flowers for . . . I will find all the flowers, even if I must steal them from the hands of our Great Leader, I will lay them at Prokofiev's feet." She had given every bit of her soul to music. The words of Goethe's *Faust* returned to her: How *great a spectacle! How great . . . But that, I fear / Is all it is.* The quiet would show her the way out. Silence would expand into a desert, a freedom, a new beginning.

She became aware of movement and felt there was a great deal of space around her, a darkness that she took for asphalt, the road, or nighttime. Where were her arms? They seemed to have detached from her body and fallen away. "My fingers have gone to gather my hair," she thought, wanting to smile, "they have gone to pick up my beautiful hair." It was useless to try to open her eyes. They were crusted shut and she had nothing to hold on to but a stabbing pain that seemed to come from deep in her lungs. Piano music came, unidentifiable. How near it was but no, the music was a prank. Who played the piano in times like these? "Oh," she thought as a trickle of water touched her eyes and then her lips, "my good hands have brought me water." She heard an echoing and then it was as if the air changed pitch, a fog gave way to rain, rain shaded into tone, tone into voices. And then one voice in particular, which she knew immediately and impossibly to be Kai. "No," she thought, the pain in her lungs increasing, "it is not good to fall into his hands." Again the sensation of movement. Then the road came away from her skin. Kai was with her. At the bottom of all these tangled impressions she glimpsed a changed idea, another way of loving someone that she had not experienced before, an attachment like that to a brother, to a friend, to a lover who could never be her lover, of a musical soulmate, a companion who might have been a lifelong collaborator. "It is a great pity," she thought, "that we will never have the chance to play *Tzigane* together because we brought something to it that had never been heard before. David Oistrakh himself would have recognized us; it is the truthfulness and the shame, no, the solitude, that comes from being at odds with oneself. It is loneliness. Only that, Kai," she thought. Yes, if only it were Kai.

"Yes, Zhuli," he said. "The Red Guards have all gone now."

There was no more time. She was moving and yet she was still on the road. She was kneeling and yet she was lying in a dark, humid room. She heard Ba Lute, she heard Flying Bear crying, and Kai saying that two of the women targeted in the struggle session were still on the road, they were dead. One, a professor of mathematics at Jiaotong, had been dragged along the pavement for a kilometre. Zhuli pushed the noise out, it was coming at her not through her ears, but through a breeze against her arms, her hands. Someone washed her, she knew it could only be Sparrow. She knew she was safe and could now open her eyes if she chose to, but she did not choose to. Silence had come to her. It did not try to connect all its pieces, to pretend they were part of the same thing. It didn't need to pretend. Silence saw everything, owned everything, eventually took everything.

Red Guards came to the house. She heard them coming nearer and nearer, they came in and things fell down, more shouting, they saw her and said they would come back. Someone was crying. It was the neighbour, Mrs. Ma, she cried, "Shame, shame!" but at whom? Zhuli didn't know, she was afraid to guess. Shame was a corkscrew inside her, winding together the selfishness, the frivolity, the hollowness of what she was, until there was no more possibility of change.

In the next existence, Zhuli decided, there would be more colours than in the human world, there would be more textures and varieties of time. This would be the world of Beethoven as he sat with his back to the audience, when he understood that sound was immaterial, it was nothing but an echo, the true music had always been inside. But take away music, take away words, and what would persist? One of her ears had been damaged. She longed for her mother and father. How brightly the core of herself flickered before her, just out of reach. What are you, she asked. Where are you?

She sat up and realized it was night. She sat up again and again, imagining herself pushing aside the sheet, walking to the doorway, to the outer room, to the fresh air outside.

Sparrow heard his cousin waking. He had fallen asleep in a chair beside her bed. She had already left the room and turned down the hallway before he fully opened his eyes. He could not move. She would see the posters that were drying on the kitchen table. Da Shan and Flying Bear had been forced to criticize Zhuli, Swirl and Wen the Dreamer, and these denunciations would be pasted up in the morning. "Call her the daughter of rightist filth," Ba Lute had instructed. "You have to. Just write it down. Don't look at me like that. It's nothing, only words."

Da Shan smudged the ink, and his father threw out the poster and made him do it again.

"Da Shan," he said, "if you don't denounce Zhuli, they'll only make it worse for her. They'll turn around and says she's a demon, that she infiltrated our lives. Let them humble us, if that's what they want. Isn't it better to be humbled? Do you want your poor father, your brothers, to lose their lives?"

Trembling, the teenager dipped his brush. Carefully, he wrote Zhuli's name.

Ba Lute had now been summoned to the Conservatory twice, where the struggle sessions had lasted a full twelve hours. Their neighbour, Mr. Ma, had disappeared, and so had Zhuli's teacher, Tan Hong. "The criticism I receive is very light, compared to the others," Ba Lute said, when he returned. He had bruises all over his body. One eye was swollen shut and his face was bloodied and lopsided, but his accusers, his own pupils at the Conservatory, had left his hands alone. People who had been labelled rightists in earlier campaigns, even those who, like Swirl, had been rehabilitated, were far less fortunate.

Twice, Sparrow had been taken away by a group of Red Guards. They had locked him in a storeroom at the Conservatory but nobody had come to criticize him or denounce him. Eventually the door was opened and he was sent away. It was as if he floated underwater, inside a bubble of air. On the streets, the students sang and wept and shouted their love. The targets who had been humiliated once were humiliated again and again, as if a familiar face elicited the most hatred, they were the ones to blame for the receding promise of modernity, the violent sacrifices of revolution, this malevolence that seemed to infect the very young. Only it was not malevolence, it was courage and they were loyal soldiers defending the Chairman. Sparrow had to protect Zhuli, he had to finding a hiding place, but where? His father had said the violence was most extreme at the universities. The radio proclaimed that, in Beijing, the writer Fou Lei, once celebrated for his translations of Balzac and Voltaire, was being subjected to daily struggle sessions alongside his wife. The family's books had all been burned and the piano destroyed. Their son, the pianist Fou Ts'ong, had applied for and received political asylum in the West. The father, Fou Lei, the quiet traitor, the poisonous needle wrapped in a silk cover, was finally being called to account.

The morning grew hotter. When Sparrow woke again, Zhuli was sitting in bed, under the window. She had left a space for her mother, as if Swirl might arrive home at any moment. With her hair cut off, she looked even younger than she was.

"It's okay," she said. "You can go back to sleep."

"I wasn't sleeping." He sat up in his chair, rubbed his face, pushing his uneasy dreams away. "No, I was only thinking."

"I'm fine now, and I know when you're telling fibs."

He smiled. One hand drifted up to the opposite arm, rising to her shoulder, finding the ends of her hair.

"Six months," Zhuli said in a low voice, "and everything will grow back." She gazed at him, and the dark smudges on her face, the bruising which had turned a sickly yellow, made her appear shadowed despite the sunlight in the room. "Sparrow, have you seen my violin?"

"Your violin," he said stupidly.

She waited, watching him.

"Zhuli," he said. He despised the quaver in his voice and pushed it down. "It was destroyed." She nodded, as if waiting for the second half of the sentence. He looked at her helplessly. "It was destroyed."

"It was," she said. "But then . . ."

"Red Guards came yesterday, no, it was two days ago. They came and smashed all the instruments. They even came in here but Ba . . . we asked them to leave. Ba Lute was denounced, he had to go to a meeting but it's finished now. He's home. The Conservatory is closed. Maybe for good."

Zhuli nodded. She seemed, to Sparrow, almost unbearably lucid.

"Where are Da Shan and Flying Bear?" she asked.

"In Zhejiang with Ba's cousin. Mrs. Ma took them by train. You need to go as well—"

"Yes," she said, and then so flippantly he didn't quite believe she had spoken. "I should have studied agriculture after all. Cousin, haven't you been listening to the radio? The campaign is everywhere. Zhejiang will be no different from here."

He did not tell her that four professors at the Conservatory had killed themselves in the last week and that Professor Tan had been locked in a room without adequate food or light. Zhuli did not mention the denunciations Da Shan had written. A wave of chanting overran the streets but they acted as if they did not hear it. It moved along Beijing Road, circling them. Zhuli asked if he had seen Kai.

"I saw him two days ago. I couldn't tell how he was."

"But he'll be protected, won't he? Nobody will harm him. They won't harm you."

The feeling in her voice came from another time, an old longing that did not know how to fade. He didn't know what to do but nod.

She closed her eyes. "I'm glad, cousin."

When she spoke again, her voice was very calm. "I'm glad," she said. She touched her hair again and then let it go. "It's like morning when the stars are painted over by daylight, Sparrow. You think it's very far away, all this light, and anyway there's a great universe of stars and other things and so you never believe they'll disappear . . . Sparrow, of all the things they say I am, they are right that I am proud. I was proud to be myself. I really did believe that one day I would play before the Chairman himself, that I would go to London and Moscow and Berlin!" She laughed, like a child at the antics of a little pet. "I know now. Those places will only ever be words to me. My pride was so great I imagined that I would stand in the room where Bach lived, I would see his handwriting, his rooms and his little bed, and I would show people what it meant to me. They would hear it. They would hear Bach in me, they would know that he was mine, too. I don't know how, I don't know why . . ."

The lucidity in Zhuli's eyes frightened him.

"There's a joke inside of it," Zhuli said, "that's why everyone laughs at me. Do you understand? All these things that we don't have are *nothing compared to the things we did have*. A life can be long or short but inside it, if we're lucky, is this one opening . . . I looked through this window and made my own idea of the universe and maybe it was wrong, I don't know anymore, I never stopped loving my country but I wanted to be loyal to something else, too. I saw things . . . I don't want the other kind of life."

Sparrow stood and went to close the door that was already closed. He went to the window, which was latched tight, he drew the curtains and tried to think of what to do. "Tomorrow," he said. "I'll take you to Zhejiang. You won't be alone. Flying Bear and Da Shan—"

"No," she said. "It would only cause trouble for them."

But what option was there? It was unbearable that there should be no escape. Think, he told himself, you must think clearly. The notebook, pen and cup beside the bed drew his attention, and he slid the pen aside and picked up the notebook. He was shaking. The sight of Wen the Dreamer's handwriting disturbed him. Where was Big Mother, where was Swirl? They alone, not he or his father, knew how to protect her. He despised his own weakness. "Zhuli," he said. "This disturbance will end. It must end."

"My poor father. What will he feel when he comes home and sees what has happened to us all?"

He didn't answer and Zhuli reached her hand to him, to the notebook. "I finished this one. Let's continue. Chapter 17, it's your favourite chapter, isn't it? Here's the box, under the bed. I had to hide it from Ba Lute."

He lifted the box out. Zhuli combed her hands through her hair, as if preparing to receive a visitor. She said, "I have this idea that . . . maybe, a long time ago, the Book of Records was set in a future that hadn't yet arrived. That's why it seems so familiar to us now. The future is arriving. We've come all this way to meet it."

"Or maybe," he said, "it's we who keep returning to the same moment."

"Next time, we'll meet in another place, won't we, Sparrow?"

"Yes, Zhuli."

Sparrow read the chapter aloud as afternoon became evening, as if reading from the Book of Records was the same as shutting and bolting the outside door. Inside the room, Da-wei would soon leave America and return home, but before his departure, a composer named Chou brings him to a rehearsal at Carnegie Hall. A hundred musicians radiate from the central figure of the conductor, Edgard Varèse, and, meanwhile, a second, smaller orchestra plays from an adjoining room. Alternating and colliding, audible but invisible to one another, they perform a single symphony using drums, alarms, scraps of song, sirens, a shouting flute, the bang and clank of metropolitan horns. The pandemonium of the symphony is the most beautiful thing Da-wei has ever heard. It seems simultaneously to include him and usher him on his way.

"Da-wei, you mustn't go back," Chou tells him afterwards. "It's too late to return."

Da-wei does not know how to answer. Before him, the orchestra has vacated the stage but their music stands wait like a flock of cranes.

"Myself," Chou says, "I left Shanghai during the worst of the fighting. The Japanese pursued us, but we managed to disappear into a crowd . . ." His face, so alive in its story, turned grey. "The army apprehended another group, mistaking them for us. They rounded them up and shot them all. They were massacred . . . You see how it is. A life for a life. I can never go back."

In the chamber, it feels as if all the hundreds of chairs are inclined towards them, listening.

"I tell you: our country has no need for us. You and I, we're all yí mín, altered people, which is to say, we will soon be the most common people in existence."

When the chapter ended, Zhuli took the notebook in her hands. She said, "I have never heard Varèse. I have heard so little modern music from the twentieth century. I wish, one day, I could go abroad and listen to what they're hearing." She said, as she if hadn't realized until this moment, "Da-wei is the shadow of my father. All these years, because of the handwriting, I imagined he was writing to us directly. To me. It was never just a book, was it? . . . Sparrow, promise me. Don't let Ba Lute burn the notebooks."

"Yes, Zhuli. I promise."

Nearly three thousand kilometres away, Wen the Dreamer arrived in Yumen City, Gansu Province. Since his escape from Jiabangou, he had crossed and recrossed the Northwest for nearly two years, no longer the same bookish young man with poems folded into his pocket. In his mid-forties, darkened by the sun and burned by the wind, old before his time, he was lithe, alert and physically toughened. He stole the identity cards of passing strangers, thereby changing his name on a monthly basis; he stopped, when necessary, to earn money or ration coupons by working in a wheat or millet field, or a cement factory. With his battered suitcase, he crossed and recrossed the desert, learning how to live in the dry moonscape of Gansu Province, how to evade capture and how to exist on air alone. One day, he found, in a book barrow in Xinjiang, a copy of Chapter 6 of the Book of Records. He stared at the pages, fearing that he was lost. Hallucinating that Da-wei, May Fourth and the Book of Records was a myth, an allegory or a system around which all their lives were knotted. Seeing his distress, the child tending the book barrow said, "My father read that book, he got it from our cousin. He doesn't have the whole book though, just a few chapters. This one's extra. He won't sell the rest."

"Where does your cousin live?"

The child raised her faint eyebrows. "Jinchang. He works in the nickel mine."

That night, Wen read the notebook without a pause, devouring it as if it were a plate of food, convinced with each turning of the page that he knew the handwriting and would always know it. In this copy, a secondary character's name had been altered: the copyist had used the character 谓 which was the wei of Wei River, whose source was in Gansu Province.

He travelled to Jinchang, a town made curious by its scattered buildings of foreign design, said to be the ruins of Roman-style houses left by a thousand exiled soldiers who settled there two thousand years ago. Their descendants were occasionally born with green eyes and startling red hair. These days, the town was more famous for its nickel and precious metals. In Jinchang, he found another chapter, also mimeographed, dated only six weeks previous, and using the same code. The owner of the book barrow was reticent, but finally he confided that he received the chapter from a honeydew farmer in Lanzhou. Wen the Dreamer followed the trail, down half a dozen roads and chapters until, one day, he knocked at the door of Notes from the Underground, the plant and flower clinic of the Lady Dostoevsky.

"My dear man," the Lady said. "It's about time. I was sure I would be dead by the time you finally got here."

She told him that Swirl was in Yumen City with her sister, where the two women worked in the local song and dance troupe. As he left, she pressed into his hand the copy of The Rain on Mount Ba, which had once belonged to his daughter and still had Zhuli's handwriting in the margins.

A week later, Wen the Dreamer appeared in Yumen, thin as a spear of grass. He came to the simple dwelling Lady Dostoevsky had described, where Swirl lived with Big Mother Knife. Lamplight flickered behind the curtain. He stood outside with his suitcase for a long time, afraid to let her see him, afraid to imagine the cessation of his loneliness, afraid of the future and also the past. He remembered how he used to watch Swirl's window in Shanghai, waiting for the lamp to be extinguished so that he could deliver a new chapter of the Book of Records. A lifetime ago. Two lifetimes. Now all the copies held a record of the places they'd been, the places they'd been forced to leave. He had tried to clip his hair, to clean himself and mend his clothes, but still he felt the uncrossable sea between who he was and who he might have been.

When he tapped lightly on the frame of the window, Swirl came to the door and opened it. She stared at him as if at an apparition.

Wen the Dreamer recited the famous line of Li Bai: "See the waters of the Yellow River leap down from Heaven, roll away to the sea, never to turn again."

"Destined," Swirl answered, "to return in a swirl of dust."

Big Mother, who was standing behind Swirl at the door, came out. Calmly, as if he came by every evening, she embraced him. And then she wrapped herself in a sweater and left them alone. She walked for a long time along the nearby ridge. Lamps from the oil refinery illuminated a web of nighttime workers. The sky was dark purple, filled with foreboding. When Big Mother returned, she saw her sister and Wen standing side by side in the shadows of the house. The stars were dimming and she had the sense that the night sky was loosening from the earth and lifting away. Not once did Big Mother see them bend or move, let alone touch one another. After having been separated for a decade, they stood so lightly, as if the ground itself could not be trusted. Maybe they talked about how, in a house like Ba Lute's, in the home of a Party hero, their daughter might have a chance to thrive. Maybe they spoke not of Zhuli, but of something else entirely, of other intimacies and unwritten lives. It was for the wind to hear, Big Mother later told Sparrow, and not for the likes of her.

Wen the Dreamer and Swirl left in the night, in a bid to escape to the borderlands. Mongolia could be reached in two days, and Wen had contacts who could help them on the other side.

The following morning, Big Mother began a letter to Zhuli, her good eye right up to the page. She would find a way to send it, along with letters from Swirl and Wen, once she felt it was safe to do so. *My heart has been heavy all day long*, she thought, remembering the poem she had recited at her sister's wedding. *Your elder sister has looked out for you. And now you are both crying and cannot part, Yet it is right that you should go on. . . .*

In the letter to Zhuli, she wrote, "I watched them depart on one small horse. Can you imagine? As if they were young again." Her tears wrinkled the page. She folded the letter and hid the words away. That evening, she went to the local Party secretary and told them her sister had slipped and fallen into the Wei River. She had tried to save Swirl, but the current had been too strong, the fetid water, polluted with waste from the factories, had carried her away. The Party secretary convened a search team. After five days, with no sign of the body and anxious about rising production quotas and the new political campaign, he pronounced Swirl dead, signed her papers and closed her file.

In Shanghai, Sparrow was taken away by Red Guards and for a week they had no word of him. A different group came for Zhuli on Tuesday and Wednesday, and then left her alone until Sunday. Sunday was the worst and the Red Guards came again on Monday. On Tuesday, Sparrow came home, starving and exhausted, but unharmed. He'd been held in isolation in a storage room and then let go. It was inexplicable. On the streets, loudspeakers blared from every corner. The official news program announced that Lao She, whose plays Wen the Dreamer had loved, and who had once been celebrated as "the People's artist," had drowned himself. To celebrate his death, joyful marching music danced from the speakers. In the middle of the broadcast, Red Guards entered the house. Despite Sparrow's begging, despite his grip on Zhuli, they took her. Her hand slipped out of his. In truth, the fear in Sparrow's voice had so terrified her, Zhuli had closed her eyes and pulled her hand free.

At first, Zhuli's classmates had been inventive. They had new slogans and methods, they had new implements like garbage pails, conductor's batons and razors. There was a comedic quality to it all, one laugh crashing down onto the next, explosive laughter, barbed laughter, tripwire laughter, questions that were not questions, the confessions they wanted that had nothing to do with confession.

On and on they sang:

The water of socialism nourished me, I grew up beneath the
    Red Flag
I took the oath,
To dare to think, to speak up, to act,
To devote myself to revolution.

They loved to sing. It was the way they looked at her, the utter implacability, the contempt, she couldn't bear. The revolutionaries soon lost interest in their own implements, and now they beat her with their bare hands. Kai said that she had always cared more about music and her desires than about the Party. He said he had tried to instruct her on the correct works, even going so far as to copy them out by hand for her, but she had rejected them. Her parents were enemies of the People and Zhuli refused to denounce them. She was loose and had no morals, she was degenerate. All passions should be subsumed to revolution, he said. He talked and talked and would not stop, but he never mentioned Sparrow's name and never betrayed him. When he ran out of words, he left and did not come back. After this, she felt she understood everything. Music began with the act of composition but she herself was only an instrument, a glass to hold the water. If she answered the accusations or defended herself, she would no longer be able to hear the world that was finally seeping into her. Loud, strange music. She kept turning her head to try to place this second orchestra, this outer room, and meanwhile the revolutionary youth kept trying to make her face forward and look at the floor. She saw their hands shouting and their mouths smiling. Silently, she berated herself. Animals, she thought, do not weep. Instead they never look away.

That day, Sparrow brought her home. He couldn't stop weeping and she realized she'd never seen him fall apart and it frightened her. But he was safe, she thought. The Red Guards had not harmed him. She thought that Kai was protecting him. Always, the pianist was just behind Sparrow, watchful, but perhaps it was all in her mind. Still, some link between the three of them could never be broken, it was the future that was to have been, if only the country had chosen a different path. She wanted to ask Kai so many questions. She wanted to tell him that whatever happened, whatever they chose, one day they would have to come awake, everyone would have to stand up and confront themselves and realize that it wasn't the Party that made them do it. One day, they would be alone with their actions. She wanted to tell him, "Don't let them hurt your hands. Your gifted hands." She wanted to tell Sparrow, "No matter what happens, you must finish your symphony. Please don't let it disappear." Did it matter more to love or to have been loved? If anyone answered her question, she didn't catch the words. I am so far away now, Zhuli thought, that words dissolve before they reach me.

How far is that, she thought. She felt terribly alone. How much farther?

With Da Shan and Flying Bear away in Zhejiang, the laneway house was quiet. On Thursday, she woke very early as she used to do. The inky darkness of the night protected her as she put on her favourite blue dress, pinned the rough edges of her hair aside, gathered what she needed and slipped through the front door. The gods of silence protected her and neither Sparrow nor her uncle woke; or if they did wake, they chose not to stop her from leaving. The night was a dream, a pure warmth that settled on her and seemed to ease her awake. She could barely walk and yet nothing hurt. She took side streets and alleyways to the Conservatory and the journey lasted a long time. Small fires burned. She came to an intersection that was piled high with books. They looked as if they had been overturned from a truck, they made a shape like a sand dune. Here and there were groups of students sleeping outside. One woke and watched her passing but seemed to think Zhuli was part of her dream; the Red Guard gazed at her and did nothing. There were posters everywhere, a mute shouting that surrounded Zhuli but no longer frightened her. She did not know how or why, but now that she understood, now that she had come to a decision, the old fears had drained away. Asleep, the revolutionaries appeared innocent, they seemed as nothing. Zhuli walked and saw buildings, littered streets, damaged lights, scraps of clothing, broken furniture. She felt the hardness of the pavement, the blue-black air and even the weightlessness of her dress. No matter which way she turned, the roads twisted and led her to the Conservatory, this had always been the course of her life. Past the gate, the courtyard was alive with shapes, small and large piles of trash which she moved between as if they were a row of empty seats. The Conservatory door had been propped open with a shoe, she did not know why, but she left the shoe in place, nudged the door wider and went inside. She thought she saw abandoned programs, lost handbags, forgotten coats and then, after a moment, the hallucination passed and she came to the staircase she had first climbed when she was a child, when Sparrow, holding her hand, had brought her to study with Professor Tan.

The Conservatory smelled of both damp and fire, a smell that seemed, as she moved through the building, to be coming from the workshop where Professor Tan had built violins using thin boards of parasol-tree wood. Zhuli stopped and looked in the door, thinking perhaps there was a violin that she could take with her and play, a violin that she could make her own. But there was nothing. Bits of wood looked as if they had been flung in joyous celebration at the windows. She went on. At the fourth floor, she turned down the hallway and saw the same posters that Kai had shown her many weeks ago. Zhuli began to pull them down. Witch. It was slow and noisy work. The papers made a terrible noise but it no longer mattered. There were so many, the posters seemed to proliferate as she removed them. She took out the red marker she had slipped into her pocket and stood before the last poster, ready to strike, but the hallway was so rigidly devoid of life she could not think of any words. Once Debussy had trickled through the walls. She heard it now, again, and was grateful, it was as if all the gods were gathering, they had come to meet her here. What had become of He Luting and and all the rest? The parents of Fou Ts'ong had taken poison and killed themselves. It was being celebrated. The rest must have gone away somewhere. Had the older generation seen everything coming and quietly dissolved before the hammer fell? She hoped so. She lifted the marker again and wrote the only words that came to her. She did not put down the writer's name, Shen Congwen, or the novel, *Border Town*. The marker moved as if of its own accord. This is what is in my mind, she thought, another person's words.

> THE OLD FERRYMAN COULDN'T GUESS WHAT THE OBSTACLE WAS, OR HOW TO FIX IT. HE'D LIE IN BED, MULLING IT OVER UNTIL FINALLY IT BEGAN TO OCCUR TO HIM THAT PERHAPS CUICUI LOVED THE YOUNGER BROTHER, NOT THE ELDER. THAT MADE HIM SMILE, AN UNNATURAL SMILE FROM FEAR. IN TRUTH HE WAS A LITTLE WORRIED, BECAUSE IT SUDDENLY OCCURRED TO HIM THAT CUICUI WAS LIKE HER MOTHER IN EVERY WAY. HE HAD A VAGUE FEELING THAT MOTHER AND DAUGHTER WOULD SHARE THE SAME FATE. EVENTS OF THE PAST SWARMED INTO HIS MIND AND HE COULD NO LONGER SLEEP. HE RAN OUT THE DOOR ALONE, ONTO THE HIGH BLUFFS BY THE CREEK. HE LOOKED UP AT THE STARS AND LISTENED TO THE KATYDIDS AND SOUNDS OF THE OTHER INSECTS, CONSTANT AS RAIN. HE COULD NOT SLEEP FOR A VERY LONG TIME.

She wrote directly overtop of the denunciations on the poster, so that "brother" appeared over "leader," "vague" over "reactionary," and "high bluffs" sat overtop "demon-exposing mirror."

Borrowed words over borrowed words, they were all attached to one another now. She turned and saw the soft shapes of paper on the floor. They had been blunted by falling and the words which had looked like joints turned out to have no weight at all. She dropped the red marker on the floor and felt consoled by its sharp clatter and went on, down the hallway until she came to the office that Sparrow shared with Old Wu. The door was closed but unlocked and Zhuli felt lightened as she entered the room. Nobody had ransacked the office. The records and books, few as they were, the portraits of Chairman Mao, Premier Zhou Enlai and Vice-Premier Liu Shaoqi, everything remained neat and ordered, as if they belonged to another time and place. She stared at the portraits and saw her own shadow in the glass. There she was finally, completely visible, the girl and the sky and fate twisted together.

"Sparrow will understand," she told herself, knowing that it was not true. But maybe he would understand, there was a devil inside her and Zhuli had no choice. She had to protect it. She could not let them restrain it.

She laid some of her cousin's records on the floor and studied them. *My first sentence was "Make revolution."* Mahler's Fifth, Bach's *Goldberg Variations*, Prokofiev's Fifth, Beethoven's "Emperor." *I took the oath, to dare to think, to speak up, to act.* She did not want to hear a violin and so the record she put on was Bach. She wanted to walk slowly, there was no longer any need to rush. Time extended inside Bach, there were repetitions and canons, there were circles and spirals, there were many voices and honest humility as if he knew that reincarnation and loss were inseparable. The music no longer seemed to come from the record player, but from some chamber of her memory. She thought of Kai and then resolved to think of him no more. In her mind, she feared most for Sparrow, because she knew him as well as she knew herself. He would let his talent burn away, he dared not admit that talent was a precious thing. She wanted to tell her mother and father that she had come to a high plateau from where she could see in every direction, and she wasn't afraid. It wasn't fear she was walking away from, but discontinuity. She could not stand the loneliness. In this brief window when she still knew who she was, before they broke her down again, she wished to choose a future and to leave. How could she put these thoughts in a note? She wanted to preserve the core of herself. If they took away music, if they broke her hands, who would she be? A note would be taken up by the Red Guards, a note would only cause further humiliation. She had a strong belief that Wen the Dreamer was alive, that Swirl and Big Mother Knife were safe, and a fervent desire that they understand her choice. When she had turned the record over and both sides had finished playing, she took the rope from her coat pocket, removed her shoes, climbed up onto Sparrow's desk, careful not to disrupt his papers. She attached the rope to a long pipe that ran along the wall. She climbed down and pushed the desk away, keeping the chair where it was. She looped and carefully tied the rope. It was very quiet and she wondered if she should say something, if she should speak and make a noise. Zhuli did not mean to weep but it was beyond her, this body and its responses, this body and its desires. She thought of the hidden library. She opened the lid and looked inside, she saw the ancient instrument on which she had first learned to listen. She thought of Sparrow, how young he was when he had opened the door that let her into this life. Was it possible to walk away, to abandon him and at the same time, to protect him? The first aria of the *Goldberg Variations* was also its end. Could it be that everything in this life had been written from the beginning? She could not accept this. I am taking this written record with me, she thought. It is mine and I'm the only one who can keep it safe. She let go.

Sparrow woke in the dark, aware of the front door opening. It seemed to remain open for a long moment before finally, almost imperceptibly, shutting. Sparrow felt as if he were groping through a dream that still continued, he had to shoulder through it, he had to make it burn away. The dream involved men walking on a frozen river and machetes hacking through the ice. Finally, it broke. He opened his eyes and the shape beside him became the outline of a window. An elongated figure widened into a bookshelf. He reached for the thin cover but it had already fallen away. After a moment he stood up and, careful not to creak the floorboards, went to the room that Zhuli shared with Aunt Swirl. He touched the empty bed.

Zhuli had gone to see the Old Cat.

He did not know how he knew this; he could think of no other reason for Zhuli to break curfew. The bed still seemed warm from his cousin's body.

In the stickiness of the hot night, his shirt had glued to his back. Sparrow poured water into Zhuli's basin and washed his face. When he caught sight of his reflection, he was surprised at his thinness. Had he fallen ill, he wondered. Had he lost weeks or months of time? In the glass, he looked as if he were still a young man, almost a student. He pondered his reflection, half expecting it to vanish. Back in his room, he changed his clothes; he pulled one of Da Shan's red armbands over his left sleeve. The armband would make him invisible. Once more, he ran his hands over his face and looked into the glass. There were voices drifting in through the closed window. Young men, Red Guards it seemed, in the alleyway. Sparrow could hear the detritus of a fire being kicked and smothered. He could smell burning. They were singing, softly, as if they were suddenly concerned about the residents of the laneway and did not wish to wake them. Slowed-down beats of music, dreaming auras of song. A young man's pure, strong tenor, sliding off the walls of the alleyway. *This is the beautiful Motherland / This is the place where I grew up.*

Later on, Sparrow came to know that he had taken the rope from around his cousin's neck. He had somehow managed to gather Zhuli in his arms, climb down and leave the room. Outside the

Conservatory, it had still been early. He took side streets and if people came up to him or spoke to him, he did not register their presence. After walking several blocks, it dawned on Sparrow that the sound of the city was dulled. Six trucks bearing water drums navigated the narrow lane, but he only became aware of their presence when he caught sight of them. There was a vibration in the pavement, and there were women at a water spigot, and there was a queue for flour, but he moved through them as if through images or projections. He kept walking and became aware of Ling running towards him, and of Zhuli in his arms as if she were sleeping. He had to focus all his mind, all his energy, on keeping her from falling. Her head against his shoulder dug into him. Red Guards came and pushed their faces against his face, but he could not hear them. There was a crowd of them. And then, he did not know how or why, he no longer saw them. He came to Beijing Road, to the gate, the narrow laneway and the maze of alleyways he had known nearly all his life. Ling was still beside him, but why had she come? Ba Lute was there. He had seen them somehow or he had been alerted. It happened so quickly, Ba Lute's approach, Zhuli taken into Ba Lute's arms, and Sparrow standing by himself in his own home. He knew his father was calling Zhuli's name, he knew because now he could hear. The room suddenly became very loud. Ling was sobbing. People had gathered in the alley-way, but nobody dared cross into the inner courtyard, it had been so polluted by crimes and spirits. Ba Lute, whose great bulk had turned so thin and old, was crying out, as if he could wake her, "What mistakes did we make? We're old, we're old now. If I sat down and wrote down all our mistakes, would that be enough? Answer me! What everlasting sins did we commit? Didn't we win this country? Didn't we sacrifice ourselves for the Revolution?" He kept shaking Zhuli as if he could drag her back to this place. Sparrow sat down on a chair. He remembered now how the tears on his cousin's face had still been wet. How long did it take for tears to dry? How close had he come to arriving in time? He thought of

Wen the Dreamer and his Aunt Swirl and his mother. He closed his eyes and tried to drown out Ba Lute's voice. Ling reappeared. She put a blanket around him and blocked out the world. He remembered the blanket that had covered him on the bus with Kai, the music that rang out, the constellations above them. He laughed and disregarded his weeping, which sounded as if came from another person. He laughed and wept until midday came, and with it the true August heat.

8 ≡

LONG AGO, AI-MING LAY beside me on my bed, holding Chapter 17 from the Book of Records in her hands. The story continued even though she had long stopped reading from its pages. In the quiet, Zhuli existed between us, older than me, younger than Ai-ming, as real as we were ourselves. Each time we set the notebook down, I had the sensation that she remained. It was we, Ai-ming and I, listening, who vanished.

≡

LONG AGO, WHEN they lived in Beijing, Big Mother Knife had taken Sparrow to Tiananmen Square. Sparrow had only been a child but he remembered, still, how the concrete felt inextricable from the grey sky, how he himself was impossibly small, like a seed in a bowl. The Forbidden Palace and Tiananmen, Big Mother told him, were built on a north-south axis that mirrored the human body. "Head!" she shouted, pointing to something he couldn't see. "Lungs! Feet!" Tiananmen Gate, festooned with imaginary animals, was the protective tissue around the heart. North-gazing animals monitored the behaviour of citizens, while south-gazing animals judged how power treated the powerless. Sparrow had imagined himself as a stone creature on the gate, wings outstretched, beak glistening in the rain.

Day after day, Sparrow read the public newspapers pinned up at the post office. Photos in the People's Daily captured the exhilaration inside Tiananmen Square, as hundreds of thousands of Red Guards lifted their Little Red Books to Chairman Mao, whose tiny figure waved back from atop the gate. The students arrived by trains for which they no longer needed tickets. They rushed into the Square like water pouring into a single container. "Ten thousand years, ten thousand years!" they shouted under the gaze of those imaginary animals. "A hundred million years to Chairman Mao!"

September blared on, wet and sticky. There was a smell in the air, a nauseatingly sweet smell of bodies left to rot in cellars or on the street. When the Shanghai students returned from Beijing, they were even more single-minded than before.

For a week, Ba Lute had been locked up in a shed with six other faculty from the traditional music department. After his release, he was barely able to stand. A letter from Swirl, sent via Big Mother Knife, arrived: Swirl and Wen the Dreamer, referred to as two bags of ribbon, had been safely received in Mongolia. They begged for news. Ba Lute's reply was only three sentences: Everyone is fine. No need to hurry back. Long live Chairman Mao and the Great Proletarian Cultural Revolution!

Every moment, Sparrow expected to be summoned but the Red Guards never came for him; everyone seemed to have forgotten he existed. He kept seeing the Conservatory, the record, the rope. During the day he tried to sleep and at night he kept watch over the bed in which Big Mother, Swirl, Zhuli, and his brothers had, at different times, slept. In the gloom, he searched for the outlines of his own hands and feet but they were camouflaged by the darkness. Night after night, he felt as if he was slowly approaching Zhuli but when morning came he saw that he had only slipped further away, and the distance between them was growing. His unfinished symphony played on in his head, unstoppable. All it lacked was the fourth and final movement, but what if the fourth movement was silence itself? Perhaps the symphony was complete after all. Too numb to weep, unable to put words to what he most feared, he bundled the pages up, intending to burn them, but in the end he hid them under the trusses of the roof.

Two months after Zhuli's death, Sparrow accompanied Kai to the house of a high-ranking official who lived on Changle Road. On the streets, there was turmoil, warfare between gangs of Red Guards over territory and influence. The official's home, however, seemed a separate country, hushed by walls of scrolls and paintings. The light that fell through the stained-glass windows was the impossible blue of sapphires.

"We recently recovered this piano," the official said, as he ushered them into a high-ceilinged room. Recovered from where, or from whom, he did not say. "As the instrument is far too valuable to remain here, the Party is shipping it to Beijing."

A young girl in a flowered dress brought out an overabundance of food and drink. Sparrow gazed at the clean edges of his dinner plate while the official spoke at length about Madame Mao, the new model orchestras and a reconstructed Central Philharmonic in Beijing. "Comrade Sparrow," the official said, dabbing his lips with a pure white napkin. "Your compositions found favour with the President of the Conservatory, didn't they? The former President, that is." He smiled in a friendly way. "He Luting was a bit stuck in his ways, don't you think? Fortunately things have changed. Now is the time for new music, a revolutionary realism befitting our Great Proletarian Cultural Revolution."

Kai said, "Comrade Sparrow's work is a model of what this new music might be."

The official nodded. To Sparrow he said, "You're fortunate to have such an admirer, aren't you?"

Above them, the ceiling fan spun, making a sound that was both monotonous and numbing.

An array of Front Gate, Hatamen, and State Express 555 cigarettes, as well foreign brands Sparrow had never seen, were arranged on a celadon platter. He sampled the Davidoff and the Marlboro, and the cigarettes left an unanticipated taste, of sweetness or sharpness, on his lips.

The official motioned Kai to the piano. Kai sat down, thought for a moment and then played, from memory, a piano transcription of Beethoven's "Eroica." The segments he played had been re-ordered and soldered together in ways that made Sparrow feel as if the music were being composed in this very moment or, more accurately, being dismantled. The word eroica, Sparrow said, turning to the official, means "heroic." The man raised his glass. "To Comrade Beethoven, our revolutionary brother!"

"To our glorious Revolution," Sparrow answered.

During the slow adumbration of the second movement, the funeral march, the official's eyes ran with tears.

How had he never noticed, Sparrow thought tipsily, just how deeply music could lie? The smoothness of all the facades–not only of the apartment, but of everyone in the room and perhaps Beethoven himself–mesmerized him.

"Conductor Li Delun has asked specifically for you," the official said. He was speaking to Kai with a calculating look in his eyes. "He says you're the most gifted pianist at the Shanghai Conservatory. Your class background is exemplary."

The ceiling fan let off squeaking, high-pitched whistles. The sounds made tiny cuts in the air. "Let the rooms be full of guests," the official recited drunkenly, "and the cups be full of wine. That is what I desire."

After dinner, when the official had dismissed them, Sparrow went with Kai to his room, the same room where they had once met with the Professor, the Old Cat, San Li and Ling.

"There are opportunities, Sparrow," Kai said. They were lying side by side, only the tips of their fingers touching. "The Conservatory is closed but the Central Philharmonic is protected by Madame Mao. Let them protect us. In Beijing, things will be different . . . Are you writing?" Sparrow shook his head. "We can't stop living our lives," Kai said. The words seemed to disintegrate as soon as they touched the air. "We can't."

We, Sparrow thought. We. He could not even say the word aloud.

"Remember what I told you?" Kai said. "My parents and sisters had no one to turn to. They came from a village that was considered less than nothing. I won't go through that again. I won't disappear. I refuse."

That night, Sparrow was kept awake by a bright seam of light beneath Kai's door. Kai's hand across his stomach was heavy, damp, and he covered it with his own. The things he felt could no longer be disowned. And yet they were not the same. They had come from such different worlds and aspired to different conditions, and the fear that drove Kai did not drive him. Panic welled up in him. He tried to control his breathing, to make it quiet. He and his father had not been able to give Zhuli a proper funeral. Prokofiev, at least, had gotten a recording and fake flowers. The authorities had taken Zhuli's body while Sparrow and his father stood by. No, they had not stood by. He and his father had praised the Chairman, the Party and the nation. They'd had no choice but, still, they had performed disturbingly well, as if words and music were only ever about repetition, as if one could just as easily play Bach as repeat the words of Chairman Mao. Pride and mastery, victory and sorrow, the orchestral language had given Sparrow a deep repertoire of feeling. But scorn, degradation, disgust, loathing, what about those emotions? What composer had written a language for them? What listener cared to hear it?

Zhuli was sitting on the edge of the mat, so alive it seemed as if he and Kai were the illusion. "Haven't you understood yet, Sparrow?" she said. He asked her what in this world a mere sound could accomplish. She said, "The only life that matters is in your mind. The only truth is the one that lives invisibly, that waits even after you close the book. Silence, too, is a kind of music. Silence will last." In the west, in the dry wind of the Gansu Desert, Big Mother and Swirl had finally recovered Wen the Dreamer. He stared at the illusion before him and wept.

The words shàng xī tiān (上西天) mean to "to go to the Western sky" or "to ascend to the Western heavens," that is, to pass beyond the western border of the Great Wall, to leave this country, to let go of this life, to die and pass away. Zhuli had not been able to wait for him. She had gone ahead to find another beginning. The idea of quiet terrified him. Sparrow wanted to follow her, but even despite the promise of an ending, of freedom, this was the life he couldn't leave behind.

In November, Kai left Shanghai and was appointed soloist at the Central Philharmonic in Beijing. The whereabouts of the Professor remained unknown and Sparrow dared not visit the Old Cat, Ling or San Li. He had heard that in the middle of a struggle session, the Conservatory's resident conductor, Lu Hongwen, had taken a copy of *Quotations of Chairman Mao* and ripped the book into pieces. A Red Guard had immediately put a pistol to his face and shot him. Since August, ten faculty and eight students had died.

The year 1967 arrived, and the Conservatory remained closed. Still, Sparrow was summoned to a meeting. The meeting turned out to be solely for him. Yu Hui, the new leader of Sparrow's work unit, had taken over He Luting's office and redecorated it with a dozen posters of Mao Zedong and a half dozen of Madame Mao in various costumes. Yu, also a composer, had a long face that reminded Sparrow of asparagus. He seemed to take pleasure in telling Sparrow that he was being reassigned to a factory in the southern suburbs.

"May I ask what kind of factory, Comrade Yu?"

"I believe you will be making wooden crates."

Yu Hui stood up from his desk. His face seemed to grow even longer.

Sparrow felt the eyes of a dozen Chairman Maos examining him. "When will I be transferred?"

"I am preparing your file as we speak. Be patient, we will inform you in due time."

"Will I be allowed to compose again?"

Yu Hui smiled, as if embarrassed on Sparrow's behalf, that he could ask such a naive question. "You know the saying: *The time has come to re-string your bow.*" He laughed at his own joke. "You're not the only one who must reform and start again. But tell me, is it really true you turned down a position at the Central Philharmonic?"

"I was not worthy of the offer."

Yu Hui smiled once more. He fluttered his hand lazily, dismissing him.

Sparrow walked out of the Conservatory and onto Fenyang Road. The intensity of the sun bled the street of colour, so that the bicycles and occasional truck seemed to vanish into the white curtain of the horizon.

At home, Da Shan had arrived unexpectedly from Zhejiang and was seated at the kitchen table, writing denunciations on long sheets of butcher paper. When Sparrow entered, his brother looked up, brush in his hand suspended, before looking down and continuing: *The most fundamental task of the Cultural Revolution is to eliminate the old ideology and culture, which was fostered by the exploiting class for thousands of years. Counter-revolutionaries like Wen the Dreamer will inevitably distort, resist, attack and oppose Mao Zedong thought. They appear to be human beings but are beasts at heart, they speak the human language to your face but behind your back they . . .* Sparrow retreated to the tiny balcony on the second floor. In the lane, a grandmother was washing her grandchild in a metal tub, and the child cooed happily. The sound lifted Sparrow from his thoughts. He still had three cartons of Hatamen cigarettes, sent by Kai from Beijing. The cigarettes, so difficult to obtain, were as valuable as a fistful of ration coupons, perhaps more. He smoked one now, reverently; these Hatamen afforded him the greatest pleasure of his day.

In the kitchen, Ba Lute was rereading Big Mother Knife's most recent letter. *Do you take me for a fool? Tell me what has happened.*

The envelope contained two further letters, addressed to Zhuli from her parents. So they had found Wen, Ba Lute thought. But was a miracle still a miracle if it came too late? He took out his lighter, lit the pages and dropped them into the brazier. "Nine lives, one death," he said, reciting an old saying, watching the paper curl simultaneously away from and into the flames. "Nine lives, one death."

Da Shan set his brush down. The poster was already four feet long. Looking up the staircase, his eyes met Sparrow's, and the boy's face flickered with emotion. Sparrow recognized grief, fear, remorse. The boy was a teenager and aspired to be an architect, but the red scarf of the Young Pioneers was knotted firmly around his neck and ink had roughened his hands. *If you want to be an architect, you should go to Tiananmen Square,* Sparrow thought. *You should see the head, the hands, the feet, the heart, the lungs. You should stand in the middle of the Square and listen.* Zhuli's shadow seemed to twist in the stairwell as if her spirit was tied to his thoughts, and unable to be free.

Da Shan waited for Sparrow to say something. Coming home, he had hoped only that his older brother would help him, that Sparrow would not allow him be sent back to Zhejiang where, to make up for the impure elements within their family, Da Shan had to take the lead in attacking teachers and other classmates. He had to break them down. Flying Bear had said that Zhuli must be guilty because only a criminal would kill herself. Flying Bear had vowed never to go home again.

"Only traitors commit suicide," Da Shan said now, staring up at his brother.

Smoke lifted away from Sparrow's fingers.

"Only the guilty kill themselves. Is that true?"

Silence.

"Is it true?" Da Shan said again. He was infuriated by the softness and the weeping in his voice. "Is it right that she killed herself? If Zhuli was really a traitor, she deserved everything that
happened."

Sparrow came down the steps and Da Shan waited for him to
act, to strike him down at last. It was this terrible quiet, Da Shan
thought, that had come between them and which he had no idea
how to undo.

When they were face to face, Sparrow touched his shoulder.
There was no weight to his brother's hand. "In Zhejiang, make
sure you're worthy of the Red Guards. That's your only family now,
isn't it?"

Da Shan burst into tears. Infuriated, his words came out as
blows. "You're worse than a traitor. Who's protecting you? You did
nothing to save Zhuli, all you cared about was your own career!"

Sparrow dropped his hand. He looked at Da Shan and
thought, You used to be so small that I could throw you over my
shoulder as if you were a sack of beans.

Their father came out of the kitchen. "Enough," Ba Lute
whispered. He was flicking his lighter on and off. "I don't want to
hear your cousin's name. Are you listening to me? It's finished
now. Finished."

Da Shan ignored his father. "You're a true coward, Sparrow.
Maybe Zhuli was a traitor but at least she knew who she was. Do
you really think you're invisible? Do you think no one can see
what you are?" The louder he shouted the angrier he became.
"You were always the most talented one, everyone said so, but
what good is talent if you have nothing inside? They'll come for
you next, I promise. No one can save you. I'll make sure of it."

In a daze, Sparrow turned towards the poster Da Shan had
written. He himself had taught his brother to write his first words
and now he took comfort in the fact that the characters were

flimsy, crooked and nearly unreadable. He turned and walked out of the room, through the front gate and into the laneway.

"My brother, the degenerate!" Da Shan had followed him to the laneway and was shouting after him. Watchful faces floated in the windows above, assessing, judging. "Have you no shame?"

Sparrow went in the direction of Beijing Road. He had neglected to take his coat and the wind cut through him. It was a chill wind, out of keeping with the season. Loudspeakers blared, speaking faster and faster. Terrified, his thoughts took on a dreamlike quality so that every face that he passed looked familiar: a friend, a student he had taught, a child he had known. The loudspeaker repeated its slogans, *Long live Chairman Mao!*

"Ten thousand years," Sparrow said. In truth, he wanted to believe. He would not feel so utterly alone if only he could give in and place his trust in a person or just an idea.

Long live our glorious Revolution! Long live the People!

Ten thousand years.

Our generation will achieve immortality!

At the Shaanxi Road intersection, children were throwing bricks at a store that sold women's clothing. Sparrow leaned down and impulsively took up a brick. In his hand, it seemed entirely pure, the weight of a newborn infant. The children were singing a familiar nursery rhyme. "The grass in the meadow looks fresh and green! But wait ten days, not a blade will be seen!"

The loudspeakers rattled on, "There is no middle road."

Paint on the walls denounced the occupant as a dissolute and immoral young woman. Lust and desire, which placed private interest over the public good, was a bourgeois luxury and a political crime. A boy swung his arm back. The brick shattered a window on the second floor. Inside the building, a girl was crying. He did not know what room the weeping was coming from. *The degeneracy of your head, your heart, your hands, feet, lungs.* Everything was finished. He thought the voice cried out, "I would have loved you for ten thousand years."

He stood with the brick in his hands until the boy took it

from him. Forcefully, the boy launched it into the air, he sent it crashing through the target's door.

Shanghai Wooden Products Factory No. 1 smelled of the earth. Each morning on waking, Sparrow shook wood dust from his pillow and his hair. In the public bath house, dust from his body turned the water orange. He hardly recognized himself, his arms and chest had thickened, reshaped by hours of stacking, lifting and hammering. Yet for the first time Sparrow could remember, his hands were immune to pain; callused, they had grown a thickened coat, a brand new shell. After his shifts, the factory fell away like an extended dream, but when he slept he still heard the factory's disjointed percussion–thumping, crashing and syncopated drumming, dotted with sirens, buzzers and bells–not so different from the musique concrète of Varèse's *Amériques*. He couldn't stop hearing this music of the everyday, and its continuity threaded together his former life and his present.

One morning, when he had been at the factory for more than a year, Sparrow's work unit was summoned to the meeting hall. Attendance was mandatory and so, long after the room was full, workers continued to squeeze themselves in.

Six televisions had been set up. Abruptly, a live broadcast began, the first televised struggle session of the Cultural Revolution. An elderly man was dragged onto centre stage by a phalanx of Red Guards. To his shock, the Red Guards were known to him; they were former Conservatory musicians who had risen to leadership positions. The stage, white with klieg lights, seemed to shear the television screen in half. Sparrow watched, frozen. Kai stood among a group at the front. He looked sturdier, more self-possessed. At first, Sparrow did not recognize the elderly man, whose head the Red Guards were forcing down so brutally his face could not be seen. A slow pandemonium unfolded. When the elderly man looked up, Sparrow saw that it was He Luting, former President of the Shanghai Conservatory.

Kill the traitor! Kill the traitor! The chanting in the meeting hall was deafening. Unable to turn or move, he felt as if the lights were being trained on him, growing brighter every moment.

Questioning began. It went on and on but He Luting stubbornly denied his guilt.

Yu Hui stepped forward, dressed entirely in olive green as if he had joined the army or a vegetable stand. "Are you so stupid you don't understand that you could be killed?" he asked. "Do you think we'll grieve if one more traitor has his head cut off?"

Knock him down!

"Before I die," He Luting said, "I have two wishes. First, I want to finish my current composition, a seven-part orchestral work. Second, I intend to clear each and every charge against me."

Unable to respond, the Red Guards took turns striking him.

"I am not guilty," He Luting cried. He looked frail, much older than his age. Another blow from the Red Guards would surely cripple him. He Luting's wife, children and grandchildren had been gathered on the stage behind him, their heads also pushed down, light reflecting off their hair. Words that He Luting had spoken to him, years ago now, returned to Sparrow. "Music that is immediately understood will not outlast its generation."

"You opposed Chairman Mao!" Yu said.

"I am not guilty."

"Disgusting traitor! You're nothing but an animal we have to slaughter–"

"Your accusations are false! Shame on you for lying!"

Around Sparrow, in the hall, people stared, bewildered at He Luting's temerity, his stubbornness.

On screen, the Red Guards, too, could not believe that this old man, this traitor and counter-revolutionary, this ridiculous musician, could possibly be challenging them. One yanked the microphone away.

He Luting reacted quickly, grabbing the microphone back.

"Shame on you!" His voice broke, but he kept going. "Shame on you for lying! Shame on you for lying!"

In an instant, they had twisted his arms so viciously that he fell to the floor. The jeering of the crowd intensified. He Luting was in terrible pain. Kai's face blurred into the screen and out. Amidst the shouted laughter, the Red Guards released him. Sparrow could see that they, too, wanted to laugh, to swell themselves up again, but He Luting was suddenly on his feet.

"Shame!" he shouted. The words ricocheted through the speakers. "Shame on you, shame on you!"

The room was shocked silent.

"Shame on you for lying!" His voice was hoarse and broken but still it cut through, by far the loudest sound emanating from the television. *"Shame!"*

The image disappeared.

Sparrow waited. The room seemed to tilt away from him, but he was held upright by the pressure of the bodies around him. The live broadcast did not resume. A newsreader appeared on the screen, but the transmission split into grey lines of static.

A buzzer sounded and and the workers returned, orderly and subdued, to their positions on the assembly line.

Punching in, Sparrow looked at the card reader and was surprised to realize that he had missed his birthday. Yesterday he had turned twenty-eight years old.

Eight months later, Chairman Mao decreed that cities were wasteful and the educated must be sent "up to the mountains and down to the villages" to experience rural poverty. All universities and middle schools still open would now be closed, all classes not yet cancelled were officially over. This new generation would be the heroic zhī qī, the sent-down youth. In early 1969, Sparrow was summoned by his work unit leader who informed him that, effective immediately, he was assigned to a factory 1,400 kilometres to the south, in Guangxi Province.

"Have you been been to the South before?" the cadre asked him.

"I have not."

"You should thank the Party. They have given you this opportunity to faithfully serve the People."

"I thank the Party and our Great Helmsman, Chairman Mao."

This time he was not so naive as to ask if he would be allowed to compose once more.

Three days later, at the Shanghai Railway Station, hemmed in by a sea of young people, he heard a woman's voice shouting his name. It was Ling.

The kindness of her expression and her obvious pleasure at seeing him surprised Sparrow, eliciting an unfamiliar pain; he had been alone for a long time.

"Tell me where you've been, Sparrow. Have you been in contact with anyone?"

His first instinct was to hide the truth. "Nowhere. No one."

"Kai's in Beijing now, did you know? He intervened and made sure we were both assigned to the South, and not to the coal mines at the Russian border." Her voice dropped. "He's done well, he performs regularly for Madame Mao." When Sparrow didn't answer, she continued. "Kai asked me to look for you. He said you might take a position with the Central Philharmonic . . ."

"But I don't write music anymore."

Ling studied him. She looked at him with a familiar intimacy, as if they were still the same people, as if nothing stood between their present and their past. "I was a month away from receiving my doctorate," she whispered. "And then the announcement came, the university was shut down and it was over. Why aren't you writing music? Listen, I still remember . . ." She hummed in his ear, so low that no one else could possibly overhear, a phrase from Bach's *Concerto for Two Violins*, and he wanted to put his hand to her lips, to quiet and protect her.

The day before, Sparrow had posted three hastily written letters: one to Big Mother Knife who was stuck in Yumen City and had not yet been granted a transfer back to Shanghai; one to Ba Lute, who was interned at a camp in Anhui Province; and one to Kai in Beijing. That night, enforcers from the Shanghai revolutionary committee had surprised the neighbourhood. They had pulled everyone from their rooms and ordered a renewed search for counter-revolutionary materials. Numbly, he had fed his books and music into the bonfires, even the three records, given to him by Wen the Dreamer twenty years ago. Sparrow had even burned the papers he had hidden up in the trusses of the roof. His beautiful Symphony No. 2, the still unfinished No. 3–they went into the flames. Nothing remained. He had watched, mesmerized, overcome by a sickening relief, as the albums and the papers, the music and the imagined music, twisted together into a kind of gelatinous mud.

All Sparrow carried in his rucksack was a light jacket, two changes of clothing, a washcloth, a sleeping mat, a cooking pot and, because he had promised Zhuli, the Book of Records.

"Have you had any news of the Professor?" he asked Ling.

She shook her head. "Even my aunt doesn't know. He was detained and disappeared. And Kai cut all ties with him . . . You heard what happened to San Li?"

A train was hurtling into the station. "Yes," he said. San Li had died, jumped from a window or was pushed. And then, more to himself than to her, "But since no one is responsible, there is no one to forgive."

She spoke directly in his ear. "There is no point in forgiveness. We need to prosper."

He could not imagine what she could possibly mean by the word prosper.

"Kai said we're being sent to a place called Cold Water Ditch," Ling said. "The closest town is Hezhou. I'd never heard of it before."

"Cold Water Ditch," he answered, wishing to make her smile. "The height of prosperity."

"Comrade Sparrow, how would you define prosperity? I believe there is no prosperity but freedom."

The doors of the train cranked open. People crushed forward. Ling gripped his arm so that, in the melee, they would not be separated.

The further they travelled from Shanghai, the more he felt as if he was breaking apart. At each station he whispered, as the older generation might have done, to the ghost of his cousin, "Don't leave, Zhuli. We have no family in the city anymore. Stay with me."

"She's here, Sparrow," Ling said. "Zhuli won't leave us."

So that when they arrived, after many days' journey, in Cold Water Ditch, it was as if Zhuli, in some invisible way, had reattached herself to Sparrow's life, to his consciousness and his being. A year later, he and Ling received permission to marry. And a year after that, they had their first and only child, a daughter, Ai-ming.

In the spring of 1970, Big Mother Knife finally returned to the laneway house on Beijing Road. There, she found her entire family missing. Even Mr. and Mrs. Ma were gone; their oleanders had grown wild, blanketing both wings of the house. She smashed all the crockery. She did it carefully, disposing of her favourites immediately, all the while singing: "Comrades, amputate the branches and tear down the leaves. . . ." Her neighbours thought she had lost her mind and backed into their doorways when they saw her coming. By the end, as she was smashing an insipid vase Ba Lute had once given her, despair overwhelmed her. When she crushed it under her shoe, the smallest pieces reminded her of little teeth.

"Make revolution," she thought bitterly. "I will make the biggest revolution of them all."

In the bedroom, she found a dress of Zhuli's and one of Ba Lute's straw shoes, and she sat down with them, uncomprehending. All the musical instruments and scores were gone. That night, she took the train west to destitute Anhui Province, where Ba Lute had been consigned to a re-education camp. It took three days to reach him and, when she finally did, they wept and argued and fought nonsensically. Ba Lute could not even speak Zhuli's name; for the last four years he had kept Zhuli's suicide from her, going so far as to make up stories about her whereabouts and her accomplishments: *At this juncture, it is not advised for Zhuli to write to you. She has been offered the opportunity to study in Paris.* Big Mother spat the words back at him. Now Ba Lute told her that he had personally written a letter to Chairman Mao, who could not possibly know all that was being done in his name. Society was in disarray.

"You wrote to Chairman Mao? You ridiculous oaf of a man."

"Our own sons denounced me," Ba Lute said, broken. "Da Shan and Flying Bear say they want nothing to do with us. But I have faith that Chairman Mao, our Great Leader, our Saving Star, will redeem us."

It was, and would always be, the only thing he ever said that made her weep. "How can he redeem us? Can he turn back time? Can he give a child back her life? You didn't even have the courage to give her a proper burial!"

"Big Mother, it was impossible. Don't you understand? It was the transformation of the world."

"That poor child," she said, turning away.

For days and then months, she thought only of Zhuli. Swirl and Wen the Dreamer had left Mongolia and crossed into Kyrgyzstan where they awaited word from their daughter, but Big Mother could not imagine telling them that she was dead and had been dead since 1966, that she had taken her own life. How could Swirl accept it? Her sister had already lost one child, the little boy who fell from the tram so long ago. Disbelief would push Swirl to come home, she would return to Shanghai at the cost of her life. If Swirl was rearrested . . . Big Mother could not finish the thought. She could not do it.

Back in Shanghai, Big Mother put in a request to be transferred to Sparrow's town, Cold Water Ditch. Finally, after a year of badgering her superiors, deploying gifts, reciting Chairman Mao's most obscure poetry, and confusing everyone with both intimidation and deference, her request was granted. Travel permit and registration papers in hand, she left Shanghai by train. A premonition told her she would never see the city again: by the time the wheel of history tumbled forward and this country awoke once more, she would be stone blind. Annoyed, she glared into the overloaded compartment and cursed every blurry face, every hand, every belly, every cadre, every little Red brat. And then, feeling guilty, she closed her eyes and cursed herself.

The decrepit train hobbled on, into the humid South. Some little turd had drawn a lopsided egg on the dusty window, or maybe the egg was a zero left behind by someone with bad handwriting. What was a zero anyway? A zero signified nothing, all it did was tell you nothing about nothing. Still, wasn't zero also something meaningful, a number in and of itself? In jianpu notation, zero indicated a caesura, a pause or rest of indeterminate length. Did time that went uncounted, unrecorded, still qualify as time? If zero was both everything and nothing, did an empty life have exactly the same weight as a full life? Was zero like the desert, both finite and infinite? Thanks to the painful slowness of the train, she had another fifty hours to think this over. Big Mother sighed and slapped her knee so violently she grunted in pain. None of the other passengers cared. "This silly melon of a train!" she shouted. "It stops at every clump of bushes! By the time we get there you kids will be grandparents and I'll be dead! We're going so slowly we might as well be going backwards!" A murmur of agreement slid down the length of the compartment, easeful and reassuring as the midnight breeze.

PART ZERO

Music which is so dear to me, and without which, more than likely, I couldn't live a day.

—DMITRI SHOSTAKOVICH

You may say that that is not love, and I would laugh at you for presuming to know what another's love isn't and what his love is.

—ZIA HAIDER RAHMAN, *In the Light of What We Know*

WHEN JIANG KAI, MY FATHER, left China in 1978, one of his suitcases was filled with more than fifty battered notebooks. The notebooks contained drafts of self-criticisms whose final pages must have been submitted, years earlier, to a superior or an authority figure. Self-criticism, samokritika in Russian, 检讨 (jiǎn tǎo) in Chinese, required that the person confess his or her mistakes, repeat the correct thinking of the Party and acknowledge the authority of the Party over him or her. Confession, according to the Party, was "a form of repentance that would bring the individual back into the collective." Only through genuine contrition and self-criticism could a person who had fallen from grace earn rehabilitation and the hope of "resurrection," of being returned to life.

I arrived in Shanghai on June 1, 2016. From my hotel room, I looked down at a city wreathed in mist. Skyscrapers and condominiums shouldered together in every direction, erasing even the horizon.

How the city mesmerized me. Shanghai seemed, like a library or even a single book, to hold a universe within itself. My father had arrived here in the late 1950s, a child of the countryside, in the wake of the Great Leap Forward and a man-made famine that took the lives of 36 million people, perhaps more. He had perfected his music, dreamed of both a wider world and a better one, and fallen in love. Day after day, Kai had bent over his desk, feverishly writing and copying pages, revising and reimagining his life and his moral code. We were not unalike, my father and I; we wanted to keep a record. We imagined there were truths waiting for us–about ourselves and those we loved, about the times we lived in–within our reach, if only we had the eyes to see them.

Summer fog slowly erased Shanghai from view. I stepped away from the window. I showered, changed and went down to the subway.

Underground, people gazed at screens or tapped at phones, but many drifted, as I did, through their thoughts. Near me, an old woman discreetly savoured cake, phones chimed and honked, a mother and daughter repeated the multiplication table and a child refused to disembark.

Unexpectedly, the train braked. The old woman stumbled, her cake went flying, and she fell into my lap.

For a moment, she was suspended in my arms, our faces inches from one another. A big whoop went up from people around us, followed by jovial applause. A child reprimanded her for eating on the train, another wanted to know what kind of cake it was. The woman laughed, the sound so unexpected, I nearly dropped her. She was in her late sixties, around the same age Ma would be now. In my imperfect Mandarin, I tried to give her my seat, but the woman waved me off as if I had offered her a ticket to the moon.

"Save yourself, child." She said something else, words which sounded like, "Enough crumbs, no? Enough."

"Yes," I said. "Enough."

She smiled. The subway hurried on.

I could feel my jet lag now; the world around me seemed far away as if I was carried in a jar of water. A man opened a newspaper so wide, it covered his wife and daughter. Behind them, in the windows, their reflections shifted, one behind the other.

In his self-criticisms, my father wrote of his love of music and the fear that he "could not overcome a desire for personal happiness." He denounced Zhuli, gave up Sparrow and cut all ties to the Professor, his only family. He wrote of how he had stood by help-lessly while first his mother, then his young sisters, and finally his father died; he said he owed his family everything, and had a duty to life. For years, Ba tried to abandon music. When I first read his self-criticisms, I glimpsed my father through the many selves he had tried to be; selves abandoned and reinvented, selves that wanted to vanish but couldn't. That's how I see him, sometimes, when my anger—on behalf of Ma, Zhuli, myself—subsides and turns to pity. He knew that leaving these self-criticisms behind would endanger others, yet to destroy them was impossible, so he carried them first to Hong Kong and then to Canada. Even here, he would begin new notebooks, denouncing himself and his desires, yet he could not find a way to reinvent himself or change.

Last week, preparing for this trip, I came across a detail: in 1949, Tiananmen Square retained its place as the centre of politi-cal power in China by reason of analytic geometry.

An architect, Chen Gang, posited the Square as the "zero point." He quoted Friedrich Engels: "Zero is a definite point from which measurements are taken along a line, in one direc-tion positively, in the other negatively. Hence the zero point is the location on which all others are dependent, to which they are all related, and by which they are all determined. Wherever we come upon zero, it represents something very definite: the limit. Thus it has greater significance than all the real magnitudes by which it is bounded."

That summer of 1966, the year Zhuli died, was the zero point for my father. Like hundreds of thousands of others, he went to Tiananmen Square to pledge his loyalty to Chairman Mao and commit himself to fānshēn: literally, to turn over one's body, to liberate oneself. Decades later, he watched on television as three university students stood before the Great Hall of the People bearing a letter to the government. It was April 22, 1989. The three lifted their arms, raised the petition high and fell to their knees, as if seeking clemency. Behind them in Tiananmen Square, more than 200,000 university students reacted in shock and then grief.

Why are you kneeling?

Stand up, stand up!

This is the People's square! Why must we address the government from our knees?

How can you kneel in our name? How?

The students, who came from every political and economic background, were distraught. But the three stayed where they were, tiny figures, the petition heavy in the air, waiting for an authority figure to receive it. Ten, twenty, thirty minutes passed, and they remained on their knees. Behind them, agitation grew. When Chinese leaders failed to respond, the Tiananmen demonstrations began in earnest.

I exited the subway at Tiantong Road, emerging at an intersection where condominiums, half-constructed, opened like giant staircases to the sky. I had been to this quarter before: Hongkou is where Swirl and Big Mother Knife grew up before the war, and it is where Liu Feng, a violinist once known as Tofu Liu, now lives.

At different times, Hongkou has been a clothing district, the

American-Japanese concession, and, during the rise of Hitler and the Second World War, the Shanghai Ghetto. In the 1930s, the Shanghai port could be legally entered without passport or visa; some forty thousand Jewish and other refugees from Germany, Austria, Russia, Iraq, India, Lithuania, Poland, the Ukraine and elsewhere arrived here, bringing not only their languages and traumas, but also their music.

I continued south, past a sidewalk argument, around three men, their bodies fully stretched out on their motorbikes, playing cards.

At Suzhou Creek, I reached the Embankment Building. Up on the tenth floor, Mr. Liu was waiting for me. I had contacted him on WeChat and, at first, when I said I was the daughter of Jiang Kai, he had been wary. But when I told him I was looking for Ai-ming, the daughter of Sparrow, he transformed entirely. Now, the first time we were meeting in person, he greeted me as if he had known me all my life. "Ma-li!" he said. "Come in, come in! Have you eaten? My daughter picked up these sugar pyramids. . . ."

Books, sheet music, compact discs, cassettes and records occupied every inch of space. After a thirty-year teaching career at the Shanghai Conservatory, he had retired last month and moved his office home. "Don't trip," he said. "I don't have insurance."

We went sideways through the kitchen and into the living room. Across the river, Shanghai's dramatic skyscrapers floated, surreal. We were a world away, but only a single generation, from the city my father had known.

Mr. Liu told me that, since the 1990s, he had watched this skyline come into existence. "When my daughter was born, none of these buildings were even a scribble on paper. These three," he said, pointing out the tallest ones, "were meant to symbolize the past, present and future. But the government's words were very boring. Instead, people call them the 'three-piece kitchen set.' You see? There's the bottle opener. The whisk. And . . . what would you say in English? A turkey baster."

I laughed. "I think the whisk is the most beautiful, Mr. Liu."
It was a cylindrical spiral like a ribbon in motion.

"I agree. But Shanghai still looks like a tool belt. By the way, don't be so formal! Please call me Tofu Liu. That's what everyone calls me, even my grandkids."

Before us, the lights of the buildings began to glow.

Tofu Liu turned his back on the city. We sat down at a little table where someone had been sorting pencil crayons. He told me that he had entered the Shanghai Conservatory the same year as Zhuli. "We both studied under the same violin teacher, Tan Hong. My father was a convicted rightist, a counter-revolutionary, just like Zhuli's father. I was a little in love with her, even while I envied her talent." During the Cultural Revolution, the Conservatory had closed. "Not one piano survived. Not one." He himself was sent to a camp in Heilongjiang Province, in the frozen borderlands of the Northeast. "We had to wear either blue, grey or black. Our hair had to be short. We had to wear the same kind of cap. That was only the beginning. The wind was glacial. We were beside a river, and on the other side of the river was Russia. We worked in coal mines. We had no skills in this work and almost every week, someone was seriously injured or killed. The Party replaced them. The only books available to us were the writings of Chairman Mao. We had daily self-criticism and denunciation sessions. This went on for six years."

In 1977, when the Cultural Revolution ended, Liu ran away from the camp and returned to Shanghai, where he sought out his former teacher, Tan Hong.

"We talked about Zhuli for a long time and about others we had known. Then Professor Tan asked me, 'Tofu Liu, do you wish to come back to the Conservatory and complete your studies?'

"I said I did.

"'After everything that's happened, why?'

"His question devastated me. How could I pretend that music was salvation? How could I commit myself to something so powerless? I had been a miner for six years, there was coal dust in my lungs, I'd broken all the fingers of my right hand, how could I possibly hold a violin? I told him, 'I don't know.' But he kept pushing me for an answer. It wasn't enough for him to hear that I loved music, that it had comforted me all this time, and I had promised myself that if I survived, I would devote my life to it. There were thousands of applicants for a handful of spots at the Conservatory. They all loved music as much as I did. Finally I told him the truth. I said, 'Because music is nothing. It is nothing and yet it belongs to me. Despite everything that's happened, it's myself that I believe in.'

"Tan Hong shook my hand. He said, 'Young Liu, welcome back to the Conservatory. Welcome home.'"

Tofu Liu showed me his mementos. These included a photo of Zhuli performing with the Conservatory's string quartet when she was nine years old and a wire recording of Zhuli and Kai playing Smetana's "From My Homeland," which Liu had kept hidden until the end of the Cultural Revolution.

"But, Mr. Liu, how could you possibly hide these things?"

He shrugged, smiling. "Before I was sent to the Russian border, I cut a small hole in the parquet floor of my bedroom in Shanghai. You know how hard parquet is! All I had was a kitchen knife. It took me two terrible weeks. I was convinced that Red Guards would burst into the room and that would be the end of me. I buried a dozen wire recordings, some photos and scores, and my violin. Ten years later, when I pulled it up, there was a nest of mice inside the violin . . . But look at this wire." He lifted the spool and showed it to me. It was pristine. "Would you like to hear it?"

I nodded, unable to speak.

Delicately, he loaded the spool into an antique wire recorder. When it was ready, he turned a knob.

The notes came to me. I half turned away.

I thought I saw curtains shift and Ba looking down at me from a window above. On the ninth floor, he leaned out. Did anyone else see him? Was it only me? My father had blindfolded himself, he had tied a piece of cloth over his face before he took his life. I had learned this only after obtaining copies of the Hong Kong police files, and the detail had broken me.

This was the first time I had ever heard Ba playing the piano. Jiang Kai seemed a stranger to me, someone who had always been more alive, more full of memory, than I could know. And yet, hearing Zhuli's violin, her measured, open voice, why did I feel as if I had known her all my life?

We listened to the recording three, four, five times. Each time I heard something different, a separation and a unity, the musicians, dust, the machine, our breathing. Music. Each time, at the end, I heard my father's voice, speaking. I had not heard it since I was ten years old. His voice like no other voice that had ever lived.

I wept. Seeing that I was upset, Mr. Liu brought me a cup of tea. "It's difficult to understand," he said. "The pressure on us was unimaginable. Don't forget, back then, your father was only seventeen years old. . . . we were all too young."

We returned to the table. I showed him my copy of Chapter 17 of the Book of Records.

"Teacher Liu," I said, "I've made tens of thousands of copies of all the notebooks. With a few keystrokes, it's possible to send files anywhere in the world, instantaneously. I want it to exist everywhere, to keep growing and changing." From my bag, I took out Sparrow's composition, *The Sun Shines on the People's Square*. "This is the piece of music I mentioned to you. It seems only right to perform it here in Shanghai. To record it. But . . . I really wonder at my sanity."

Liu took the pages. Slowly he read through them.

I watched the curtains move and the wind alter; Ba and Ma had left this world, yet I was here in Shanghai. I still breathed and changed and dreamed.

After a long time, Liu looked up from the score. "Ma-li," he said, "I'm sure you know that, without obsession, there is no life's work. But where does this attentiveness come from? Have you asked yourself? Surely it's what we each carry, in greater and greater quantity as we age, remembrance." He used the word jì yì, which has two meanings: 记忆 (to recall, record) and 技艺 (art). He was silent for a moment, looking down at the pages. "The music reminds me of something Zhuli said when we were rehearsing Prokofiev. She said the music made her wonder, Does it alter us more to be heard, or to hear? Is it better to have been loved, or to love? Of all his compositions, this is Teacher Sparrow's most extraordinary."

He opened his violin case and lifted the instrument out. A phrase filled the room, it seemed to move both backwards and forwards, as if Sparrow wished to rewrite time itself. Note by note, I felt as if I was being reconfigured.

When Teacher Liu set the violin down, he asked me, "Do you play the piano?"

"I never learned."

"Then I'll arrange everything. Teacher Sparrow meant for this music to be heard here."

"Thank you, Professor."

Before I left, I showed him a photograph of Ai-ming.

"Why, it's Zhuli isn't it?" he said in surprise, staring at the image. "It must be. No? It's Teacher Sparrow's daughter? Ai-ming. Ah, well. How remarkable. She has the very same face as Miss Zhuli."

Tofu Liu gave me the recording to keep and I gave him a copy of Sparrow's music. I remembered, then, something that Ai-ming had said. *I assumed that when the story finished, life would continue and I would go back to being myself. But it wasn't true. The stories got longer and longer, and I got smaller and smaller. When I told Big Mother this, she laughed her head off. "But that's how the world is, isn't it?"*

S PARROW WAS PEDALLING SLOWLY home from Huizhou Wooden Crate Factory, pushed forward by a steady breeze. It was late August, just after rainfall. Along the road, loudspeakers announced a special program: "Tonight in Beijing, the Philadelphia Orchestra, under Eugene Ormandy, will perform for Madame Mao. This is their third concert in the city, one of a total of six performances in China."

The newsreader had said the date, September 14, 1973.

But it was 1976. The concert had been almost three years before.

Others, too, were staring up at the loudspeakers, just as baffled. It had been nearly a decade since the radio had broadcast any music besides the eighteen approved revolutionary operas. Now, music exploded above them, the feverish opening crescendo of Respighi's *Pines of Rome*. Sparrow coasted to a stop, bewildered by its detail, the cheerful, almost absurd piano and the tinkling brass.

By the time he reached home, the second half of the program had begun. His daughter ran out to meet him. "It's a new work by Madame Mao!"

Sparrow smiled, despite himself. "No, Ai-ming. This is Beethoven and it comes from another century." This is a fragment, he thought, of something that once existed but that no longer grows here, like a field cut down.

He went inside. The Sixth Symphony, Beethoven's *Pastoral*, trotted gaily through the rooms. Even Big Mother was lost in thought. He thought the walls were creeping nearer to him, they brushed his arms and scraped the back of his neck. You could close a book and forget about it, knowing it would not lose its contents when you stopped reading, but music wasn't the same, not for him, it was most alive when it was heard. Year after year, he had wanted to play and replay it, to take it apart into its component pieces and build it once more. And then, finally, after six years, after seven, and then a decade, his memory had gone quiet. Without trying, he had stopped remembering. But this broadcast, what was it? Were they hearing the future or was it only the final outburst of the past? Long ago, He Luting had shouted, "Shame, shame. You should be ashamed," and Zhuli said, "I will make Prokofiev himself proud." If the concert truly took place in Beijing, Kai must have attended. A sound inside a sound. But what if all of this was only in his mind?

The applause that came was so fierce, he feared the radio might topple over. Violent catapults of applause, rhythmic, sustained.

From the opposite side of the room, Big Mother said, "What bloody change is coming now?"

The music was nothing more than a broadcast, a simple program, but he turned and saw exultation on his daughter's face. Little Ai-ming had pressed her forehead up against the radio, his daughter was overjoyed, she had been transported, she looked as if all her nerves were alight. She looked like Zhuli. For a moment he had no idea where he was. He wanted to pull her back, to take the machine away and bury it noiselessly in the ground. Trembling with cold, he walked across the room and switched the radio off.

Because her father was so quiet, Ai-ming had, from an early age, turned to Big Mother Knife; her grandmother was her confidante, her teacher and also her pillow. No one in this life cared about her as Big Mother did, and so she took great pleasure in climbing over her, sleeping on her and fluffing Big Mother's curls. Ling, her actual mother, had been reassigned to Shanghai nearly five years ago, and only visited once each year, during Spring Festival. Her father, Sparrow, was the Bird of Quiet.

"Don't be fooled," Big Mother once told her. "He's not moving, as usual, and he's not thinking either, sadly. Your father is empty as a walnut shell." She had leaned close and whispered in Ai-ming's ear: "The world is like a banana, easily bruised. Now is the time to watch and observe, not to judge. Ai-ming, believing everything in books is worse than having no books at all."

For weeks after, Ai-ming wondered about these words. On the August night when the Philadelphia Orchestra performance was broadcast, she had spied on her father as he listened to this Beethoven, and she observed how, for at least a year afterwards, the radio returned to its usual music, playing only *Shajiabang* and *Taking Tiger Mountain by Strategy*. Once, though, there had been a broadcast of Albanian music, and it had made Sparrow stop what he was doing and turn towards the radio, as if it were an intruder. In school, as the daughter of a class enemy she was forbidden to join the Young Pioneers, among other injustices. This was a new word for her, injustice, and she liked to roll it on her tongue for the shock of it. In school, they recited essays about what made a good revolutionary. She began to wonder what made a good father, a good grandmother, a good enemy, a good person. Are you a good person, she thought, looking at her teacher, or are you a good revolutionary? Are you a good revolutionary, she thought, looking at Big Mother Knife, or are you a good grandmother? Was it even possible to be both?

The game intrigued her. How pleasurable it was to bury words inside the soil of her thoughts. She imitated her father's expression, a studied emptiness. But sometimes his expression failed him. Sometimes Sparrow looked at her with so much anxiety, she felt her hair stand on end. Ba, she thought, are you a good person or a good worker? Is Chairman Mao a good person or a good leader?

One morning, Big Mother unlocked the battered suitcase that was used primarily as their dining table. Inside the trunk was a single straw shoe, a pretty blue dress, a sheaf of music in jianpu notation, and a cardboard box full of notebooks. Her first observation was that the books were grubby.

"Your mouth is hanging open," Big Mother said.

Her grandmother fanned the notebooks out, removed three and told Ai-ming to close the suitcase. When it was latched and locked, Big Mother set the notebooks down and opened the first one: the pages looked even older than her grandmother. Big Mother's face swooped down as if to taste the paper. From this position, she turned her head and looked at Ai-ming. "This," she whispered gruffly, "is what excellent calligraphy looks like."

Ai-ming went in for a closer look. The characters seemed to hover just above the paper, like ink over water. They had the pristine cleanliness of winter flowers.

"Waaa! Isn't it strong?" Big Mother said.

Delight squeezed Ai-ming's heart. "*Waaa!*" she whispered.

Big Mother straightened, grunting her approval. "Of course, the calligraphy is not as robust as Chairman Mao's but still, it's pretty good. Refined yet with a depth of movement. Maybe . . . you want to read some to me. Chapter 1, but no more. You're still far too young."

It was early morning. Her father was at the factory which, last year had been reborn. Now it was Huizhou Semiconductor Factory No. 1, and he had gone from building wooden crates to making radios. The Bird of Quiet could assemble the new Red Lamp 711 shortwave radio in the shake of a feather.

Outside, loudspeakers were chiding the world. Rain fell in continuous sheets, beating the tin roof like a regiment of horses, so they hid under the blankets. The many wrinkles on Big

Mother's face reminded Ai-ming of the dry, patient earth in February, thirsty for spring.

How can you ignore this sharp awl that pierces your heart? If you yearn for things outside yourself, you will never obtain what you are seeking.

And so the novel of Da-wei and May Fourth began once more.

It pleased Big Mother Knife that Ai-ming did not appear to notice the transition from the original Book of Records to the new chapters written by Wen the Dreamer. Unable to recover the rest of the book, he had simply continued on from Chapter 31. He, like the character of May Fourth, would spend the greater part of his life in the deserts of Gansu, Xinjiang and Kyrgyzstan, where, they said, more than three hundred ancient settlements lay beneath the sand. Their traces–documents on wood and paper, silks and household objects–had endured, preserved by the dry air. In the new chapters, Wen continued the old code, hiding their where-abouts inside the names of characters. Sometimes the code was descriptive: wěi 暐 (the bright shining of the sun), wēi 溦 (a fine rain), or wēi 潿 (a cove, or a bend in the hills). Sometimes heart-breaking: wèi 未 (not) or wéi 潷 (to flow backwards).

Throughout her childhood, little Ai-ming asked for Chapter 23 to be reread so many times, the words must have shown up in her dreams. What the child pictured, or how she made sense of it, Big Mother could not say. "This literary resurrection of yours," she wrote to Wen the Dreamer, "has won another admirer." She meant Ai-ming but Wen the Dreamer imagined Zhuli, now grown. It was 1976, and Zhuli would have been twenty-five years old. Big Mother had begun letter after letter, telling Swirl that her daughter was gone, but she did not have the courage to send a single one. In September of that year, she wrote that Zhuli had received permis-sion to study at the Paris Conservatory: their beloved child had crossed over into the West. Big Mother half believed her own letters. It was the first time since the start of the Great Proletarian Cultural Revolution that such a lie was even remotely credible. My beloved

Swirl, she thought, I fear you will never forgive me. She sealed the letter and entrusted it to their messenger, Projectionist Bang, who travelled the hinterlands showing movies in the villages, and was a trusted confidant of Wen the Dreamer.

That same September, the end of the beginning came.

In the morning, loudspeakers cried out the same turbulent song: "The Esteemed and Great Leader of our Party, our army and the People, Comrade Mao Zedong, leader of the international proletariat, has died. . . ." Big Mother walked the shrouded streets. She stood before the newspaper boards and squinted at the text. Squinting made no difference; these were yesterday's papers. She thought of her sister and Wen, of her lost boys and Ba Lute, the unwritten music, the desperate lives, the bitter untruths they had told themselves and passed on to their children. How every day of Sparrow's factory life was filled with humiliations. Party cadres withheld his rations, demanded self-criticisms, scorned the way he held his head, his pencil, his hands, his silence. And her son had no choice but to accept it all. He let them pour all their words into him as if the life inside him had burned away, as if his own two hands had knotted the rope around Zhuli. Yet Big Mother thought she understood. In this country, rage had no place to exist except deep inside, turned against oneself. This is what had become of her son, he had used his anger to tear himself apart.

Yes, how simple a thing it was to weep, she thought, gazing out at the frenzy of grief and uncertainty around her. She tried not to think of Da Shan and Flying Bear, of Zhuli, of all the names that would disappear completely, relegated to history so as not to disturb the living. White paper flowers, the traditional symbol of mourning, inundated every tree. She wept with rage and helplessness at all the crimes for which the death of an old, treacherous man could never answer.

Ai-ming was six years old and had never seen a foreigner before, but she thought the tall Chinese man with the shiny shoes and the pristine shirt with buttons must be from another province, if not from another age, perhaps the future. He had wavy hair, immaculate eyebrows, round eyes, a clean-shaven face and in his pocket, bright as sunlight, a golden pen. She had not known, initially, that there was a stranger in the house. When the music began to play, she had turned, as if in a dream, and rushed towards it. Looking through the open door was like peering into a cave. They were facing her, New Shirt and her father, but they were so busy looking at something, that she snuck inside and melted against the wall. If her father didn't know she was there, how could he make her go away?

As her eyes grew accustomed to the darkness, the two men sharpened. New Shirt was clearly listening to the music, but Ba looked all chewed up. His elbows and knees contorted, he was folded up as if to protect his hands. Music held them within its downpour. Ai-ming squeezed her eyes shut and popped them open again. No, they were still there. Her father stared at nothing. The music, a joyful dance, made her think of the poem "Famous pieces and grand words," and of the carcasses of dead radios Sparrow sometimes carried home, tinkering with them in his spare time. Now the music coiled into another feeling, it seemed to start all over again but suddenly it ended. New Shirt reached out to a square box that had a big whisker. He lifted a circle from the square, so shiny black it was almost blue, and he turned the circle upside down. He flicked a switch and pushed the whisker down. Her father said, "No, it's enough. Don't play the second side."

Another switch was turned. Ai-ming felt as if the remains of the music were treading silently from the room. Through the doorway, the light sagged in, pinkish grey.

"Kai, your performance tomorrow . . . what time will it be?" Even Ba's words sounded smaller.

"You must come." Kai reached into the pocket that held his golden pen. He retrieved a square of paper and gave it to her father. "It's in the factory buildings. We're doing Beethoven's

'Emperor,' Dvorak's Symphony No. 9 and an American composer."
He said so many foreign words, Ai-ming wanted to cry out at the
strangeness of it. "Li Delun is conducting."

Her father held the paper and stared at it as if he could not
read.

"All through the Cultural Revolution, we were able to perform," Kai said. "Seiji Ozawa visited the Central Philharmonic
last year. Did you know he was born in Manchuria? Not everything disappeared, it was only put aside."

"What happened to He Luting? The last time I saw him was
on television. . . . Years ago now, 1968."

"I heard it was Chairman Mao himself who ordered He Luting
released from prison." The man's voice was smooth, like unmarked
paper. "A few years ago, the charges were dropped and his name
cleared."

Kai picked up a square of cardboard and looked into its image.
"These recordings are so rare now, Sparrow. Last October, people
in Beijing began to unearth the records they had hidden. After
Madame Mao was arested, we thought everything would go back
to the way it was but . . . People know the Cultural Revolution is
finally over, it was all the work of Madame Mao, the Gang of Four,
and so on, that's what the government says, but they can't help
being cautious. Not many records have resurfaced. I did meet a
professor at Beijing University who has a small treasure of scores,
but that's all. Isaac Stern will visit Beijing and Shanghai, have you
heard? Next year." Sparrow said nothing, Kai adjusted his long
legs and continued. "When Ozawa came, he said our ability to
interpret the music had fundamentally changed. . . ." He extended
his hands as if he were carrying two eggs. "As if an entire emotional range was lost to us, but we ourselves couldn't hear it. Every
musician in the orchestra knew they'd been cheated. But until
that moment, we never had to face it so directly."

"Maybe some people always knew," Sparrow said. "Maybe
they never stopped knowing what was counterfeit."

Kai brushed his fingers against his own mouth, as if to rid himself of dust.

Now Sparrow addressed the other man as if he were a student, or a younger brother. "Now that things are changing, what will you do, Comrade? Do you still hope to study in the West?"

"Sparrow, please don't misunderstand."

Her father shifted his cotton pants, pulling them up slightly as if he was sitting outside and the sun warming his ankles.

"We've started auditions at the Shanghai Conservatory," Kai said. "There are over a thousand applicants for a handful of spots. He Luting will be reinstated as President. The old faculty will be invited back. Your father, too. And you. He Luting specifically asked me to visit you."

"My father is in Anhui Province. I'll write down the name of the labour camp for you."

"Sparrow, some of the applications are from your former students. Remember Old Wu? They don't forget. Some of them thought they might never touch a violin or a piano again."

They spoke of names and places Ai-ming didn't know. In fact, she had never heard her father string together so many sentences in a row. It was as if the Bird of Quiet had taken off a coat of feathers, or put one on, and become another creature. Outside, her grandmother was calling for her, but Ai-ming burrowed even further into the shadows. Eventually Big Mother shouted something about eating frozen pineapple on a stick, and creaked away.

" . . . but Shostakovich died."

"When?"

"Two years ago. Li Delun managed to get hold of his last symphony, which none of us had heard. And Symphony No. 4, which he withdrew, remember? And a series of string quartets . . . Where are your brothers?"

"In the Northwest. Flying Bear is in Tibet. Da Shan joined the People's Liberation Army."

"Do they come to see you?"

"No, they don't have permission."

Kai said, "These reforms will give us back what was taken. I honestly believe this. You must have faith, Sparrow."

There was more music. As they listened, Sparrow and the man sat so close together, they made a single confused shape.

"Sparrow, I've been thinking about Zhuli–"

"I can't . . . Tell me instead, what record is this?"

"This? Don't you remember, it's Stokowski's transcription of Bach. The chorale preludes. 'For every vital movement in the world around us, there is a corresponding movement within us, a feeling.'"

They used foreign words to describe the sound, which made her feel as if the night sky had been slipped into her pocket.

"Since the reform and opening up, I've tried to – it's very difficult – I can't stop thinking about her, about Zhuli. Do you find that strange?"

"No, Sparrow. But . . . no one is responsible for what happened."

"That isn't true."

"Come back and teach at the Conservatory. You'll be able to write again, to continue where you left off. What happened to your symphonies?"

Her father laughed and the sound chilled her. "My symphonies . . ."

Ai-ming must have slept because when she opened her eyes again, Kai was gone. It was only Sparrow sitting in front of the square box, leaning towards it as if to another, more beloved, child. When Big Mother lit the lamp and found her curled up on the floor, she gave Ai-ming the needle eye.

"I was listening to music," Ai-ming said. "And I had a stomach ache." She smiled because her own words sounded preposterous.

"Who gave you permission to have a stomach-anything!"

The Bird of Quiet paid no attention.

Early the next morning, she found him sitting outside, smoking peacefully, oblivious to the breakfast Big Mother had prepared. One by one, Ai-ming ate all his spicy cucumbers.

The Bird of Quiet was a shy creature. One had to approach him softly, as if he were a goat. "Who built that singing box?" she whispered.

He started. She feared that everything she did unsettled him, and it made her so mad she wanted to shout at him and slap herself.

Sparrow said it wasn't a singing box, it was an "electric singing engine," a record player.

"I want to see it."

He brought out the box once more. When he lifted and let go of its sturdy whisker she could not tell if her father was bothered or tired, or only lost. The piece of music with the slow, spare notes turned out to be Variation No. 25 of Bach's *Goldberg Variations*. She told her father that hearing the music was like looking into a radio. What she meant was that, even looking at the innards of the sets her father brought home, even staring into the belly of the machine, *into the thing itself*, electricity and sound remained as exquisitely mysterious as the night sky.

He looked at her with such sadness, as if she were someone else entirely. He taught her the first foreign names she ever learned: the first, Bā Hè (Bach) and the second, Gù Ěr Dé (Glenn Gould).

Inside Sparrow, sounds accumulated. Bells, birds and the uneven cracking of the trees, loud and quiet insects, songs that spilled from people even if they never intended to make a noise. He suspected he was doing the same. Was he, unconsciously, humming a folk song or a Bach partita, had he done it when he walked with Ai-ming at night, hoping to turn her eyes to something larger? The hiss of small, soldering devices crackled in his ears, the same tired jokes, the same clanking and capacitors, resistors and minuscule shunts, the high-pitched pain in his hands, the sly meetings and self-criticism sessions, the repeated slogans like a knife sharpened to dullness: sound was alive and disturbing and outside of any individual's control. Sound had a freedom that no thought could equal because a sound made no absolute claim on meaning. Any word, on the other hand, could be forced to signify its opposite. One night he dreamed that he sat in a concert hall. Around him programs fluttered, voices hummed, bags opened and closed, the orchestra keened towards harmony. Giddy with joy, full of nervous anticipation, he awaited the performance of his own Symphony No. 3. A chime summoned the last members of the audience. The lights dimmed. Quiet settled. He watched, unable to move, as Zhuli walked onto the stage in a long blue dress. She searched the auditorium for him. Her hands were empty. He woke.

In the Cultural Palace of the People, on the grounds of the Huizhou Battery Factory, Sparrow presented his ticket, expecting to be turned away. Instead he was shown to a row of reserved seats. Everywhere was movement. Upwards of a thousand people pressed into the hall, Party cadres (grey), office workers (white), assembly line workers (blue), filing beneath a cascading banner that read: *Fully expose and condemn the treason committed by the Gang of Four!*

Sparrow found his seat. Beside him, a woman in her mid-twenties, dressed in a pale green skirt and a flowered blouse, was turning heads. A few months ago, the flowered blouse would have been deemed unacceptable, even criminal; but today it was merely odd. The young woman, confusingly familiar, wore her hair loose. Unbraided, it curled in arabesques. There was a mark on the underside of her chin, the shape of a thumb, a violinist's mark. She turned and met his gaze. Sparrow blinked, embarrassed to be caught staring. He turned back to the stage. Eventually the conductor of the Central Philharmonic, Li Delun, stepped forward. From the podium, Li stared out with a quivery calm. The two pens in his breast pocket shone extravagantly. Li introduced the concert program (Mahler, Beethoven and Copland) and then began speaking, at length, about the successor to Chairman Mao, Deng Xiaoping. It was extraordinary that Deng had come to power. He, too, had been brought down by the Cultural Revolution, his political career destroyed and his family targeted. His eldest son had been tortured by Red Guards and, in 1966, fell, or was pushed, out of a third-storey window, the same as San Li. But father and son had outlasted the turmoil, the son now famous in his wheel-chair. Deng had out-manoeuvred Madame Mao and her admir-ers, who now languished in prison. Now, with the backing of the Politburo, he was unrolling a series of economic and political reforms. In the auditorium, Li's speech was a kind of song in itself, in which people intermittently cried out, "Ashes burn once more!" and "Strive to implement the Four Modernizations of Comrade Deng!" The Great Helmsman's name, xiǎo píng, meant "little bottle" and so, in the trees just outside, someone had hung a collection of small green bottles, along with colourful banners that read, "Deng Blue Skies." The glass tinkled in the breeze, a hope for better days.

Facing waves of applause, Li cried out, "Let us build a just society, a revolutionary China fit for a musical people!"

Beside Sparrow, the young woman sighed as if wishing to propel herself onto the stage where the musicians were now filing out in solemn rows.

The Central Philharmonic wore their everyday clothing, grey or blue slacks and short-sleeved button-down shirts. Sparrow's heart was beating so oddly, he felt it was detaching from his body. The sound of the orchestra tuning chilled him; strings, woodwinds and brass made their simultaneous climb or descent to a sustained A, and an oboe fluttered up the scale like a thought set loose. Sparrow had not seen a score since 1968, and the ones used by the Philharmonic appeared to be hand-copied. The music stands, too, were makeshift, held together by tape, string and wooden splints. He felt the clattering tap of Li Delun's baton on the music stand as if the conductor had rapped on Sparrow's own spine.

Mahler's Ninth Symphony rose in a tentative hum.

The house lights had remained up and every face in the audience, every small reaction, was visible. No one fidgeted. On stage, the musicians leaned forward, as if they were sliding across the same tilting boat. A bright red banner gave way at one corner, "Premier Zhou Enlai lives forever in our hearts." It folded diagonally but didn't fall.

Danger seemed to come from every side. The young woman's hands were covering her face and he wanted desperately to take them and place them in her lap. *You must not let them see,* he thought. *If they see that you are devoted to it, they will take it from you.*

The reverie of the first movement sharpened to a hallucinatory edge. Sparrow silenced the music by thinking about Mahler himself. Late in life, the composer had discovered, in German translation, the poets Li Bai and Wang Wei, and their poetry had provided the text for Mahler's song symphony, "Das Lied von der Erde" (The Song of the Earth). The poems had been translated into French, and then into German, and from there Mahler had made his own additions so that the poems, copies of mistranslated copies, were almost untraceable to their beginnings. But some were known, including Wang Wei's "Farewell," familiar to everyone of his and his mother's generation, even if they no longer recited the lines. "At odds with the world, return to rest by the south hill . . ."

Over the next hour, Sparrow succeeded in pushing away the sound of the orchestra. It was warm in the hall and his shirt was damp, the damp hardening to an icy cold.

There was no intermission. As the piano was being wheeled out for Beethoven's "Emperor" Concerto, Li Delun came to the microphone again. "We dedicate this Concerto No. 5 to our resurrected comrade, He Luting, President of the Shanghai Conservatory," he said. "Long live Chairman Deng! Long live the Communist Party of China! Long live our country!" In the hall, surprise and consternation but also sustained applause and even, Sparrow thought, cautious jubilation. Amidst the noise Kai came forward and took his seat at the piano. It was small, the kind a well-to-do family might have kept in their home before the Cultural Revolution. It was the first piano Sparrow had seen since 1966.

Kai sat with his back rigidly straight. He had no score in front of him. Sparrow could see where his trousers, cuffed unevenly, lifted to expose his ankles. The pianist waited, both hands on his thighs, as the concerto opened in controlled exclamations, vibrating across the auditorium. Kai began, traversing the scales with a familiar clarity, only the tips of his body—head, fingers and feet—moving. Inside Sparrow's head, multiple versions played; he simultaneously saw the performance and heard a memory, a recording. He listened to the immense space between then and now. When the allegro began, Sparrow closed his eyes. Up and down the scales again, as if Kai were telling him there is no way out, there is only the path back again, and even when we think we're free, we only endlessly return. The concerto's beauty was even more impassioned than he remembered, and also more piteous and quiet and restrained, and he clasped his hands together to absorb both the grief and joy in his body. He remembered, long ago, playing Flying Bear's violin for Zhuli. Beside him, the young woman's eyes were glassy with tears that did not fall. Sparrow could not imagine weeping openly. He inhaled and found himself, against his will, listening. Near the end of the movement, the first, jubilant chords repeated, but the notes no longer conveyed the original feeling. Underneath was an ending, a buried movement, the sound of one life held captive by another. The concerto swept on, never pausing to dwell on its own astonishing constructions.

On stage, the first violinist played with his whole body and then, suddenly, as if remembering the audience, he closed up again. Sparrow tried to place Zhuli before him. Beneath the violin, her supporting arm had always appeared so pale. He remembered her humility before the music, even as a child she had felt accountable to it. The notes went on, as if living another life. He could have followed Kai to Beijing. But he had never known how to write music, to perform music, and yet be silent.

Tumultuous applause swept over him. Kai stood, all the musicians stood, their white shirts, damp with sweat, feathery against their bodies. The encores came.

Sparrow saw the young woman staring straight ahead and he recognized in her an ambition, a desire, that he was certain he no longer possessed. Would he ever contain that hunger, that wholeness, again?

Late that night, he played a series of nothings on an erhu that Kai gave him. Songs broke off and became other songs, *Shajiabang* sliding into "Night Bell from the Old Temple," breaking into a fragment of Bach's *Partita No. 6* as if music blew through his mind like scattered pages. He kept on this way, playing the beginning of one piece and the end of another, and Kai lay back and gazed at the nearness of the ceiling. Kai had the key to this room where the Philharmonic's instruments and record players were stored, but they could have been in Room 103, in Shanghai, in the remote Northwest or the far South, anywhere with four walls and only the two of them. Sparrow let himself believe they had found their way back to an earlier time. Kai asked him to play "Moon Reflected on Second Spring," and Sparrow played it once, and once again, realizing that he could not recall the last time he had heard it. Perhaps on the radio in 1964. After that, it had simply disappeared. He felt a humming in his hands and a renewed, almost unbearable, pleasure. By the time professors from the Central Conservatory had discovered the composer of "Moon Reflected," the blind erhu player, Ah Bing, was in his seventies. "If only you had come ten years earlier," Ah Bing had famously said, "I could have played better." The professors captured six songs on a recorder before they ran out of wire. When the songs reached the capital, Ah Bing was acclaimed as one of the nation's master composers. He died only a few months later, and those six recorded songs became all that survived of his work. "Moon Reflected on Second Spring" was an elegy, a spiral of both radiance and sorrow.

Kai had other records. Overcome with curiosity, Sparrow set the erhu aside. Going through the collection, he felt like a child standing before a wall of colours. He chose Shostakovich's *Symphony No. 5.* Kai pushed blankets under the door to dampen the sound and opened another bottle of baijiu. They lay side by side on the thin mat, the tops of their heads grazing the record player.

"Shostakovich was criticized for the fourth movement," Kai said. "Do you remember? The Union of Composers said it was inauthentic joy."

"But inauthentic joy is also an emotion, experienced by us all."

"The censors are always the first to recognize it, aren't they?" Kai smiled and time ran backwards. *Biscuit.* The name came unexpectedly to Sparrow. He had known the young woman in the pale green skirt and flowered blouse. She had been a violinist. She had been the same age as Zhuli.

Kai was still speaking. "Later on, Shostakovich reused pieces of the fourth movement in his patriotic work, cantatas to Stalin and so on. Did you know? All those fragments of inauthentic joy. In 1948, when his music was banned, he publicly accepted the wisdom of the Party. But, each night, after the long meetings, he went home and composed. He was working on his *Violin Concerto No. 1* and, for the first time, he hid his name inside the work."

Sparrow knew but had not thought of it in years. The signature, D, E-flat, C and B, which in German notation read D, Es, C, H, curled like a dissonance, or a question, in Shostakovich's music.

The Fifth was everything Sparrow remembered, tortured, contradictory, lurid, gleeful. The room ceased to exist, the record itself became superfluous, the symphony came from his own thoughts, as if it had always been there, circling endlessly.

Sip by sip, the wine loosened their reserve. Kai said that in Beijing, in 1968, the struggle sessions had started up all over again.

Mass denunciations were moved into stadiums. He saw a student humiliated and tortured in front of thousands of Red Guards.

"For what crime?"

"He said the children of political criminals shouldn't be persecuted. That class status shouldn't pass down across generations."

The children of class enemies. Like Zhuli. Like Ai-ming. "What was his punishment?"

Kai turned, surprised by the question. "He died."

When Sparrow asked how, he said, simply, "They shot him."

Kai wiped his hand over his mouth. "Ozawa has promised to bring a few of us to America. I have this hope . . ."

The last time they had been alone, Shanghai was on the verge of change. This small room seemed to Sparrow like a hidden space inside the Conservatory. When he left this room, perhaps the door would lead him back to the hallway of the fourth floor, where the walls were covered with posters. He would arrive in his office before it was too late, he would tell his cousin that all things, even courage, pass from this world. Everything passes. But he could not get there in time. When he entered the room, he saw her again, just as she was. Each year, as he grew older, as the Zhuli in his memory grew younger, as Da Shan and Flying Bear drifted further away, he knew he should let them go. But how could he explain it? The person inside him, the composer who once existed, would not allow it. And Sparrow, himself, could not erase the composer. The composer wanted to tell Kai that no one, not even Deng Xiaoping, and nothing, no reform or change or disavowal, could return those years to them.

"Sometimes I think of leaving. If you had the chance to go overseas, Sparrow, would you?"

He smiled, wanting to make light of himself. "Even taking the train to Shanghai during Spring Festival feels like crossing the ocean. I never thought I would grow accustomed to the South but, after all this time, I feel at home here." When he heard the words spoken aloud, they felt true.

Kai gestured towards the ceiling as if it were Inner Mongolia. "All the educated youth are going out of their minds, trying to get back to the city. And in Shanghai, they're rioting, there are no jobs. Sparrow, look at it from their perspective. It would be unimaginable to them that someone could turn down a position at the Conservatory."

"I prefer to wire a circuit board than to compose a symphony." Inside the factory, Sparrow's hands had learned another language entirely. His body had altered. Chairman Mao had not been wrong, to change one's thinking, one had only to change one's conditions.

Kai lit a cigarette and gave it to him. They were the luxury Phoenix brand, which Sparrow had never even seen before. Kai lit another for himself, holding it out to one side. The ashes fell harmlessly onto the concrete floor. The ceiling disappeared behind smoke.

"I used to hear music in everything," Sparrow said, but the sentence hung between them. He did not know how to finish it.

"Dear Sparrow . . ." As Kai exhaled, he changed position so that the crook of his left arm partially covered his face. "I'm sorry for everything, I'm truly sorry. . . . we were all alone but Zhuli's situation was the most desperate. We all betrayed ourselves in some way. Not you . . . but I responded in the only way that I knew how. All I wanted was to protect those years of effort, to protect what I loved. I know I was wrong." The words seemed to come from a far corner of the room, detached from Kai. "We all made mistakes. . . . but can't you see that it's finished now. More than a decade has passed. . . . She always said your talent was the one that mattered and she was right. What happened to your Symphony No. 3? It was your masterpiece. It was so full of contradictions, so immense and alive. I haven't heard it in ten years, but I could still play it. . . . You must have finished it by now."

"I can't even remember how it began," he said. He wanted to ask Kai if he had denounced Zhuli, but he couldn't bring himself to say the words. And it was true that everyone had denounced another to save themselves, even Ba Lute, even his brothers. Kai's answer wouldn't bring her back. "You loved her, too, didn't you?"

"Zhuli is gone," he said quietly. "Many people are gone, can't you see?"

"I don't see."

Kai turned onto his side and looked at him, a beseeching look. He crushed out his cigarette and unthinkingly lit another, unable to bear the silence.

"At Premier Zhou Enlai's funeral," he said, "I went to Tiananmen Square, I read the posters and the letters people had left behind. I memorized them. *Let me tell you, world / I do not believe / I don't believe the sky is blue / I don't believe that dreams are false / I don't believe that death has no revenge.* Everyone read them and I wondered: what happens when a hundred thousand people memorize the same poem? Does anything change? Around Tiananmen Square, there were so many mourners . . . hundreds of thousands of workers. Crying openly because for a day or two, they could grieve in public. The police came and gathered up all the funeral wreaths. People were outraged. They gathered in the Square shouting, 'Give us back our flowers! Give them back!' They shouted, 'Long live Premier Zhou Enlai!'"

Sparrow wanted to listen to *Symphony No. 5* again, to the reflective and reflecting largo. Shostakovich was a composer who had finally written about scorn and degradation, who had used harmony against itself, and exposed all the scraping and dissonance inside. For years his public self had told the world that he was working on a symphony dedicated to Lenin, but no trace of that manuscript had yet been found. When he was denounced in 1936, and again in 1948, Shostakovich answered, "I will try again and again." Did the composer inside Sparrow have the will to do this? But if he knew the will and the talent were gone, what good would it do to begin again?

"Sparrow, remember the classics we memorized? The words are still true. 'We have no ties of kinship or even provenance, but

I am bound to him by ties of sentiment and I share his sorrows and misfortunes.' We've waited our whole lives and now the country is finally opening up. I've been thinking . . . there are ways to begin again. We could leave."

The possibilities before Sparrow, which should have given him joy, instead broke his heart. He was no longer the same person.

I used to be humbled before music, he thought. I loved music so much it blinded me to the world. What right do I have, do any of us have, to go back? Repetition was an illusion. The idea of return, of beginning over again, of creating a new country, had always been a deception, a beautiful dream from which they had awoken. Perhaps they had loved one another, but now Sparrow had his parents to care for. They relied on him, and his life was not his own, it belonged to his wife and to Ai-ming as well. And it was true, factory work had brought a peace he had never known before. The routine had freed him.

Kai's mouth was against his shoulder, the skin of his neck. They lay like this, unable to move forward, unable to continue.

Kai said, "What you said is true. I loved her. I loved you both."

"There was no shame in that."

"No," he said quietly. "But I was ashamed."

"We were young."

"It was a kind of love, only I didn't comprehend."

"If you have the chance to go to America, you must go. Don't let the opportunity pass. After all you've seen, all that's been done, don't turn back. Your family, and Zhuli, too, would have said the same."

Kai nodded.

Was he weeping, Sparrow thought. The alcohol and the cigarettes had cleared his head and heightened his desire. There was no need to weep, he knew. They were fortunate, they had seen through the illusion. Even if the country went on, they could never be made to forget. I loved you both, Sparrow thought. I love you both.

"I'm sorry, Sparrow," he said. "I would sacrifice anything to be a different person. Please. Please let me help you leave."

"No," Sparrow said. Zhuli is here, he thought. And the composer had long since gone away, only Sparrow himself had failed to recognize it. But he need only to look down at his tired, calloused hands to know. "My life is here."

Ten years later, at the Shanghai Conservatory, Ai-ming was impeded by every kind of music: trills and percussion, a violin reciting a flotilla of notes. The Bird of Quiet walked ahead of her. In the new trousers, baby blue shirt, and leather shoes that Ling had given him for 1988 Spring Festival, her father looked taller. Or, maybe he only looked this way because, when he wore his usual clothes, the uniform of Huizhou Semiconductor Factory No. 1, Sparrow never stood up straight.

Her father ran up the narrow road of the Conservatory as if someone up ahead was calling him.

Beside her, Ba Lute moaned, "Ai yo! These young pianists have no understanding of contrapuntal anything. Loud and fast, that's the only thing they know."

"But it sounds good, grandfather."

"Because you have no ear. You never had one, poor kid."

Which was true. Just the other night, when he tried to give her an erhu lesson, he had screamed at her, "How can a budding scientist be incapable of keeping 4/4 time? Even a buffalo can do it!"

Now Ai-ming took his papery hand. Ba Lute had gotten plump in the belly but not in the legs and he resembled a pear on toothpicks. She feared he would totter over and be crushed.

"Hey, you! Little Sparrow! Slow down," he shouted.

When her father turned, Ai-ming imagined the sparrow he might have been when he was a boy, a burst of song and a rush of feathers. Big Mother had told her that in the early 1960s, Conservatory students had been sent out to the fields to wage war. They played their instruments loudly and dissonantly from morning until night so that no little birds could land in the fields and eat the grain. Day after day, thousands of sparrows, killed by exhaustion, had fallen dead from the sky. "Yet another solicitous idea from Chairman Mao," Big Mother had said solemnly. "Who said Western music never killed anyone?"

Something so barbaric would never happen now. To mark the beginning of 1988, Big Mother had given her a New Year's calendar with the words, "Happiness Arrives," written in running characters above the plump faces of the Gods of Harmonious Union. Those words lifted her thoughts as she tugged on Ba Lute's hand. *Happiness arrives.* Pretty violinists, wearing brightly coloured dresses, parted around them. She would like to be a musician, Ai-ming thought, simply to look like them. But no, she had always preferred to dismantle a record player than to listen to any old sonata.

"Oh, oh," Ba Lute said. "This old fart is running out of air."

"Don't rush. We're not going anywhere."

"How true, how true."

The Bird of Quiet remained where he was, waiting patiently, as if he existed in a different dimension from the students zipping past. They were electricity, Ai-ming thought excitedly, sizzling electrons, and her father was the electron gate. Or they were time and he was space. Ai-ming remembered how, when Chairman Mao still breathed, she had regularly written criticisms of her father. ("I cry bitter tears knowing that I am the daughter of a bad element, capitalist-roader. . . ." "In this war, there are no civilians!") She'd been only a kid at the time, so her father had to help her write the tricky characters. When Chairman Deng came to power, criticisms like these were no longer so common. She and her father had never talked about them. Now, it seemed almost funny to remember that she had called him a snake or a demon, and even a snake–demon, that she had denounced him so naturally. He had taught her how to protect herself by hiding inside the noise.

"Why did we come anyway?" Ai-ming asked. "The Shanghai Conservatory only makes him feel bad."

"Eh, it's not my fault. Your father wanted to come. He has old friends here, you know."

But there were no old friends, or none that came out to see him. He went into one building and out another, searching for someone, and she and Ba Lute waited under various flowering trees. Before they left, her father went into one of the practice rooms. Ai-ming sat on a chair in the corner as her father played the piano, she had never heard him do so before, had not quite realized he was even capable. His entire body, the way he moved, changed. Most of the pieces she recognized from the records (Bach's Partita No. 6, Couperin, Shostakovich) but there was another piece, a complex figure that seemed to disassemble as she listened, a rope of music, a spool of wire. It seemed to rise even as it was falling, to lift in volume even as it diminished, a polyphony so unfathomably beautiful it made the hairs on the back of her neck stand up. When it stopped, tears came abruptly to her eyes.

After a moment, her father pushed the bench back. He closed the lid without a sound.

"What music is that?" she asked.

He turned to her and smiled. Ai-ming grinned, too, unsure. She felt an inexpressible sorrow welling up in the room.

"It's nothing," Sparrow said.

"Nothing?"

He stood up and went to the wall. "It's mine," he said. The lights were off so when he hit the switch they turned on, and he stared up at them, confused, and flicked the switch once more. The number 103 was stencilled in neat black ink on the wall.

"What do you mean it's yours?"

"It's me," he said, more to the light switch than to her. "Music I wrote a long time ago, part of a symphony I never finished." He went out. In the courtyard, the sun's glare faded all the colours. "I hadn't expected to remember, I was sure that after all this time it had completely disappeared."

She followed him out, the music circling in her mind.

She wondered how many things a person knew that were better forgotten. Her father had looked at the piano as if it were the only solid thing in the room, as if everything and everyone else, including himself, were no more than an illusion, a dream.

From the moment she had first looked into the belly of a radio, Ai-ming had known her vocation: to study computer science at Beijing University and to be part of the technological vanguard. Wasn't it obvious to everyone? Computers would one day hold up half the sky.

When she made this grand announcement to her family, Ai-ming had been six years old. Her father had continued eating but Big Mother had applauded, saying, "So not everyone in this house is half-dead after all." That year, 1977, the competition had been epic: more than five million people wrote the university entrance examinations, competing for 200,000 precious places. Chairman Deng Xiaoping had reopened general admissions, and this was the first time since 1966 that university entrants would not be selected by the Party. In town, during the student parades, Ai-ming had even waved a banner ("The People love the students!"). How entrancing they were! Exhausted from studying yet defiantly awake. On the day of the exam, the first bells signalling the start of test-taking had brought everything to a stop, no traffic, no noise, no bickering, even Big Mother stopped shouting at passersby. Many weeks later, when the results were announced, the university entrants became the new heroes, young men and women who sweated over books instead of ploughs, who held up not one Little Red Book, but a giant stack of possibilities that teetered towards the skies. Their minds were ever-expanding factories crunching through raw material and spitting out answers. To get an education, Ai-ming thought, is glorious. To go to Beijing University one day would mean freedom.

In 1988, after studying sixteen hours a day for a full year, it was finally Ai-ming's turn to endure three days of testing on nine subjects. *Happiness arrives*, she told herself. The first essay question was: "Light and shadow—'All the variety, all the charm, all the beauty of life is made up of light and shadow.'—Leo Tolstoy. Discuss.'" The second was: "Take inspiration from the philosophy expressed by Ruan Yuan's 'Poem on Wuxing.'" She wrote more than nine hundred characters on each and, by the end of the first day, was giddy from nervous exhaustion. The overhead lights were distractingly bright, they made warning signals in her eyes. The exam was followed by an interminable wait, by tears and sleeplessness and tantrums. Her impressive scores got her hopes up but in the end, although she made the cut-off for South China Institute of Technology, her scores were not good enough for Beijing University or Tsinghua, or her third choice, Fudan. She would not be able to leave the province. All that week, comrade neighbours fell over themselves to congratulate her father and grandparents because Ai-ming was the only one from Cold Water Ditch going on to university. The neighbours couldn't understand why Ai-ming was inconsolable, curled up in her room, crying her eyes out.

The Bird of Quiet gave her two pieces of advice. *Study hard.* And: *It is good to be cautious.*

They were eating dinner and Ai-ming, still weeping, said. "Oh, Ba! What's the point in being timid?"

Sparrow chewed his barbarian eggplant and refrained from giving her Big Mother's answer ("Oh, you new generation! You think you're so worldly-wise. You have no idea the rice is already cooked!") or any answer at all. There had been a time in Ai-ming's life when her father's quiet had seemed like another person in their midst. Quiet was alive, like a toy you could just keep hitting. Once, when she was twelve, she had asked him, "The music you used to write, Ba, was it criminal music?" He could only say, "I don't know." That same night, he wrote a new banner for the front door which read, *May the Red Sun keep rising for ten thousand years*, in calligraphy that was accomplished but empty, a fixed smile. He might as well have written Joy! on a plastic bucket.

Big Mother shouted, "Good question!"

Ba Lute whispered, "Symphony No. 7 in F Minor, 'Timid,'" and giggled at his elderly joke. He leaned across the cluttered table, wanting to wipe her tears, and instead smeared them all over her cheek.

In retirement, Ba Lute was the most content of all. He was forever banging on something or other and making old-time music, and he made Sparrow play music, too, even though Sparrow said his hands were useless. Ba Lute was such a funny-looking old man, too big for his skinny legs. Big Mother would curse him tenderly, "I like you more now that I can see you less." On sunny mornings, they sat outside like a dragon and a phoenix guarding the gate, or like two flowery portraits of Marx and Engels, Big Mother with her pants rolled up to catch the sun on her knees, and Ba Lute with his vest rolled up to catch the sun on his belly.

Ai-ming got up to clear the plates. Until the arrival of the university results, 1988 had been a year of prosperity, there had been meat on the table twice each week and they had a sewing machine, a sofa, the latest Red Lamp upright radio, and quality bicycles for every member of the family. Ma had her own television. She'd just been promoted to news editor at Radio Beijing, and had moved to the capital. When the university results arrived in Cold Water Ditch, Ai-ming realized that fortune had indeed arrived, but had found her wanting.

By the time she finished washing up, her left eye was swollen shut from crying.

She rejoined Sparrow in the courtyard where he was waiting with the record player. A few of the neighbour kids were there too, playing cards, their mouths smeared ridiculous, with some kind of barbecue sauce. They were squabbling and she wanted to kick dirt in their faces. It was Sunday evening, the only night she was allowed to listen to Western music though, in reality, all these years, she had only been keeping her father company. Did her father honestly believe she wanted to spend hours listening to the agonized rumblings of Shostakovich? His Tenth Symphony made it clear life was hopeless.

"You choose, Ba." She only hoped he wouldn't choose Bach, whose uptight fugues made her feel like she was trapped in a barrel rolling down a hillside.

"Mmm," Sparrow said, rolling his cigarettes. His special Xinjiang tobacco had a damp earth smell. "Prokofiev?" he suggested.

"I'll get it."

She found his favourite, Prokofiev's *Violin Concerto No. 1*, inside the cardboard sleeve that had a picture of big-jowled, lantern-faced David Oistrakh. She put the record on. Music seeped into the air and Sparrow listened with one elbow on his knee, his entire body curved like a trigger.

Prokofiev composed his pretty music, as if he had not a care in the world.

As a result of yearly gifts from Ling and Big Mother Knife, her father had accumulated one of the largest record collections in Guangxi Province, but he still insisted on hiding them. The first thing they did when they got home each Spring Festival was dig out another part of the floor and bury another stack of music. Her father was paranoid.

What kind of life was this? A record was a kind of storage in which music lay waiting, love letters from Canada stored words that kept Sparrow awake at night. She knew because she had opened the letters and sneakily read them all. But for anything to be alive, it required motion: the current must run, the record must turn, a person must leave or find another path. Without movement or change, the world became nothing more than a stale copy, and this was the trouble with Ba's elegant calligraphy, his patient life, it was frozen in time. His tomorrow would always be, somehow, yesterday. Ai-ming knew she was by nature more impulsive, less patient.

In the courtyard now, Sparrow lifted the record player's thin arm and set another album down. Ai-ming had to fight with all her strength not to push the record player over and smash it on the ground. This was Smetana's *From My Homeland*, and it made Ai-ming so irretrievably unhappy her tears started up again. The Bird of Quiet paid no attention. She pulled hard on the skin between her thumb and index finger to extinguish the pain in her heart.

"Ai-ming," he said.

She lifted her head. The music had finished without her noticing.

"If Beijing University is where you wish to go, then study for another year and write the exam again."

As if she would ever be accepted into Beida! She felt such bitterness she almost laughed.

"I requested a transfer to Beijing Wire Factory No. 3 and it's been approved. You know the factory, they make radios and also the new mini-computers. We'll both move to the capital and have Beijing papers. Your mother used all her connections. . . . anyway, it's done now. She's supposed to telephone tonight, that's why I hadn't said anything . . . When your mother calls, try and act surprised."

She stared.

Sparrow explained, "The university cut-off scores are lower for those with Beijing residency."

Ai-ming knew that, of course. The cut-off was a full hundred points lower, and she would have passed easily this year, if only she'd had Beijing papers. Worse, their province had only been allocated fifty spots at Beida. The deep injustice of the world flared up inside her all over again and made her want to scream.

"We can move to your mother's apartment in Beijing or stay here. It's up to you."

Ai-ming could barely nod her head. She felt shame crawling through her body like an old self-criticism. "I want to go, Ba."

Sparrow smiled, delighted.

She began to cry again, she felt a debilitating mix of joy and panic.

"I haven't been to Beijing since I was a teenager," he said. "Don't be upset, Ai-ming. Nothing is ever complete, it's only a matter of turning one's head, of focusing on a new place . . . and I wouldn't mind the chance to hear something new. The Central Philharmonic is in Beijing. . . ."

She didn't know what he was talking about. Her father had turned his attention back to the record player. One record after another was lifted up in his hands and then set down again. She intervened. She chose Shostakovich's Jazz Suites, and the album opened with Waltz No. 2, which was glorious and lopsided and entirely unapologetic. Sparrow returned to his chair, he gazed up at the clouded night. He closed his eyes.

When Sparrow said, "It is good to be cautious," in the same sure way he might quote Chairman Deng, "To get rich is glorious," he had swayed a little bit because, these days, he was drinking too much. His hands bothered him, a phantom pain he couldn't relieve. One evening, a few days before they were due to move to Beijing, Big Mother asked him, "What are you waiting for? What do you need, my son?"

"I'm content."

"Ba Lute says the conservatory in Guangzhou offered you a position but you said no. Is it true? You're so stubborn. I don't know who gave birth to you."

He smiled. After a moment he said, "What could I teach? I haven't written in twenty years. There's a new generation of composers now, better suited than me." He changed the subject. "You should come to Beijing with us."

"Beijing! Surrounded by cadres and bureaucrats. Eating dust. I'd rather live in Mao Zedong's coffin."

"I fear that would wake him."

Big Mother burped. Carefully, she placed her copy of the Book of Records, still in its shoebox, on the chair beside Sparrow. She nudged it towards him. "Don't wait anymore," she said at last, standing up. "Swirl and Wen aren't coming home. I don't even know what's happened to Projectionist Bang. And your two brothers. They could be Americans by now for all I know." She sighed slowly into the house. "Long, long, long," she said. "So long is the Revolution."

Sparrow remained outside. At last, he opened the shoebox.

He lifted out Chapter 42 from the stack of notebooks, its pages were almost pristine, as if it had never been read before. In the chapter, Da-wei has come back to Northwest China. He and his wife are searching for their daughter who has been missing for many years. One day, they come to a mountainous village where all the peasants, cadres and educated youth are too busy to speak, they are engaged in a monumental task: they have been ordered to construct a great dam, and to do so, they must demolish their local mountain piece by piece. Da-wei and his wife can only stand and watch in amazement. The air is choked with the dust of the ground and the dust of the heavens. The peasants are singing a hymn to Chairman Mao, and when Da-wei's wife asks them if they have seen this girl, the peasants refuse to even look at the photograph.

"My daughter would be grown now, a young woman," she volunteers, but the peasants shake their heads and continue to haul their baskets.

Someone answers, "Everything comes to rest at the bottom of the river," but Da-wei and his wife are certain she is not there.

They travel on but year by year the Taklamakan Desert wears them down, their clothes, their shoes, their faith, until the photograph, too, disintegrates. Even their tears refuse to last. The hot sun immediately dries them, leaving behind only flakes of salt. Da-wei tells his wife that the time has come to return home and she answers, "Tell me where our home is, and I'll go." They want to make a spirit offering to their lost child, but they have nothing, no money and no goods. It is 1988 and on the former Silk Road, there are no longer any merchants or trains of camels, and countless villages have been abandoned.

They come to a blue oasis in the wilderness, shrouded in mist, where birdsong twists between them. It seems like the edge of the world, but in fact it is the ancient city of Khotan, for they have reached the southwestern edge of the Taklamakan Desert. Da-wei thinks of his lost brothers, of May Fourth and now his own child, a girl named Zhuli, and he wonders if he and his wife are the last to pass through this gate. Where does the future exist? If they continue west, they will reach the disputed lands of Kashmir. Do they turn around or keep going? To which side do they belong? On the walls of a school, someone has copied out a letter or a poem and the words read,

> I came into this world
> bringing only paper, rope, a shadow
> Let me tell you, world
> I do not believe. . . .

His wife no longer has a photograph to show to strangers, and she simply crouches down against the wall, exhausted. The twisting cascade of her hair has fallen from its hold.

Da-wei touches the words on the wall. *A new conjunction adorns the sky now / They are the pictographs from five thousand years / They are the watchful eyes of future generations. . . .*

"I know she's gone," his wife says. "I know it, but how can I let her go?"

A young man in the schoolyard is playing music. He is playing a violin, what they called a xiǎo tí qin, a small, lifted zither, and Da-wei, recognizes the song. Bach's Concerto in D Minor, written for two violins, but the man plays alone, the counterpoint is gone, or never was. Da-wei thinks of the duties of a father: there should be gifts of money to see his daughter through the underworld, oranges for sweetness, silk to cover her. His pockets are empty and he is ashamed that he has nothing to give her, in this life or for the next. This music, and the great distance it has come, confounds him. He wants to tell his daughter to return home, but the roads have changed and nothing in this country is familiar, if she turns back towards the cities of the coast, she might lose her way. How can he help her? Why has he been so powerless? Da-wei hears the counterpoint as if it were real, a melody line he knows intimately, having replayed it again and again from the radio station, into the safekeeping of the air. *I came into this world bringing only paper, rope, a shadow*. . . . In surviving the present, did they sacrifice the future? The world he once believed in has changed its shape once more.

His daughter left so long ago. But he himself does not know how to be free.

"Help me," his wife says. "Help me to let her go."

Sparrow closed the notebook. He heard music trickling from somewhere, a radio left on, a memory. Zhuli, he said. He listened as the air answered.

Ai-ming sat up in bed. She could hear a recording of Bach's *Concerto for Two Violins* circling through the house, starting and then stopping. When she crept out of her room, she saw her father seated on the floor, his back to her. He lifted the needle and held it there, as if something in his mind could not be decided, and then he set it back again. The first tension of sound, the air that came before the music, seemed to crackle up from the floor itself. Oistrakh performed the piece with his son, and the two violins circled one another, sometimes warily, sometimes harsh with accusation, disclosing a covetousness, but also an immense feeling, for which she had no words. She watched her father, thinking of Beijing and the future. What if everything was unprescribed, she wondered. What kind of world would that be? What if everything, or anything at all, had the capacity to change and begin again?

FROM THEIR TWO-ROOM FLAT beside the Muxidi Bridge, in a traditional Beijing hutong–a maze of alleyway housing–Tiananmen Square was just fifteen minutes away. It was only fifteen minutes but still, pedalling down the wide boulevard, Ai-ming felt as if she were lifting off into outer space. Growing up, she must have seen thousands of pictures of the Square, but the reality was defiantly modern: shadowy couples, long-haired drifters, teenagers listening to rock music, singing, "The world is a garbage dump!" Small children wobbled by in their padded coats, moving at the same sedate pace as their grandparents, as if they had all the time in the world. Today, the afternoon wind had an unkind bite, April could not let go of winter.

Her bicycle leaned on its kickstand. Ai-ming sat on the paving stones and gazed, proprietorially, out into the Square. For as long as she could remember, right and wrong had been represented by the Party through colour. Truth and beauty, for instance, were hóng (red), while criminality and falsehood were hēi (black). Her mother was red, her father was black. But Beijing, resting place of Chairman Mao, turned out to be softly ochre and even the colossal boulevards had a camel-coloured hue. Red existed only in the national flag and the Party banners, but all that red couldn't make a dent in all this yellow. Sometimes the wind brought sand from the Gobi Desert and the dust got into everything, not only her perceptions but also her food, so that silky tofu tasted crunchy.

"Come on," a boy whispered, "don't be like that," and the girl who leaned on his shoulder said, "If you like her, just tell me honestly. I'm not old-fashioned. I won't do something foolish . . ."

Ai-ming closed her eyes and pretended not to be eavesdropping. People in Beijing were different, she thought. They were surprisingly dignified, they were more subtle yet more hopeful creatures.

Today was Ai-ming's eighteenth birthday. She had undone her braids, emulating the city girls. Pedalling down the eight-lane thoroughfare of Chang'an Avenue, she had felt its soft heaviness floating behind her. Yesterday, instead of studying, she had altered the line of her best dress, and now the cotton tugged firmly at her breasts and hips, giving her a feeling of heightened containment. In the centre of the Square, she looked up at the ochre sky and thought, "Let me tell you world, I wish to believe."

Alone, she did not feel lonely at all. It was as if she walked upon some miraculous circuit board that made her more powerful. But later on, at twilight, when she met her parents at the Square's northern edge and they walked to Ai-ming's favourite restaurant, Comrade Barbarian, she began to feel as if her lungs were being crushed. Her mother radiated anxiety, or perhaps only regret. After dinner, when Ling paid to have their picture taken in front of Tiananmen Gate, Ai-ming had a sudden image of what they must look like: Sparrow, the factory worker, Ling, the diligent cadre and Ai-ming herself, the good student. They even dressed in the bland, inoffensive colours of a model family.

"Don't even breathe!" the photographer said. "Hold it, hold it. . . ."

She fixed her gaze on a point behind his right ear, where three slim boys in matching windcheaters stood beneath an enormous banner: "Study Hard and Make Progress Every Day."

She thought to herself, *I must make myself fortunate.* But what was fortune? She had come to believe it was being exactly the same on the inside as on the outside. What was misfortune but the quality of existing as something, or someone else, inside? Since childhood, she had been reading Sparrow's diary, which her father used to write and submit to his superiors every week. Until 1978, her father had been categorized as a criminal element, but with a diary this dull, there was no way he could be a hooligan. Only now did Ai-ming realize she'd underestimated the Bird of Quiet.

Even Big Mother hadn't known about the bundle of foreign letters hidden in a Glenn Gould album sleeve. At first, it had been the stamps that drew her to them: such glorious images of Canadian mountains and frozen seas, such thick Western paper. *Are you writing? Will you send me your recent compositions? My beloved Sparrow, I think of you constantly.* Who was this Jiang Kai and what did she look like? How was it possible that the Bird of Quiet had a secret love?

The photographer's shutter made a big clap.

"Good," Sparrow said. "Done!" He turned to Ai-ming. There was a tiny piece of fluff on his factory shirt. She removed it.

Ling counted the coins in her purse and gave them to the photographer. The coins made a clicking like a handful of beans.

Sparrow pointed up to a dragon kite in the air. He didn't seem to realize she was no longer a little child, and could not be so easily diverted. "How beautiful."

At home, in the tiny room that served as her study, magazines occupied her. Not the candy-coloured women's magazines that had begun to appear in Beijing kiosks but serious journals such as *Let the Natural Sciences Contend.* She had an affinity for probability theory and Riemannian symmetric spaces, which she continued to study, neglecting politics and English, which had been her downfall the first time around. One of their neighbours, Lu

Yiwen, was a glamorous first-year student at Beijing Normal University. She had given Ai-ming a copy of Miyazaki's *China's Examination Hell: The Civil Service Examination of Imperial China*. It was thick. Yiwen had laughed and said she didn't need it anymore. Now, Ai-ming glared at her desk and felt the ridiculousness of it all. These high towers of books made a futuristic city around her. She hid inside and dozed off, her dreams intersecting like airplanes in the sky. A voice in her head kept saying, nonsensically, "Yiwen is airy like a cloud." "The Central Committee of the Chinese Communist Party announces with deep sorrow . . ." She turned and as she did so, a page of *Let the Natural Sciences Contend* crumpled under her cheek, she reached out to wipe it off, "–long-tested, loyal Communist fighter, Hu Yaobang, a great proletarian revolutionary–"

Big Mother Knife, she muddily thought, used to mutter "yào bāng" when she scrubbed their only rice pot. The words meant "brilliant country," and they also happened to be the name of the General-Secretary of the Party. The disgraced, former General-Secretary.

"The utmost efforts were made to rescue him. . . ."

Ai-ming opened her eyes.

"At 7:53 a.m., April 15, 1989, he died at the age of seventy-three." Her chair shifted. The scratching of wood against wood seemed to come from her own bones. One shoulder burned with pain and the other felt loose and long. She thought she could hear people weeping. The crying came nearer, it entered with the rain that was dripping down and darkening the concrete walkway outside the door. Today was Saturday, but both her parents were at work. She walked across the room and sprawled out on their bed, too restless to study, and watched the rain for a long time.

When Sparrow arrived home from the factory he turned their own radio on straightaway, even though they could hear the neighbours' radios just fine. He had been caught in the rain and his wet hair looked sad on his forehead. Ai-ming took a towel and rubbed it violently over his head.

"What did you study today?" he asked, muffled.

"Everything. Are we bringing flowers to Tiananmen Square?"

He pushed a corner of towel out of his face. "Flowers?"

"Look, all our neighbours are making them." She could see into the rooms across the narrow alleyway, and also the rooms adjoining their kitchen, where the Gua family were folding white paper chrysanthemums, the symbol of mourning. "For Comrade Hu Yaobang! He died today, you know."

"Mmm," Sparrow said. He was tilted over, trying expel water from his ear. Now his hair was standing straight up and he looked like a porpoise.

She said nonchalantly, "You know, when he was asked which of Chairman Mao's policies might still be relevant in China, Hu Yaobang said: 'I think, none.'"

"You know better than to repeat such things."

"If the General-Secretary can say it, why can't I?"

Her father straightened. "Since when did you become the General-Secretary? And wasn't he purged?"

On the radio, Red Guards were shouting ridiculous slogans at a disgraced Hu Yaobang. This was the 1960s, before Ai-ming was born, and the frenzied sound clip lasted only a few seconds before moving on to better days. Here he was in the new economic zones, here he was with cadres in the Northwest. *After the Cultural Revolution and the downfall of the Gang of Four, Comrade Hu worked for the rehabilitation of those who had been wrongly accused. . . . He travelled through 1,500 districts and villages, all the way to remote Xinjiang and Inner Mongolia, to see how Party policies manifested in people's lives. . . .*

It rained harder. Ai-ming slowly peeled an orange.

In the alleyway, Yiwen walked by wearing a new pink dress, it swayed against her hips as she went, floating against her long pale legs. Ai-ming felt as vulnerable as this naked orange in her hand. They were the same age but she was a child compared to Yiwen, who was an actual university student. Yiwen had a portable cassette player and she was always listening to music as she walked. It was very modern and deeply Western to listen to music that no one else could hear. Private music led to private thoughts. Private thoughts led to private desires, to private fulfillments or private hungers, to a whole private universe away from parents, family and society.

The squeak of Sparrow's plastic slippers interrupted her thoughts. Ai-ming gave him the peeled orange and he smiled as if she had given him the sun. He went to the record player and Ai-ming flicked off the radio, silencing Hu Yaobang in mid-sentence.

She crawled into bed even though it was still early. The fugue of Bach's *Musical Offering* circled in the darkness like a dog chasing its tail. Ai-ming heard her mother come home, and the routine words her parents exchanged. *Same bed, different dreams.* The old saying described Sparrow and Ling perfectly. How could it be that her mother was such an independent, modern creature? Why did her father love someone so far away from his present reality? How could Ai-ming live a better life than theirs? To her, the only essay question that mattered was, How was it possible for a person to write her own future?

On Monday, Ai-ming ran into the neighbour Yiwen at the water spigot. "You're going to Tiananmen Square this morning, aren't you?" the older girl asked.

Taken aback, Ai-ming could only say, "Why?"

The girl laughed. She lifted her full water bucket, staggering backwards. "Yes, why?" Yiwen said, still laughing. "I almost believed you! Ai-ming, you really tricked me. What a straight face! If I ever need someone to give an alibi for me, I'm coming to you first."

Ai-ming smiled. She watched Yiwen's pink dress float down the alley.

Back in her room, she stood for a moment looking at the stack of books on the desk. The university examinations were still three months away. She drew the curtain across the window, changed her dress and left the apartment.

She pedalled slowly, in love with the wind against her face. Long before Jianguomen changed into Chang'an Avenue, she saw bits of flowers, paper and ribbon all over the road, accumulating like clouds until, at the Square, she arrived at an unreal scene. Thousands of funeral wreaths, with their paper ribbons, were pulsating in the breeze. Just off the Avenue, factory workers were having a public meeting, some girls were reciting poetry, and a group of university students huddled on the ground with ink, brushes and paper, writing essay-length posters. She walked deeper into the Square, searching ludicrously for Yiwen. The concrete seemed to expand from her own feet like an endless grey footprint.

At the Monument to the People's Heroes, three grandmothers were muttering subversively. "Heart attack." "Just like that! Right in the middle of a Politburo meeting." "Those foxes humiliated him, they bullied him until his heart gave out. . . ." A colossal black-and-white Hu Yaobang towered above them, the photo blown up so big that Comrade Hu's nose was the height of a man. Posters were everywhere, on the ground, affixed to the Monument, on makeshift boards. *The ones who should drop dead still live. The one who should live has died.* Just reading the poster made Ai-ming feel as if she had cursed the government or ratted out her father.

She actually lifted a hand to cover her eyes. Still the words on the posters slipped between her fingers. *Why is it that we can't choose our own jobs? What right does the government have to keep a private file on me?*

She turned around only to find herself facing another wall of paper.

Is it not time to live like human beings?

Do you remember?

I am lonely.

She stepped closer, squinting at the characters. *Do you remember?* What illegal thoughts. *The ones who should die . . .* But actually, why should anyone's thoughts be illegal? In the distance, the concrete was shifting, it metamorphosed into a small crowd. The small crowd seemed to replicate itself, more and more demonstrators appeared with banners elongated like ships above their heads. *"Arise, slaves, arise! We shall take back the fruits of our labour . . ."* A Tsinghua University flag dipped and slid sideways, and there were others, too, flags announcing the Institute of Aeronautics and People's University. The students met a line of police. From far away, it looked like a grey wave gulping up a string of fish. The police disappeared and the crowd grew fatter. A banner floated, delicate as a finger, towards her, "Long live education!"

She couldn't help but wonder how the first-years among them had answered the examination question, "Leo Tolstoy. Discuss." Turning awkwardly, she tripped over a schoolbag. The owner apologized and kicked the bag carelessly away from them, she thought she heard something snap. When he smiled the shadows under his eyes widened. The boy asked what department she was in and, when Ai-ming stared, he pointed to a pendant above his head ("Education Department") and then, answering a question she hadn't asked, he said, "An official re-evaluation of Hu Yaobang's life and career. An end to the spiritual pollution campaign. That's number one and two. And also . . . we're asking the government to free those arrested in 1977 for speaking the truth. The heroes of Democracy Wall, you know. Twelve years later, and they're still in prison!" It turned out he was speaking to someone behind her. Humiliated, she stepped sideways and out of his line of vision. His glasses had no nose rests and the frames were sliding down. She wanted, tenderly, to push them up. The students started shouting, "Yaobang forever!"

The sweetness of a piece of cake she had eaten earlier in the day persisted in her mouth. Bits of paper carnations were stuck to her shoes and Ai-ming tried to scrub them off against the grey concrete, not wanting to trail them, like evidence, back home. She found her bicycle and pedalled slowly back, against the constant stream of Beijingers moving towards the Square.

That evening, she crouched with Yiwen in the courtyard and they washed dishes together. "Okay, tell me," Yiwen whispered, "what exactly is revolution?" Ai-ming coughed softly and said, "What?"

"Okay, okay," Yiwen said, "just joking. I thought I would help you study! But, seriously, don't you think citizens should own themselves, be their own people? Isn't a self only a body combined with a system of thought?"

"A self?"

A plastic dish slid out of Yiwen's soapy fingers and spluttered back into the water. She was wearing sneakers, a white T-shirt that served as a dress, and a pink bandana. She'd recently gotten a violently short haircut. Ai-ming had noticed that she carried a spray bottle and every now and then would squirt a big cloud of homemade insect repellent at her bare legs. When she got bitten, she roughly slapped her calves and thighs as if they belonged to someone else.

"My Beida boyfriend," Yiwen said, as if she had other boyfriends at other universities, "says that thousands of wall posters calling for reform have gone up in the last twenty-four hours. His best friend carried a banner to the Square last night. You know what it said? It said, 'The Soul of China.'" She sighed and scrubbed her family's rice pot. "The job assignments are pitiful these days . . . Who knows where they'll unload us once we graduate? I have a cousin who works alone in a closed-down factory in Shaanxi Province. Completely alone! She's supposed to be an accountant. What kind of job is that?"

"If you study at a Beijing university you end up with a good job. Don't you?"

"Beijing!" Yiwen made a face. "We should all go to the West. America owns the past and they own the future, too. What do we own?" She slapped the water. "Hey, what kind of rock music do you like?" Her T-shirt dress had soaked over her thighs and soap bubbles slid down her knee.

"Are there different kinds?"

Yiwen giggled. "Like Northwest Wind style. Do you like that? Let's sing something. You know anything by White Angel? Or Mayday?"

All afternoon, Ai-ming had been reading *Let the Natural Sciences Contend* and her head was full of geological disturbances. "I'm not good at remembering lyrics."

"Ai-ming, little country girl. My father told me that your father used to be a musician! Is that true? Like a rock musician? Hey, come on, you're not really this shy. Are you?"

This was worse than the national examinations. Ai-ming had no idea what the correct answer could be. Fortunately it didn't matter because Yiwen had her own monologue going. Now she started singing by herself: *"I've never stopped asking you, When will you come with me? But you always laugh at me because I have nothing! I'm giving you my aspirations and my freedom, too."*

One of the neighbours, a little boy known as Watermelon, started singing along. He was small but he had big, wet voice. *"I want to grab your hands. Come with me . . ."*

Yiwen stood up, the little dress too small for anything.

"Want to come to the Square, Ai-ming?"

"I can't."

"Tomorrow then." Yiwen tipped over the bucket of soapy water, dumping it out, and then put the clean dishes inside.

"What's your boyfriend like?" Ai-ming asked.

Yiwen got to her feet, swaying slowly, the dishes clattering like rattled birds. She smiled teasingly. "I like it when you leave your hair down."

Ai-ming plunged her hands into her own dish water and said, "Yiwen, where did you get your cassette player?"

"From Fat Lips, on the corner. You want one? He always gives me a really good price."

"I want one. For my father."

"Sure, anytime. Knock on my window. We'll go together."

"We're not Red Guards! We're the surviving remnants of the May Fourth generation. Can't you tell the difference?" Ai-ming's alarm clock hadn't sounded yet, it must be early. Or maybe it was late, the middle of the night, but Yiwen's voice was instantly recognizable.

"Queen Mother of the West! We put aside every dream for you and look what a terror you've become." Ai-ming sat up in bed. Yiwen's father sounded exhausted. His voice seemed to split into three parts as he shouted louder. "Protesting the government at Zhongnanhai in the middle of the night! Getting arrested! You're not really my daughter, are you?"

Yiwen's mother kept repeating the same words over and over: "Calling the leaders by their first names!"

"So what if I call Li Peng by his name? They're just people," Yiwen shouted. "People have names! Why can't you see that? You had the Revolution to believe in, but what do we have?"

A door slammed. Someone, it must be Yiwen, was crying. But perhaps it was Yiwen's father.

Ai-ming sat up. Nobody talked like that so the whole interlude must have been a dream. Patiently, she waited to come to her senses. Shadows fell in waves across the bedclothes and nothing in the room seemed still. She hugged the sheet and remembered Yiwen's pink dress which expanded, covering her, smelling of jasmine, even as the argument went on, fitfully, only partially overheard, lulling her back to sleep.

"If you can solve a physics problem, you can solve this." The Bird of Quiet was looking over her shoulder, later that morning, examining the study questions on Ai-ming's desk. "All you have to do in this essay question is demonstrate correct political understanding.

I think you should do a more careful study of Mao Zedong–Marxist-Leninist thought, especially this chapter on methodology, and matter or materialism as objective reality. . . ."

Two cantaloupe seeds had stuck to his hand, and she noticed two on her left hand as well. These four seeds blocked out everything Sparrow was saying.

After her father had closed the door again, she returned to staring out the window. Of course, the people outside, the neighbourhood aunties, Yiwen and Watermelon, could see her as well as she could see them. They were taking down the laundry before the rain resumed, and no one paid any attention to her sitting miserably between her stacks of books. Yiwen's eyes were puffy. She was singing mournfully to herself,

> I grew up beneath the Red Flag.
> I took the oath.
> To dare to think, to speak up, to act.
> To devote myself to Revolution.

The air had the icy kiss of winter, which was perfect, really, for a funeral. Hu Yaobang would have approved. A week had passed since the announcement of his death, and today, a Saturday, the whole city was going to Chang'an Avenue to pay their respects. Sparrow, however, said they weren't going, Tiananmen Square had been barricaded off, so they would watch it on the neighbourhood television. Television was better, he said. Her father had allowed one of his co-workers to give him a haircut, she didn't know how much baijiu the comrade had drunk, but it all looked a little lopsided. She found it difficult to argue with him, that bad haircut evoked too much pity. Meanwhile Ma unexpectedly announced she was going to the funeral procession because it was the correct thing to do. "You can come with me, Ai-ming. If you like."

To go or not to go? In the end, the bad haircut won.

"It's okay. I'll keep Ba company."

If Ling was hurt she didn't show it. She put on her good shoes and walked elegantly out. Her mother was unfailingly elegant, as if she were a stranger in her own house, which she was. Ai-ming hadn't lived with her since she was three years old, and even though it wasn't Ling's fault, she still felt as if Ling was only impersonating a mother. Ai-ming had always felt more at ease with her great-aunt, the Old Cat, a rare books collector who ran a mobile library, she drove it around in the back of a vegetable truck. The Old Cat lived by herself in Shanghai—"I'm a single modern woman"—and was almost seventy years old.

The funeral was due to start at 10 a.m., so Ai-ming and Sparrow had a slow breakfast. He read the newspaper and she alternated between Collected Letters of Tchaikovsky and Sun Tzu's The Art of War, and the only sound was the crackling of the pages and her father grunting softly in response to an article or maybe just an advertisement. Radio Beijing was announcing things that everyone already knew, and then repeating them again. For security, Tiananmen Square had been closed to the public, people would have to gather on the surrounding boulevards, etc., etc. Ai-ming realized she was looking forward to the few seconds of silence during the funeral because, finally, the radio would have to stop lecturing.

Sparrow poured her a glass of pear juice. "It's strange that the government would close the Square. I suppose Comrade Hu Yaobang was very popular . . ."

Oh, poor Hu! she thought. She had seen pictures of Hu Yaobang all her life, his perfectly egg-shaped head, the man who thought he could change China from within, introduce economic freedom step by step, serve prosperity one sip at a time. Ai-ming wondered: could such a method ever work? Was there anyone in this world who could taste something delicious—economic freedom and political reform—a taste that was salty and fattening and sweet and promising, and only be satisfied with one mouthful? Who could wait patiently for nearly a billion other people to also have a taste? No, anyone would try to get a second mouthful, a third, a whole bowl for themselves. Of course Hu Yaobang had failed, and of course he had been purged! Her thoughts disturbed her. All sorts of private thoughts had been opened up by the sight of Yiwen's pink dress. Even in these modern times, few people wore pink and Ai-ming supposed Yiwen had dyed the dress herself. What about that boy with the glasses slipping down his nose? She had wanted to reach out and touch his slender waist and ask him . . . ask him what? *Doesn't it all seem absurd to you? Why do we have no words for what we truly feel? What's wrong with our parents?*

She went into her bedroom and, because it was cold, dressed under the covers, her left foot, and then her right, struggling to find their way through her jeans. She lay in bed with just her jeans on and no other clothes, her hand moving between the bare skin of her stomach and the thickness of the denim. She imagined that all the world existed between these two sensations, nakedness and clothing, softness and roughness, within and without. What would it be like to leave the country entirely? Here, a change in Party policy could abruptly exile you to the deserts. She pulled on a shirt and then a sweater. Her bare skin felt as if it were waiting for something that would never happen. Nothing fit properly, she would have to alter all her clothes and re-cut everything differently. I want to live, she thought, but nobody here knows how.

Her father suddenly announced he, too, wanted to go to Tiananmen Square to pay his respects to Hu Yaobang, that it was better to go now because the streets would no longer be crowded. It was as if he had just woken up and realized who had died.

"Okay," Ai-ming said. "I'll come with you."

The Bird of Quiet sat down at once to fold two paper carnations. When he was done, he pinned the first carefully to Ai-ming's coat and the second to his own.

They put on their shoes, untangled their bicycles and ped-alled slowly out of the alleyway. How lanky her father was.

Maybe it was unavoidable that a man who did wiring all his life would start to look like a wire himself. The streets outside were not crowded. A few teenagers were sitting on a flower pot at the Muxidi Bridge, none as attractive as Yiwen, whose skin was as pale and fragrant as the flesh of a pear. Ai-ming rode up alongside Sparrow, who began humming Beethoven's Fifth, as if to amuse her.

"Ba, let me fix your haircut."

He smiled, coasting. "Old Bi told me this haircut would make me look young."

"It's a bit crooked, that's all." All warfare is based on deception, she thought, and depends on the element of surprise. "Anyway, what if I applied to universities in Canada?"

She noticed no alteration in his pace, only a slight tipping of his bicycle towards the sidewalk which he immediately corrected. She pressed on. "Yiwen said that almost everyone she knows at Beijing Normal has sent out applications to America. Canada is less expensive though. Imagine if I won a scholarship! You could come with me. Because . . . I wouldn't want to go alone." Her recklessness seemed to come from the streets themselves. This is what happens when politicians die all of a sudden, she thought. It's like a table leg collapsing and things go sliding off.

"Everyone says it's very cold in Canada," Sparrow said. He sped forward. "And isn't your worst subject English?"

"Your daughter can be good at anything if only she applies herself."

Sparrow had no ready answer for that. Fortunately for him, the road suddenly got crowded. He detoured south, into the smaller alleyways inside the Second Ring Road. Turning a corner, he nearly collided with a line of city workers sweeping the street, but they kept on working as if he had never existed and never would. Some of them looked fifty years older than Big Mother Knife.

"Ai-ming," he said when she caught up to him again. "First it was Beijing. And now it's Canada. Once we get to Canada, maybe it will be the moon."

"Others have done it. Even the moon."

"I used to imagine I would go to the West, too, and that I would bring my family with me."

She waited for him to continue, but her father's thought remained a half-thought. The street was bottling up, but still he pedalled headlong into the mourners, pushing between people like a dumpling between noodles. The sky was so white, as if all colours had been sheared away, there were paper flowers in the trees and on the ground, on the coats of everyone around them, and the air smelled not of dust but of a rich and mouth-watering broth. Along the road, families were sitting down to lunch. Faced with this immovable congestion, Sparrow finally dismounted and they began walking, conspicuously, against the flow of the crowd. She and her father were completely out of tune with the moment. Ai-ming walked with her head down; the grey propriety of Beijing, the ochre goodness of it, belonged to people who knew when to arrive for funerals and what time to eat lunch.

She became aware of a new crowd approaching. They were chanting and at first she couldn't make out the words, the loud-speaker they used was weak and tinny. Eventually she saw two young men, each wearing a red armband, carrying a banner that read, "We are young. Our country needs us." The two were un-usually tall, and their banner swayed high into the air. Behind them, the students were sweating, their formal clothes had come untucked, some looked like they had been fighting. And they were crying. Their devotion to Hu Yaobang was sincere, Ai-ming thought suddenly, while hers had always been impersonal.

"Do we love our country?"

"Yes!"

"Are we willing to sacrifice our future for the Chinese people?"

"Yes!"

"Did we do anything wrong?"

Sobbing, "No! No!"

They were passing now, linked to one another, like paper dolls.

The lunching families looked up from their tables. Some got to their feet. Sparrow, too, had stopped walking and was staring at the student procession. *What's happened, what's happened*, the words rebounded from person to person. A boy disengaged himself from the long line and was immediately surrounded. He said that student representatives from the universities had tried to present a petition to the government. Three young men had knelt on the steps of the Great Hall of the People, and had remained on their knees for forty-five minutes while all around them the students and Beijing citizens had yelled at them to stand up, to stop kneeling. Yet they had remained, holding the petition up in the air as if they were children before their father, or slaves before an emperor. But no representative from the government had come out. Lines of police, twenty men deep, had stood between the crowd and the Great Hall. Last night, 100,000 university students had walked to Tiananmen Square and slept there overnight, so that when the Square was closed off in the morning, they would already be inside. "We only wanted to pay our respects to Hu Yaobang, just as those before us have always paid their respects in times of mourning." Even the police had called for the students to stand up. "They asked us why we had to address the government on our knees, but nobody could answer." Officials had stared at them from inside the glass doors and only one, a professor from Beida, had finally come out and tried to pull the young men up.

"But there was no violence," the boy said. "There was no violence. The police agreed with us. Some of them were weeping, too. We're all brothers."

He looked stunned. He turned away and rejoined the procession, buckling himself back into the connected arms.

"Boycott classes!"

"We must have the courage to stand up!"

A placard floated by, "According to the Chinese Constitution, Article 35, the citizens have the right to free speech and assembly." Applause rippled down the avenue. Dust had gotten into Ai-ming's eyes, she tried to rub it out but the rubbing only made it worse. The students looked crushed, their paper flowers were flattened against their chests. In fact, she thought, they looked as if they had come from another country, even though they had only come from a few blocks away. In her distraction, the bicycle slipped from her hands and smacked hard against someone's knee. She dropped her head and began to apologize, expecting someone to call her an idiot country fool, but instead the bicycle righted itself and floated back into her hands. "Good for you students," a woman said. Her voice was scratchy, she was rubbing her knee. "You're braver than we were. Much braver. When my generation gathered in Tiananmen Square, it was a different world." Ai-ming looked up, but either the woman had melted away or Ai-ming couldn't affix the voice to the face. All around her, older people were looking at her as if she had given them lucky money. She could not see properly. She felt as if the sidewalks, the tables and chairs were all shifting, but she was frozen. "I'm sorry," she whispered. Everything flowed before her, the crowd grew denser and then it slowly loosened. It was not until they had nearly reached the Square that she could feel her own weight again, her two legs, the solidity of the bicycle.

Sparrow, too, was quiet. He had lost his paper flower and his coat looked naked. His bicycle creaked. She unfastened her own flower, pulled him to a stop, and pinned it to him. Behind him, the last remnants of the student procession turned right, north towards the university district. What world had they come from and to what world were they returning?

"Ai-ming, what are you thinking?"

What had the Square looked like this morning when the sun rose on a hundred thousand youth curled together on the concrete? She felt embarrassed because, in response to her father's question, she, a young scholar, could only think of Yiwen's favourite song, *It's not that I don't understand. It's that things are changing so fast.*

Sparrow rephrased. "What were these students thinking?"

They had entered the Square now. The phalanxes of police remained, guarding the Great Hall of the People, even though it was probably empty. The day was quickly getting on. A conscientious few students were meticulously picking up garbage, but they left the paper flowers, which tumbled like pollen whenever a breeze came. The oversized Hu Yaobang gazed sorrowfully down from the Monument.

"I came here when I was a small child," Sparrow said. "Big Mother brought me. She told me the Square is a microcosm of the human body. The head, the heart, the lungs . . . She told me not to get lost."

"Did you get lost?" Ai-ming asked.

"Of course. The space is so large. It takes more than a million people to fill it. Even in 1966, the Red Guards couldn't do it."

"Ba," Ai-ming said. "I want to go abroad." There was some part of her that remained untapped, she thought, that would never come to life unless it was given space.

"A person needs money to go abroad. Your mother and I don't have that kind of money."

"The ones without money try to find outside sponsorship."

Sparrow was quiet.

The Art of War, Ai-ming thought, ashamed. Be subtle! be subtle! and use your spies for every kind of business. "If you know someone in Canada who could sponsor me, I could go."

Her father looked at her as if from a great distance. Had she been too direct? Was it obvious she had invaded his privacy?

"Yiwen told me," she said hurriedly, baldly lying. "She said she has an uncle in America. That's why she applied to go overseas. I thought we might know someone."

"But why would I know anyone in Canada?" Ba said. His voice was piercingly gentle, cutting her like a toothpick.

"I don't know. . . . you must know musicians who went away," she said wretchedly. "With my grades. If I studied hard, I could . . ."

"Beida is a the best university in the country. Your mother and I don't want you to study in Canada, it's so far away."

"But you could come with me!"

Sparrow shook his head, but not in a way that said no.

She said, "Once you told me that when you were young, you wanted to go abroad. To write your music. To hear other influences. Why is it too late? Ba, you've been working in the factory for twenty years and this is a long time in a person's life. I think . . . I have a sense that things are changing. The whole point of Hu Yaobang's reforms was to give opportunities to people like you, people who were unfairly treated."

"Is that what you think, Ai-ming, that I was unfairly treated?" He touched the flower she had pinned to his coat, as if he had just noticed it.

She wanted to curl up into a ball. Even though her intent was good, the directness of her words made her feel as if she was poking him repeatedly with a sharpened stick.

After a moment, Sparrow said, "And what about your mother?"

"Ma lived nearly twenty years away from us. What difference would it make to her?"

"She lived far away because the government assigns our jobs and our housing."

"But why? Why can't we choose for ourselves?" Across from them, in the emptiness of the Square, there were posters asking this very same question. She was not alone in her thinking, she had nothing to fear. Ba doesn't even know how afraid he is, she thought. His generation has gotten so used to it, they don't even know that fear is the primary emotion they feel.

"I chose my life, Ai-ming," he said. "I chose the life that I could live with. Maybe it doesn't seem that way from the outside."

She wondered if he believed his own words. She said, "I know, Ba."

They stood together in the Square where funeral wreaths softened the emptiness. The architecture was intended to make a person feel insignificant, but Ai-ming felt confusingly large, there was so much room here, a child could run in any pattern, make any shape, never encounter anyone or anything.

"I want to know what it's like in a young country with lots of space," she said. "If you say something out loud, you hear your own voice differently."

Sparrow nodded.

She said, "Canada."

In Sparrow's mind, lines of Chairman Mao came back unbidden.

We had much to do
and quickly.
The sky-earth spins
and time is short.
Ten thousand years is long
and so a morning and an evening count.

Near to them, in front of the Great Hall of the People, the first line of police, too, seemed to be melting. It could be, Sparrow thought, that a person does not even know that they have gone quiet. Qù could be a substance that begins as a strength and transmutes, imperceptibly, into loss.

They had reached the southern edge of the Square.

Now Ai-ming asked him, "Why did the students kneel down?"

"I imagine . . . they wanted to show respect. They followed the ways in which petitioners have always approached the government."

"But why did no government official come out?"

"Because . . . even though they were kneeling, if a member of the government had come and addressed their demands, the students would have been in a position of power."

The sun was luminous but the wind was cold. His daughter hugged herself tightly. Paper flowers jumbled over the ground, paper carnations grew from the trees, though some had fallen and been mashed by the everlasting stream of bicycles. He heard their tinkling bells and also a music in his head, shaken loose, the Twelfth *Goldberg Variation*, two voices engaged in a slightly out-of-breath canon, like a knot that never got tied. He could still write music. The thought jolted him. It might be possible to procure a piano, he could visit the Central Conservatory and ask for the use of a practice room. But then Sparrow had an image of himself, waiting beneath their turning fans, and smiled to think of himself appearing in his Beijing Wire Factory No. 3 uniform and his blue worker's cap. The absurdity of it made a deep impression. His age struck him forcefully, as if some blindfold had momentarily loosened and allowed him to see things as they were.

He wanted to take Ai-ming's hand. Sometimes, when Ai-ming bruised her knee on the table or suffered some psychological melancholy, it seemed to lodge inside him as well. Where did the line between parent and child exist? He'd always tried to refrain from pushing her in one direction or the other, ever fearful he might drive her towards the Party, but what if his silence had let her down or failed her in some crucial way? But maybe, he thought, a parent should always have failings, some place into which a child can sink her teeth, because only then can a child come to know herself. He thought about those young students kneeling with their petition. Eventually, they would be arrested. It was inevitable.

"What happened to all that music, Ba? What if . . . I wish you'd been able to get away, to the West or some other place. I think, if it weren't for me, maybe you would have tried to live a more honest life."

Had he been dishonest, Sparrow wondered. To whom had he been dishonest? Hadn't he said what needed to be said?

"Forgive me for speaking so directly, Ba. Only . . . you raised me to think my own thoughts, even if I couldn't say them aloud, isn't that so? I think the time has come to say, sincerely, what I feel."

The brutality of children never ceased to surprise him.

He had to stop and rest. His heart was beating strangely and his hands felt full of paper cuts, even though there was no visible injury. Ai-ming caught hold of his arm. She looked suddenly alarmed and he wanted to smooth the terror from her face. Big Mother Knife and Aunt Swirl used to trace their fingers over his forehead, his eyebrows; when he was a child, it would help him fall asleep. But that was almost fifty years ago, when Shanghai was occupied. How funny, Sparrow thought, to think that he had been a child of a former world. When had he ceased to be that person? Ai-ming pulled him to a sidewalk bench and then she ran to fill her tea thermos. She also came back with fish balls on a stick. They looked so unappealing his mouth twisted in disgust. Relieved, Ai-ming laughed. He drank the tea and she ate the fish balls, savouring their saltiness as only a young person can. He fought the urge to put his arm around her. Did he want to hold on to her to keep her safe, he wondered, or just to keep himself from being lonely? Ai-ming was eighteen years old and she was ready to find a new beginning, entirely different from his own. This realization shocked him: Ai-ming was still so young, and already she had judged him.

Over the weekend, the Square came into Sparrow's thoughts like a continuous sound. He had heard from his co-workers that hundreds of thousands of people continued to gather there, they were writing public messages, using Hu Yaobang's funeral as a pretext to mourn others, those who'd never been given a proper burial.

On Tuesday, when Sparrow arrived home from work, Ai-ming and Ling were engrossed by the apricots they were eating and barely noticed him. He changed out of his factory clothes. The previous night, while his wife and daughter slept, he'd written a wall poster to bring to the Square. Now he tucked the narrow roll of paper into his coat.

By the time Sparrow reached Tiananmen Square, it was twilight; thousands of others like him had come to feel the breeze of the open air. Walking across the Square's infinite greyness, he felt as if he had been exiled to some distant moon. The memorial to Hu Yaobang remained, more flowers had arrived and more posters. In 1976, after Premier Zhou Enlai died, similar events had taken place. Beijingers had come to the Square and mourned openly, provocatively; his death had allowed people to demonstrate loyalty to the disappeared, to people like Zhuli. The government must know that allegiance to the dead was a stubborn loyalty that no policy could eradicate.

He took the poster from his coat. Nearby two girls were mixing glue, and he asked for their assistance. "No problem, grandfather!" one said. She had a Shanghai accent. "I'll stick that up for you." She read over his poster, nodded with a kind of bureaucratic approval, and pasted it up in a prominent position. Sparrow had copied a quote from the scholar Kang Youwei, whose treatises he had read in Kai's room, with the Professor, San Li, Ling and the Old Cat, and still remembered: "And yet throughout the world, past and present, for thousands of years, those whom we call good men, righteous men, have been accustomed to the sight of such things, have sat and looked and considered them to be matters of course, have not demanded justice for the victims or offered help to them. This is the most appalling, unjust, and unequal thing, the most inexplicable theory under heaven."

The contours of Hu Yaobang's portrait were disappearing bit by bit. In the openness of the Square, he allowed himself, for the first time in many years, to remember. Zhuli was in Room 103 playing Prokofiev. His Symphony No. 3 had been finished in his head a thousand times, but he couldn't hear the ending. Perhaps the places in ourselves that appear empty have only been dormant, unreachable.

Zhuli, he thought. I'm sorry that I came too late. Of course he knew that she had forgiven him long ago, so why did he hold on to this guilt? What was the thing he was most afraid of?

The next afternoon, Sparrow gazed once more into the chassis of the Model 3812 radio. At the next work station, Old Bi and Miss Lu were arguing over the ongoing demonstrations, which had spread to a boycott of classes at thirty-nine universities by sixty thousand students. Despite the fact that university students were now banned from factory grounds, someone had managed to smuggle pamphlets into the cafeteria, "Ten Polite Questions for the Chinese Communist Party."

Bi's foot kept kicking the table leg to punctuate his words, which seemed to be directed at no one. "Donkeys, donkeys, donkeys!"

"Just last month, fifty people here got reprioritized," Miss Lu said placidly. "They've no jobs and no rations. Modernization stinks."

"But we need to be practical." Bi made a triple kick. "We don't need a million kids in the Square. We need a few smart bosses who know how to run the shop."

The young woman beside Sparrow shouted, "Fuck this wire! These new 1432s are shit." Her name was Fan and she was hot-tempered. "Old Bi, if you kick the table one more time, I'm going to stab both your eyes."

"Give it to me," Sparrow said. He took the chassis, realigned a crooked filter capacitor, connected it straight to the chassis, soldered it with his hot iron, checked the circuit ground and the alignment, and handed it back. It made him think of an electrified violin.

"Comrade Sparrow has the fingers of a little girl," Dao-ren joked.

Radio Beijing was playing Tchaikovsky's *Violin Concerto in D major*. Ever since the announcement of Mikhail Gorbachev's visit to Beijing in May, they had been bombarded by Tchaikovsky and Alexander Glazunov.

"The fact is," Fan said, pointing her soldering gun at Old Bi, "these Beijing kids took one look at our lives and decided it wasn't for them. I thought I would study at Fudan University and become a doctor, but look where I am now, not that you comrades aren't a daily joy to be with! I didn't see my parents or my siblings for fifteen years! I know for a fact that Comrade Sparrow here hasn't seen his brothers since they were kids! These days, if you curse the wrong person, you might as well shoot yourself! My sister's kid complained about his corrupt boss. Poor little shit was re-prioritized and hasn't been assigned a job for three years! He's going to the Square every day now!"

Sparrow pivoted the chassis and began working at it from the opposite corner.

As the others argued, Tchaikovsky's triplet configurations and double stops rained from the speakers like the beating of a thousand wings. When at last the shift ended and they all shuffled towards the exit, Sparrow felt as if a century had passed. On the way home, he nearly fell asleep on the crowded tram, pinned between the window and someone's dried beans. His fingers were completely numb. When he finally tumbled out at Beijing West Railway Station, a large crowd was jostling in front of the post office. Lunch tins cracked against his elbows. Sparrow tried to push his way through but was impeded by the cart of a candy maker. *If we let this turmoil go unchecked, a China with a bright future will become a chaotic China with no future.* Loudspeakers were broadcasting the seven-o'clock news, which meant he had gotten home later than normal. "These children are creating political turmoil?" people around him were muttering. "Counter-revolutionaries? Is that the verdict?" The broadcast continued: *Under no circumstances should the formation of any illegal organizations be allowed.* He would have to . . . pain sparked along his arms, as if strings had been tied around his fingers and slowly tightened. Wasn't this what Red Guards had done to . . . he couldn't think. The bystanders around him were staring malevolently at the speakers. "Are they kidding?" someone asked. "Do they plan on using tanks on a bunch of math students?" Uneasy shifting. "This is turmoil? This is like the Cultural Revolution? I've seen more political turmoil in my soup pot."

Sparrow pushed his way around the candy man. The vendor tried to interest people in the fantastical shapes he created by pulling sugar syrup, he made words and even the heads of famous figures. Sparrow had loved these sweets when he was a boy. He bought three, one that seemed to be in the shape of Chairman Mao, another that was clearly Beethoven, and a third unidentifiable. He pushed his way through the crowd.

Home at last, he could smell the starchy sweetness of the rice Ai-ming had prepared. His daughter had already laid out pickled turnips and spicy eggplant. On radios and speakers up and down the hutong, the government verdict on the student demonstrations repeated: *This is a serious political struggle confronting the whole Party and People. . . .* The announcer let it be known that the editorial would appear in People's Daily the following morning, April 26, and the Party urged all citizens to study it carefully. Sparrow thought he must ask Ai-ming to design a device that surreptitiously turned off other people's radios.

A translation of the Collected Letters of Tchaikovsky sat on the television. Why in the world was Ai-ming reading this? He turned its thin pages. He couldn't concentrate on the words but in the photos, he observed that Tchaikovsky had the large belly of a fortunate man. The composer looked stout and stylish.

He turned the pages of the book as loudly as he could, hoping Ai-ming might emerge, missing her company. The letters of Tchaikovsky were full of banter, he seemed to have several brothers. Here Tchaikovsky was, writing to one brother about the composition of his famous Violin Concerto in D major, Opus 35: "It goes without saying that I would have been able to do nothing without him. He plays it marvellously. When he caresses me with his hand, when he lies with his head inclined on my breast, and I run my hand through his hair and secretly kiss it . . . passion rages within me with such unimaginable strength. . . ."

Sparrow stared down at the page.

Where was the record player? This was a fever pervading his limbs, causing turmoil in his thoughts. He felt such an intense longing for music that he was almost a child again, listening to his mother and Swirl as he waited beneath a teahouse table. And where were Kai's letters? They were missing from the record sleeve where he normally kept them. For years, he had heard nothing of Kai and then, out of the blue in 1985, as reforms intensified, a letter had gotten through. Only then did he learn that Kai had left the country. In 1978, after visiting Sparrow in Cold Water Ditch, he had crossed the border into Hong Kong where he applied for asylum. Within a year, he had married, left for Canada and had a daughter. The first letters had trickled into Cold Water Ditch, arriving every six months. Now, in Beijing, the letters from Canada came every few weeks. Kai said he no longer played the piano. This turning away from music was impossible to explain, he was haunted by people and events; he felt he had been sleeping all these years. He wanted desperately to return to China, however briefly, but his defection made it impossible. The government refused to grant him a visa. Could Sparrow come and see him in Hong Kong? He had already looked into all the particulars. Kai would wire money that might serve as a guarantee for Sparrow's exit visa. This detail was entered into the letter as if it were an ordinary passing thought. Sparrow did not comprehend, but the texture of Kai's writing, the inability to picture either of them in a foreign country, the inability, in truth, to picture the outside world at all, embarrassed him. Sparrow wrote a hesitant reply. And then, last month, Kai had written to him. *Long ago, you told me* not to turn back but I know now that you were mistaken, I knew it then, Sparrow, but I was too afraid to see it. I was too selfish. And what right did I have to ask you for anything? But Sparrow, the future depends on knowing what we loved and who we have become . . . Please, if you can, please come to Hong Kong. There are too many things between us. There is a lifetime. I recently learned that the Professor was imprisoned and survived the turmoil. He passed away in 1981. We never reconciled. How could I not know of his death until now?

Even when he tried to remember, it came to him like another life. Love was his devotion to his parents, to Ling, to Ai-ming, to this life. But if this was love, what was the other?

"Ba, what's wrong?"

Where were the letters? He had looked at them only a few weeks ago, and had left them hidden in the sleeve of a Glenn Gould album.

"What are you doing on the floor?" Ai-ming said.

"I'm looking for the record," he said.

"What record?"

In the evenings, before the lamps were lit, a person could mistake her for Zhuli. The same querying eyes. The same persistent observation. Leave me, he thought. One day, won't Zhuli leave me? But the thought shamed him.

"Is it your hands? They're giving you pain again, aren't they? Come and sit on the sofa."

Kai had a daughter, too.

How did a person know, he wondered, what was love and what was a facsimile of it? Did it matter? Was the thing that mattered most the action that one took—or failed to take—in the name of that feeling?

"Tell me what record it is, Ba."

Those radios outside kept up their warnings. *This is a planned conspiracy and chaos. Its essence is to negate the leadership of the Party and the socialist system once and for all.*

Ai-ming was kneeling on the floor beside him.

His daughter chose a record. She chose Scarlatti's Sonatas in D. Sparrow had a sickly desire to crawl into the machine. In 1977, he remembered hearing that, during the Democracy Wall protests, a man his age named Huang Xiang had pasted up a poem he had written during the Cultural Revolution. Throughout the 1970s, as he wrote the poem, he had covered each page in plastic, wrapped it around a candle, then added another layer of wax around it. When the Cultural Revolution ended, he melted the candles and removed all 94 pages of his poem. Was this a real story, Sparrow had wondered, or was it something like the Book of Records, an imagined survival? How was it possible that people of his generation had taken part in such acts and yet these acts remained so desperately hidden? What happened if you melted a person down layer by layer? What if there was nothing between the layers, and nothing at the centre, only quiet?

Grief for Comrade Hu Yaobang is being used to confuse and poison people's minds.

Yes, he thought. This is what grief does. It is a confusion, perhaps a poison, that breaks us apart until finally we become something new. Or had he been lying to himself? What if he had failed to create someone new?

"Father . . ."

She put a glass in his hand and he tasted baijiu. How sweet the alcohol was on his tongue, a few quick sips and it might numb his body, thereby releasing him, as in the old saying, "When wine sinks, words swim."

"Ai-ming," he said. "No matter what happens, you must write these examinations. You must do well." University was the only way, he thought, to force open the door.

"Ba," she said, "it's not too late for you to go abroad. Don't you still need to write your music?"

Why did everyone keep mentioning his music? Couldn't they just let it go? He drank the liquid down, pretending he had not heard her properly. Before the watchful eyes of Ai-ming, he felt exposed. As if the weakness of the times had lodged inside him, slowly pulverizing all that was unique and his alone, because he had allowed it to do so.

To his great relief, Ai-ming stood up and left him.

He sat in front of the record player. The composer inside him had fallen silent because Sparrow had allowed him to do so.

All revolutionary intellectuals, now is the time to go into battle! Let us unite, holding high the great red banner of Mao Zedong Thought, unite around the Party's Central Committee. . . . But no, those words, that editorial, had come from a different era, a different movement. It was only a memory.

Hidden in the record sleeve of Beethoven's "Emperor" Concerto, conducted by Leopold Stokowski with Glenn Gould as soloist, along with the letters from Kai, was a photo of the three of them together: Sparrow, Zhuli and Kai. His cousin was in the middle, fourteen years old, the only one who looked straight into the camera, the only one with nothing to hide. She had been learning Prokofiev, it had been around the time of Spring Festival, and he remembered how much she had fallen for that composer. "Sparrow, do you think it's possible to love something too much?" She had grasped his hand, the way a child does. She had still been a child in that summer of 1966. "But each phrase is so full, if I tried to hear all its overtones and undertones, nothing would ever get played!" Yet she had learned to hear a great deal, he thought. She'd heard too many voices and given credit to them all. They had been taught, through the lessons of Chairman Mao and the ecstasy of revolution, that death could preserve a truth. But death preserved nothing, he thought. It removed the wholeness of those left behind, and the truth they once knew vanished, unrecorded, unreal, like sound dissipating. He had lived only half a life. Without intending to, he had silenced Zhuli. He remembered how much of himself he had poured into that Symphony No. 3. He could have left the papers in the trusses of the roof, he could have hidden them with the Book of Records. Why had he not done so? Why had he destroyed them with his own hands?

A line from Big Mother's most recent letter from Cold Water Ditch came back to him: *There is no way across the river but to feel for the stones.*

YIWEN HAD TOLD AI-MING that students from every Beijing university would be demonstrating the following day, in defiance of the April 26th editorial. "I'm going," Yiwen had said. She had been in the middle of braiding Ai-ming's hair and unconsciously gave the braid an angry tug. "I don't care what my parents say. We went to a funeral and the government called us criminals! Do they expect us to just shut our mouths? We're not the same as they are. . . ."

In her study, Ai-ming closed her eyes. She missed the companionship of Big Mother's snoring hulk. In her memory, she was back in Cold Water Ditch, she was the same nosy child snooping into Big Mother's book trunk. Here were the forty-two notebooks of the Book of Records, a girl's blue dress, as well as a pamphlet with a yellow cover, and on the cover the words, "Gods and Emperors."

The pages had fascinated her. Later, she understood it was a political tract and an answer to Deng Xiaoping's celebrated Four Modernizations. "We want no more gods and emperors," the writer had proclaimed. "No more saviours of any kind. We want to be masters of our own country. Democracy, freedom and happiness are the only goals of modernization. Without this fifth modernization, the other four are nothing more than a new-fangled lie."

When she opened her eyes, she looked out and saw Yiwen's mother sitting in the courtyard, washing clothes. The pink dress rose briefly from the water before it was pushed under again, re-emerging tangled up in the arms of a shirt.

As soon as her parents left for work, Ai-ming shut her books. She went outside, walked calmly to the north gate of the alleyway and retrieved her bicycle. She hopped on. As she pedalled away from the books, she felt suddenly free, airborne. At the Chinese Academy of Sciences, she swerved across the intersection, dodged a cart loaded with water drums, and continued on under the big trees of Yuyuantan Park.

Sidestreet and delivery lanes opened up before her, and she flew north until she reached the Third Ring Road. Here, noise pummelled the buildings. At first all she could see were hundreds of green-hatted police. But behind them, just visible on the other side, were the edges of innumerable banners, mostly red and gold, like a wedding. The loudspeakers, out of sync, blurted out garbled warnings, "Demonstrations without official approval are illegal and will be banned! Demonstrations without official approval . . ."

On Ai-ming's side of the police lines, two old men in white vests were holding a neatly written banner: "The way ahead is long and far, yet I will search far and wide," but the two, who reminded her of Ba Lute, already seemed tottery on their skinny, grandfather legs.

Ai-ming locked her bicycle to a grate and squeezed onto the overpass. Looking down, she saw the students pressed right up against the police line, where the officers had hitched themselves together, arm in arm. The students were using the sheer mass of their numbers to slowly, tectonically, exert pressure. It was fierce and sweaty work.

I was a silly egg to think I would be able to find Yiwen, she told herself, blushing at the unexpected thought. The mass of young people disappeared into the horizon, as if the crowd stretched all the way to Beijing University itself.

A boy who had climbed up a lamppost called out that comrades from the University of Politics and Law had banded together and broken through a blockade at the Second Ring Road. Noise rioted up, vibrating the overpass. She watched as ladies coming to or from work, in factory blues, pink aprons, and green smocks, tried to sweet-talk the officers into letting the students through. Old people sat on their balconies as if watching opera, shouting at everyone to get on with it. Even as it grew increasingly tense, it was clear to Ai-ming that the police had no intention of pulling out their weapons. They were simply placing their bodies in the way.

Minutes passed, another half-hour, and still the agonizing pushing went on.

The students, all neatly dressed, attractive with their earnest glasses, began chanting the words of Comrade Deng himself: "A revolutionary government should listen to the voice of the People! Nothing should frighten it more than silence!"

On this side, the residents joined in, so that the police were pinioned between two tidal waves of sound. This went on for half an hour before everyone stopped to rest. Meanwhile up on the overpass, it was shoulder against shoulder, chest against back, with still more people arriving. Ai-ming was so sweaty she feared she might be squeezed, like a slippery fish, off the bridge.

The students were reorganizing. All the young women had been sent up to the head of the line. A few men around Ai-ming laughed dirtily. A soothing female chorus rose up:

"Raise the incomes of the police!"

"Brothers!" a young woman called. "You have been working hard all morning! Citizens of Beijing! Bring water to the People's police!"

Amidst laughter and cheering, water materialized. Ai-ming scanned continuously for Yiwen. A few police lifted off their peaked caps, withdrew colourful handkerchiefs, and mopped the sweat from their faces. They smiled shyly at the girls, who giggled. Everyone exhaled, like a rest between sets.

The students managed to reformulate themselves so that boys and girls were mixed together once more. Meanwhile, the overpass took up the chant, "What's so hard? It's like cutting cabbages and melons!"

By now, Ai-ming had been on the overpass for almost three hours and she, too, felt the moment had arrived. She couldn't stand to be further compressed. From the boulevard of protesters, more cries came, rolling forward with piercing intensity.

"Reject the verdict of the *People's Daily!*"

"We are not a mob, we are civilized members of society!"

Under this sustained pressure, Ai-ming could see the sweating police beginning to fray. The students pressed their advantage, all the while chanting, "The People love the People's police!"

The students heaved through the centre and the green police lines dissolved to the sides like a soft leaf curling open. Ai-ming heard an uprush of sound that felt as if it were coming from the concrete and the buildings themselves. Residents leaned so far out she was afraid they would all tumble off the flyover together. Her own shouts of both astonishment and relief were lost in the tumult. Even though the success of the students seemed inevitable, it also seemed impossible, and everyone looked mildly stunned. A police hat flew nonsensically up onto the overpass, and Ai-ming, finding it in her hands, gently tossed it down to a bareheaded officer, who gazed up into the sun, looking for her. She waved. Carts of water and icy tea appeared. Beside her, a toothless old man was throwing popsicles down to the crowd. A huddle of police were talking into radios, a few were grinning, and students patted their shoulders as they went by. A banner passed, "A new path is opening up: the path we long ago failed to take."

The marchers moved forward, surrounded on all sides by student marshals with red armbands. Ai-ming ran to unlock her bicycle from the grate. Pushing it beside her, she slipped between the lines of students. Everyone's clothes were rumpled as if they'd all been wrestling or turning over and over in their sleep.

They weren't asking for anything impossible, Ai-ming thought. Just room to move, to grow up and be free, and for the Party to criticize itself. A red banner from Beijing University read in proud, golden characters, "Without the Communist Party, there would be no New China."

The closer they came to the Square, the more the crowd seemed to become a part of her own body, so that Ai-ming herself expanded limitlessly as students from other universities continued to arrive, connecting at intersections between the First and Second Ring Roads. Cooks in tired hats and white aprons stood outside their kitchens, waiters smoked passionately, shopgirls teetered out of department stores, so that around six in the afternoon, when office and factory workers came off their shifts, they were all crushed together in the smaller roads. People her parents' age kept pressing water, ice cream sandwiches, frozen fruit, and Inch of Gold candies into her hands. Sugar-struck, Ai-ming thought she saw the dazzling pink of Yiwen's headband. She followed it as if following torchlight.

"Yiwen!" she shouted. Her lungs were bursting. "Yiwen!" Without her realizing that it was happening, what she appeared to be on the outside, and who she was on the inside, had become the same. Rapture felt so strangely light. A knot of journalists from the People's Daily passed by holding hands, they didn't bother to hide their badges. One carried a signboard that read, "Free Thoughts! Free Speech!" The air was inundated with words like this, banners and posters that covered the street like moveable type, as if the sidewalk itself was an enormous banned book. It was difficult to believe that what she witnessed was real and not a counter-revolutionary's hallucination. And, stranger still, there was no weeping, no regret or anxiety about the past, and none of the day-to-day insincerity which was a normal part of everyday life. And here was Yiwen, just ahead of her. Ai-ming halved the distance between them and halved it again. The police had evaporated as if they, too, belonged to some other Beijing. And had someone pulled out the wires of the loudspeakers? Ai-ming ran up to her friend. The uneven pavement made the bicycle bell jingle and, hearing it, Yiwen turned, saw her and broke into a luminous smile.

"What is revolution?" Yiwen said, half laughing, half crying. "Ai-ming, what is revolution?" Could it also look like this, Ai-ming wondered. Yiwen reached around, hugging her waist. "This is revolution," she said, her mouth brushing Ai-ming's hair. Because of her father's low political status in Cold Water Ditch, she had never had a true friend before. They were walking like family who had lost and then found one another. Tiananmen was a gate, the passageway to a square with no walls, no obstacles, just the wind and space to breathe, and even a call to abandon oneself. Couples embraced, they clung to one another in wide-eyed desire. Maybe, she thought, by the time the examinations arrived, the content of her thoughts would be permissible, the only thing that would need measuring would be the quality of her argument. If so, this change had occurred suddenly, with so little forewarning, and before she had even thought to ask for it or dared to imagine that overnight a society could change. Yiwen was singing, "Now your hands are shaking, now your tears are falling. Maybe what you're saying is, you love me, with nothing to my name, come with me, come with me!" She wanted Yiwen's arm never to lift from her waist. Maybe, if China could get better, she would no longer desire to escape abroad.

Celebration rattled the streets. Ling's bus entered the Third Ring Road before coming to a standstill in the face of bicycles and crowds. She stepped down as if into a different city. Even here, several kilometres away from Tiananmen Square, she could hear the chanting. There were explanations on people's lips but none that made sense. "The student demonstrations broke through three thousand police. . . ." "The Square is blocked off so they've filled Chang'an Avenue. . . ." "All they did was present a petition and our government called them counter-revolutionaries!

Shame!" "Enjoy it while it lasts. No flower can live a hundred days...." Red bits of banners clung to trees just as, only two weeks ago, funeral chrysanthemums had blanketed the boulevards.

At home, Ling pushed her shoes off, went to the dining table and hung her purse on the chair. The apartment was quiet. She knocked at Ai-ming's door and, receiving no answer, opened it. Sparrow was writing. When he looked up, it was as if he had no idea where he was.

Ling took a breath. The room smelled of alcohol. "Has Ai-ming gone to the Square?"

"She was already gone by the time I came home."

His hand covered the sheet of paper before him.

Outside, the street noise grew, dissolved and came again, like an explosion.

"Every citizen is on the streets tonight it seems. Except you, dear Sparrow."

She came nearer, looking closely at her husband's face. He was extremely pale. "What's happened?" she asked. "Are you worried about the demonstrators? The government won't arrest the whole city. They can't."

He couldn't look at her. "What are the students asking for?"

"I'm not sure they know anymore. The government accused them of inciting chaos. They compared them to the Red Guards and the students don't agree. Nobody does."

Sparrow stood up. "They have no idea of the risk," he said. He moved towards the door as if this room was too crowded.

Ling followed him out. The sheet of paper, turned over, remained where it was.

"But what if . . ." she said, following him into the kitchen. Suddenly exhausted, Ling sat down at the table. "Those students are rebelling against us, too. Against our generation, I mean."

Sparrow said nothing.

When had they last had an honest conversation, she wondered. Could it be months, or even years, since they last confided in one another? "We let the Party decide our jobs, our fates, our homes and the education of our children. We submitted because . . ."

"We thought some good might come."

"But when did we stop believing it? Look at me, I edit transcripts and I'm grateful for the job. My life is a mountain of paperwork and a sea of meetings." She laughed, but found her own laugh alarming. "Unlike us, these young people have literally no memory. Without memory, they're free."

"Yes," he said.

"I've been thinking about my life, Sparrow. Not the past but the future. Don't you ever think about yours?"

"Yes, of course, but here in Beijing . . . sometimes I imagine that I . . . but we–"

Ai-ming burst into the apartment, elated. Ling caught a glimpse of another girl darting down the alleyway, a flash of neon colour. It was the neighbour's wild daughter, Yiwen.

Sparrow turned towards the door. "Where have you been?"

"At the Square, of course! You should see it, all the people– "

He began to berate her. Ai-ming stared at her father as if he were a stranger.

"How can I protect you?" he yelled. "How?" He had drunk more than Ling had supposed. She stood up from the table and went towards him. Sparrow kept on: "The government is right. You're no different from the Red Guards! You think you know everything, you think you can judge everyone, you think you're the only ones who love this country. You think you can overturn everything in a day, a moment!"

"Sparrow," Ling said.

"They stole everything," Sparrow said, turning to her. "But why did we let them do it? Why did we give in? I remember everything now. My brothers. I couldn't . . . Zhuli. They needed me to help them, but I didn't. Why did we throw away everything that mattered to us?"

Ling's heart was breaking. She had never seen him come apart, she had stopped thinking that he could. It was as if someone had cut a single wire inside him on which everything had depended. "Sparrow, let it go."

"How?"

"Ai-ming," Ling said, wanting to shield their daughter. "Go to your room." Ai-ming obeyed. Tears streamed down her face.

"How can I forget?" Sparrow's face was drained of colour. He looked at Ling as if she had always known the answer. "If I forget, what's left? There's nothing."

All she wanted was to lie down, close her eyes and rest, but she had to get out of this room, out of the falseness of this home. Ling picked up her purse from the chair. The walls were pressing in on her and she couldn't breathe, thinking of everything she had given up for her family, but most of all for the Party. She looked once more at her husband, who had covered his face with his hands. "Don't you see?" she said. "Things are changing."

He didn't answer.

"Live your life, Sparrow. It's the best thing either of us can do for our daughter." She went out the door, through the alleyway, and into the street.

When Sparrow woke, the room, the city, was quiet. He got out of bed, lit the lamp and took the letter out of its hiding place. On the kitchen table, the paper gleamed whitely.

Even if I had the means to leave

I was content in my life

The night sky was a thickening dark. He would like to have a piano, he would like to sit, right now, in the darkness of a practice room. Music, for him, had always been a way of thinking. He pushed the pages away. Sparrow could not imagine leaving his daughter behind. Ai-ming was so much like Zhuli. Were they similar because of him, had he failed to give his daughter the room she needed? In the eighteen years of Ai-ming's life, he had never been separated from her, not for a day. He covered the letter with his hands and chided himself for being mournful. If he could sweep away all this mournfulness, which must only be a kind of dust from his previous lives, he would be a better father and a kinder husband. Ling's confidence and goodness had always sustained him. He had no right to grieve. Their neighbour was listening to the radio, Sparrow could hear the anchor's even drone but not the words. Music began, echoing through the alleyway, but it was music he couldn't recognize, music from an era he didn't know, music composed in the present.

Ongoing disruptions in the street, in the factory and in his home continued. He suspected Ai-ming was going to the Square every day, but neither he nor Ling had the will or influence to stop her. On the May First holiday, he telephoned Cold Water Ditch on the neighbourhood phone. Big Mother came onto the line and shouted, "Workers' Day? We live in a Communist country. Every day is workers' day!" He could hear Ba Lute giggling behind her. Big Mother grumbled, "Tell that lazy Ai-ming to study hard." When he said there was unrest in Beijing, she said, "Good! Nobody should be at rest."

How, he wondered, when he put down the phone, had Big Mother managed to raise a son like him? It was impossible not to believe in the mischief of the gods.

The May Fourth demonstrations came and went, as large as the preceding April 27th demonstration, and included a contingent from Sparrow's own Beijing Wire Factory No. 3. But he did not go.

Sleep became impossible. Sparrow took to walking at night. Even at two or three in the morning, bicycles roamed the streets, students flitting from one place to another. Time felt elastic, stretching into unfamiliar shapes, so that he could be both in Beijing and in Shanghai, an old man and a young man, in the world and in his thoughts.

One night, he came across three men and two women playing music at the closed gates of Jade Pond Park. The musicians made

time disappear. On Chinese instruments, they played the dignified promenade from Mussorgsky's "Pictures at an Exhibition."
Mussorgsky's ten movements depicted an imaginary tour of an art
collection, and the composition had been written in honour of his
friend, a painter who had died suddenly at the age of thirty-nine.
A deep and unfamiliar calm pervaded Sparrow. On a nearby pillar,
someone had pasted up a letter, "I've been searching for myself,
but I didn't expect to find so many selves of mine." When morning
came, the musicians packed up their instruments. Sparrow
bought a dough stick and savoured it as he watched the night
workers go off duty and the day workers go on.

One evening, he arrived home from the factory to find a gift
from Ai-ming. She had bought one of the new Japanese cassette
players, small enough to fit into one hand. His daughter was so
delighted with the gadget, she could not restrain herself from
testing all the buttons and trying the headphones herself, adjusting and readjusting the volume. They might have toyed with it all
night had Ling not dragged them out for supper.

He continued his nighttime walks, listening to the Walkman.
Ai-ming had made a dozen tapes for him, copying them, she said,
from someone called Fat Lips. Lately, she had friends all over the
place. One evening, Sparrow walked all the way to the university
district listening to Bach's *Goldberg Variations*. In the darkness, one
could always hear better. The music became as real as the concrete
sidewalks and stout brick walls. Elderly guards at the entrance to
Beijing University were immersed in their midnight card game,
and so Sparrow passed through the gate unimpeded. Perhaps in
his innocuous clothes, he had been mistaken for a cleaner or a
parent visiting from the countryside.

Low lights flickered in the student dormitories where, now
and again, excited figures were visible in the narrow windows. The
tape ended and he hit the eject button, removed the cassette and
turned it over. The machine made satisfying clicks. Cannonades of
laughter came from the dormitories, arriving in staggered bursts.

Posters clung to every surface, banners wept from the windows, the ground was a deluge of papers and empty bottles. Workers were sweeping up the debris, twig brooms scratching the cement. The Variations started up again. The cassette was Glenn Gould, Ai-ming had told him, but a different, 1981 recording of the *Goldberg Variations*. In the opening aria, each note seemed to Sparrow as if it had been pulled open rather than pressed down. Occasionally, he heard Glenn Gould himself, humming. Why had Gould gone back to record the same piece of music again? No one could tell him. Fat Lips only had this one edition, Ai-ming had said, a copy of a copy that a foreigner had given him.

The counterpoint folded over in his mind. The further Sparrow walked into Beijing University, the greater the quantity of political posters. Even the trees had not been spared. Torches had been set up, and here and there boys wandered by in shorts, reading the posters, just as people of Sparrow's generation, at the post office and elsewhere, studied the newspapers displayed in their plastic boxes. More posters were being pasted up over the old ones, making an ever-thickening book of protest. In 1966, Beijing Red Guards had written, "We must tell you, a spider cannot stop the wheel of a cart! We will carry socialist revolution through to the end!" Twenty-three years later, Beijing students wrote, "Democracy takes time to achieve, it cannot be accomplished overnight." But several proposed an immediate hunger strike that would occupy Tiananmen Square before the arrival of Mikhail Gorbachev in four days' time.

A tall boy gestured menacingly at him, but Glenn Gould prevented Sparrow from hearing the shouted words. Sparrow pushed his headphones off. "I said, don't think of tearing anything down!" the student said impatiently. "I know you're a fucking government spy!" Sparrow was so surprised he mumbled an apology.

He backed away, nearly tripping over a gracefully written pennant with the words, "A society that speaks with only one voice is not a stable society."

The breeze cooled him. He left the grassy hill and exited through the gates of Beida, to the tree-lined edge of Haidian Park. In this unfamiliar city, Glenn Gould seemed his only confidant, the most familiar presence. Do I really look like a spy, Sparrow wondered. Are there spies who behave like me?

A hundred radios passed through Sparrow's hands.

In the evenings, when he went to Tiananmen Square, the boulevards had a serene yet haunting openness, the wide streets themselves seemed to promise an end to this impasse. The government had not reversed its condemnation of the student protest, but had begun to speak in soothing tones. General-Secretary Zhao Ziyang, who had worked closely with the deceased Hu Yaobang, had used a May 4th speech to air his own point of view. The students, he said, were calling on the Communist Party to correct its mistakes and improve its work style, and these criticisms were in line with the Party's own assessment of itself. "We should meet the students' reasonable demands through democracy and law. We should be willing to reform and we should use rational and orderly methods." To Sparrow's great surprise, the press had begun reporting on student demonstrations that were occurring not only in Beijing, but outside the capital, in some fifty-one cities. A fracture had appeared in the system, and now water was rushing in to widen it. Ling said that even within her work unit at State Radio, the consensus was that the government had been too harsh. The demonstrations offered an opportunity: if the Party could prove its sincerity, it would win the loyalty of a further generation.

The nights continued, growing ever warmer. He wrote to Kai to say, "Yes, I will come," and having sent the letter off, lost himself by walking the Muxidi alleyways, listening to another of Ai-ming's tapes, this one Shostakovich's Fourth Symphony, which had gone unperformed for twenty-five years. What would it be like to go to Canada at this stage in his life? What if Kai could sponsor Ai-ming? He would pay the money back. But what about Ling and this life? What about his parents? In what way was he still a composer if he had made not a sound for more than twenty years? There were no answers to his questions.

Yet the knowledge that he would see Kai brought him an undeniable, undiluted pleasure. Upon sending the letter, Sparrow had felt abruptly changed. That a few simple words could transform him, *Yes, I will come*, unsettled him. But why should he continue to fear? Wasn't society changing? Nearly a month had passed since Hu Yaobang's death, a month in which Beijing students continued to boycott classes. There were rumours that high-ranking members of the Communist Party were prepared to sit down with the students, face to face, and take part in a televised dialogue. If so, this would be the first time such an event had occurred in Sparrow's lifetime; he could not fathom it, and remembered, still, He Luting, his head forced down by Red Guards.

A change in the system of government had the power to change the fundamental construction of the world he knew. He would go to Hong Kong. A truthful end could come at last. He and Kai were no longer young, they had families of their own. It was difficult to move on without an end ... but move on to what? He could not think so far into the future and if he thought of Ling, all his childish imaginings evaporated. Everything changed in a day, an hour, a moment. In the past, he had misread events, he had reacted too slowly. Sparrow had made mistakes but he promised himself he would not make them again. Now, in the afternoons, when he came home from work, Sparrow sat down at Ai-ming's desk and composed. The old Symphony No. 3 was gone, he could no longer retrieve what it might have been, and so he had started a new work, a simpler piece, a sonata for piano and violin. The Japanese composer Toru Takemitsu once described his own work as "a picture scroll unrolled," and Sparrow felt a kinship with this image. He could hear this sonata in his head as surely as he could hear Bach and Shostakovich on the cassette player. The sonata was real and had already been created. One's own mind, the saying went, concealed more information than five cartloads of books. It was like learning to breathe again, not just with his lungs but with his whole mind.

On May 13, the students went on hunger strike. Sparrow was working in Ai-ming's room when the announcement was broadcast on the radio. He sensed that the piano and violin piece was unfolding at a sped-up tempo, and he erased the last hour's work and began again, re-counting the measures, altering the space between development and return, two themes supporting one another. The line of the piano was difficult to hold, but the violin felt supple and unceasing. It was not heroic, it wished only to play for itself alone, even if it knew such a thing was not truly possible.

A commentator on the radio argued that these revolutionary youth were part of a deliberate attempt to humiliate the government and the nation. "Why else begin a hunger strike two days before our historic summit with Mikhail Gorbachev? This is the first visit from a Soviet leader in forty years. . . ." Another said the students' intentions were good, but their methods were immature, and it was imperative that they refrain from damaging the nation's image. The news also seemed to be wrestling with its own head; the newsreader announced that General Secretary Zhao Ziyang favoured far-reaching press reforms, so that content and analysis would be decided by news editors and not Party officials. A sharp pain in Sparrow's back flared unexpectedly, and he felt like an old piano that couldn't be tuned.

At work the following day, the factory was unproductive. Half his co-workers had signed on to the new independent workers' union operating from under a tarp on Chang'an Avenue. They had gone so far as to identify themselves by their real names, even showing their work badges. His co-workers only wanted news of the Square. Sparrow hadn't yet signed on, he was trying to imagine himself boarding the plane for Hong Kong. Kai had been true to his word and Sparrow's exit visa had been approved. For the first time in his life, he would travel out-side China. Kai had begun to float other ideas. *We could teach at the Hong Kong Conservatory. I have also made inquiries at the Vancouver Conservatory of Music. What have you been composing? Send me what you have.* He began to suspect that Kai was living an illusion more complex than his own.

Fan, who worked the line with him, tapped her pencil on his desk. "Comrade Sparrow," she said. "You look hideous. Do you have a fever? Is it contagious? Maybe you should get home and rest."

Fan was still so young, Sparrow thought suddenly. If Zhuli were alive, she would be thirty-seven years old. These days, she entered his thoughts freely, as if some barrier between them had broken down.

"I'm not . . ."

"Go on. Production is non-existent anyway." Fan got up, he could see her in the next aisle talking to the floor supervisor, known to everyone as Baby Corn, Sparrow didn't know why. His hands were trembling. Perhaps he did have a fever. Baby Corn came over, deferential, as if Sparrow were his ancestor.

"Comrade Sparrow, you're looking dead on your feet. Take the afternoon off. You're back on shift tomorrow anyway, aren't you?"

"I would prefer to stay." Sparrow was afraid he would be criti-cized, later on, for not working to his full capacity. They would use this weakness to reprioritize him and lay him off. If he lost his job, they might revoke Ai-ming's Beijing papers, and she would not be allowed to sit the university examinations.

"I insist," Baby Corn said, distracted. He wandered a few steps away and gazed into the large face of his brand new watch.

"Come on," Fan whispered. "He's a real pain when he's angry. Besides, you look *awful* . . . Did you injure your back? At your age, you've got to take better care of yourself."

As he left, he heard the newsreader saying that talks between the government and the students, scheduled for the morning, had been cancelled. Outside, even the breeze felt sticky. He had started cycling to and from work because the buses were not reliable. Ling had told him that youth from across the country were pouring into Beijing by the tens of thousands. They were painting democracy slogans on train cars so that wherever the trains went, the student messages, too, would go. Sparrow pedalled slowly across the factory grounds, ashamed of his exhaustion. If he was not careful, they would all be calling him Grandfather, which was ludicrous because he was not even fifty.

He ended up on Chang'an Avenue, his bicycle inching through traffic as if he were part of a larger procession. He hadn't meant to go to Tiananmen Square, it was only that he neglected to turn right after the Muxidi Bridge, and had continued straight. Chang'an Avenue was jammed; now he couldn't turn around even if he wanted to. He had grown up in Shanghai, the most modern of Chinese cities, and yet he felt like an outsider here, out of his depth. The flood of Beijingers carried him forward until, glimpsing the Square, he saw that it was once more overrun with banners representing more universities than he could count. And now Sparrow truly did not wish to be here. Loudspeakers were broadcasting continuously. A young woman's frail voice crackled over the street: "The country is our country. The people are our people. The government is our government. Who will shout if not us? Who will act if not us?"

Sparrow got down from his bicycle and began to push it. The young woman was using the exact words of Chairman Mao, written when Mao Zedong was a young fighter.

Beside Sparrow, an enormous man with a grizzled face was reading the newspaper as he walked.

"This hunger strike," Sparrow said to him. "Is it real? Will the students really refuse food?"

"Ai! These kids . . ." The stranger's badge, stamped with the words Capital Iron and Steel, trembled from a clip on his shirt. "It'll be over in a few hours. Old Gorbachev will be escorted into the Square tomorrow and the Party will shake the kids off

Tiananmen like ants from a stick." He folded the paper in half. "That's what my son tells me anyway."

"And all these people?"

"Exactly. I came to see what's gotten everyone so worked up. Of course, I admire their ideals. Who doesn't? But even a nothing like me can see that the students and the government aren't speaking the same language. Everyone wants to fix the country, but everyone wants power, too, don't they? That's what we're talking about in my danwei. . . ." He tapped his badge. "Our work unit alone has over 200,000 workers and if we support the hunger strike, that changes everything, doesn't it? That's a bloody revolution." He took a bag of buns, as if by magic, from his other hand and offered one to Sparrow, who accepted. The man ate half of one in a single bite. "Any kids, Comrade?"

"A daughter."

"Not a university student, I hope."

"Thank heavens, no."

The man swallowed the bread in his mouth and washed it down with a gulp from his tea thermos. "Frankly, I don't understand what's wrong with us. The stupidity we went through, a whole generation slapping its own head . . . how come we keep arriving at the same point?" He screwed the lid back on his thermos. "Hey, you're not a plain coat are you? Someone told me there are thousands of plain coats snooping around."

"A spy?" Sparrow smiled. "No, but other people have thought the same."

"Because you're so unthreatening," the man said. "Don't take offence. It's just that you've got such a listening face."

It was twilight. Behind the Monument of the People's Heroes, hundreds of students were lying on the ground. They were guarded by other students, wearing red armbands, who made a kind of human barricade around them. Sparrow felt that a world he had been living inside was being forced open. But weren't these students also living inside a world of their own construction? The hunger strikers had the brightest futures in the entire country. As Beijing university graduates they would be responsible for their parents and grandparents, for their siblings if they had any, yet here they were, lying on the bare concrete. He felt a gnawing fear scraping against his lungs. Three boys on one bicycle rolled by, acrobatic, joyful. They shouted, "We won't eat fried democracy!" and a ripple of laughter came from the pyjama-clad students. Where were their parents? he wondered. But now a boy with a red armband came to him and said sternly, "Don't take this the wrong way, Comrade, but only we are allowed here. It's for the security of our hunger strike revolutionaries." Sparrow nodded, backing away. The recording on the loudspeaker began again, it was the same fragile voice as before, "Today freedom and democracy must be bought with our lives. Is this fact something the Chinese people can be proud of?"

Sparrow looked up, trying to find the source of the broadcast, but the endlessness of the sky made it difficult to see what was near.

I have grown old, he thought. I no longer understand the ways of this world.

The following morning, as they stood beneath Fan's flowery umbrella outside the factory gates, Fan gave Sparrow a pamphlet that listed the demands of the hunger strikers. There were just two: immediate dialogue on an equal footing, and an acknowledgement of the legitimacy of the student movement. Fan told him that the workers of Beijing Wire Factory No. 3 would be marching in support of the students on May 16. She had heard that almost all of Beijing's factories, as well as scientific and educational institutes, were planning the same. Fan was unusually subdued, and when Sparrow asked if she was well, she told him that her sister in Gansu Province had suffered a work accident but Fan didn't know the severity. "And I've been going to the Square every night after work," she said, "to help out where I can, because these skinny kids haven't eaten in three days, and the government has yet to lift a finger. How did we come to this?" Fan's troubled face turned away from him. "And I don't want to make radios anymore." She looked back and laughed, a lost, unhappy laugh. "Does anyone want to make radios?" she said. "Oh, damn your second uncle!"

This was a special Beijing curse and it made Sparrow smile.

Fan raised her eyebrows, which made her ears wiggle slightly. She leaned mischievously towards him, so close their noses nearly touched. "What would you like to do, Comrade Sparrow, if you were free to choose a vocation?"

He didn't hesitate. "I'd like to play the piano."

Fan let out a honking laugh. Someone coming up the stairs dropped their lunch tin in surprise and let out a sad, soft, *Waaaaa!* "It's never too late to learn!" Fan shouted.

Sparrow smiled. "I suppose."

"But the piano kind of thing, Comrade," she said, turning serious, "is a hobby and can be done in addition to a steady job and what I meant with my question is the kind of vocation that requires a lifetime's commitment. I wanted to be a doctor, I think I told you once, I wanted to open a clinic in my sister's town but you know how it was back then. It wasn't up to me."

Rain battered dully on the umbrella. I want to see my daughter grow up, Sparrow thought. The premonition scared him so much he reached out his hand, intending to grasp the wall, and caught only air.

Fan didn't notice. Her fingers were idly tapping the handle of the umbrella, playing an imaginary instrument. "Speaking of pianos," she said. "Remember that musician in 1968, the composer from Shanghai, the tall one with the long face, what was his name? They locked us in a room and made us watch his struggle session. Old guy was being kicked around on live television and we still had to call him names."

"He Luting."

"That's it! Right on television, they were going to make a big example out of him. I haven't thought of him in years. Do you remember it?"

"I remember."

"Oh, boy. Everyone had to watch, it didn't matter whether you worked upstairs or in the basement. So we all heard it when he shouted, 'How dare you, how dare you. . . . *Shame on you for lying.*' That's what he said, he kept yelling out, 'Shame! Shame!' Those Red Guards couldn't believe it. I can still see their faces, big eyes and dumb-dumb mouths. Nobody could believe it, the nerve of this guy. I wonder if he's still alive."

"I think so," Sparrow said.

"*Shame on you!* I'll never forget." She disappeared for a moment into her own searching. "We all knew that, once the cameras were switched off, pow, that would be the end of him. They wouldn't let him get away with it."

"But afterwards, were you yourself different?"

Fan looked at him, startled. "Comrade Sparrow, what kind of question is that?. . . how could anyone be different?" She gave an irritated sigh. "Sure this He Luting proved that it was possible to fight back, to stand up . . . but I still didn't know how it was done. The Red Guards back then, the youth, you know how vicious they were . . ." She reached into her pocket and took out a handful of candies. "You like these, don't you? White Rabbits. Have a few of these and don't ask me any more questions. All right, I'm a coward! But damn your questions, they make me feel like I belong in a factory and will never deserve better."

"Don't be upset," Sparrow said, accepting the candy. "I'm the same as you. I had the desire, but never the will."

"And now?" Fan asked.

He shook his head, but it occurred to him that now, finally, when he had the will, desire itself might have disappeared. For twenty years, Sparrow had convinced himself that he had safeguarded the most crucial part of his inner life from the Party, the self that composed and understood the world through music. But

how could it be? Time remade a person. Time had rewritten him.
How could a person counter time itself?

That night, when Ai-ming came home in tears, Sparrow helplessly
gave her the candy. He knew that Ai-ming stayed in the Square
each day and passed herself off as a student. His daughter said
that hundreds of students had lost consciousness, they were on IV
drips. She had spent the day trying to keep a path clear for the
stream of ambulances. How could he yell at her? More than three
thousand had joined the hunger strike and some were threatening
to set themselves on fire. But he saw, when he passed the neighbourhood television, that this confrontation with the government could not go on indefinitely. He watched clips of Gorbachev's
arrival in Beijing, all the members of the Politburo standing stiffly
on the tarmac, their faces as grey as their colourless coats. General-
Secretary Zhao Ziyang had met with Gorbachev, they had sat on
chairs too large for their bodies. Comrade Zhao said that some
young people had doubts about socialism, that their concerns
were sincere, and for this reason reform was crucial. The anchor
read without looking up. The grand celebration that had been
planned for Tiananmen Square, intended to celebrate the first
visit by a Soviet head of state since 1959, had been cancelled.

The following morning, Wednesday, Sparrow met his work-
mates at the Muxidi Bridge. Everyone was neatly turned out in
their dark blue uniforms, while around them Chang'an Avenue
swelled in a kind of euphoria and sadness. People from factories
across the city arrived continuously in trucks and re-purposed
buses. Fan was busy giving orders, she had a voice sharp enough
to crack glass. Old Bi was there, too, with Dao-ren, who carried
one side of a banner that read, "We can no longer stay silent."
Even the floor supervisors, managers and superiors were walking with them. He had heard that some, including Baby Corn,
had children who had joined the hunger strike, and it was true,

Baby Corn did not look well. An enlivening breeze made all the banners crease and ripple, and an expression of Big Mother's caught in his mind, *Those who sow the wind will reap the whirlwind.* At last they set out, behind the banner of Beijing Wire Factory No. 3. The sky was like a yellow curtain they could never quite pass through.

The air was tumultuous as Tiananmen Square came into sight. He saw banners announcing the Beijing Bus Company, Xidan Department Store and, shockingly, the Beijing Police Academy. Ling was here, too, walking alongside her co-workers at Radio Beijing. Men from Capital Iron and Steel waved orange flags that caught the sun. They were sturdy and mountainous, and had taken it upon themselves to direct traffic. Life was in flux, orchestral and completely unrecognizable. Through the loudspeakers a student was saying, "Mother China, witness now the actions of your sons and daughters," while foreign journalists, having come to report on the Sino-Soviet summit, were so numerous they seemed to be replicating themselves from moment to moment. Journalists and editors from the *People's Daily* walked under a red-and-gold banner, the colours of sunset. Everywhere, students, almost drunk with exhaustion, collected donations, and their plastic buckets and biscuit tins overflowed. The workers around Sparrow started buying up all the water, nourishing biscuits, popsicles and sticks of frozen fruit, and carting them to the hunger strikers. Sparrow felt as if all his past lives, all his selves, were walking beside him.

"Comrade Sparrow," Fan said, taking hold of his arm, "are you okay? We should find some ice for your back injury–"

"I'm fine," he said. His voice was hoarse. "I never imagined so many people . . ."

Fan's smile was so wide he was surprised to realize she was weeping.

On the loudspeakers, a scholar was addressing the crowds, "There are things that I can't accept from the government, and there are extreme elements within the student movement. But history is this kind of process, it's all mixed up. . . ."

In two weeks, he would fly to Hong Kong to see Kai, yet he had neglected to tell Ling or his daughter this important detail, and the fact that he was hiding so many crucial things could no longer be brushed away. Chanting reverberated off all the bodies and all the buildings: *Can lies go on forever?* When he reached the Square, he thought, So this is what Tiananmen Square looks like when it is truly full. Even Chairman Mao never lived to see it like this. Mao's portrait on the gate, so familiar it might as well be the moon in the sky, appeared smug and overdressed for the spring humidity. Despite the million demonstrators, the only visible police were the ones marching in support of the students. The student loud-speakers were exhorting the hunger strikers to be orderly, to "sleep neatly," and to refrain from playing cards, because such behaviour would compromise the purity of their goals. The fasting students had no mats or tarps to lie on, only sheets of grubby newspaper. A sign read, "The Party maintains its power by accusing the People of fabricated political crimes."

Sparrow could not imagine what this scene would like through Zhuli's eyes, at the age she would be now. How many deceits had the Red Guards accused her of? How many crimes had the government fabricated? How could a lie continue so long, and work its way into everything they touched? But maybe Ai-ming would be allowed to come of age in a different world, a new China. Perhaps it was naive to think so, but he found it difficult not to give in, not to hope, and not to desire.

Everyday there were more demonstrations: a million people on Wednesday, and another million on Thursday despite rainstorms. By now the hunger strike was in its sixth day and even the official *People's Daily* was reporting that more than seven hundred strikers had collapsed. When Sparrow went out, no matter the hour, he could hear ambulances racing to and from the Square. His factory, perhaps every factory in the city, had all but closed. His new composition was almost done. Reading it over, he heard a counterpoint to Gabriel Fauré's Op. 24, a similar descending sweep, and the three twisting voices of Bach's organ prelude, "Ich ruf zu dir," which he had always loved. But perhaps, rather than a counterpoint, the other works were sounds overheard, lives within lives. He no longer knew. The structure of his sonata felt unbalanced, even monstrous, and even though he knew it was nearly finished, he had no idea how it would end.

He called it, tentatively, *The Sun Shines on the People's Square*, a title that echoed Ding Ling's novel of revolutionary China, *The Sun Shines over Sanggam River*. But the Square in Sparrow's mind was not the Tiananmen Square of 1989. Instead it was multiple places from throughout his life: the Tiananmen Square he had walked on in 1950 with Big Mother Knife. The People's Square of Shanghai. The square courtyards of the laneway house, the sheets of Zhuli's music, the portraits of Chairman Mao, the bed he shared with Ling, the square record jackets he had burned, the frames of the radios that he built every day. The ancient philosophers believed in a square earth and a round (or egg-shaped) sky. The head is round and the feet are square. The burial tomb is square. What might cause something to change shape, to expand or be transformed? Weren't the works of Bach, the folded mirrors, the fugues and canons, both square and circular? But what if the piece of music in his mind could not be written? What if it *must not be finished*? The questions confused him, he knew they came from that other life inside him.

Ai-ming appeared in the doorway. "Are you writing, Ba?"

He put down his pencil. She was wearing clothes he didn't recognize, a dress that must have come from the neighbour, and it made Ai-ming look more grown up, more like a northern city girl.

"Yiwen asked me to bring some blankets to Tiananmen Square," she said. "These are donations from the neighbours, but she couldn't carry them all. Ma is going to help me. Do you want to come, too?" Ai-ming appeared thin, exhilarated. In the last few weeks, she had said nothing of Canada.

It was almost midnight. Sparrow said yes. Yes, he would go with them. Perhaps tonight he would tell them both that he was leaving for Hong Kong. He would be gone briefly; before they knew it, he would be home again. He would not abandon his life, but find a new beginning that included them.

Outside, Ling was stacking the blankets onto their bicycles, securing them with twine. Every movement she made was precise, intentional. He had always loved this quality of hers.

"You've been composing," she said.

"A new sonata. It's nearly finished."

"I'm glad, Sparrow." Her face was guarded yet, in its curiosity, open to him.

He wanted to tell her that attachment, to another person, to the past, was shifting from moment to moment. Set in motion again, his own life was finally becoming clear. But Ling knew, he thought, of course she already knew this. So many people, sent to labour camps like Ba Lute, taken away like Swirl or Wen, reassigned to distant provinces like Ling and Big Mother, had been denied a basic freedom, the right to raise their own children.

They set off, Ai-ming leading, turning through the maze of alleyways that bypassed Chang'an Avenue. Ahead of Sparrow, Ling's hair twisted in the breeze. Her movements were strong and graceful, and the almond scent of her skin seemed to float back and hold him, once more, in thrall, following her, he had the sensation of rising up a flight of stairs.

Even now, so late at night, there were people everywhere. Banner after banner read, "Chairman Deng Xiaoping, step down!" He pedalled faster. He was side by side with his wife and daughter now, and they were folded into the tens of thousands who occupied the perimeter of Tiananmen Square day and night.

They got down and began pushing their bicycles, Ai-ming leading the way. Inside the Square, a student marshal with startlingly long arms recognized her and came to assist. When they reached the hunger strikers, Sparrow unknotted the twine and was about to carry the blankets inside when the long-armed student stopped him. "Only students," he said sharply. "No outsiders." Ai-ming had run ahead. In the lamplight, he could see the faint glow of her shape. She was speaking to a tall, pale girl with very short hair, the neighbour's daughter, Yiwen. The girl looked desperately thin. Some of the hunger strikers were fast asleep, a few boys were singing quietly, the camp smelled of urine and garbage. Doctors and nurses in smocks and blue jeans hurried past. One nurse was slumped over a table. "Quiet, quiet," another whispered loudly, "can't you see they're trying to rest!"

A wiry old man in a blue uniform ran up. Excitedly, joyfully, he announced that the new independent workers' union had officially called for a city-wide general strike. Sparrow was stunned, but no one else seemed to react. Ling, too, was speechless. She whispered to him, "How do they dare? How do we dare?" Minutes later, a girl ran in and said that General-Secretary Zhao Ziyang and Premier Li Peng were on their way to the hunger strike command headquarters. The tent hustled into activity, and then nothing, as if news continuously arrived, burst, rained down, evaporated and was no more. Ai-ming had wrapped her arms around the neighbour girl, they stayed that way for a few moments, their eyes closed, the girl rocking back and forth, weeping. An old woman came by the entrance, she was delivering water donations and at the same time eating a fried dough stick, and the guard hissed at her, "No food here! No food!" and the old woman, pale with shame, turned and fled.

Ling tried to intervene. "She's a citizen only trying to help."

"No food here!" the student shouted.

"Be quiet," the slumping nurse cried. "Just be quiet, please!"

Ai-ming emerged, crying freely, and together they pushed their bicycles around the scattering of people. It was late and they were hungry, so Ling led them to Comrade Barbarian. The kitchen was still open, though the menu was limited, the waitress said that the owner was making regular deliveries to the Square to support the student marshals and volunteers. They ate in silence and Sparrow finally said, "Ai-ming, you have to look after your health." His daughter stared at her plate. Streaks of dried tears had left white patches on her skin. "But what about you, Ba?" she said. "In a week, you've aged a decade." Ling sighed. "Come on. Everyone eat." When they went back out, speakers were being dragged around even though it was almost three in the morning. People had come out all over again because the student broadcast centre was repeating the news that General-Secretary Zhao Ziyang had indeed arrived, along with Premier Li Peng, and they were meeting with representatives of the hunger strike. After Deng Xiaoping, they were the highest-ranked leaders in the country. Sparrow was so exhausted, he felt as if his shoes were glued to the concrete. He did not know how many minutes passed before a staticky broadcast finally dribbled out of the speakers. It was now four in the morning. The sound was not good, words were lost. General-Secretary Zhao kept clearing his throat and starting over.

The first clear words that filtered through were, "Students, we came too late."

The Square itself seemed to widen, like something pulling apart.

"Students, I am sorry. Whatever you say and criticize about us is deserved. My purpose here now is to ask your forgiveness."

He saw a look of pain pass over Ling's face. Only it wasn't pain, he realized, but fear. The General-Secretary's voice was reedy, he seemed to be struggling against overwhelming emotion. "You cannot continue to . . . after seven days of hunger strike . . . to insist on continuing only until you have a satisfactory answer. You are still young and have much time ahead of you."

People from the restaurant had all come out now, Sparrow saw the waitress and two cooks, and a few old diners in their undershirts. A jumble of teenagers. "It's the same as always," one of them shouted. "They want us to be obedient and go home!" Murmuring all around, approval or disapproval, Sparrow could not tell.

"You are not like us," Comrade Zhao continued. "We are already old and do not matter. It was not easy for the country and your parents to nurture you to reach university. Now in your late teens and early twenties you are sacrificing your lives. Students, can you think rationally for a moment? Now the situation is very dire, as you all know. The party and the nation are very anxious, the whole society is worried, and each day the situation is worsening. This cannot go on. You mean well and have the interests of our country at heart. But if this goes on it will go out of control and will have various adverse effects. All in all, this is what I have in my mind. If you stop the hunger strike, the government will not close the door on dialogue, definitely not! What you have proposed, we can continue to discuss. It is slow, some issues are being broached. I just wanted to visit you today and at the same time . . . tell you how we feel, and hope that you will calmly think about this. Under irrational circumstances, it is hard to think clearly. All the vigour that you have as young people, we understand because we, too, were young once, we, too, protested and we, too, laid our bodies on the railway tracks without considering the consequences. Finally, I ask again sincerely that you calmly think about what happens from now on. A lot of things can be resolved. I hope that you will end the hunger strike soon and I thank you."

The broadcast devolved into static.

Sparrow looked up at the sky, it was too bright in the city to see any stars, everywhere he looked was a deep blue, a never-quite-black.

"What does it mean?" Ai-ming said.

Ling was weeping.

"I want to go home," Ai-ming said. She was still so young but why did she already look so empty? "I want to go home."

Now it was Sparrow who led them, silently, as if they were thieves, through the dark night, past speakers where Zhao Ziyang's address was being replayed, "Students, we came too late, I am sorry..." past groups of people listening for the first time, past blossoming trees and a row of magnolias whose flowers he couldn't see, but whose fragrance remained in the air, unrelenting, intoxicating.

Late the next morning, when he woke, disoriented, he heard Yiwen telling everyone that General-Secretary Zhao Ziyang had been removed from office. Someone inside the Party had leaked this information. Demonstrations had broken out in 151 cities and the government intended to declare martial law. The army had already arrived at the perimeter of the city.

The national examinations still had to be written. To Ai-ming, the entire process was plainly ludicrous. Theory and practice, practice and theory, if she analyzed another poem by Du Fu she might go into exile herself. She was curled up on the sofa, eating a cucumber, when Sparrow appeared, groggy, all the hair on his head mashed to one side. After wishing him good morning, she asked him, "Were you fighting someone in your sleep?"

Sparrow smiled confusedly. He took the cucumber from her hand and started to eat it.

Radios blared in the alleyway, families were shouting at each other about matters big and small, but she and Sparrow both pretended they heard nothing. Ai-ming told him that, early this morning, she had been determined to study. She'd opened the exam catalogue and found herself at the 1977 questions. That year, the national essay had been: "Is it true that the more knowledge, the more counter-revolutionary? Write at least 800 characters." What if a similar question appeared on this year's test? For over an hour, she'd struggled to compose an opening line. The page was still blank. She could no longer make sense of the word counter-revolutionary.

Sparrow crunched the cucumber and listened.

"How can I write the examinations?" she said. "How should I..."

"Don't worry so much about the essay question." Her father's voice sounded thick, like a full sponge. "Why don't you go back to studying literature or mathematics?"

She nodded but this wasn't what she meant. It was the whole idea of answering, the fear that every word had multiple meanings, that she was not in control of what they said.

Sparrow said that he was going to the factory to see what was happening.

Had he forgotten what year this was? And why did he look like he was in pain? It was only now that she realized he was wearing his factory uniform. "But Ba!" she said. "Everyone says the army will come in from that side, from Fengtai."

He nodded without hearing. "Ai-ming, don't go to the Square today. Promise me." He looked at the door then back again. "Where's your mother?"

"Radio station."

"Oh." He nodded but his eyes were glassy. "Ai-ming, I have a friend in Canada who might sponsor you. I'm willing to do everything I can. I'm going to meet with him in Hong Kong in June–"

"What friend? You're going to Hong Kong?"

"–but first you must write the examinations and you must do well. Without a high score, even sponsorship won't help you . . ."

He was talking in a kind of perturbed state. Was it a trick, she wondered. So that she would stay where she was, live inside books, ignore what was happening to her thoughts? And who was this friend?

"I'll excel in the examinations."

When she said this, the Bird of Quiet looked incredibly glad, like a child. She tried to steel herself against her father's innocent smile.

"You're a good child, Ai-ming. A good daughter. I'm a lucky father."

Sparrow left for the factory. Ai-ming changed her clothes, pulling on a dress of Yiwen's. In the courtyard, she took Yiwen's clothes down from the laundry line, stuffed them into a bag along with a toothbrush and washcloth, books, and a few coins her mother had given her. She hopped onto her bicycle and hurried out.

The city seemed loosened by the heat. She pedalled hurriedly to Tiananmen Square but found it unexpectedly quiet. One of the student marshals, a physics student who called himself Kelvin, told her that Yiwen had gone out with a "battalion" to the western suburbs in an effort to blockade the roads and prevent the army from reaching the Square. Ai-ming turned around and cycled back the way she had come.

At the Muxidi Bridge, nobody could pass: bicycles, buses with punctured tires, burned-out sofas, shouting people, and stockpiles of wood overflowed the intersection. When Ai-ming finally made it across, she glimpsed broken glass, swerved hard and nearly collided with a scooter. The driver's "Sorry, sorry!" fluttered backwards. Her front tire made a sad, sucking noise before going flat. She got down and began pushing the bicycle on. The scraping of the rim against concrete made her teeth ache. Unable to see through her tears, Ai-ming locked the stupid, useless, unforgivable bicycle to a tree, took the bag of clothes and kept walking. Her whole body was coated in sweat. A bus came and she jumped on, but almost immediately the bus stopped. She tumbled out with the other passengers: here was the army now.

Army trucks, stretching as far as she could see.

Ai-ming walked towards them. Tears, confusion, hysteria. The military trucks were surrounded by people. "Brother soldiers!" an old man was shouting. He lurched in front of Ai-ming. His blue factory uniform sagged around him like a riverbed. "Do not become the shame of our nation! You are the sons of China. You, who should be defending these students with your lives! How can you enter our city with guns and bullets? Where is your conscience?"

A few officers tried to make themselves heard above the commotion, they said their only mission was to keep the peace. Everyone was hysterical and calling out.

An ancient grandmother had taken it upon herself to lie down in the road, in front of the trucks. "Who are you retaking the streets from, eh?" she said hoarsely. "I'm no rebel! I was living here when your great-grandfather still wore short pants!"

A man in a factory uniform, carrying dozens of individually wrapped cakes, began dropping them, indiscriminately, over the railings of the trucks. "My daughter is in the Square," he said. "My only child. I appeal to your courage! I appeal, I appeal . . ."

Ai-ming could not see Yiwen anywhere, it was a thousand times more crowded here than it had been at Tiananmen Square. She hugged the bag of clothes to her chest and stood in the mayhem, hungry, thirsty, shivering with fear, ashamed at having disobeyed her father. A soldier her age stared at her with palpable longing. How did I end up here? Ai-ming thought. This is my country, this is the capital, but I don't belong in Beijing. Where is Yiwen? If I only I could find Yiwen, I would know what to do.

The afternoon was disappearing but the crowds only grew larger. Some soldiers climbed out of their vehicles and stood in the road, humiliated. Some were in shock, some looked angry, some wept.

On the fifth floor of the factory, all the seats were empty. Sparrow sat at his work station, basking in the absolute stillness. This was the first peace he had known in days, and the quiet inside him now felt freed, it sat on the table, uncaged, like a house bird. Despite the emptiness, he felt as if his co-workers had left an afterimage: every work station belonged unassailably to someone. Perhaps, in a moment, Dao-ren, Old Bi and Fan would reappear, and it would be Sparrow himself who would dissolve, as if he had always been the illusion. The freedom of departure comforted him, and he put his head down on his arms and fell into a sound, peaceful sleep.

It was nearly ten at night by the time Ai-ming found Yiwen, huddled with two other girls. One was called Lily and one was called Faye. The girls were draped over one another and looked like a single body with three heads. Yiwen's father had told her that, until she quit the student demonstrations, she was no longer welcome at home. She had been sleeping in Faye's dormitory room.

After learning that all three had been part of the hunger strike, which had officially been called off this afternoon, Ai-ming coaxed them to a nearby noodle stall.

The vendor was a sleepy-eyed woman with a thick northeastern accent. "Take your money back," she said to Ai-ming, after the other girls had floated away to a table. "No, no, I mean it. I've got nothing to offer you kids but these noodles. They're good noodles but they won't change the world."

Embarrassed, Ai-ming thanked her.

"So, what do you study?" the vendor asked.

Ai-ming looked into the woman's puckered, hopeful face. "Um, Chinese history."

The woman pulled her head back like a bird. "What's the use of that? Well, at least you know that my generation was tossed around by Chairman Mao's campaigns. Our lives were completely wasted . . . We've pinned all our hopes on you."

"The other girls study mathematics," Ai-ming said, trying again.

"That's what we need!" the vendor said, smacking her chopsticks against the metal pot. "Real numbers. Without real numbers, how can we fix our economy, make plans, understand what we need? Young lady, I don't mean to be rude but you should really think about studying mathematics, too."

"I will."

She carried the noodles to their table. There was something wary in the girls' eyes, but they softened when they saw the food.

"What will you do now?" Ai-ming asked.

Lily swallowed a mouthful of noodles. "What can we do? I'm afraid to go back to the university. Maybe it's all a trap and they're waiting to arrest us on campus. In 1977, Wei Jingsheng got seventeen years in solitary confinement for writing one wall poster."

"We can't let them take the Square." Yiwen's voice seemed to come from the plastic tabletop. "We have to stop them here, in the streets, we have to fight the army. We can't let them through."

"The Square is our headquarters," Lily said. "If we lose the Square, we lose everything. Everything. Do you even know what they did to the protesters in 1977? That's what scares me. Nobody even remembers."

The table was low compared to the height of the chairs, and it made them all lean forward as if they were planning a conspiracy. Lily, Faye and Yiwen kept talking, using other military terms. How could they talk about fighting the army? Ai-ming found her thoughts drifting nervously; if she didn't hear them, she wouldn't be implicated. Yiwen picked up her hand and held it, squeezing it so hard that a jolt of pain flashed in Ai-ming's eyes. On the public speakers, the grating repetition of the martial law announcement had started up again. *In accordance with Article 89, Item 16, of the Constitution of the People's Republic* . . . Waves of sound broke through the street, "Down with Li Peng! Down with Li Peng!" Still the voice on the loudspeaker crept out, insistent: *Under martial law, demonstrations, student strikes, work stoppages, are banned* . . .

"We've got to sleep here in the road, right in front of the trucks," Faye said. She had sleepy eyes and a demure chin, making her words all the more shocking. "I don't care what happens to me anymore. I don't care. What future is there for us anyway?"

"I'm so tired," Yiwen said. "Doesn't it seem a lifetime ago that Hu Yaobang died and we all brought flowers to the Square? That was April 22. All we wanted was to deliver a funeral wreath to the Great Hall of the People. That was the beginning, wasn't it? What's the date today? May 20. Only four weeks since Comrade Hu's funeral."

Was that really how it had begun? Ai-ming wondered. Could it have been so simple?

Girls at a nearby table sang an old Cultural Revolution song, and the words seemed both to lull the students and rouse them.

"All these songs," Yiwen said. Her hand felt small and damp. "I never understood. I thought they were real."

"They were just words," Ai-ming said.

Lily looked at her, forthrightly, calmly. "But what else did we have?"

When they finished eating, Lily and Faye went off to look for friends from Beijing Normal, and never returned. Ai-ming and Yiwen joined the other students sleeping on newspapers on the ground. Ai-ming lay on her back. From here, the tanks appeared even more monstrous. Frightened, she closed her eyes against the increasing clarity of the stars. The most important people in her life were Sparrow, Ling, Big Mother Knife, Ba Lute, and now Yiwen, and it was like they had all been raised on different planets.

"It's easy to say we'll sacrifice our lives for the country," Yiwen said quietly. "At the beginning it feels very brave. Is that what you meant, Ai-ming? You said it was just words. You think that the things that matter are more difficult than words—to retreat from a confrontation, for instance, to work at changing something, truly changing something." She lifted her hand towards the bodies and the tanks. "Ai-ming, you're studying history to prepare for the examinations. What if revolution and violence are the only way?"

Beside them, army soldiers were speaking softly in their uncomfortable trucks. They were so crowded that the soldiers had to take turns even to sit down. Ai-ming tried to clear her thoughts. All these slogans and songs had been handed down, she thought, and if the words were not theirs was the emotion that propelled them borrowed, too? What about the students' desire, their idealism, their righteousness, how many contradictory desires did it serve? Once idealism had belonged to Chairman Mao, the revolutionaries, the heroic Eighth Route Army. Had their generation inherited it? How could a person know the difference between what was real and what was merely illusion, or see when a truth transformed into its opposite? What was theirs and what was something handed down, only a repetition? The loudspeakers kept cutting into the air: *Under martial law, soldiers are authorized to use all necessary means, including force....* Hadn't the government, too, stolen their words from somewhere else? *People are forbidden to fabricate or spread rumours, network, make public speeches, distribute leaflets, or incite social turmoil....* As if words alone could make reality, as if there were no people involved, as if words alone could make someone a criminal, or conjure crimes from the air. Hadn't the Red Guards tried to destroy the old language and bring to life a new one? What if one had to create a whole new language in order to learn to be oneself? She said to Yiwen, "I think we keep repeating the same mistakes. Maybe we should mistrust every idea we think is original and ours alone."

Yiwen's head nodded against her shoulder.

They both smelled the same, like the noodles they had eaten and also the ashy ground. How did Yiwen see her? Was she a sister, a friend, a confidant, something else? Here is the one thing in my life, Ai-ming thought, that has no parameters. She wanted to tell Yiwen how she felt, but she was afraid to damage everything they had.

"I can't sleep," Yiwen said. "Tell me a story."

Ai-ming could think of nothing, no words that belonged to her. I'm eighteen years old, she thought, and I still haven't begun to know my own thoughts. She felt as if a part of herself was being left behind. She squeezed her eyes shut and recited the only words that came to her, the poem at the opening of Chapter 41 of the Book of Records: "'Of course, no one knows tomorrow. Tomorrow begins from another dawn, when we will be fast asleep. Remember what I say: not everything will pass.'"

It was dawn by the time Sparrow cycled home from the factory. The 1981 recording of the *Goldberg Variations* rippled through his headphones, and the music felt both long and momentary. For this new recording, Glenn Gould had instilled a continuous tempo, a pulse, so that all thirty variations more clearly belonged to a unified piece. A few weeks after the 1981 recording was released, Glenn Gould had died suddenly at the age of fifty. Sparrow had not learned of Gould's death until years later, and convinced himself the radio announcer was mistaken. So much so that, a few months ago, when a letter from Kai mentioned the death of Glenn Gould, Sparrow had been upset by it all over again. What kind of man had the celebrated pianist been? he wondered. If Gould had been prevented from playing the piano for twenty years, what other form might his music have taken?

It must have rained not long ago. The air felt renewed, the dawn light was the colour of pearls, unreal against the pavement.

Turning onto Guang'an Road, he almost fell off his bicycle when he saw the army trucks. They were surrounded by a restless crowd, people in their nightclothes and others on their way to work. Hastily, he swung his bicycle around and detoured south. The Goldberg Variations continued in his ears. But when he tried to reach the centre, he met checkpoint after checkpoint. Beijing, with its grid of ring roads and bridges, had been solidly designed to protect its heart, Tiananmen Square and the Forbidden City. Smaller roads were manned by students, but along all the major thoroughfares, Beijing residents had set up human barricades, crowds so dense no army truck could hope to cross without meeting violent resistance.

He pressed on through ever more congested streets.

Sparrow smelled bonfires even though nothing burned. The smell brought back an image of Wu Bei, struggling to stand on his tiny chair as the Red Guards humiliated him. *The monster is waking, Teacher! You have stepped on its head countless times, and now the monster is crawling out of the mud.* At the barricades, as if in uneasy counterpoint, people chanted, "We must turn over and awaken! We must sacrifice and serve the Revolution!" Yet Gould continued, unrolling one variation and tipping in slow motion towards the next. By the time Sparrow reached home, it was nearly ten in the morning. The rooms were empty. He sat at the table and drank a cup of tea. Noise from the ongoing demonstrations filled the room. Radio Beijing didn't broadcast music anymore, instead the loudspeakers kept repeating the fact of martial law. He regretted all the radios he had ever built. He wanted to find some way to cut all the wires, to hush all the voices, to broadcast stillness, quiet, on this city that was coming unmoored.

Late in the afternoon, he woke suddenly. Here was his daughter's face hovering above him, slowly sharpening. "Ba," she said. "Ba!" She kept repeating that representatives from Wire Factory No. 3 were in the living room. He got up. Ai-ming brought him a basin of cold water. Sparrow dunked his face, thinking he had been reprioritized out of his job. Instead, he came out to find Miss Lu and Old Bi, in their factory uniforms, sitting on the sofa, eating peanuts. They smiled nervously when Sparrow said, "Have you just come off your shift?"

Miss Lu recovered a peanut that had fallen between two cushions. When she had it firmly between her fingers, she pointed it at him and said, "Old Bi and I have finally decided to join the independent union. They've been canvassing in Tiananmen Square, you know? The Beijing Workers Autonomous Federation." She cracked the shell and threw the peanuts into her mouth.

Old Bi leaned forward. "Let's just say we're tired of sitting on the hilltop and watching the tigers fight. Maybe you are, too, Comrade Sparrow, and if so we should stick together."

Ai-ming had followed him out, he could hear the flat squeak of her slippers behind him.

"Yes, okay."

Old Bi and Miss Lu kept looking at him, as if they were still waiting for an answer.

How could he learn to see around corners? What mistake was about to lunge towards him?

Miss Lu said, "You need to show your work unit ID and register your real name. We understand if you'd rather not. After all, you've got a family to think of . . ."

"Wait. I'll get it."

Sparrow went to the bedroom, found his ID card and put it into his pocket. A new letter from Kai was sitting on the dresser, in plain sight. Ai-ming must have placed it there. She had followed him in the bedroom, but before she could say anything, he told her he was going to the Square. "I want you to stay inside." He said it sharply, as if she had already disobeyed him. He picked up the letter and placed it, too, in his pocket.

"But, Ba . . ."

"For once, Ai-ming, do as I ask."

Outside, he watched, lightheaded, as Old Bi unlocked his bicycle. As they left the alleyway, Sparrow pedalled behind them. Miss Lu was balanced on the back of Old Bi's bike, and her old-fashioned cloth shoes sat daintily in the air. She stretched a hand out, handing him a cigarette. It was a good brand, Big Front Gate.

"Baby Corn was on the barricades last night," Miss Lu said. "He told us two million Beijingers are on the streets. He said he ripped up his Party membership card."

The cigarette tasted opulent in his mouth.

"It's all getting so emotional," Old Bi said. "All these tears and threats are obscuring the bigger issues. We could help these students steer the ship but who listens to the older generation?"

Smoke clouded from Miss Lu's mouth. "That's right. We had our day and look how well we served the country. Oh yes, we Red Guards were very first class, very rational."

Old Bi pretended he hadn't heard.

They came to a large tent on the northwest corner of the Square, temporary headquarters of the independent union, where a lineup of uniformed workers stretched along the boulevard. Jokes were passed from person to person like midday snacks. Two hours later, upon reaching the front, Sparrow signed his name below thousands of others. He felt too afraid to be afraid. A giddy volunteer informed him, hands gesticulating, that workers were organizing themselves into various battalions, some were in charge of gathering supplies, some would battle the army at the roadblocks, and others had joined the Iron Mounted Soldiers, a motorcycle reconnaissance network.

Distracted by the sound of helicopters, Sparrow told the volunteer he would do whatever was needed, but he didn't own a motorcycle.

"Oh-oh," Fan said, suddenly appearing with her booming voice. "Be practical, Old Sparrow! You're not a kid anymore! I don't see you leaping up on barricades, just falling off them!"

"Falling down is also a form of obstruction."

Fan rumbled a laugh, gave him a stinging slap on the back, and then another.

On a nearby bench, Old Bi and Miss Lu were sharing a cigarette, entranced by the workers' radio broadcast, read by a young woman with a heart-shaped face and a soprano voice.

Sparrow went outside and onto the Square. Conditions had deteriorated, the students looked bedraggled and destitute. There was garbage everywhere and the camp smelled very bad. One after another, people scrambled up to the microphone, identifying themselves as teachers, intellectuals, or student leaders.

He watched for a long time. Their speeches ("No kneeling!") grew increasingly vehement until, driven by their passions ("No compromise!") and by the high tide of emotions, they, too, finished by asking the protesters to stand firm and risk everything ("No retreat!"). The sky opened and heavy rain broke free. Tarps collapsed onto the huddled students, and he heard them cry out, a mix of laughter, groaning and cursing. Banners drooped, flags stuck to their poles, a pair of abandoned shorts and a few wet T-shirts sat like turtlebacks before the portrait of Chairman Mao. Sparrow saw a tall girl standing alone, a pink headband in her hair, and wondered if it was Yiwen, the neighbours' daughter. The rain blurred her figure, and he felt he was looking into the past, or into a future that would not arrive. He heard footsteps behind him and turned. Fan was running towards him, a graceful hop-skip-jump-jog, holding a bright blue umbrella like a prize in the air.

He was assigned to the blockade at Muxidi Bridge, which was so close to home it was like watching over his backyard. Sparrow and a dozen neighbours took up a position on the roof of a city bus, whose tires had been punctured. Songs from the 1920s and 1930s proliferated around them, and neighbours, including Ling, handed out candy nougats, tea and pastries. All night, he followed Ling's figure in the crowd below. She was distributing copies of an unauthorized supplement to the *People's Daily*, printed covertly by the newspaper's staff. In the last week, Sparrow had hardly seen her. Ling was never home, she had thrown all her energy into the ongoing dispute at Radio Beijing. Journalists and editors, including Ling, had come down firmly on the side of the students and were no longer waiting for official approval before broadcasting their reports. The Ling he had first met in Kai's room, the sharp-eyed philosophy student, had been biding her time and here she was now, as if she had never been away. In fact, all over Beijing, people who had seemingly resigned themselves to always wearing ten layers of coats were now shedding them all at once. They carried themselves differently, they were proud, even joyful, in bloom.

Battling sleep, Sparrow found himself remembering the swaying of the Wuhan bus, when he and Kai had gone in search of Comrade Glass Eye, when a red-cheeked girl had fallen asleep in Sparrow's lap as he played "Bird's Eye View." He, too, had felt purely happy then. The music had seemed to scour everyone clean. Perhaps the messages of the students had done something similar: simplified ideas had set in motion a train of desires. A slogan on a headband or a T-shirt, "Give me liberty or give me death," had led to a hunger strike and a political impasse, and both the will and desire to change one's conditions.

On the second night, Sparrow was told to bring a cotton mask, towels and handkerchiefs, because the army was expected to use tear gas.

And yet, and yet. The next morning, the People's Liberation Army started up their convoys, and began reversing out of the neighbourhood. The exhausted soldiers waved as they departed, some weeping and others laughing. Bright ropes of flowers flooded the streets they had left behind.

On Saturday, Ai-ming came home breathless, jubilant. She said that the students had entered into discussions with the government, and agreed to a full withdrawal from Tiananmen Square. "Yiwen is coming home." She turned to Sparrow and said, "You don't have to sit on that broken bus anymore pretending to be a fighter."

When he touched his daughter's cheek, Sparrow felt almost harmed by the softness of it. "Will you eat at home tonight, Ai-ming?"

"I'll even cook. And you'll be sorry you asked!"

Ling went out to buy groceries. The news of the students' decision had not yet been broadcast, but in the alleyways, everyone seemed to know what had occurred. The streets vibrated with a hopefulness she had not witnessed since the first years of the Republic, as if all the years between then and now had only been a hallucination or a detour. Returning home, she ran into Yiwen's father at the water spigot. Yiwen had not been home since the start of the hunger strike, yet it was her father, Comrade Zhu, who had lost so much weight. Seeing Ling, he said, "These children, ah! You give your life to them and they crush your heart!"

Ling took out the good cut of beef she'd bought and gave it to her neighbour. He lifted both hands, refusing. "Take it," she said. "The students have called off the demonstrations. Now you can welcome Yiwen home."

Water overflowed the bucket and Zhu turned the tap off. "You see how it is," he said, accepting the gift, and beckoning her into his flat. "We sacrificed everything so that Yiwen could get a good education. She's our only child. When Yiwen was accepted into Beijing Normal, I held the letter in my hands and wept. The first time I had wept in forty years! I thought I might have a heart attack. Yiwen is the first in both our families to go to university. She's smarter than anyone I've ever known. I tried to make her understand how fortunate she was, to be born into this time, to have opportunities we never had." He shook his head. "But these kids think it's all up to them. They have no understanding of fate." He took a container from his ice box and gave it to her. It was a chicken, already marinated. She tried to refuse but he wouldn't hear of it.

"Perhaps it was us," Ling said, picking up where they had left off. "We understood fate all too well."

"Ah," he said. "You're right about that. Our children have 'stood up,' and now it's we, their parents, down on our knees and begging forgiveness! But okay, okay, whatever. Look," and Zhu pulled a small badge from his pocket. "I even joined the Beijing autonomous residents' federation. You should join, too. There are all sorts of initiatives under discussion."

Late that night, Radio Beijing announced that the students had overturned their own decision. They had decided to stay in the Square after all, until the Party conference scheduled for June 20. The date jolted Sparrow. It was the same day he was scheduled to fly to Hong Kong to see Kai. The radio also announced that General-Secretary Zhao Ziyang, who had already been removed from his post, had been stripped of all remaining duties and placed under house arrest.

Through the window of the little office, he saw Ai-ming and Yiwen sitting in the courtyard. They were holding hands and looking up at something in the sky. At the stars, he thought, or at the helicopters, maybe one could no longer be untangled from the other. His sonata for piano and violin, the first piece of music he had written in twenty-three years, was finished, he could do no more. He made a clean copy, signed his name and wrote the date, May 27, 1989, and the title, *The Sun Shines on the People's Square*. He put the copy in an envelope to send to Kai. He wished to hear it performed, and he remembered how, despite his protests, Zhuli used to play all his half-finished pieces. When he looked over the music, he couldn't shake the feeling that it had come from someone else entirely, or more accurately, that it had been written by himself and another, a counterpoint between two people alive and awake, young and old, who had lived entirely different worlds.

Outside were the usual voices—rainfall, laughter, a radio, sirens, good-natured bickering—but here in this room was music that existed in silence. In the Shanghai Conservatory, he remembered, paintings showed musicians playing the qin, a silk-stringed zither, only the qin had no strings as if, at the moment of purest composition, there was no noise. Sparrow had never made a sustained sound, the music came in beginnings and endings like the edges of a table. The life in the middle, what was it? Zhuli, Kai. Himself. Twenty years in a factory. Thousands of radios. A marriage and family. Nearly all of his adult life: the day after day, year upon year, that gives shape to a person, that accrues weight.

He saw himself putting down his pencil and standing up from the desk. He saw himself walking out of this room, this alleyway, this city, without turning back.

The following morning he woke early, put on his uniform and returned to work.

As I waited in Shanghai, one life unexpectedly opened the door to another. Three days after I met with Tofu Liu, he telephoned me. His niece at Radio Beijing had put him in contact with someone I should meet: Lu Yiwen, the close friend of a Radio Beijing editor who had passed away in 1996. This was the same Yiwen who had known Ai-ming and her parents in 1988 and 1989. I felt the impossible had occurred: I had plucked a needle from the sea.

Tonight, June 6, 2016, I went to her flat on Fenyang Road, near to the Shanghai Conservatory.

Yiwen was a tall, strikingly beautiful woman in her mid-forties. She wore jeans, a T-shirt, and sandals, and her long hair was tied up in a loose knot. She spoke with an intensity that I found riveting. She was restless, she made large gestures as she spoke, as if she were drawing on a screen. We spoke in English. After graduating with a degree in Chinese language and history from Beijing Normal, she had overturned her life and applied to study electrical engineering at Tokyo University. To her surprise, she had been accepted. She had only returned to China the previous year. She was divorced and had a teenaged daughter.

Yiwen had much to tell me. A story is a shifting creature, an eternal mirror that catches our lives at unexpected angles. Partway into our conversation, I opened my laptop and showed her a scan of the composition, *The Sun Rises on the Peoples' Square*. I began humming the notes.

"This is Sparrow's music," Yiwen said immediately. "But . . ."

"How do you know?"

"He was singing it all the time. I used to hear him in the evenings, walking home late at night. In 1989, we lived in the Muxidi Hutong, all the flats were small and very close together, we were living almost one on top of the other. Sparrow would pass by my window on the way to his flat. And I could hear him in the little study, where he used to do his writing. His music was like something in the air." Yiwen leaned closer to the computer. "But how on earth did you get this?"

"A friend performed it for me. A few years ago. I've learned to read the music a little."

"But how did you find a copy of the music? It was destroyed in 1989. Ai-ming had only nine pages. I saw it destroyed."

I told her that Sparrow had sent it to my father in a letter dated May 27, 1989. That I had only found it a few years ago, in a Hong Kong police file. It had been among my father's possessions when he died.

Yiwen became suddenly emotional. "Ai-ming thought it was gone."

"Do you know where Ai-ming's mother is? I've tried to find her but the address I have—"

"Ling? But she died in 1996."

A wave of emotion gathered in me; I had always suspected Ling had passed away, yet still I had hoped. I thought for a moment, collecting myself. "Ai-ming had a great-aunt who used to own a bookstore. She was very elderly. . . ."

"The Old Cat. She lives in Shanghai. She turned a hundred this year and when you ask the year of her birth, she says she's been alive forever. I'll write down her address for you. She doesn't have a telephone."

Yiwen continued, "In 1996, Ai-ming came back from the United States."

"Sometime in May," I said.

"Yes, mid-May. She came to Beijing for her mother's funeral. The situation was difficult. Her U.S. visa had never come through and she didn't have a Chinese hukou, a residency permit, any longer. She took a risk and went to the public security bureau to request one, but they denied her . . . I saw her a few times while she was in the city. Her mother's death was unbearable for her. Ai-ming wasn't well. She told me she was going to live with her grandmother in the South. Later on, about a year later, so 1997 or 1998, she wrote me a letter. She said she was going to Gansu Province in Western China. She asked me to come with her. I was living in Tokyo at that point. I asked her if she was kidding, why in the world was she going to the desert in the middle of summer? All I wanted was for Ai-ming to come to her senses, to see reason. But I said things . . . I was extremely harsh in my letter, I said too much . . . I never heard from her after that. It must have been . . . early 1998."

The dates matched my own. The things I felt were inexpressible.

"I was young, I didn't understand. Everything that happened during the demonstrations, the way it ended, the way people died, had left me angry and cynical," Yiwen said. "Ling's death changed everything for Ai-ming. Actually . . . after Ai-ming went away the first time, to Canada in 1990, I became very close to her mother, I admired Ling and saw how courageous she had been. I began to see my life in a different way. She was the one who encouraged me to apply to the University of Tokyo. Ling made it possible for all of us to start our lives again, but she herself never had the chance." Yiwen stood up and went out of the room. When she came back, she carried two items. The first, a picture of Ling,

Sparrow and Ai-ming taken in 1989. They were standing in the centre of Tiananmen Square. The second, Chapter 23 of the Book of Records, which Ai-ming had copied out and given to Yiwen for her twentieth birthday.

"I didn't know how Ling was connected to your family in Canada. I only knew that a lot of letters went back and forth. But Ai-ming never told me the details, even when she came back in 1996."

"And Ling, she never told you?" I asked.

Yiwen looked at me searchingly, as if I was the one with the answers to give her. "It was just the way life was back then," she said finally. "People lost one another. You could be sent five thousand kilometres away, with no hope of coming back. Everyone had so many people like this in their lives, people who had been sent away. This was the bitterness of life but also the freedom. You couldn't live against the reality of the time but it was still possible to keep your private dreams, only they had to stay that way, intensely, powerfully private. You had to keep something for yourself, and to do that, you had to turn away from reality. It's hard to explain if you didn't grow up here. People simply didn't have the right to live where they wanted, to love who they wanted, to do the work they wanted. Everything was decided by the Party. When the demonstrations began, the students were asking for something simple. In the beginning it wasn't about changing the system, or bringing down the government, let alone the Party. It was about having the freedom to live where you chose, to pursue the work you loved. All those years, our parents had to pretend. To see the future in a different light takes time. But we thought everything could begin with this first movement."

We sat in silence for a moment. The notebook–Ai-ming's handwriting, Chapter 23–felt both real and weightless in my hands, so near and so far away. "What made you decide to come home?"

Yiwen set the notebook on the table, beside a photograph I had given her, showing Ai-ming, Ma and me, in 1991. "The first movement is finished. It will never come back again. But, Marie, how can I put it? It might be finished, it might be over, but that doesn't mean I've stopped hearing it."

Just recently, I began listening to the transcriptions and reimaginings of Bach's music written by the Italian pianist Ferrucci Busoni; these albums had been part of my father's music collection and now they are part of mine. Two hundred years separate the births of Bach and Busoni, yet I find these transcriptions intricate and terribly beautiful. Why did Busoni transcribe Bach? How does a copy become more than a copy? Is art the creation of something new and original, or simply the continuous enlargement, or the distillation, of an observation that came before? What answer would my father give?

In 1989, when he left my mother and me, he waited in Hong Kong for Sparrow to come. I was so young when he abandoned us; the regrets he carried can never be known to me. I fear to imagine his suffering and yet the details I do know will not leave me. Pills and drinking, my mother was later told. A debilitating depression. Gambling. Perhaps he felt that what had happened to Sparrow must be his fault somehow, that the Hong Kong visa, the travel papers, the ticket, had made Sparrow a target. Of course, it wasn't true, but Ba couldn't know that, and he came to what seemed to be a logical explanation. He had betrayed my mother and me, and didn't know how to go back, to become what he was. Sparrow, Zhuli, the Professor, his own family, they were gone; all the selves he had tried to be, everything that he had lost, could no longer be denied. My father had loved Sparrow almost all of his life; of this I have no doubt. It was early in the morning, still dark, when he went to the window of his ninth-floor room. He climbed out. Nobody looked up, nobody saw him; he was entirely alone. I understand that he wanted to stop his heartbreak, no matter the cost, and to end the enormity of his emotions. Maybe he hoped we, his family, would forget, but my mother and I, waiting in

Vancouver, held on to the person we had known. Ma had truly loved him–the part of him that he had shown her.

Many lives and many selves might exist, but that doesn't render each variation false. I don't believe so. If Ba were still alive, this is what I would tell him.

Throughout my life I have struggled to forgive my father. Now, as I get older, I wish most of all that he had been able to find a way to forgive himself. In the end, I believe these pages and the Book of Records return to the persistence of this desire: to know the times in which we are alive. To keep the record that must be kept and also, finally, to let it go. That's what I would tell my father. To have faith that, one day, someone else will keep the record.

ONDAY AND TUESDAY FELT like a single continuous day in Sparrow's life.

Production had slowed to almost nothing, Old
Bi and Miss Lu were listless, and Dao-ren looked as if she was
dismantling radios rather than building them; but Sparrow felt
glad for the distraction of work and actually surpassed his quota
for the day. Music joined all the movements he made, it slid
between his thoughts like a staircase reaching in multiple directions, until he was nothing more than sound. Around him conversation continued: rumours and truth crumpled together.
Someone said that the People's Liberation Army was planning a
coup. Miss Lu reported that police had arrested a dozen members
of the Iron Mounted Soldiers, who had renamed themselves the
Flying Tigers. Old Bi said that high-ranking generals in the army
had been purged, and that new battalions of the PLA would re-
enter Beijing tonight.

"Tomorrow," Miss Lu said.

"Never," said Fan.

Meanwhile, in the Square, Hong Kong entrepreneurs had
donated hundreds of brand new tents and the students had
erected a statue, the Goddess of Democracy. A new open-air

forum, the Tiananmen University of Democracy, had been inaugurated the previous night.

On Wednesday, Fan did not arrive for her shift.

By Thursday, the temperatures were reaching forty degrees and the wires in Sparrow's hands felt alive. On Radio Beijing, a powerful member of the standing committee said that the youth were "good, pure and kind-hearted," and were not the problem. It was the workers, in particular the leaders of the autonomous union, who had created a cancer cell made up of the "dregs of society."

But where was Fan?

On Friday, Old Bi came in late. His normally neat and clean hair was damp with sweat, and he had to smoke three of his Big Front Gate cigarettes in quick succession before he could tell them what had happened. Old Bi described the crowds in front of the public security office on Qianmen Avenue. "They've been arresting people all week," he said. "So I went up there to find out what happened to Fan. These bastards asked me why I was looking for a counter-revolutionary. A political criminal! They said, 'Run along home before we arrest you, too.' 'Oh, really?' I said. 'For what crime?' 'Comrade, you're in violation of martial law.' 'Fuck me,' I said. 'You're in violation of the Constitution!'" Old Bi took out another cigarette. "Idiot that I am, I was wearing my ID card on my shirt. They wrote everything down."

Miss Lu yanked the cigarette out of Old Bi's mouth. "You shouldn't have gone by yourself! You have no self-control."

Sparrow poured him a cup of tea.

"I'm going back tomorrow," Old Bi said, grabbing back the cigarette. "They can't arrest us all."

That night, Sparrow called Cold Water Ditch. Big Mother Knife was out of breath from being summoned to the neighbourhood phone. After she had huffed for some minutes, she told him that the student demonstrations had spread to Shenzhen and Guangzhou. When he asked if she had joined the protests, she shouted, "Deng

Xiaoping and those old farm tools in Beijing should retire! All those old men, it's like they breathe through the same nostril!"

Beside Sparrow, the caretaker of the phone, Mrs. Sun, was smoking and pretending to read the *People's Daily*. Her children clambered around her like sparks going off.

On the other end of the line, Big Mother had grown quiet and Sparrow thought she was done speaking.

He was in the middle of saying goodbye when Big Mother interrupted to tell him she had news. Last week, she had received a letter from Aunt Swirl and Wen the Dreamer.

"Ma," he said.

"Don't interrupt!" she shouted. And then, sighing, "I'm getting old. I keep losing my train of thought."

Now Big Mother filled in the years, speaking rapidly as if she were running across a narrow beam. Back in 1977, Wen had nearly been rearrested. If it weren't for his friend, Projectionist Bang, they could never have gotten away. They had retreated deeper into Kyrgyzstan. Last year, word finally reached them that Big Mother's petitioning had been successful: during the reforms initiated by Hu Yaobang, the convictions against Wen the Dreamer had been overturned and his criminal label had been removed. "It only took ten years," Big Mother said bitterly. Swirl and Wend were coming home. In the letter, Swirl said they'd already crossed Inner Mongolia and reached Lanzhou. After nearly twenty years in the desert regions, they wanted to visit the sea. They planned to stop in Beijing before continuing on to Shanghai and Cold Water Ditch. Big Mother had already given them Sparrow's address, even though it would be another few months before the official paperwork reached them. He should expect them in the winter.

"Will you recognize Swirl?" his mother asked.

"Always," he said. Sparrow shifted the phone to his other ear. "Do they know everything that's happened?"

He feared he had inadvertently pushed his mother off the balance beam and that she had toppled over and fallen into the quiet. But Big Mother's voice, when it came back, was steady. "She knows. They both know."

Over the line, the faint echoes of other conversations broke through and fell back.

"My son, have you been writing music?"

Sparrow, surprised by her question, answered truthfully, "Yes."

"Well, what is it?"

"A sonata for piano and violin." He wanted to tell his mother about an entirely different recording, Bach's six sonatas for the same two instruments. Throughout his life, Bach had returned to these six pieces, polishing and revising them, rewriting them as he grew older. They were almost unbearably beautiful, as if the composer wanted to find out how much this most of basic of sonata forms–exposition, development, recapitulation–could hold, and in what ways containment could hold a freedom, a life.

His mother sounded illogically near. "What did you name it? I hope you didn't just give it a number."

Sparrow smiled into the phone. He was aware of Mrs. Sun staring up at the ceiling, at a particularly large spider. "I called it *The Sun Shines on the People's Square*."

"Did you?" She gave a big, round pop of a laugh.

He couldn't help but laugh as well. "Yes, I did."

"You'll find a way to play it for Swirl and Wen the Dreamer?"

"Of course."

"It's a joyful title, isn't it?" his mother said.

He nodded, surprised by the grief that overtook him. He remembered something Zhuli had once said. *Luckily, joy seeps into all your compositions.* Some part of him had always existed separately, it had continued even after he had ceased to listen. "Yes."

The next day, Saturday, Ai-ming slept until noon. It was so hot, even the bed felt as if it were melting. Last night, she and Yiwen had stayed late at Tiananmen Square, where the rock star Hou Dejian had given a concert, his voice reverberating up to Chairman Mao's portrait like a dream they were all letting go.

Now Ai-ming sat up, sweaty, nauseous, the whine of electric guitars pulsating in her head. She felt as if she had not slept at all. The racket of the helicopters continued, they were circling Beijing again, dropping pamphlets. She sat up. The calendar said June 3, the month of May had vanished, dissolved by history. Today, Ai-ming would copy Chapter 23 of the Book of Records as a birthday present for Yiwen. This evening, she would go to Tiananmen, but she would come home early, she would have a good rest.

At home that afternoon, Sparrow fell into a deep sleep that went undisturbed by the loudspeakers, whose broadcast repeated stubbornly: *Beginning immediately, all Beijing citizens must be on high alert! Please stay off the streets and away from Tiananmen Square! All workers should remain at their posts and all citizens should stay at home to safeguard their lives.* What did he dream? Later on, Ai-ming often wondered because, when Sparrow came out of his room around dinner time, he was calm, even elated. He was carrying a small bundle of papers that were taped together and folded, accordion style. He sat down on the sofa beside Ling, oblivious to the broadcaster's repeated warnings. Perhaps Sparrow, like Ai-ming, did not believe that the army would re-enter the city. Sparrow was humming a piece of music, an enlargement of the pattern of notes he had been humming for weeks. Directly above him, the Spring Festival calendar showed two plump goldfish: good fortune gliding over his head like clouds.

Ai-ming listened to his humming. The music was not a lament, and yet it had a lifting, altering sadness impossible to pin down.

Ling was reading yesterday's paper. She stared, as if hypnotized, at the same page. Side by side, Ai-ming's parents appeared joined at the hip, although Ling leaned slightly away, as if to make space for another person. Ai-ming studied her father closely. His bad haircut had grown out a little, making the Bird of Quiet look like someone who had once been very handsome.

She stretched out her hands. After three hours of copying Chapter 23, when May Fourth arrives in Hohhot and begins her journey into the desert, all the little bones in her fingers hurt.

The noise of the helicopters was maddening, as if their only purpose was to agitate everyone's nerves. A sharp sound cracked against the windows and then the door. She and Ling jumped but Sparrow simply turned, as if he'd been expecting an intruder all along. A woman's raspy voice cried out, "Comrade Sparrow! Comrade Sparrow!"

When no one else moved, Ai-ming went to the door and pulled it open.

The woman had a narrow nose, surprisingly large eyes and a small, pointy chin. What was the stain on her dress? Mud. Dried red mud. And she had a new bruise, very swollen, just below her left eye.

"Fan," her father said.

"Sparrow, help us . . . please." Fan was shuddering as if from cold. "Old Bi, Dao-ren, we have to bring them here. . . ."

Ai-ming stepped away from the door.

"They were hit at Gongzhufen. We have to hurry. The army is coming in!" She stared at Ai-ming with an unreal placidity, blank terror.

"Gongzhufen . . ." Sparrow said.

Ling was looking at Sparrow's sheaf of papers, she had picked them up off the sofa and was staring at them as if no one and no sound had entered the room. Sparrow went and spoke into her ear. Ling stood up.

"Ai-ming," her father said, turning. "Stay with your mother. Do you understand?"

"Yes," she said.

"You promise to stay here?"

She nodded.

"Ai-ming, promise me that you won't leave the house. I have to go now."

Why was he shouting? Or perhaps he wasn't shouting. He was speaking quietly yet his voice seemed to be pounding in her ears.

"Yes, Ba."

He paced the room in a confused way, looking for something. His coat? His ID? The bundle of papers? A letter? Whatever it was he had wanted to bring with him, he abandoned it. He gave Ling one last look, a smile to reassure her, before hurrying after Fan.

Ai-ming followed them to the door.

"She's a co-worker," Ling said. "She works at the wire factory."

Ai-ming saw her father's bicycle wobbling down the alleyway into the shadows. A vanishing colour caught her eye, a pink dress, a flash of orange light. The stuttering vibration of helicopters made it impossible to think.

"Shut the door, Ai-ming."

She turned to find her mother beside her.

"Shut the door," Ling repeated, doing it herself.

Her mother was holding that sheaf of papers and Ai-ming saw line after line of musical notation, a language she had never learned to read. At the top, three words were visible, For Jiang Kai. "He'll be home soon," Ai-ming said. Her own voice sounded silly to her, flattened.

"What do you know about it? What have you ever known about your father?"

Dazed, Ai-ming said nothing.

"Do you know he could have composed for the Central Philharmonic, he could have studied abroad, he could have had a different life, if only he was a completely different kind of person. . . ." Ling shook the papers slightly. "But he wouldn't be with us, he wouldn't have chosen us, would he? If he'd been given the choice." The papers in her hands seemed to proliferate. "Your father has always been a good man but kindness can be a downfall. It can make you lose perspective. It can make you foolish."

Ling sat down on the sofa.

"Ma?"

"Why did he go with her?" Ling said. "Doesn't he know what's happening out there? Does he think that this life doesn't matter? Does he really believe that he can carry on as if he is invisible?"

At first, the gunfire had been intermittent, shocking, but now it came steadily, a drilling in the night. When Ai-ming could stand it no longer, she hid in the study, surrounded by her books, *The Collected Letters of Tchaikovsky*, *The Analects*, *The Rain on Mount Ba*. In the courtyard outside, the scramble of voices grew increasingly frantic.

Two hands rapped softly on the glass. The pink headband in Yiwen's hair was as startling as daylight. Ai-ming pushed open the window.

"Come out," Yiwen whispered. Her eyes were wide, she'd been crying.

Ai-ming looked around the room. A pair of plastic sandals, her mother's, were turned over beside the book trunk. Ai-ming slipped them on. She climbed onto the desk and dangled first one leg and then the other out the window. She felt Yiwen's warm hands gripping her ankles, pulling her insistently down. She jumped.

Halfway out of the courtyard, Ai-ming realized she'd forgotten to close the window. "Wait, wait, Yiwen," she whispered, turning to go back. As she reached the window, she saw a figure hovering in the doorway, moving towards her. She told herself that the shadow was only in her mind. Ai-ming pushed the glass closed.

"Ai-ming!" she heard. "Ai-ming, where are you going?"

She kept running.

"Ai-ming, come back."

These streets, covered with smoke, could not be hers. Ai-ming's bicycle swerved around the debris: overturned chairs, bricks that seemed to have come from nowhere, tree branches, abandoned cars, a wagon in which two children were sitting, staring mutely out. Behind them, at the Muxidi intersection, she saw overturned buses and smoke billowing from at least a dozen fires.

"Yiwen, where are we going?"

But the other girl kept pedalling. "How could they," Yiwen said. She was somehow both calm and distraught. "How could they?" She pedalled furiously as if someone was chasing them.

Small clusters of bicycles moved in every direction. A truck filled with boys, heading towards Muxidi, swerved past. The boys shouted that they were on their way to the barricades. To her relief, Chang'an Avenue grew less chaotic as they approached Tiananmen Square. On and on the boulevard went, the sounds of fighting diminishing. The Square rose before them, she saw the tent city, grey and sturdy against the concrete, and the Goddess of Democracy, shining like a trick of light.

"We can't go back," Yiwen said. "They're killing people at Fengtai. They're killing people at Gongzhufen. Right in the street, at the intersection. I saw it, Ai-ming. I saw it. At first it was only tear gas but then there were real bullets, there was real blood, they're following people through the alleyways–"

"Gongzhufen?"

"I don't know, I don't know."

Ai-ming's legs kept moving, the bicycle rushing forward, but she felt as if she were falling. "I have to go back. My father's at Gongzhufen."

"Are you crazy?" Yiwen was crying so hard she could not possibly see in front of her. "They're shooting. The People's Liberation Army is shooting. I saw three or four people hit right in front of me. The bullets, it's as if they explode inside the person–"

"No, the army wouldn't dare. They must be rubber bullets."

"They wouldn't!" Yiwen shouted, hysterical. "People were crying, Why are they shooting us? Why are they shooting? And then they couldn't run away because of the roadblocks. Our roadblocks. All the roadblocks we set up. They couldn't climb over them."

In the Square, an immense crowd of students was still gathered at the base of the Monument to the People's Heroes. Yiwen's bicycle rolled to a stop.

"But what now?" Ai-ming whispered.

Yiwen was looking directly at her, but Ai-ming had the disturbing sensation that she, Ai-ming, was not really there. She saw stains on Yiwen's dress, the muddy darkness of blood. Someone else's? she thought, her heart pounding, surely someone else's.

"What have we done?" Yiwen said. "What have we done?"

Sometimes the army trucks burst forward without warning, heedless of who stood in the road. Every moment there were yet more soldiers and yet more people, as the ones trying to escape collided with those who had only been onlookers, or who had been standing outside their buildings, or had been on their way to or from work. Sparrow and Fan had run almost all the way back to Muxidi and they were both gasping for breath. In the alleyways, soldiers materialized as if they were born from the ground. The crowd was not running away, but only back and forth, back and forth, like toys on a string. Electric buses, which had once formed a barricade, were now wrecks of charred metal.

"Don't let them pass," Fan was saying. "They're murderers. Don't let them get through to the Square."

Teenagers stumbled by, carrying an injured girl in their arms.

A voice on a loudspeaker said, "Go home, go home." Someone was crying for help.

The tanks came forward again. He heard the dull knocking of bricks against metal.

"Fascists, fascists..." Sparrow turned. Was it Fan? He couldn't see her. How neatly and quietly the soldiers had appeared behind him, shoulder to shoulder, their guns raised. But they walked past Sparrow as if he was not there. Behind them, a woman lay injured on the road. Two men ran and began to pull her backwards. The soldiers shot repeatedly at a single person he couldn't see.

Fan was shouting, "Animals! Inhuman animals!" Smoke fell as if from the trees.

The loudspeaker broke though the noise, "Go home go home go home."

"Little Guo, where are you? Little Guo!"

"He's hit, he's hit! Someone help us!"

Fan was supporting a man who leaned heavily on her shoulder, he was tall, heavy-set, and wearing a navy blue worker's uniform, and his full weight came down like a falling pole as Sparrow rushed to help. Stumbling forward, Sparrow feared he would bring them all down. He caught hold of something, a piece of metal. He pulled away as it began to singe his hand.

"Careful, careful," Fan mumbled, as if she were in a dream, as if she were guiding a line of small children across the road. "Don't let them reach the students."

His hand felt as if it were melting. The man leaning against him said, "Please don't leave me. Promise me, please. You can't leave me."

"I won't leave you. Tell me your name." The steadiness of Sparrow's voice felt unreal and far away. "Where did you get hit?" The blood had covered up the original wound.

"It's inside me," the man said, crying now. "They did this to me."

Another person rushed over with a flatbed tricycle, everyone was shouting, the wood of the cart was slick with blood and a thick grime. The big, injured man was jostled in, alongside the woman Sparrow had seen earlier. Her eyes were open, they looked at him with a question. The driver began to pedal, they tried to help him by pushing the cart on both sides. "Which way?" the driver shouted. "Which way?"

"Go west, get to Fuxing Hospital." "No, no, get him over to the centre on Zhushikou–"

"Wait, wait, there are more people here . . ."

Two more bodies were hurried into the cart.

"Save yourselves!" the injured man moaned, feverish. "Can't you see they're shooting?"

Sparrow thought of his bicycle, he would need it but where had he put it? A man was pouring gasoline on a hulk of metal, crying, "Animals! Butchers! Down with the Communist Party!" Smoke rushed into Sparrow's chest, it filled his throat and vision. He felt an anger that had seemed long gone, or had never existed in him before. Through the jostling crowd, he thought he saw Fan and went towards her.

At the Muxidi intersection, Sparrow found himself on streets that he knew, and he recognized familiar buildings and the houses of his neighbours, things that made him feel irrationally safe. The noise was overpowering, exploding canisters of tear gas, people shouting, petrol bombs flaring along the road, crawling up over the army tanks. A long vibration suddenly exploded somewhere near. If he closed his eyes for too long, rows of buildings might be erased, just as lines of people, too, were vanishing. The soldiers had been singing the words of Chairman Mao: *If no one attacks me, I attack no one. But if people attack me, I must attack them.* Sparrow walked towards the armoured trucks where soldiers moved in glacial, melting shapes: Kneeling. Shooting. Standing. Creeping forward. Their olive green uniforms, the hard shell of their helmets, seemed out of keeping with their young faces. Too young, they looked the same age as Kai and Zhuli had been long ago. They walked impossibly slowly, as if the soldiers' bodies were balloons and their guns were made of lead. He heard the flat crack of a concrete block hitting an armoured tank. Sound accelerated. One tank rushed towards the place he had been standing only a moment before. He thought he was still there, watching the tank grow larger. The people running appeared to be suddenly unmoving. All of the shapes he saw became sound, the cracking of trees, the swinging of a rifle, the edges of a bayonet. He felt the whistle of bullets passing near, but the crack of the rifles was delayed, the noise coming a second, two, three, later.

Sparrow did not know where Fan was. He recognized the closed storefront of a train ticket office, and saw a couple huddled there. Loudspeakers above continued urging them to *Go home, Go home. . . .* but PLA soldiers were coming out of their trucks and infiltrating the small streets and alleyways. The man was dressed smartly and had wavy hair and a thin face, the woman was carrying a small child in her arms. "We have to go," the man was saying. "No, no," she whispered. "We're trapped, they're shooting back there." The surreal sound of a pop song was tinkling down from above, someone had left a radio or a television on. Gunfire punctured the alleyway, making sparks of light. Sparrow wanted to protect them, but did not know how to give them the same terrifying invisibility that he seemingly possessed. The woman's dark hair gleamed wetly, and he saw now that a long stain of blood was moving from her hair, down her clothes, over the child in her arms, and dripping onto the sidewalk. The man was sweating. His dress shirt had the softness of an old newspaper. "Give her to me," the man begged. The woman refused, hugging the child closer. "Why are they shooting?" the man said brokenly. "How can they?" More armoured trucks were rushing along Chang'an, as if they were late for an appointment further ahead. "Don't be scared," the woman said to the motionless child. "We're almost there, stop crying. We're almost there." Now the trucks stopped and more soldiers poured out. "Fascists, fascists!" an old man shouted. He was wearing shorts and a white undershirt. He was instantly surrounded by three soldiers. Sparrow saw a teenager with a camera, the camera hovering in front of his face. The soldiers turned and shot him. Sparrow began to run towards the teenager, shouting. The soldiers kept firing. One came forward in a vicious motion and bayoneted the boy in the stomach. The teenager gripped the bayonet with both hands, screaming, trying to pull it out. By the time Sparrow reached them, the soldier was gone and the student was curled up on the ground, blood and internal organs coming out of his body. The strap of the camera, twisted around his wrist, was moving in a hallucinatory way. Bricks rained down on the soldiers and one fell, the crowd suddenly doubled, tripled, surrounding the vulnerable soldier. A burning mattress flew in slow motion onto an army truck. Someone had thrown it from an apartment above, and the mattress was exploding as it fell. "Why have you come here?" a woman wept. "You're not wanted here. Don't you understand? They've tricked you. It's all lies!" *If no one attacks me, I attack no one!* "How can you turn your guns on us?" "We won't kneel down anymore!" But *if people attack me, I must attack them.* "Murderers, murderers . . ." "Shame, shame on you!"

Sparrow crouched beside the teenager, who stared up at him as if towards a face he knew, the only visible person. "Tell me your name," Sparrow said. He was shouting, he worked anxiously, trying to stop the flow of blood with his hands and then with his shirt. The boy said his name was Guoting and that he was a student at People's University. "What did they do to me?" the boy asked curiously. Sparrow did not have the words. It seemed only yesterday that he was walking his baby daughter around and around the courtyard of their home in the South, whispering lullabies, *Ai-ming, turn your eyes to the sky, don't look at the ground. Look elsewhere, Ai-ming . . .* But this year, he had turned forty-nine years old and time, which for so long had seemed to stretch unbearably, was now contracting. He held the boy's hand and saw blood expanding towards him. "Guoting," he said firmly to the boy. "Don't be afraid. I won't leave you. Look up at the sky. See how it belongs to us . . ." The soldiers were not leaving any room for people to turn back or retreat. The noise of the crowd shattered his thoughts. A soldier who had fallen into the hands of the crowd was crying out for mercy. The boy on the ground was dying. Could the middle of his life have come now, delayed, twisting around again, retrieving him? Minutes later, Sparrow stood up and the boy's lifeless body was carried away on a cart. The streets seemed simultaneously empty and full.

The couple he had seen earlier were now standing in the intersection. Lights from the tanks found them, and the woman carrying the child darted into an alleyway. The man, frozen with fear, remained where he was. *My love*, the woman cried, desperate. *My love.* All the noise of the street came to Sparrow as he began to run towards the line of soldiers, it ran beneath all the sound in his head. He no longer felt any fear. Big Mother's voice came to him: "Never forget: if you sing a beautiful song, if you faithfully remember all the words, the People will never abandon the musician." As a child, he had hidden away in the practice rooms of the Conservatory, repeating Bach's canons and fugues until his fingers were numb. He had not been afraid, then, that his hands, his eyes, his mind, had given themselves over to something else. Zhuli played the opening aria from *Xerxes* for her mother. He wrote the words, *I will come*, and mailed this letter to Kai. He remembered the train platforms crammed with young people, the great exodus of a million people to the countryside, an endless motion of blue and grey coats. He remembered carrying Zhuli home. The weight of her body, her head against his shoulder. He saw Kai seated before the piano, playing the symphony never completed. The words and passages he remembered surprised him. All the pages had glued themselves together, he saw there had never been any hope of reaching the end. The lights from the trucks and tanks were blinding. The woman's voice no longer called, and he knew that the father had gotten away, he was safe. He stopped running, his hands up for them to see. His daughter, his wife. What had any of them done that was criminal? Hadn't they done their best to listen and to believe? There was nothing in his hands and never had been. The crack of the gun was delayed and came to him too late, but the sound gave him the sensation of closing a thousand doors behind him. Light from the tanks found him, as if they could collect all the irreconcilable parts of his life. No matter how many lights they shone, they could never take away the darkness. Daylight was blinding, but in the dark he still existed. What did they see, he wondered, his hands still open. Of all the people he had loved and who had loved him, of all the things that he had witnessed, lived and hoped for, of all the music he had created, how much was it possible to see?

At the base of the Monument to the People's Heroes, Ai-ming lay on the concrete, looking up at a sky grey with smoke. Despite the humidity, someone's thin blanket covered her feet, and another was draped over her shoulders. Dishevelled, hysterical students kept arriving, crying out that the army was shooting in Muxidi, that the hospitals in the west of the city, from Fuxing to Tongren, were overrun with the dead, that the wounded numbered in the thousands. Street by street, no matter how many Beijing residents stood on the road, the People's Liberation Army was forcing its way into the centre. She pulled Yiwen closer to her. "We have to leave before it's too late. Please."

Yiwen stroked Ai-ming's hair in a listless daze. "It's already too late," she said. She was no longer crying, it was as if she had already gone away. "Hours ago, it was already too late."

Rumours kept circulating as the minutes dragged on. Dead at Fengtai, at Muxidi, at Xidan. The loudspeakers jolted into life again, only now it wasn't the student broadcasters but the government who had control: *For many days the PLA has maintained the highest degree of restraint, but it is now determined to deal resolutely with the counter-revolutionary riot. . . .* She closed her eyes. How could it be so humid and cold at the same time? An air of unreality pervaded everything she saw. *Citizens and students must evacuate the Square immediately. We cannot guarantee the safety of violators, who will be solely responsible for any consequences. . . .* The concrete shook as if from a disturbance directly below them. "What time is it?" Ai-ming said to no one, and a handful of voices answered. *Three o'clock, two minutes after, almost three.* She had not seen the fire in the northwest corner begin, but now it rushed high into the night, scattering light on the waiting soldiers. The fire consumed the ransacked tents, the makeshift tables and all the papers of the independent workers' union. "I hope they burned their lists," Ai-ming said. "I hope they remembered to make all the names disappear." *Rioters have savagely attacked soldiers of the PLA. Cooperate with the PLA to protect the Constitution and to safeguard the security of the country. . . .*

A boy with an enormous rifle was dragged screaming out of a tent. The boy wept that the soldiers had shot his older brother in the back. "My brother is dead!" he shouted. "He's dead, he's dead! I'll kill them! Let me kill them!" A student marshal smashed the rifle again and again on the concrete until it snapped. "Do you want to get us killed, too?" he said. Another put his arm around the boy's shoulder and pulled him away.

What could anyone say? Yiwen's fingers in her hair moved slowly, as if winding down.

Now the army had them surrounded. A professor, Liu Xiaobo, and the musician, Hou Dejian, had been on hunger strike in support of the students, and now they hurried from their tents, running back and forth to the regiment of soldiers a few hundred feet away. They were trying to negotiate a retreat. Clusters of people followed them, broke away, rejoined. Meanwhile, leaders gave speeches about the necessity of non-violence and the purity of sacrifice. "I am not afraid," Yiwen kept whispering, her entire body trembling. In a burst of shouting, soldiers who had been hiding in the National Museum now marched out, thousands of them, the long bayonets on their rifles lifted in a glittering parade. Around the perimeter of the Square, Ai-ming could see tanks. She felt almost grateful when the lamps in the Square clattered off, the loudspeakers were cut, and this new quiet surrounded them like a tunnel. It was too late to leave, too late to turn around.

The students huddled up on the first tier of the Monument were in chaos, shouting through their loudspeakers, trying to organize a vote in the darkness.

"Who is determined to stay and who wishes to leave?"

Hou Dejian managed to get hold of a loudspeaker. "Students, a peaceful evacuation is still possible." He said that the army had agreed to open a corridor and let them exit through the southeast corner of the Square. They would not be harmed.

"Shame! Shame, cowards!" The hissing around Ai-ming nearly drowned him out.

A few voices shouted that a rebel army, led by Zhao Ziyang, was on its way to rescue them.

A student beside Ai-ming stood up. "We have to hold out until 6 a.m. The United States Army is going to intervene."

"Hou Dejian, shame! Shame!"

"We must stay. Out of our sacrifice will be born a new China!"

At the northern perimeter of the Square, the soldiers began shooting into the sky. The cracking of hundreds of rifles made it seem as if the air itself was exploding. A lamp above them was blown out. A boy beside Ai-ming was so terrified he fainted. He was shaken roughly back into the present.

The vote began. Each person called out, simultaneously, their vote. She herself shouted, "Leave!" and beside her, Yiwen countered, "Stay!"

The voices died down. She heard the buzzing of the lamps, already dark but still burning out, and Yiwen's exhausted, almost inaudible voice, "Stand firm, stand firm. How can we let it end like this?"

The soldiers were moving quickly. She saw the rustling of their lines rising towards them.

"We're leaving!" a girl ahead shouted. "They voted to leave."

Her words were met with rage. "It's not true!" "We want to stay!" "More people voted to stay!"

Yiwen stumbled to her feet. "Other people died for us!" she cried. "Now we're going to collaborate with their murderers? Have we no shame?" Others called out similar words, but the shouting mutated into exhausted crying. They had been in the

Square more than five hours, and only now did Ai-ming find herself breaking down, thinking of the promise she had made to her father, unable to comprehend how Yiwen was ready give up her life and the lives of others. For what? To hold Tiananmen Square, which had never belonged to them.

"Line up, line up in rows of ten . . ."

"Get in your battalions! Lock arms!"

She joined arms with Yiwen and with a tiny girl beside her. There were thousands, perhaps several thousand, students still here. University banners were awkwardly raised, they shook as if already falling. Yiwen and Ai-ming were displaced and found themselves walking under the flag of Beida. This is the first and only time, Ai-ming thought, that I will belong to Beijing University. The achievements she had once wanted for herself seemed a lifetime away, they were the aspirations of a completely different person.

Tanks were entering the Square, they made a shattering vibration. People around her began screaming and Ai-ming turned and saw the place where the Goddess of Democracy had been standing. The statue was light, almost constructed of air. The army, she thought numbly, did not need tanks to push her over. They could have done it with their bare hands. The shaking of tanks and helicopters continued, as if the concrete itself was being ripped apart. Would they have a parade now? she wondered. Now the soldiers were pressing in from both sides, funnelling the students between a narrow corridor of bodies. She saw a soldier strike a boy ahead of her with his baton. Behind him, a girl turned and spat in the soldier's face. But still the procession kept pushing inexorably forward. The people around her were weeping. At the front, the student leaders began to sing the Internationale.

Arise, slaves, arise!
Do not say that we have nothing.
We shall be the masters of the world!

The soldiers stared.

The students left the Square. She and Yiwen broke off from the procession and walked home. In a daze, they scrambled down side streets, avoiding the sound of gunfire. By the time they arrived back in the alleyway, the sun had risen and the sky was white.

DAY AFTER DAY, they went to the hospitals to search for Sparrow but finally, after three weeks, Ai-ming refused to pretend. Instead, she let her mother go alone while she sat in the little room, staring at the sheaf of pages taped together like an accordion book. Unfolded, Sparrow's composition hung down on both sides of the desk and touched the floor. This music, she thought, was the record of something her father had never heard with his own ears, he'd had no access to a violin let alone a piano. It had only ever existed in his mind and now here, silently, on paper. On the back, he had copied out a quote, "Beauty leaves its imprints on the mind. Throughout history, there have been many moments that can never be recovered, but you and I know that they existed." The afternoon disappeared and twilight retreated into darkness. She heard a rattling at the glass and looked up expecting to see her mother, but instead it was Yiwen, impossibly pale, impossibly beautiful.

"Ai-ming, Mrs. Sun sent me to find you. Someone's looking for your father, they've called in on the neighbourhood line."

Yiwen's face reminded her of something or someone else. What was it? *Won't you come with me! I want to grab your hands. Come with me . . .*

"Give me your hand, Ai-ming. Let's go together."

Ai-ming began folding up her father's composition and then stopped and left it where it was. The window scratched her bare legs as she climbed through, and she wondered if she'd grown to a monstrous size. The things she touched seemed out of proportion to the shape of her body. Outside, the concrete against her bare feet was warm, a heat that burned through her body and vanished into the air.

They went to Mrs. Sun's flat, which normally housed the telephone station in the window. The phone had been moved inside. "For security," Mrs. Sun was saying now, as she pulled Ai-ming into the room. It was crowded with too much furniture, as well as the Sun grandparents, nephews, son and grandchildren, but they all squeezed back, away from Ai-ming as if she were an unpleasant, desert wind. Mrs. Sun appeared, leading Ai-ming firmly towards the telephone. In Ai-ming's hands, the receiver felt slippery, as if it was sweating. She held it close and said, "Yes."

"Hello?" The caller had a smooth, melodious voice. His Shanghai accent was odd, slightly flattened. "I'm looking for Comrade Sparrow."

She felt as if the walls had grown fifty pairs of eyes. Mrs. Sun's youngest grandson had sidled up to her and was hugging Ai-ming's knees. "My father isn't here. I'm sorry, who's calling?"

He said his name was Jiang Kai, that he was calling from Hong Kong and that he was a pianist. He might as well have been speaking in code, the words made no impression on her whatsoever. "When will your father be home?" he asked. "It's urgent that I reach him."

She recognized the man's name, but in the confusion of the room, whatever knowledge she had dissolved like a lump of soil in her hand. "I don't know."

"Tomorrow?" Jiang Kai said hopefully. "I was afraid . . . I've been following the news on television." His voice appeared and disappeared. "Do you know when I might speak to him?"

"I don't know."

"Are you Miss Ai-ming?" his asked. "Is this Ai-ming?"

"Yes."

"I need to speak to your father, Ai-ming. Is everything okay? Please trust me . . ."

"We checked the hospitals," Ai-ming said.

"The hospitals?"

"I don't know." She was afraid her voice would break and if she began crying again she would never be able to stop. The phone felt preposterously large against her ear. "You should write to my mother. I don't know."

"What's happened? I'm a friend of your father's, Sparrow was my professor at the Shanghai Conservatory. I live in Canada and I can help, please let me help."

She felt nauseous. The letters, the foreign stamps, the record player, the stranger with the pure white shirt. The name Kai could be written, or overheard, so many ways. She had never guessed it always was the same person. "You should write to my mother. I don't . . . I can't." She was crying now, out of confusion. "He always wanted to play the piano."

"What?" There was a pause and then, "Ai-ming, are you still there? Please don't hang up!"

He was shouting and she was sure the Sun family and Yiwen could hear the panic spilling out of the phone, and this realization terrified her.

"I don't know if you'll see him soon," Ai-ming said. "He isn't here. I don't know. He isn't here."

"Ai-ming," he said.

"I have to go."

"Wait, please—"

"I'm sorry, I'm very sorry that I can't help you. I'm sorry you can't help him."

She pulled the receiver away from her ear and held out the phone to no one.

Mrs. Sun bundled forward. Her eyes were red, as if she had been squeezing them shut. She took the receiver. Jiang Kai was still speaking. Mrs. Sun broke into the crackling noise. "Comrade Sparrow hasn't come home since the night of June 3. Don't upset his daughter. She really doesn't know, poor girl. She's only a kid . . ."

Yiwen was holding her hand. Who was trembling? Was it her or the other girl? Why were they shivering so much?

The wall of Sun family members had broken into conflicting voices. "Didn't you hear they were burying bodies in a schoolyard not far from here? The school is complaining about the smell . . ." "What nonsense! When will you learn . . ."

Ai-ming stepped carefully over the children and around the Sun grandmother who had sunk deeper into her chair. More people had come into the flat, but she and Yiwen pushed between them, out through the crowded doorway and into the alley. Whispering voices seemed to catch like needles on her clothes, on her hands and feet. To scrub them off, Ai-ming ran ahead, straight out of the laneway, afraid that if she screamed, if she let any noise escape, something terrible would happen. On the street, she collided with a couple walking by, the woman jolting into the man, the man stumbling sideways and dropping his bag of fruit. Behind her, Yiwen was already apologizing, and the man, irate, yelled at them to be more careful. "Imagine if we'd been . . ." But he didn't finish his sentence. "Look," he said, picking up his plums. "They're all bruised now."

The street was surreal in its regularity. Someone had cleared the rubbished bicycles away. Night workers were sweeping the sidewalks, the grocer pulled down his metal shutter, copies of the People's Daily were pinned up on bulletin boards. Ai-ming stopped to read a page, "The pernicious effects of bourgeois liberalization and spiritual pollution are to blame for this counter-revolutionary riot . . ." There followed a report about the heroic sacrifices of the People's Liberation Army. But other parts of the paper wrote of heavily armed soldiers and machine gun killings, as if the paper itself was fracturing into different voices. Ai-ming turned away. Yiwen was telling her that at Beijing University, Tsinghua and Beijing Normal, Premier Li Peng was being denounced as an enemy of the people and tens of thousands of students were throwing their Youth League or Party memberships into a heap, and setting them on fire.

"But the government won. It's over," Yiwen said. "It's finished, isn't it?"

Ai-ming could say nothing. Everyone said that the foreign newspapers were reporting a massacre in Tiananmen Square, but she had been in the Square. She had seen the students walk away. Didn't they know the tanks had come from the outside? Didn't they know about the parents, the workers, the children who had died?

She remembered, in April, riding her bicycle down Chang'an Avenue, how this wide street had felt like a path not only to the middle of the city, but to the centre of her life. The open, unwalled space of the Square. She thought of the records of Prokofiev and Bach and Shostakovich that Sparrow used to bury under the floor in Cold Water Village, she thought of Big Mother Knife and Ba Lute who were on their way to Beijing. She thought of her mother's face, once so impassive, now incapable of hiding her pain. How could this be the same street? How could these be the very same walls? How could she ever pretend that it was?

They walked back down the alleyway. The door was open. In a dream, Ai-ming entered, thinking that Sparrow had come home. All the cupboard doors in the kitchen had been flung open. She heard a noise in the back room, her bedroom.

"Wait," Yiwen said. "Don't go in."

Ai-ming pulled her hand out of Yiwen's. She kept going. In her parents' room the dresser had been overturned.

She could hear voices, a woman and a man.

She turned the corner and entered. All her books lay jumbled on the floor. Neither the woman nor the man were familiar to her, nor were they wearing a uniform of any kind. The woman asked for Sparrow's residency permit and his factory badge. Her voice was almost kind. Ai-ming shook her head. The man was busy rummaging through papers. He tore up her study notes. He began to tear up the piece of music that had been sitting on the table, her father's composition. The man did it tiredly, almost without thinking, that's what it looked like to Ai-ming, as if he was just folding laundry or washing dishes. She began to cry for help. Yiwen was there, she shouted at the strangers to get out, to leave them alone. The woman told them to find Sparrow's work unit ID because they would be back. For reasons Ai-ming could not understand, the man and woman went out through the window, climbing out into the alleyway. Yiwen tried to pick up the pieces of the composition but Ai-ming said, "Leave it, leave it." She knelt down on the floor. She pulled the pieces from Yiwen's hand and began to tear them up into smaller and smaller pieces. She wanted it all to disappear. Yiwen kept shouting at her, calling her name, grabbing pages back. It was only later, when Ai-ming finally stopped shaking, that she saw what she had done.

Yiwen salvaged what she could. But in the end, she and Ai-ming were only able to piece nine pages back together. The rest of Sparrow's composition was gone.

Ling opened the front door soundlessly, slipped off her shoes and went into Ai-ming's room. The moon was faint, the night was utterly quiet, and her daughter slept, curled up on her side, one hand splayed open. The book Ai-ming had been reading weeks before, The Collected Letters of Tchaikovsky, lay on the floor beside her, still open. Three days had passed since officers from Public Security had entered the apartment. Ai-ming had tidied the room and gotten rid of the mess the agents had left behind, but still Ling imagined she could see their footprints beside the desk, as if they had been chiseled into the floor.

Ling sat down on the floor, beside the footprints.

Ai-ming seemed to turn slightly. In sleep, her daughter's fear lifted momentarily, so she appeared younger, more like the child she had been.

She wished to crawl into the bed beside Ai-ming, to fall asleep and wipe away her own thoughts. Since June 4, her colleagues at Radio Beijing had been pressured, one by one, into writing denunciations of the student movement; a few had been purged. Life had gone on; it had slipped backwards. It was only a matter of time, Ling knew, before she, too, gave in. The new political study sessions, mandatory for everyone, required them to pledge their support to the Party. If someone believed differently, dreamed differently, society could make sure there were no longer jobs, or space, for them. How easily the day-to-day had resumed.

In any case, her colleagues, too, had seen what she had seen, and they, too, had joined in the weeks of demonstrations. But Ling had gone to the hospitals alone on June 4. She had seen all kinds of people jeering the soldiers, screaming, weeping. Businessmen in suits, cadres from the street offices and residents' committees, nurses, construction workers, factory men. At Fuxing Hospital, on the ground and in the courtyard, and in a bicycle shed, were bodies. Two long sheets of paper affixed to a wall listed the names of the known dead. She had seen the corpse of a young man, the strap of his camera still looped around his wrist. She had seen women her own age. Bodies lay even at the entrance. A nurse came, begging her to give blood. The hospital had run out, she said, and people were needlessly dying. "At Muxidi. At Xidan . . ." Around Ling, people moved too fast or too slow. She had given blood in a chaotic room, and then continued on to the Children's Hospital, the Post Hospital, and then to the Beijing Medical Centre. The injured multiplied and became never-ending. She had looked into every face and examined every piece of clothing. Looking at feet and shoes, at mouths, at eyes, multiple gunshot wounds, wrecked bodies. In the morgue, they were laid on straw mats or strips of stained white cloth. There was a book of records. If the name was unknown, the nurses and doctors had listed the deceased's sex and estimated age, the objects in his or her pockets, the colour of a jacket or the pattern of a shirt. After leaving People's Hospital, she had run into soldiers. They had fired at civilians in a senseless, indiscriminate manner, shouting out that the passersby were counter-revolutionaries. Hooligans. Ling had pedalled blindly home, too distraught to be afraid. When she reached her own door, she had gripped the handle, unable to move, an icy numbness spreading out from her heart. In the first few days, she had felt almost nothing.

Now, in Ai-ming's bedroom, she could see, as clearly as if it were in her hands, the statement she had written but had not yet signed, supporting the use of force by the army against the demonstrators. Pledging her allegiance to Deng Xiaoping, to Premier Li Peng and the Communist Party. She saw the hospitals. She thought of Kai, the Professor, Zhuli, the Old Cat. She saw decades of deception and love, and also a lifetime of fidelity. She saw false surfaces that slice through everything, two-dimensional edges that could cut to the very centre of things.

Moonlight slid against her daughter's face, making it appear angular, smooth and cold. She stood up and went to the outer room. Sparrow's record player had a film of dust that bothered her and she instinctively took a cloth and proceeded to wipe it carefully, every side of it. When she was done, she opened the lid. The record inside was a recording by Glenn Gould and Yehudi Menuhin, Bach's Sonata No. 4 in C Minor. What was the last thing Sparrow had said to her? What was the last look he had given her? Their lives were bound together, Ling knew. She set the needle down and music swayed into life, the steady river of the piano, the lyrical exactitude of the violin.

Afterwards, when she lifted the record and replaced it in its cardboard sleeve, Ling found letters. All the letters written from Canada and Hong Kong.

At work the next day, the new director of the station summoned Ling to his office. He informed Ling that her husband's body had been recovered on the morning of June 4, and that he had already been cremated.

"His body?" she said. The ceiling fan spun so slowly, as if all the electricity in the building was being funnelled out.

"You should collect his ashes from the crematorium. I have the address here. Within three days, if the ashes are not collected, the crematorium will have no choice but to dispose of them."

"How did my husband die?" she asked.

He stared at the papers in front of him. "A stroke."

They both looked at one another. Ling wanted to close her eyes, but her mind refused to let her. "But where did he suffer this stroke?"

The director slid the sheet towards her. "At home."

She stared down at the page, and the space awaiting her signature, unable to react.

"Actually, since you're here," he continued, "we're having difficulty with another matter. Your daughter is registered to write the university entrance examinations next month. Unfortunately, since she's a relatively new Beijing resident, we've run into some obstacles. Political background checks, you understand . . . of course, I'll do all I can to secure a place for her."

He closed his hands together as if they contained something precious.

"It appears your husband was in contact with a number of people who harbour resentments towards the Party. Any information you can provide would help us in our work. Some are already charged and are in detention. This is a serious class struggle and we must each do our part. The Party will not let you down. The Party understands that many good cadres were led astray by a dangerous few. The Party says: to those who confess, leniency; to those who resist, severity."

What shook Ling most was that she wasn't even angry. Anger,

too, could dissipate, but this emptiness that took its place might never be released.

"He's already dead," she said at last. When the director said nothing, she asked him, "What more do you want from him? I gave my life to the Party. I gave my life. What more do you want from me? I have nothing more to say."

When she looked up, the director appeared genuinely ashamed. He remained silent.

She picked up the pen and signed her name.

Afterwords, the world outside was made only of intersecting flat surfaces, angle after angle, peel it back and she would only find more of the same, yet another surface. A lifetime of carefulness and sacrifice meant she had no one in whom to confide. At the crematorium, she was given a cardboard box of ashes. They had run out of wooden boxes. Perhaps inside the paper would only be another box, and then another and another, and so on until infinity. Trembling, she undid the string and lifted the lid. Around the bits of bone, the ashes were matted together, they had a softness and a lightness that broke her. She replaced the lid, tied the box to her bicycle and pedalled home.

Nothing remains unchanging, she thought. Her legs pedalled quickly as if they could leave her self behind. She had seen too much. Yes, things could still change, not for her, not for Sparrow, but for Ai-ming. She could not stop her own heart from breaking. But for her daughter behind this mountain was another mountain, behind this sea, another sea.

CODA

I N MY MIND, AI-MING'S story has a hundred possible endings. Perhaps she simply wanted to leave the past behind and she took on a new identity and a new life. Perhaps she became involved in something she could not speak of to us. Perhaps her counterfeit papers came back to haunt her. In recent years, this last possibility consumed me, for there were stories of Chinese migrants lost in the maze of detention centres; many had arrived in the United States in the years following the 1989 Tiananmen demonstrations and had never obtained proper papers. In the early 1990s, the United States had passed the Chinese Student Protection Act, offering permanent residence to students involved in the protests. However, they were eligible only if they had arrived in America between June 5 1989, and April 11, 1990. Ai-ming had crossed the border in May 1991. Ten years later, in 2001, when detentions in the United States skyrocketed, those without papers were swept up in the crackdown.

Sometimes, in Vancouver, I go to the apartment where my mother, my father and I used to live. I imagine that Ai-ming and I, in the most extraordinary of circumstances, will meet one another there. The street is the same, the apartment blocks have barely changed. Sometimes people's lives fold back together, sometimes all they need is a meeting place, good fortune, faith. Years ago, Ai-ming told me that her mother used to stand in the intersection of Muxidi, waiting for Sparrow, remembering, long after his life had ended.

June 20, 2016. In Shanghai, two lamps shone by the window where Professor Liu stood holding his violin. With his great, white eyebrows, he reminded me of a snow lily. The pianist, Mrs. Wang, in a midnight-blue silk dress, sat at the piano, ready.

Beside me, Professor Liu's daughter, our sound engineer, gazed sternly into her laptop. She dragged her headphones off, massaged her forehead and dropped the headphones back on. In Shanghai dialect, she asked for a sound check. The musicians played the opening of Bach's Sonata No. 4 in C Minor.

There were thirty people in the room, mostly musicians and composers, some of whom had known Sparrow decades ago. In the first row, Yiwen was hugging her daughter to her side. To her left was Ai-ming's great-aunt, the Old Cat.

The room stilled. Professor Liu lifted his violin. Sparrow's Sonata for Piano and Violin, dedicated to my father, began.

At first, the violin played alone, a seam of notes that slowly widened. When the piano entered, I saw a man turning in measured, elegant circles, I saw him looking for the centre that eluded him, this beautiful centre that promised an end to sorrow, the lightness of freedom. The piano stepped forward and the violin lifted, a man crossing a room and a girl weeping as she climbed a flight of steps; they played as if one sphere could merge into the other, as if they could arrive in time and be redeemed in a single overlapping moment. And even when the notes they played were the very same, the piano and violin were irrevocably apart, drawn by different lives and different times. Yet in their separateness, and in the quiet, they contained one another. Long ago, Ai-ming copied out a poem for me:

We told each other secretly in the quiet midnight world
That we wished to grow together on the earth, two branches of
    one tree.
Earth endures, heaven endures, even though both shall end.

Sound waves walked across the computer screen, recurring yet unpredictable, repeating yet never the same. I saw the Old Cat's head, nodding. Against the window, the curtains continued to move.

In this room, there was only the act of listening, there was only Sparrow, Kai and Zhuli. A counting down and a counting up, an ending that could never be a true ending. The not yet was still to come, and the book remained unfinished. We loved and were loved.

Ai-ming, I thought, you and I are still here.

Around us, the first movement expanded, turning like smoke.

≡

IN DUNHUANG, in the far west of China, Swirl, Wen the Dreamer and Projectionist Bang were sorting through photocopies. It was 1990. Ai-ming sat across the table from them, watching the slight movement of their three grey heads. They were all staying in the rooms of Projectionist Bang, resting for several weeks so that onward travel arrangements could be made. Here, the summer sky was a deep, silvery white.

Projectionist Bang, who had a face like a dried pink plum, made his living sweeping the grounds of the famous Mogao Caves. Ai-ming liked to hear about the caves, and so she asked him now which was his favourite. Projectionist Bang welcomed the interruption. He said that some of the Mogao Caves were painted with visions of paradise, images that dated to the fourth century. "But the painters' idea of paradise was only a copy of life on earth," he said. "Dancing, wine, books, meat and music. Paradise offers all the things we've never learned to properly distribute, despite the excellence of our residents' committees and our people's communes."

Behind his small brick house, the dirt road led out into the shifting sands of the Taklamakan Desert. Just this morning, a camel train had swayed by, returning home after a seventy-eight-day journey across the Gobi, the emptied humps of the animals sagging over like devastated pillows. Having never seen a camel in her life, Ai-ming had thought their humps were injured. Projectionist Bang had laughed so hard, his hearing aid had fallen out. Ai-ming had wanted to disappear into the ground, or though the nearby gate of Jiayuguan, the Gate of Sorrows, where the western reach of the Great Wall came to an end. She had once fancied herself a scholar, but she didn't even know that a camel's hump emptied and grew soft like a deflated balloon.

Swirl had intervened, reminiscing of a camel she had known in her thirties, during her time at Farm 835. The camel's name had been Sasha.

Now, again, Projectionist Bang was struggling with his hearing aid and it looked like he was trying to reattach his ear. "Oh," he said, when he had managed to get it right. "About the piano you wanted, I found one. The pianist is an old rightist, exiled to Dunhuang in 1958, used to be a physicist. His sentence finally ended last year but he hasn't got around to going home. It's just like the old books say, 'Even the Emperor is an exile on these dusty roads.' Anyway, we looked over the piece of music, those nine pages, and he said he could prepare it in a few days. Stitch it together somehow. At least we'll get an idea of what it sounded like."

"Projectionist Bang," Swirl said, "if you play the violin part, I think it will be just right. Can you do it on your erhu?"

"Sure, sure," Bang said. "We're a bloody orchestra out here."

Ai-ming, Swirl and Wen the Dreamer had been travelling together for five weeks, 2,500 kilometres, by train, bus, cart, moped and foot. Her great-uncle and great-aunt, already in their seventies, had the tenacity of llamas. Everything they owned was packed in a single suitcase, a piece of luggage meticulously cared for, yet so battered it looked as if it had lived ten thousand lives. Swirl and Wen could survive on hot water and radishes, eating sunlight and dusty air. She wasn't sure if they slept because whenever she opened her eyes, at midnight or 3 a.m. or dawn, they were always awake.

Wen had told her stories of the desert, Comrade Glass Eye and her own father, the Bird of Quiet. Swirl told her about Big Mother Knife, Lady Dostoevsky and Zhuli. Sometimes Ai-ming cried for no reason, even when the story was a happy one. Sometimes, when the story was sad, she felt nothing, not even the beating of her own heart.

Now, Swirl was sorting through the pages of another set of the Book of Records because they had fallen on the ground and gotten out of order. Ai-ming was watching Wen the Dreamer. His face had an angular sharpness, an immense calm. In the sunlight, his white hair was nearly transparent.

Wen had decided to hand-copy the last chapter. He was using the cursive script and, as he drew each character, the brush barely left the page. There was something circular, watery and eternal about it all.

He looked up at her and set aside his brush. The word he had just written was 宇 (yǔ) which meant both *room* and *universe*. "Child, do you know where you want to go?"

She remembered walking with her father to Tiananmen Square and how she had said to him: *Canada*. Now she said, "I don't know. I just want to leave everything behind."

He looked at her sadly. "But after doing even that, one day you might have to find another way to continue."

"How?" she asked.

He didn't answer. His picked up his brush and continued writing. The small stack of notebooks beside him seemed to lift slightly, like the ribs of an accordion. She studied the photo he kept beside him. Zhuli was holding her violin as if it was the instrument, the wood and strings—and not her thoughts, not her future—that needed protecting. What if this is where I should stay, Ai-ming wondered. What if I can't survive on my own? She felt like a stranger to herself, as if her body was in fact a giant house, but she had only ever bothered to visit one room.

"How to continue," Wen said. "Your father wondered this too. For many years he didn't write music at all. Chairman Mao gave us one way of looking at the world, and so did Marx, Engels and Lenin. All the poets and writers, all the philosophers. They agreed on the problems but never the solutions. Shostakovich and Bach gave your father another way of listening. I think about your father every day . . . Perhaps, later on, when he composed again, he tried to hear these different voices simultaneously with his own, so that his music would have to come from broken music, so that the truths he understood wouldn't erase the world but would be part of it. When I was alone, I often asked myself, Can a single hand cover the sky? How can we live like this and see so little? Ai-ming . . . I have so many regrets. Everyone tells me how much you resemble Zhuli. Don't ever try to be only a single thing, an unbroken human being. If so many people love you, can you honestly be one thing?"

She didn't understand.

His brush came to the end of a line. Chapter 42, when May Fourth reaches the end of the desert. She's aged so much, and her friend Da-wei has long since passed on from this world.

"Uncle Wen, how many chapters do you think there are?"

"Once I asked my wife the very same question. She told me, Wen the Dreamer, it's foolhardy to think that a story ends. There are as many possible endings as beginnings.'"

The desert air made Ai-ming feel lightheaded. She had taken to sleeping early, waking late, and to napping after lunch and before dinner. Each time she opened her eyes, she felt as if her head was enormous, her hands tiny, and her lungs crushed. One afternoon, she woke up and heard the voices of her three caretakers and Big Mother Knife, who had arrived from the South to be with them, and had managed to obtain false papers for Ai-ming. Big Mother could see very little now, and sometimes, when she thought too much about Sparrow and her boys, tears leaked from her good eye, itself now failing. Ai-ming had never seen her grandmother mourn, she would gently wipe the tears and Big Mother would grumble, "Who's that?" "It's me." "Ah, you."

"If my granddaughter crosses into Kyrgyzstan," Big Mother was saying now, "what's the next logical step?"

"Are you kidding? If she makes it even that far, the next step would be a generous cash offering to the Queen Mother of the West." This was Projectionist Bang.

"What about arranging passage through Istanbul? She says she wants to go to Canada."

"Canada?"

"Sparrow has a friend there. A musician." Big Mother paused. "Sparrow had."

Ai-ming stared unblinking at the bright room. The truth was, she was terrified of the future. She would never study at Beijing University, never follow Yiwen, never join the Communist Party and then never renounce her membership, never leave flowers at Tiananmen Square. Ai-ming had written the examinations, she had scored high, but when the results came, she had told her mother she would not, could not, stay. Ling had not seemed surprised. "Your father wanted you to be able to choose," she said. But what if it was all a mistake? What if she simply didn't have the courage? It would take courage to continue living in Beijing. Her mother had already quit her job at the radio station, and moved back to Shanghai to be with the Old Cat. Ai-ming was afraid that life, which had seemed to be expanding forward, had stopped and turned around. That it would carry her forever backwards.

She thought she had been weeping soundlessly, but Swirl came into the room. She was as graceful and beautiful as a written word, but any word could be so easily erased. One day, Ai-ming thought, unable to stop the flow of emotion, I'll open my eyes and every one of you will be gone, and I'll be all alone. Swirl stroked her hair. When her great-aunt looked at her, what did she see? Am I truly a construction? One day, will someone become a construction of me, a replica?

"I'm so afraid, Aunt Swirl. I'm afraid to be alone."

"I promise you, Ai-ming, it will get easier in time."

She slept and when she woke again it was dark. The voices of Swirl and Big Mother circled in the night.

"And the camp that Wen escaped from . . ."

Swirl said, "Did I ever tell you? He went back to see it but it had disappeared. The entire camp has been swallowed by the desert as if it never was."

"Do you remember . . ." The stop and start of Big Mother's voice broke Ai-ming's heart.

"The Red Mountain People's Refreshment House," Swirl said.

Big Mother murmured.

"Shanghai during the Occupation," Swirl said. "The green hat you made for Sparrow. The words to 'Jasmine.' The Old Cat. Da-wei and May Fourth. Zhuli snoring in our little hut, and kicking you off the bed."

"The four widows you lived with."

"The little boy who led the line of blind musicians, hand to elbow, elbow to hand. The three of us walking the length of the country."

"So many children," Big Mother said.

Ai-ming heard the sound of a cup set down.

"You'll come back to live with me, won't you? You and Wen."

"You won't be able to get rid of us," Swirl answered.

"She was a good child," Big Mother said. "A courageous girl."

Swirl was humming a fragment of music, a small piece of the unending sonata that Sparrow had written. Big Mother took the words from "Song of the Cold Rain," from "In That Remote

Place," and joining in, sang them over Swirl's music. The melodies came from songs and poems Ai-ming half recognized, songs her father had sung when she was a child. The harmony was rich and also broken, because the two women were so much older now, and they had loved and let go of so many things, but still the music and its counterpoint remained. "Destined to arrive in a swirl of dust," Big Mother sang. "And to rise inexorably like mist on the river."

Ai-ming sat up in bed. She listened.

$$\equiv$$

AI-MING CARRIED A small suitcase. At the beginning it was full and heavy, but it was depleted little by little over the course of a journey that took more than three months.

An elderly woman who had once been a translator met her at the Kyrgyzstan border and went with her to Istanbul.

From Istanbul, she flew to Toronto.

In her suitcase she had packed a single change of clothes, toothbrush, washcloth, soap and a tea thermos; a photograph of Zhuli, Kai and her father; a letter from Yiwen. She felt like Da-wei crossing the sea, like a smuggler or a piece of code. Her father had never had the chance to cross the borders of his country.

I have done these things for my parents, she thought, and for myself. Could it be that everything in this life has been written from the beginning? Ai-ming could not accept this. I am taking this written record with me, she thought. I am keeping it safe. Even if everything repeats, it is not the same. It was just as Wen the Dreamer said: she could take the names of the dead and hide them, one by one, in the Book of Records, alongside May Fourth and Da-wei. She would populate this fictional world with true names and true deeds. They would live on, as dangerous as revolutionaries but as intangible as ghosts.

In Toronto, she waited for my mother to call her.

In Vancouver, I reached out and took her suitcase.

It is a simple thing to write a book. Simpler, too, when the book already exists, and has been passed from person to person, in different versions, permutations and variations. No one person can tell a story this large, and there are, of course, missing chapters in my own Book of Records. The life of Ai-ming, the last days of my father: day by day, year by year, I try to see a little more. In Shanghai, Tofu Liu told me that Bach reworked psalms and folk songs, Mahler reworked Li Bai and Wang Wei, Sparrow quoted Prokofiev in his own compositions, and others, like Zhuli and my father, devoted themselves to interpreting this music that was never written for them. The entire book of records is lost, but some objects and compositions remain. In Dunhuang, where Ai-ming stayed with Swirl and Wen the Dreamer, forty thousand manuscripts were recovered in a cave sealed around 1000 AD. In 1900, when an earthquake caused the rocks to split, an abbott, the guardian of the caves, discovered the cache, towers of pages preserved by the dry air of the desert. Mixed in with Chinese prayers were documents in Sanskrit, Tibetan, Uighur, Sogdian, Judeo-Persian, Syriac and Khotanese; a Parthian fragment written in Manichean, a tantric instruction manual in the Uighur alphabet, a past due bill for a camel. Ballads, inventories, circulars and donations. A letter to a husband that reads, "I would rather be a pig's wife than yours." Astronomical maps. Board game instructions. A guest's apology for getting drunk and behaving badly. A poem for a beloved donkey. The sale of a brother. Variations of Sparrow's complete composition, *The Sun Shines on the People's Square*, can be heard all over China. In shopping malls, public parks, private homes, on personal computers, in night clubs; on headphones in Tiananmen Square, that place that Chinese architects once imagined as the zero point, the location that determines all others. Maybe no one knows where the original recording came from, or that it arrived, like a virus, over the internet. The composer's name may ultimately be lost. Mathematics has taught me that a small thing can become a large thing very quickly, and also that a small thing never entirely disappears. Or, to put it another way, dividing by zero equals infinity: you can take nothing out of something an infinite number of times.

To date, Yiwen and I have left innumerable copies of the Book of Records online and even in bookshops in Beijing, Shanghai, Dunhuang, Hong Kong. When I met the Old Cat in Shanghai, she showed me her copy of the thirty-one chapters of the Book of Records copied by Wen the Dreamer back in 1950.

The Old Cat told me that one day in the near future this library, which itself had gone through so many transformations, would pass from her hands into Ai-ming's keeping. She said, "I understood from the time I was a child that the boundless vista is at the perilous heights." Later, as if speaking to another, she said, "Ling, you must give my regards to the future." And then the Old Cat, who was wearing a suit as she sat in her wheelchair, who carried a bright silver pen in her pocket, smiled at me. She said, "My goodness. How much you resemble your father."

When she said this I understood that these pages, too, are just one variation. Some must remain partial chapters, they have no end and no beginning.

I continue to live my life, to let my parents go and to seek my own freedom. I will wait for Ai-ming to find me and I continue to believe that I will find her–tomorrow, perhaps, or in a dozen years. She will reach up for a book on a shelf. Or she will switch on the radio, she will hear a piece of music that she recognizes, that she has always known. She will come closer. At first, she will disbelieve and then a line will come back to her, words she overheard on the street long ago but has never fully forgotten.

Tomorrow begins from another dawn, when we will be fast asleep.

Remember what I say: not everything will pass.

ACKNOWLEDGEMENTS

To Charles Buchan and Sarah Chalfant, my gratitude and love. Your confidence and wisdom have sustained me.

Thank you to Lynn Henry at Knopf Canada, Bella Lacey at Granta Books and Christine Popp at Luchterhand Literaturverlag, for their profound insight, generosity and commitment to this book of records. I am deeply fortunate to have traveled this road with you.

I am grateful for financial support from Simon Fraser University, University of Guelph, Nanyang Technological University Singapore and the Conseil des arts et des lettres du Québec. Thank you to Katharina Narbutovič and the DAAD Berliner Künstlerprogramm who hosted my partner, and welcomed me not only as family but as an artist in my own right. Do Not Say We Have Nothing began in the freedom and openness offered to us in Berlin.

To my students and fellow faculty in the MFA Program in Creative Writing at City University of Hong Kong, which was closed down as a result of internal and external politics, and to my friends in Hong Kong, thank you for six beautiful years.

A small group carried me through difficult times, financially, artistically and spiritually. Thank you Ellen Seligman, Y-Dang

Troeung, David Chariandy, Sophie McCall, Steven Galloway, Sarah Blacker, Phanuel Antwi, Johanna Skibsrud, Amanda Okopski, Priya Basil, Xu Xi, Sara O'Leary, Anita Rau Badami, Elee Kraljii Gardiner, Michelle Garneau, Dionne Brand, Guylaine Racine, Tsitsi Dangarembga, Claudia Kramatschek and Tobias Wenzel.

To Emily Wood and John Asfour, and to my mother, Matilda Thien, who left this world far too soon. As John wrote, "When death catches me on the sidewalk of a poem, I will only regret not having had you in my arms long enough."

To my father and Katherine Luo, for their love and faith. To Rawi Hage, for everything.

Not everyone who supported and strengthened this story can be named. To my beloved friends in Shanghai, Hangzhou, Beijing and Dunhuang, thank you for accompanying me through this book of records and an alternate memory of history. Remember what I say: Not everything will pass.

21. "Watch little by little the night turn around . . ." Adapted from Pink Floyd lyrics for "Set the Controls for the Heart of the Sun," adapted from Tang Dynasty poet Li Shangyin's "Untitled Poem(iii)", from *Poems of the Late T'ang*, transl. by A. C. Graham (New York: New York Review Books, 2008), 147.

30. "You and I are forever separated by a river . . ." "A Trip to Xinjiang", News Plus, China Radio International, Beijing. November 1, 2013. Radio.

Lyrics from a folk song translated from Russian to Chinese, collected by musician Wang Luobin who once dreamed of studying at the Paris Conservatory. At the age of 25, he encountered and fell in love with Xinjiang music and, over decades, traveled throughout the region, collecting and adapting more than 700 songs into eight albums. He spent 19 years of his life imprisoned.

30. "My youth has gone like a departing bird . . ." "A Trip to Xinjiang."

38. "I would also like to be wise . . ." Bertolt Brecht, "To Those Born Later," transl. by John Willett, *The Faber Book of Twentieth-Century German Poems* (London: Faber and Faber, 2005), 71.

71. "The marriage of a girl, away from her parents . . ." Adapted from Wei Yingwu, "To My Daughter on Her Marriage into the

Yang Family," in Witte Bynner, *The Jade Mountain: A Chinese Anthology, Being Three Hundred Poems of the T'ang Dynasty, 618–906* (New York: Knopf, 1930), 212.

72. "When the mind is exalted . . ." adapted from Wei Yingwu, "Entertaining Literary Men in My Official Residence on a Rainy Day," *The Jade Mountain*, 208.

87. "How can you ignore this sharp awl that pierces your heart? . . ." From a song by Jesuit missionary, China scholar and musician, Matteo Ricci (1552–1610), as quoted in *Rhapsody in Red: How Western Classical Music Became Chinese* (New York: Algora Publishing, 2004), 59.

99. "These kids have never even seen an instrument in their dreams!" Li Delun, who brought donated musical instruments to Communist headquarters at Yan'an in 1946, and became the founder, instructor and conductor of the orchestra. As quoted by Sheila Melvin and Jindong Cai in *Rhapsody in Red*, 176.

111. "We told each other secretly in the quiet midnight world. . . ." Adapted from Bai Juyi, "Song of Everlasting Sorrow," in Witter Bynner, *The Jade Mountain*, 120.

145. "I am lovesick for some lost paradise . . ." adapted from Ch'u Tz'u, or *Songs of Ch'u*, "The Far Journey," transl. by J. Peter Hobson, *Studies in Comparative Religion*, Vol. 15, No. 1 & 2 (Winter-Spring, 1983).

146. "Family members wander . . ." Adapted from Bai Juyi, "Feelings on Watching the Moon" http://www.chinese-poems.com/bo3.html

151. "Moonlight in front of my bed . . ." Li Bo, "Quiet Night Thoughts," transl. by Burton Watson in *Columbia Anthology of Traditional Chinese Literature* (New York: Columbia University Press, 1996), 204.

151. "The streets our brushes . . ." Vladimir Mayakovsky, "An Order to the Art Army," December 1918. Transl. Anna Bostock, as quoted in John Berger, *Art and Revolution: Ernst Neizvestny,*

Endurance, and the Role of the Artist (New York: Vintage, 2011), 44.

152.   "Yellow dust, clear water under three mountains . . ." Li He, "A Sky Dream," in Tony Barnstone and Ping Chou's *The Anchor Book of Chinese Poetry* (New York: Anchor, 2005), 199.

160.   "We shouldn't be afraid of our own voices. . . ." adapted from Chin-chin Yap's interview with Ai Weiwei, *Ai Weiwei: Beijing–Works, 1993-2003* (Hong Kong: Timezone 8, 2003), 41.

197.   "The beauty is in the machinery," Prof. Henryk Iwaniec, from Alec Wilkinson, "The Pursuit of Beauty: Yitang Zhang solves a pure-math mystery," *The New Yorker*, February 2, 2015.

198.   ". . . deletes 16 percent of all Chinese internet conversations" David Bammam, Brendan O'Connor and Noah A. Sing, "Censorship and Deletion Practices in Chinese Social Media," *First Monday*, 17.3 (March 2012).

199.   "Could I awake now and cross towards her?" Inspired by "Thus, in fainting we yunguoqu 暈 過 去 'faint and cross away', and in awakening we xingguolai 醒 過 來 'awake and cross toward here,'" Perry Link, *An Anatomy of Chinese: Rhythm, Metaphor, Politics* (Cambridge: Harvard University Press, 2013), 9.

211.   "Even the beautiful must die . . ." Friedrich Schiller, as quoted by Jan Swafford in *Johannes Brahms: A Biography* (New York: Knopf, 2012), 463.

211.   "A birch tree, a spruce, a poplar is beautiful . . ." Excerpted from the section of Schiller's letter to Körner of February 23, 1793, which is entitled, "Freedom in the appearance is one with beauty." This translation is taken from Friedrich Schiller, Poet of Freedom, Vol. II, Schiller Institute, Washington, D.C., 1988, pp. 512-19. See http://www.schillerinstitute.org/transl/trans__schil__essay.html

212.   "Those representatives of the bourgeoisie who have sneaked into the Party . . ." Mao Zedong, "May 16 Circular", as quoted in Michael Lynch's *Mao* (London: Routledge, 2004), 181.

215.   "Leave their allotted space and march to the centre of the

stage" adapted from Jonathan D. Spence, *The Gate of Heavenly Peace* (London: Faber and Faber, 1982), 22.

229.   "All revolutionary intellectuals, now is the time to go into battle . . ." Nie Yuanzi, "What have Song Shuo, Lu Ping, and Peng Peiyun Done in the Cultural Revolution?", *Peking Review*, Volume 10, May 25, 1966.

242.   "We wash away insects, and are strong," Mao Zedong, "To Guo Moruo," in *The Anchor Book of Chinese Poetry*, 360.

266.   "The water of socialism nourished me . . ." Lyrics from the song, "Longing for Mao Zedong", arranged by Li Jiefu. Hongweibing gesheng [The voice of the Red Guards] (Beijing: Houdu dazhuan xuexiao Hongweibing daibiao dahui, 1969), 99.

269.   "The old ferryman couldn't guess what the obstacle was . . ." Shen Congwen, *Border Town* (New York: Harper Collins, 2009), 96.

272.   "This is the beautiful Motherland . . ." From the famous patriotic song, "My Motherland", lyrics by Qiao Yu and music by Liu Chi.

278.   "Let the rooms be full of friends . . ." He quotes high-ranking official Kong Rong in chapter 11 of Luo Guanzhong's 13th-century classic, *Romance of the Three Kingdoms*, translated by C.H. Brewitt-Taylor. Web edition published by eBooks@Adelaide, https://ebooks.adelaide.edu.au/l/literature/chinese/romance-of-the-three-kingdoms/index.html

284.   "The grass in the meadow . . ." Ibid. The children's nursery rhyme from *Romance of the Three Kingdoms*, ch. 9.

284.   "There is no middle road," Editorial of the *Liberation Army Daily* (Jiefangjun Bao): "Mao Tse-Tung's Thought is the Telescope and Microscope of Our Revolutionary Cause," June 7, 1966. *The Great Socialist Cultural Revolution in China* (Peking: Foreign Languages Press, 1966), III, 11-17.

286.   "Before I die," He Luting said, "I have two wishes." Based on the life He Luting, as described by Sheila Melvin and Jindong Cai in *Rhapsody in Red: How Western Classical Music Became Chinese* (New York: Algora Publishing, 2004), 238 and referenced by

Alex Ross in *The Rest Is Noise: Listening to the 20th Century* (New York: Macmillan, 2007), 564.

294. Shostakovich's letter to Edison Denisov, as quoted by Laurel Fay, *Shostakovich: A Life* (London: Oxford University Press, 2005), 199.

295. "A form of repentance that would bring the individual back into the collective . . ." Kang Sheng, torturer and high-ranking member of military intelligence for Chairman Mao, as quoted in David Ernest Apter and Tony Saich's *Revolutionary Discourse in Mao's Republic* (Cambridge: Harvard University Press, 1994), 288. Kang was instrumental in aligning Chinese support for Pol Pot and the Khmer Rouge in Cambodia.

297. "Zero is a definite point from which . . ." Quote adapted from Friedrich Engels, *Dialectics of Nature*, as quoted by Wu Hung in *Remaking Beijing: Tiananmen Square and the Making of a Political Space* (London: Reaktion Books, 2005), 8.

298. Students Zhang Zhiyong, Guo Haifeng, and Zhou Yongjun kneel on the steps of the Great Hall of the People, April 22, 1989. Between 1989 and 2002, Zhou, a student at the China University of Politics and Law, served five years in prison. In 2008, while attempting to re-enter China to visit his ailing father, Zhou was re-arrested by Hong Kong police and renditioned to China. Initially charged with political crimes, he was sentenced to 9 years in prison for financial fraud. He has not been heard from since 2014. All efforts have been to find the source of this widely-shared photograph, to no avail. Please contact the publisher if you have information about the photographer or rights to the image.

301. Tofu Liu's method of hiding artefacts, based on photojournalist Li Zhensheng, *Red-Color News Soldier* (London: Phaidon, 2003).

313. "For every vital movement of the world external to us we behold the image of a movement within us . . ." Philipp Spitta, *Johann Sebastian Bach, His Work and Influence on the Music of Germany, 1685-1750*, Volume 2 (London: Novello, Ewer & Company, 1884), 602.

323. "Let me tell you, world / I do not believe . . ." Bei Dao, "The

Answer," *The August Sleepwalker*, transl. Bonnie S. McDougall (New York: New Directions Publishing, 1990), 33.

324.   "We have no ties of kinship . . ." from *Romance of the Three Kingdoms*, ch. 11. Ibid.

335.   "I came into this world bringing only paper, rope, a shadow . . ." *The August Sleepwalker*, 33.

351.   "All warfare is based on deception . . ." Sun Tzu, *The Art of War* (Stockholm: Chiron Academic Press, 2015), 33.

370.   "We want no more gods and emperors . . ." Quotation condensed from Wei Jingsheng's "The Fifth Modernization," as quoted by George Black and Robin Munro, *Black Hands of Beijing: Lives of Defiance in China's Democracy Movement* (New York: Wylie, 1993), 50.

379.   "I've been searching for myself . . ." I believe this is a quote from Xi Chuan, Preface to *Depths and Shallowness*, but can no longer find the original source.

381.   "A society that speaks with only one voice . . ." Zheng Yi during 1989 demonstrations, as quoted by George Black and Robin Munro, *Black Hands of Beijing*, 177.

383.   Toru Takemitsu as quoted by Alex Ross in *The Rest Is Noise*, 564.

385.   Student radio broadcast, from Chai Ling's "Declaration of a Hunger Strike," as quoted by eds. Liang Zhang, Andrew J. Nathan, Perry Link, Orville Schell in *The Tiananmen Papers* (New York: Public Affairs, 2008), 154.

392.   "There are things that I can't accept . . ." Adapted from a quote by Liang Xiaoyuan in *The Gate of Heavenly Peace*. Directed by Richard Gordon and Carma Hinton, Boston: Long Bow Productions, 1995. Documentary film.

397.   Zhao Ziyang's speech to the students in Tiananmen Square, May 19, 1989. Wikipedia entry on Zhao Ziyang. https://en.wikipedia.org/wiki/Zhao—Ziyang

402.   Noodle seller's words adapted from interview with Wu Dingfu in "The Tiananmen Father," from Liao Yiwu's *The Corpse Walker* (New York: Anchor, 2009), 217.

406.   "Of course, no one knows tomorrow. Tomorrow begins from

another dawn . . ." Bei Dao, "Stretch Out Your Hands to Me . . ." *The August Sleepwalker*, 55.

412.   "I held the letter in my hands and wept . . ." Zhu's dialogue, adapted from Liao Yiwu's interview with Wu Dingfu in "The Tiananmen Father," *The Corpse Walker*, 217.

440.   "Beauty leaves its imprints on the mind . . ." Original source lost.

456.   "Even the Emperor . . ." Projectionist Bang quotes *Romance of the Three Kingdoms*, ch. 14.

462.   "Mixed in with Chinese prayers were documents in Sanskrit, Tibetan . . ." Partially adapted from Colin Thubron's *Shadow of the Silk Road* (New York: HarperCollins, 2009), 94. Further expanded based on public domain data from The Dunhuang Project. "Beside the mass of Chinese prayers are documents in Sanskrit, Tibetan, Uighur, Sogdian, Khotanese, Turki in a melange of scripts; a letter in Judeo-Persian, a Parthian fragment in Manichean script, a Turkic tantric tract in the Uighur alphabet, Nestorian scriptures. Ballads, inventories, wills, and deeds. Personal letters, chance intimacies. Somebody pens a whimsical argument between wine and tea. A guest's apology for behaving indecorously drunk the night before. A funeral address for a dead donkey." http://idp.bl.uk/

MADELEINE THIEN IS the author of the story collection *Simple Recipes*, which was a finalist for the Commonwealth Writers' Prize, a Kiriyama Pacific Prize Notable Book, and won the BC Book Prize for Fiction; the novel *Certainty*, which won the Amazon.ca First Novel Award; and the novel *Dogs at the Perimeter*, which was shortlisted for Berlin's 2014 International Literature Award and won the Frankfurt Book Fair's 2015 Liberaturpreis. Her novels and stories have been translated into twenty-five languages, and her essays have appeared in *Granta*, *The Guardian*, the *Financial Times*, *Five Dials*, *Brick* and Al Jazeera. Her story "The Wedding Cake" was shortlisted for the prestigious 2015 *Sunday Times* EFG Short Story Award. The daughter of Malaysian-Chinese immigrants to Canada, she lives in Montreal.